ALLAN MAYER

Tasting the Wind

TASTING THE WIND

Published in 2008 by YouWriteOn.com

First Edition

Published by YouWriteOn.com

For my wife, Alison for all of your love, support and advice,

and without whom...

For my family- Mum and Dad (Betty and Ron,) Ronald,

Philip and Karen,

Deane,

Michael and Enid.

For Brian, Peter, Anita, Richard, Kim, James,

Philip and Sharon, and to all of those people who survive the

perpetually changing care system with their spirits intact.

In memory of David Heffer

-Acknowledgements-

Thanks to my readers for their encouragement, ideas and greater

mastery of spelling and grammar than my own:

Linda, Trish, Heather V.,

Heather H., Emma, Carolyn, Christine, Darren, Andy, Janet.

Thanks to Lynn, my friend and coach, for helping me realise my goal.

It is not at the greatest level, the cosmic and the eternal, that mankind is divided, but at the level of the microscopic and transient.

What unites man can be measured in universes and aeons because each and every one is made of the same stardust, given a spark of the same divine nature and a place in the same eternal pattern.

But what divides man can be measured in millimetres and seconds- the millimetres of physical proportion which are perceived as 'attractive' or 'ugly,' the microscopic gap in the chromosome or few minutes of oxygen deprivation at birth that affect the whole being.

And it is a truth beyond doubt that a man can even die for no other reason than that he looks 'different.'

'Eddie's Diaries' (1962)

ALLAN MAYER

TASTING THE WIND

TASTING THE WIND

-Prologue-

24th December 1976

For as long as he could remember, Frankie Adams had worn socks as gloves. He had never chosen to wear them in this way, but was now so resigned to their presence that even in his dreams he pictured himself as a man with no fingers. The socks were always grey, but rarely a matching pair, as they were either faded to varying degrees, or had originally belonged to different owners; and he could never take them off, as they were always tightly secured at the wrist with a bracelet of sellotape.

There had been one memorable morning, Christmas morning in Frankie's forty- second year, when someone had removed his saliva-saturated night-time 'gloves' and had forgotten to put on a fresh pair. What Frankie remembered mostly was his hands feeling sensitive and vulnerable, as if they were those of a new-born baby, and that everyone who came across him that day stared at him, some of them laughing, because he looked somehow different and strange. The memory stayed with him, and every Christmas he hoped that it would happen again.

But it never did.

TASTING THE WIND

The evening of this particular Christmas Eve had started like any other, the day staff leaving, everyone put to bed, and the cacophony of unrequited communication *gradually subsiding to a resigned, drug- induced hum. Nurse Cahill sat at her desk, her head nodding to the tinny beat of her radio earpiece. Her heart had only just begun to settle from something that had happened half an hour previously, when she had clearly heard a woman's voice say:*

'Their heads were green, their hands were blue.'

She was used to patients, at least the ones who could talk, coming out with meaningless gibberish, but as this was an all male ward it had caused her to jump from her chair, pulling the waxy earpiece from where it lodged. She inspected each bed before returning to her desk, and checking that her radio was correctly tuned. As she feasted on chocolate liqueurs a lean figure stepped from the shadows behind her and drifted forward to where he could hear her slurping the syrup from her chubby fingers. He peered over to leer at the outline of her breasts, trying not to notice how the lamp emphasised the down on her arms and upper lip. As he grabbed her shoulders she let out a yell- the word scream would conjure up something far too high-pitched and feminine- and, spinning round, landed a hefty right hook which left her attacker sprawled on the linoleum.

'Wha...?' said the stunned auxiliary, as he wiped the back of his hand across his bleeding lip. 'Merry Christmas to you too.'

'How the hell did you get in here?'

'I did ring the bell, but you didn't hear it. Anyway, I've got these' he said, triumphantly jangling a set of keys. 'They're dropping like flies with this throwing up bug; even Sister Claire has gone down with it. There aren't enough agency nurses to go round, so it looks like we're in charge.'

Laughing, the two angels of mercy kissed, and in the glow of the desk light looked momentarily devilish.

'Thank God I'm getting out of this shit-hole.' said the fat nurse, looking round at the twenty-odd sarcophagal beds.

' You got your transfer then?'

'No. I've given up on that. Haven't you heard? All of these places are closing. There's no future in it. I'm going to retrain, go into Social Services. That's where it's at now: Care in the Community.'

Frankie listened and, unknown to them, as it would have been to anyone else who had ever worked with him, took in every word. He wished that he was getting out, that he could be cared for in this 'community' thing, instead of being punished here for something he couldn't remember doing as a child. He let out a small groan as the pain in his stomach mounted again, but tried not to complain too loudly, as he had been chastised earlier for keeping the others awake.

Frankie had a curved spine, which meant that he could only lie comfortably on his left side. The thin boy in the next bed had the opposite problem, so every night they lay looking into each other's eyes. Neither of them could talk, and no one ever questioned what one thought of the other, or if either of them even had the capacity of thought. All that Frankie knew was that in the five years that they had occupied those beds, the boy's gaze had been his only source of comfort, understanding and fellow feeling.

The nurse made her way down the lines of beds, tucking the patients in, the ambulant ones particularly tightly, so that they would be discouraged from wandering. The thin boy was never going to go anywhere, but noticing that his top sheet was not conforming to the hospital standard the nurse bent down to insert it tightly between base and mattress, while the other sat with his feet on the desk, guzzling a can of beer.

Frankie watched the stiff skirt rise up, revealing legs that were each as thick as the thin boy's body. He wanted to touch where the blue uniform slid over the black mounds. He knew it was all right to do that because he had seen the boy nurse do it, so he pulled himself up using the cot-side and reached out with his shaky, grey-socked hand, guiding it like the hand of a puppet to its huge beach ball of a target.

Then an involuntary spasm sends his hand shooting out, and pinching, through the baggy material of the sock, a roll of nurse-flesh. The nurse bellows and spins round, her large hand raised like a conductor's as the background noise of crying and babble ceases at the recognised signal of threatened violence.

Then the hand falls, but instead of the anticipated slap it grabs the flapping toe of the outstretched sock.

'I'm sick of you, you vicious little bastard.'

11

TASTING THE WIND

She pulls at the sock until it stretches, winds it around a bar of the cot-side and ties it, then stalks over to the other side of the bed and does the same with Frankie's free hand.

'I'm sick of your pinching and whining. You can stay like that now, it might teach you a lesson.'

The thin boy watches as the male nurse, whispering and giggling, kisses the fat nurse and goes with her through the blue door opposite his bed into what they call the 'punishment room.' He listens as the screaming and grunting sounds coming from the room mingle with the resumed din of the ward, and the first retching sounds from Frankie. He watches helplessly as Frankie struggles to turn onto his side. He hears Frankie starting to choke on his own vomit. Then he hears nothing, sees no more movement.

From the other side of Frankie's bed the long white face of a young boy rises like a new moon. The boy is wide-eyed, his expression of fright enhanced by the stiff brush of hair which crowns the top of his head. He limps round to the foot of the bed, and climbs up, patting Frankie and whimpering, stroking his face and removing vomit from around his mouth and nostrils.

When the nurses emerge, the boy is sitting at the foot of Frankie's bed, his red pyjama jacket smeared with sick, a crimson urine patch spreading on his crotch as he swings his bare feet, rocking, and chanting:

> *'Whose in the cupboard?*
> *Rang the bell,*
> *Kissed the nurse*
> *Made the noise,*
> *Naughty Mr. Hill.'*

Then they see Frankie's still form, and rush to untie him, their minds already fabricating a tale of how they tried to save him, as the moon-faced boy mutters 'he's gone to our Lord.'

The boy drops down from the bed, his feet slapping on the linoleum floor, 'I'm going to set my dog on you,' then throws himself at

the fat nurse, barking and clawing and biting. Although she is so much bigger than him, she screams in fear, until her accomplice helps her to drag him to the punishment room, where he is locked in for the night.

Then one of them is desperately cleaning up the vomit- 'what the fuck are we going to do?'- as the other changes the socks on the dead man's hands- 'we tidy up, there are no witnesses'- she gestures to the thin boy, then to the punishment room- 'he can't speak, and that one's in gaga land, so shut the fuck up and bin these socks.'

Thus the ward is restored to its sterile status quo, where everything is clean, and every patient cared for, up to and beyond the line where complete care becomes complete control.

And the thin boy saw all of this. Whether he understood what he had seen or not nobody knew, or cared. Either way, he was never going to tell.

-Chapter 1-

31st October 1986
2.30 a.m.

When I was a kid I taught myself to puke at will. As an adult I've not found much use for it, but back then it was my most powerful weapon in the battle against evil. If you were to ask me why, when most kids were concentrating on using 'clackers' without bruising their wrists, I was perfecting my aim with projectile vomit, I'd say it was because of an enormous handicap I had at a very early stage of my life, in the form of an educational psychologist called 'Ricky.' Ricky had been brought in to help me when my dad was ill and my behaviour had started to register on the 'bizarre' scale. Now unless you count developing a lifelong fear of enclosed spaces and losing the ability to ever totally trust another human being, I would say that I coped well with his behaviour modification techniques (which eventually included shutting me in the cupboard under the stairs.) What really screwed me up was discovering that if not before and during, then certainly not very long after my dad died, he was shagging my mum.

Like I said, I haven't had much call for projectile vomiting since I was a kid. Now I'm all grown up I've found a much better way to self-induce sickness, which takes longer but is much more fun. At least at the beginning of the night. As it happens, I'm at the end of the night, well early hours of the next morning actually, and I can't remember ever being this pissed. Here it comes again: whoosh, it hits the water like the result of a successful hara-kiri, the sharp sword driven in and the innards let out with a big heavy splash. One small flush, one giant leap and...

'She's gone.'

I say the words out loud because somebody- it was probably Rick the Prick- once told me that naming the event and not just ignoring it would somehow help me to face up to it and to 'master my feelings.'

So how do I feel then?

I feel like I've just dislocated my sodding jaw, that's how I feel. And the worst thing about it is that there's nobody here to say 'there there, Martin,' or even 'you can sleep on the couch tonight you drunken git.'

Not that I could sleep anywhere yet. This is 'Stomach Clearance Sale: Everything Must Go.' I'll probably be here for the rest of the night, feeling round the toilet rim as if I'm trying to turn an egg-shaped steering wheel, THE BIG ROW- the one that finished us off-repeating again and again in my head.

'It wasn't so much your being out of work I was objecting to', she'd said, 'as your cavalier attitude towards losing your job.'

'Cavalier attitude? ' I'd said, pretending to know what the fuck she was on about, 'cavalier attitude?'

'It's just the way you treat your whole life, she'd screamed, 'you just coast along with no purpose, and *I've* become part of the furniture. You take as much notice of me as you do of this sodding chair.'

To demonstrate, she had picked up the chair, a wooden one with a worn green cushion, and on the word 'chair' launched it at the wall. She didn't usually do that sort of thing; usually she freaked out if anything got damaged because we rented the flat, and very little had got broken in the four years, ten months and eleven days we'd lived there.

I remember when we first moved in. It might only have been a flat over an oatcake shop in a small North Staffordshire town, but waking up each morning to the aroma of freshly griddled pikelets blending with that of Jo's perfume made it feel like Heaven. That was at first. But like everything else, eventually it's just there, then after a while you don't even notice it. According to Jo our relationship, that is my contribution to our relationship, had gone the same way. The not noticing I mean: like not noticing if she'd had her hair done, or was wearing a new shade of nail varnish, or a dress I'd not seen her in before. If you were to ask my opinion I'd say that she'd just perfected her hobby of finding things to criticise me over to a fine art.

Funny word that, 'opinion.' We use it as if it makes things vague and subjective, when in reality an opinion can change your whole life. I can see us now, just sitting there in silence, staring at the kitchen chair with its broken, splintered leg, knowing that we were losing each other just because we had different opinions about what was important.

'Does this mean we're finished?' I'd asked.

'Wake up Martin,' she'd said, 'and smell the oatcakes.'

And that, I suppose, was the last time I saw Jo.

Until tonight...

***

I was saying goodbye to the guys at the club.

'Besht wishesh mate,'

'Thanks mate,' I'd said to Neville, as he crushed my fingers, 'I'll come back and see you.'

I've known Neville for about a year now but, if I'm honest, it wasn't through choice. I suppose it started with the bank that Jo worked for, and the negative publicity it was getting because of its investments in South Africa. There had obviously been a brainstorming session at head office about how to put on a human face without actually risking the returns on their investment, and some bright spark had suggested that attention could be drawn from their stance on South Africa, which was, after all, a long way away, by making links with local charities. This meant not only donations, but also staff (In T-shirts with bank slogans) acting as volunteers. Jo, believing that it would not only be a nice thing to do but that it would do no harm to her chances of promotion, chose to help out at 'Breakaways,' which is a youth club for mentally handicapped kids. She said she thought it might also be good for my soul to do something for somebody else, so I reluctantly went along with her. At first it was just to prove her wrong about me, but then I found that I liked it and stayed, even after she packed it in. It would change my life for good.

Neville continued with his bone-crushing handshake, and looked me straight in the eye as if he was about to give me some really important advice. He always dressed in black for some reason, and tonight, as it was disco night, it was the black jeans and 'Motorhead' T-shirt.

'You sort 'er out,' he said, 'that Mrs. Thasher'

'I don't think I'll be seeing her Nev, London's a big place, but if I do...'

'Promish?'

'I'll do my best.' That seemed to reassure him. ' But what'll you do without me here to pull your arse out of trouble?'

'Gerra job.'

'What sort of thing?'

'An'fing. Just want to earn some...' Neville scratched the palm of his hand. 'Do your old job at the Factory if I was clever enough.'

'Clever enough?'

We were shouting over the music, and standing as close as we could without touching, like a couple of drunks at chucking out time.

'All I did Nev, was take things out of cardboard boxes, split them up, and put them into smaller cardboard boxes, then pass them on to somebody else.'

'Thatsh it?'

'You said it.'

And it was shit. And I hated it. But it was a job, although I suppose that's my dad talking. He had been a miner, and had brought me up to believe that it was better to be employed and pissed off than to be happy and idle. But since his day the employment options and the boredom factor had altered out of recognition for the unqualified youth of Stoke-on-Trent: the pits and pot banks are no longer there, just dead chimneys and old slag heaps that look like green burial mounds; it was the electronics industry that took on me and most of my school mates, all of us wondering how we could apply the stuff we'd done at school about Henry the Eighth, simultaneous equations and Eskimos to soldering things onto circuit boards, pushing pallet trucks and, in my case, opening deliveries to the stores and dividing them into numbered jobs for the shop floor.

As me and Nev talked, Vicki had danced her way round to face us. Although he had known her all through school, Nev just couldn't cope with the fact that she had recently regenerated, Dr. Who-like, into a new version who wore short skirts, make-up and perfume, and definitely had the hots for him.

'Come on Ne'll, Dance.'

TASTING THE WIND

Neville's bottom lip jutted out as he folded his arms and swung away from her. Shoulders sinking, Vicki hung around for a minute or so, before tearfully shuffling back to the dance floor.

'What's up Nev, Do you only dance to head bangers? Why don't you give Vicki a dance and make her night?'

'I not dance with her,' said Neville, continuing to look away, 'she an'capped lady.'

I just looked at him. The corners of his mouth were drawn down, his forehead furrowed and his eyes questioning, as if I should have understood why he wouldn't want to dance with Vicki. Would I? Well of course I would, I had done lots of times. But that was as a volunteer at a special club, and I know that there's dancing and there's *dancing*. There's dancing like you do with your elderly aunt so that she can join in the party, and there's the other kind. And Vicki wanted the other kind, but when Neville looked at her his first thought was exactly the same as other people have when they see him- 'Down Syndrome', or perhaps even 'mongol'- and the poor sod didn't realise the irony of it.

Neville also had no idea of the concept 'out of your league,' as he looked across the dance floor to where a small blonde in a little black dress had formed an arm-swinging circle. She was a new volunteer, and seemed to think it was what you did at that sort of club. Next thing, Neville was there, not too close, but close enough to be seen, hands in pockets and head down, his tongue sticking out further than it needed to. She turned around and noticed the poor lad, all on his own, nobody to dance with, held out her hand, and then bingo, the circle broke up as the smoochy section started and the new volunteer ended up in full clinch with Nev.

'I see Neville the Devil's doing his cute little Down syndrome act again.'

Jo.

I hadn't even seen her come in, and she was standing right next to me. The heartbeat started. The mouth dried. I took a deep breath and was about to say: *don't take things seriously? Just coasting? Well I'm shipping out and I'm going to London now. I'll show you who's got no purpose. You'll be begging me to come back you bitch.*

But all I could manage was:

'Jo?'

'Martin.'

'How are you?'

'Fine. How are you?'

'Fine. In fact, I'm happy.'

Happy.

Well I *was* happy. Happy about the fact that I could speak. I glanced over at Neville, who was having fun with his little blond piece, dancing and singing along to 'Move closer till it feels like we're really making love,' his hands sliding further down the little black dress, as Vicki sat crying by the bar.

'I thought...' my words were whittling down to a dry little squeak, so I coughed, took a deep breath, and looked her full in her dimpled chin.

'I thought you didn't come here anymore.'

She did that nervous hair-twiddling thing. 'I'd heard that you were going to be here tonight, and I wanted to say goodbye, and to ask you...' *You want to ask me to stay don't you? You've realised you made a mistake and you want me back.*

She turned away from me, the slowly changing disco lights picking out a well of tears, making her brown eyes blue, then yellow, then red.

'...I wanted to ask you if you were leaving because of me.'

Of course I'm leaving because of you, why else do you think I'm packing up and travelling two hundred miles away if it's not some stupid male gesture conceived in a drunken stupor from the inside of a toilet bowl.

So I said: 'No. Well not entirely. I just haven't got much to hang on for around here have I? And I'm twenty-five now. That's a quarter of a century. I don't want to spend the next forty years opening boxes.'

'But why London?'

Yes, why London? I suppose it just has more of a dramatic edge to it than 'I'm running off to Scunthorpe.'

'I couldn't get anything I fancied round here. There were pages of jobs down South though.'

Jo looked at her watch, and then, for the first time, the penny dropped: no matter what foolhardy plans I could come up with-running off to London, holding her rabbit, Baldric, hostage, cutting off my balls and presenting them to her as earrings- she would not be getting back with me. And there was one major reason for that.

'Jo...is there somebody else?'

Sighing, she looked down and said 'Yes. His name's Ken. He's a bank manager.'

'Barbie not available tonight then?'

'Martin!'

'Sorry.'

It always used to be like that. I'd say something outrageous, she'd say 'Martin', I'd say 'sorry', but more often than not we'd collapse in a giggling heap. Not tonight.

She put her hand on mine and I felt a trail of goose bumps run from it up to the top of my spine.

'I'll have to go.'

She hadn't asked me to stay. She wasn't going to ask me to stay. She took a card from her handbag and, giving it to me, leaned over and kissed me on the lips. And for once I did notice that she was wearing a different perfume, and that it was obviously a more expensive one than I used to buy her.

'I just wanted to let you know,' she said, 'that there's no hard feelings. Take care while you're out there changing the world. Maybe you could drop me a line?'

As she left, the lights came up. I didn't want it to end like that. I wanted to go after her, tell her how I felt, that I knew she could never be happy with Flash Harry and that she should swallow her pride and come back. I started for the door, but nearly knocked over a small figure who had positioned herself right in front of me. I looked down, and Vicki was standing there, her face pink and puffy, her hands behind her back.

'Before you go,' said the youth club leader at the mike, 'we have a little presentation to show our appreciation to one of our volunteers, Martin Peach, who is leaving us tomorrow to go on to greater things.'

A car started up outside, its headlights tracking across the curtains as it pulled out of the car park. Vicki handed me a wrapped present, about the size and shape of a pen box, then flung her arms around my neck, pulling me down so that her tears formed a warm wet patch on my shoulder.

'Do you know, Vicki,' and this one always did the trick when she was crying over one of Neville's rebuffs, 'your face looks like a pound of tripe.'

But it didn't work this time.

It occurred to me that we were both pretty much in the same boat, Vicki and me: found wanting and dumped. I gave her a squeeze, and felt her shoulders start to move as if they were pumping out the tears.

There was a point where I felt like I might start joining in, until I reminded myself that this was something I didn't do, couldn't do, and pulled away from her just in time to avoid making a fool of myself.

***

Back in the rat-arsed present I find myself rising, viewing the world as if through hazy polythene, which distorts and bulges as I pull myself up using the sink. I stare at the mirror until the two images of myself fuse into one. Now work this one out: I've got a pale, freckled face, with   hair that is red- tinged but murky, like clay that's just been dug out of the garden. I've got a good nose, which is well formed, midrange size and slightly turned. Silver rimmed glasses hide brown eyes that are so deep that you can hardly tell where the colour begins and the pupil ends. My cheeks aren't chubby, but they aren't hollow either. I've got full lips and - no kidding- a cleft chin like Kirk Douglas. So why, with all of this, am I not good looking? I've decided it can only be one thing: proportion. I've got all the right parts, but not necessarily in the right proportions.

It takes several laps of the flat, but I eventually make it to the bedroom. I identify it as the bedroom because I recognise the picture on the wall that is propping me up. It's one of those crappy student posters that Jo put there just before she left me, which says:

Tomorrow is the first day of the rest of your life.

The picture is of an orange sunset reflected in a calm sea.

Failing to see the straining holdall which contains all of my worldly goods, I trip over it, but luckily end up crashing onto the bed. I can see a crumpled newspaper cutting on my bedside cabinet, which is the job advert that I'd found in Jo's 'Guardian.' My efforts to focus on it are totally unsuccessful, which is a shame really, because I can't for the life of me remember what the job is. I can just about make out the bold print at the top, which says:

Wanted: Graduates.

Yes, I know it says graduates, and I've only got art 'A' level, but in my book it's as good as a degree, and I had managed to get hold of a certificate. That was the easy bit. The biggest problem had been the fact that I needed a reference. Mr. Foster wasn't going to give me one, because he'd sacked me, so I wrote my own and got Foster's secretary, Gill, to intercept the request and send out the fake. I just love it when a plan comes together.

The intention had never been to get a job. The idea was that at some stage Jo would find out that I was planning to move two hundred miles away and would come back, begging me not to go. But she

didn't, and after tonight I know why. So here I am, no girlfriend, no job, no family to speak of, and no future.

Unless I go tomorrow.

On the way from the club to the pub tonight I'd just about decided the opposite. I'd have had to disappoint my mate Dave, who was due to move into the flat with his latest lay at the weekend, but he'd have got over it. Problem was, when I got to the pub there was a surprise party for somebody, with a buffet, a pile of presents and posters saying 'Bon Voyage.'

'Looks like there's a do on,' I'd said to Dave, 'whose leaving?'

'You are, you dozy tosser,' he'd said, 'you are.'

It was only then that it occurred to me that maybe I should go ahead with it. Maybe I did need to get away from everything I'd known, and make a fresh start. What had I got to lose?

As I begin to drift into unconsciousness, the last thing I'm aware of is the poster, which is directly ahead of me on the wall at the foot of the bed.

Tomorrow is the first day of the rest of your life.

I'd never noticed before, but there is a yacht bobbing up and down upon the water. And it *is* bobbing up and down. And it *is* starting to sail away from me. As I watch it's progress I can see a figure on board and it takes a while before I realise that it's Jo, and that she's waving goodbye.

I sit up with a start- not an easy thing to do when you're on the cusp of drunkenness and hang over. Bleary eyed, I stare at the orange poster. It's just a setting sun. There mustn't have been a yacht on it in the first place. The bedside lamp casts my shadow over the picture, and somehow, in the half-light, its colours have changed, giving the message a whole new meaning.

Tomorrow is the first day of the rest of your life.

But now, instead of a bright sunset and the promise of good times ahead, dark clouds hang ominously over vast and dangerous looking seas. No longer buoyed up by the alcohol that had carried me through the evening, I look at the picture and get a deep sense of foreboding, a feeling which, if I were superstitious, I would see as some sort of premonition.

-Chapter 2-

3rd November 1986
09.05 a.m.

Through the translucent plastic strips that covered the side entrance of the hospital, small amber baggage trucks droned in and out like bees, carrying piles of bright yellow plastic sacks marked 'for incineration.' In front of the reception area, an orange brick afterthought of about one hundred and thirty years, a man in a blue overall and a flat cap was herding a group of patients onto a minibus. A short, obese woman in a grey raincoat and white plimsolls without laces struggled to climb the step. The man poked her in the back, and when she screamed in defiance swiped her across the head with an audible crack, before looking around to see if anyone was watching. When he saw Jamie approaching he ruffled her hair affectionately, then grabbed both shoulders of her coat and pushed her onto the vehicle. The door of the bus slammed shut and it set off down a slope to the right of the building, disappearing behind a line of trees.

The hospital was just one of the many Victorian giants that circled the city, huge yet virtually invisible. It had a central clock tower, a tall belching chimney, and a water tower. It had Yellowing patches of ivy that looked like an impetigo rash on its grey skin. And it was dying.

Even when he had worked there as a nursing student, Jamie had known that the arguments for its existence were as antiquated as the building itself. The Victorians had believed that the people they institutionalised were ill, and it followed that if people were ill they should be in hospital.

24

The right answer, thought Jamie, *to the wrong question.*

As was eugenics, which said that left to their own devices 'idiots' would breed and produce idiot offspring, who would cause the

average intelligence of Englishmen over the following centuries to fall, and for manners and culture to become a thing of the past. Jamie smiled as he recalled what his colleague, Colin, had said only the night before:

'The eugenics argument falls flat doesn't it, when you realise that despite separating so many so-called 'defectives' from the gene pool the average Englishman is thick as pigshit. I mean, if 'Eastenders' is meant to represent the state of the nation...I rest my case.'

Jamie made to follow in the direction of the bus, but as he passed by the hospital entrance a small man with black, greased-back hair, broke rank with the mob that jostled to be first in line for the returning vehicle, and made a limping run toward him.

'Wait a minute, please... wait.'

Despite the fact that he couldn't have been much more than five foot tall his jeans were too short in the leg, and were of a faded, nondescript colour, which blended with both the hospital and the day. By complete contrast, his jumper was lime green, decorated with a polka dot pattern that Jamie realised as he drew closer comprised of holes and cigarette burns. The man stood in front of him, wringing his hands.

'Can I help you?' asked Jamie, assuming an old-fashioned air of politeness.

'Are you a S-Social Worker?'

Easy mistake to make, thought Jamie.

His face was particularly pale today, and the cold wind had done nothing to help his eyelids, which were dry with eczema. Wearing a combat jacket and hair scraped back into a ponytail, revealing a single stud earring, he had an air about him when entering the hospital grounds of someone who was on a mission in enemy territory.

'Sort of,' he said, 'I'm a Senior Residential Social Worker, but call me Jamie.'

'Can you tell me then: when can I go home?'

TASTING THE WIND

Jamie looked across the void, desperately wanting to be a bearer of good news, but feeling like an apocalyptic messenger announcing the down side of the second coming: *it's not for everyone.*

'What's your name,' asked Jamie.

'Timmy Weekman.'

'I'm sorry Mr. Weekman, you're not on our list, but maybe someone else will...'

'Please take me, I've been good. I don't want to stay here, I will be good, please let me come with you...'

Timmy started slapping his own face with one hand, and biting the soft flesh between the thumb and forefinger of the other. As a thin stream of blood began to run down the man's wrist, Jamie's instinct as an ex- nurse was to elevate the hand and to apply pressure to the wound, but he knew that if he tried to do that it was likely that he wouldn't just be being faced by a manic patient, but by a manic patient who was also bleeding profusely and choking on a lump of his own flesh. What he needed was a distraction.

It came with a ripple of laughter from the crowd, which quickly developed into a chorus of clapping and shouting. Timmy Weekmen switched instantaneously from mania to manic laughter, as the crowd parted to reveal a breathless middle-aged nurse, chasing a laughing man in red pyjamas across the gravel forecourt. The man had a thick mop of hair like a brush perched on his head, and a long, pockmarked chin, which reminded Jamie of the man in the moon from a childhood storybook. As he crunched his way in tartan-slippered feet across the orange gravel, he swung a holey 'Tesco' carrier-bag like an incense shaker, and called out:

'Nee naw nee naw nee naw'

And the people who were grouped around and about the old building and slouching in its doorways echoed him:

'Nee naw nee naw nee naw....'

He stopped abruptly and, looking over his shoulder, called:

' Come on Pansy, here boy.'

The pet bounded up to him. He stroked it's thick fur, then as It jumped to lick his face, it caused him to giggle and clutch the bulky carrier bag to his chest, before racing on. And although there was nothing there, the man saw the pet so clearly, and mimed playing with it so precisely, that whenever Jamie recalled the scene he could never do so without seeing a real dog.

The nurse looked at Jamie with a forced smile of recognition.

'I bet you're not taking that one.'

'No,' said Jamie, ' Actually, I was hoping that I might manage to track down Mr. Doyle today, I think he's been avoiding me. Do you know where I might find him?'

'Your best bet, as usual, is the 'Happy Owls', but I think you're flogging a dead horse there. Oscar is quite happy where he is.'

'I'm sure,' said Jamie 'that if we just got a chance to talk to Mr. Doyle and to put what we have to offer in an unbiased way, he'd be quite happy to...'

'It has been put to him in an unbiased way,' she snapped, 'I told him myself what it would mean. He's happy here with the care that we provide.'

'I'm sure he is, but...'

They were interrupted by a loud 'Nee-naw' as the moon-faced man returned, this time chasing his dog. The nurse, having got second wind, pursued him back into the hospital. A minute later, the latter day 'Wee Willy Winky' was running up and down the fire escape, singing 'climb climb up sunshine mountain,' and had inspired a popular uprising, as patients refused to get onto the newly-returned mini bus for fear of missing the entertainment.

The 'Happy Owls' Social Club was still decorated for the Halloween party, which had taken place on the previous Friday night. *No trick or treating for me that night,* thought Jamie, yawning. He had managed to get to bed relatively early, after rushing from the hospital to meet another new staff member at the tube station. He had been working long shifts since Ed, the manager, had had his breakdown and left. Ed had initiated and carried out the first visits to the hospital, at the same time as overseeing the building and equipping of the Bungalow. Then he had been found, crying hysterically, under his desk.

Jamie had seen people burn out before- the last mental handicap hospital he had worked at was across the road from one which specialised in mental health. It was well attested that there was a nurse who had spent most of her working life at one, and was now enjoying enforced retirement at the other. There was an overlapping period at each hospital where people coming across her for the first

time could not tell if they were dealing with a member of staff or a patient. But Ed was the first person Jamie had seen burn out before a project had actually got up and running.

Jamie had met the new Residential Social Worker on Friday night and taken him to his lodgings, where he'd had the weekend to settle in. Today he was being briefed and given rudimentary training. Tomorrow he was starting at the hospital. Since meeting him, Jamie's excitement about his mission to rescue victims of the institution, as he saw it, had become tinged with doubt regarding the quality of the staff they were attracting. The first advertisements had, at a cost, turned up only half the number needed. It was Des Machin, the area manager, who had the idea of putting, in large letters, the word 'GRADUATE' at the top of the next advertisement. The job description and reimbursement were the same, but it would, he had argued, uncover a whole new seam of applicants. Des had read somewhere that the concept of the 'graduate job' was becoming a thing of the past for arts graduates. 'What do you say to an arts graduate with a job?' asked the contemporary joke: 'Big Mac and fries please.' So there should be, Des had argued, a market for those after their first job who would value a year or two of work experience in the 'real world.'

So far, only two had turned up: there was Jane Vertue, a small, mousy theology graduate, who seemed at first reserved, but was proving to be an intelligent and incisive advocate for the rights of the patients... and there was Martin Peach.

And if he's a graduate, thought Jamie, *I must be Maggie Thatcher.*

But beggars, he reminded himself, could not be choosers. Word was that even the normally unflappable Des was starting to panic. Firstly he had lost his manager, then recruitment just hadn't turned up enough suitable candidates among the usual clutch of inadequates, social misfits and perverts. The level of pay was such that it would only attract two types of person: those with a real vocation or those who just couldn't get anything else. Then people were turning up and leaving after a few days because they said it hadn't been made clear to them about the level of handicap they'd be working with, so Des had taken it upon himself to phone the others to check that they knew what they were coming to. To recruit enough people to staff a whole new service may realistically mean that interviewers could not be as choosy as they would wish, but if Martin Peach was typical of what was being attracted, Jamie had grave doubts about the future of the Bungalow.

The 'Happy Owls' had a morning aroma of burnt toast and bleach. Patients in faded blue overalls were being directed by staff in wiping tables and mopping floors, the screeching of the table legs on the tiles competing with 'the Birdie Song' on the jukebox, and with the sound of a children's counting rhyme from the television in the lounge area.

About twenty years before, the 'Friends Society' had decided to raise funds for a patients' social club. The nearby village of Oulston was home to the retired stockbroker, Church of England foxhunting set, and some of the residents were descendants of the same well-meaning Victorians who had originally backed the building of the hospital, so had a sense of hereditary ownership over it and the goings on of those who lived there. If a social centre was built on site, they felt, it would give the patients somewhere to meet, something different to do, and may also discourage them from wandering to the village pub.

At the first meeting of the 'Friends of Oulston' someone had said 'there should be a cafeteria and a lounge area.' (The possibility of a bar never arose.) Then there were hours of debate about which one should be on the left, and which on the right of the foyer. At the second meeting the issue of a name for the club was mooted. After two hours of brainstorming, the name 'Happy Owls' was agreed, at the cost of only one resignation from a 'friend' who had lobbied for it to be named after a distinguished ancestor.

So the 'Titschlinger club' was not to be. Instead it was the 'Happy Owls.' 'Owls' because of the name of the hospital, 'Happy' because it was a place where people could go... to be happy. A local artist contributed by painting a mural on the outside wall of three small owls and a large one, all smiling and winking in a way which made them look more sinister than happy. And since his student days this was how Jamie thought of it: the 'Sinister Owls.'

Twenty years after its creation the lounge furniture of the 'Sinister Owls' had not changed. There were several big soft chairs and settees, all covered in the same mottled burgundy plastic. Closer up the coverings were full of holes, and the occasional attempt to wipe them exposed a much earlier, much happier light red. There was a pool table, and in one corner a large tableau with nursery rhyme figurines, which Jamie considered aesthetically and ethically offensive.

Jamie thought through his brief, which had seemed simple enough to begin with. The first task had been to meet with the individuals who had been chosen for 'resettlement' and offer them a place at the new Bungalow, but somehow, until now, Oscar Doyle had managed to completely avoid him.

Once the offer had been made the interview process was initiated, which meant that everyone who knew the patient, and in some cases the patients themselves, were questioned on their history, their routines, their likes and dislikes, their medical background, and so on, until as complete a picture as possible was built up in order to ease the transition. Another part of this was contacting family members- a feature which in many cases was not proving easy. Some families kept in touch, visiting regularly or having their son or daughter home for holidays. Others had disappeared. Either they had died, or wished to forget all about that child who had not turned out quite as expected.

Jamie was well aware that in these cases it was important to reassure families that the intention was not to reintroduce the person to the family home. It was more about 'personhood.' All human beings have a history, and an essential part of restoring the humanity of the patients was to create a picture of who they were before they had emerged out of the fog to find themselves on a hospital ward, or in the unimaginative surroundings of the 'Happy Owls.'

Sitting on one of the burgundy chairs, his stocking-feet on a coffee table, was a small stocky man with a receding hairline and thick 'jam jar' glasses. Although they were both grey, his holed socks were odd, and dangled at the toe. He was absorbed in a schools' Maths programme on the TV, which was mounted high on the wall.

'Excuse me' said Jamie, in an excited but almost quietly reverential voice, like David Attenborough coming across some lost tribe, 'are you Oscar Doyle?' Oscar was watching the TV intently, as if he was presenting a review of schools' programmes later that day, and appeared not to notice Jamie as he sidled up to him, pulling up a spare stool which had trespassed into the lounge from the cafe area.

'Er, excuse me.'

The man turned his head slowly, trying not to miss the lesson about making up the correct bus fare from a selection of change.

'Yeah?'

'Are you Mr. Doyle?'

'Yeah.'

'Well, my name is Jamie Heffer. I'm a Senior Residential Social Worker.'

His bottom lip jutting a little, Oscar looked at Jamie over the top of his glasses.

'I've come to invite you to move back to the Borough where you lived before you moved here.'

Oscar's bushy eyebrows raised, and he turned his head to face Jamie full on.

'Would you like to do that?'

Oscar took off his glasses, pulled out a shirt flap and wiped them.

'What's it like?'

'Well it's a lovely new purpose-built Bungalow. You'll be sharing with five other people from the hospital. You'll be able to learn a lot of skills that you haven't had the opportunity to use here. What I mean is things like doing your own shopping, your own cooking and washing up, and you could even go out and do a proper job, earn some money instead of having to sit here watching the telly all day.'

Oscar stared silently at Jamie, then jiggled his little finger in his ear.

'So what do you say?'

Oscar looked him up and down, glanced back at his TV programme, then turned completely around to face him, just long enough to say 'Piss off,' before resuming his previous position.

This, thought Jamie, *is not going to be easy.*

-Chapter 3-

31st Oct 1986

7.30 pm

I'm a firm believer in the fact that human beings were never meant to do factory work. The problem is, I suppose, that if we continue to insist on having those microwave ovens and custom kitchens it doesn't leave us with much choice. I remember the first day I worked at the factory, looking at my watch, expecting it to be near to dinnertime and finding it was only nine o'clock. Even the first break, where I had to learn to drink a hot cup of tea in ten minutes, was a whole hour away.

As the years went on, and I learned the ropes, I got into the habit of going to the toilet at nine to break the monotony either by just sitting, or reading a page of newspaper that I'd folded and put in my pocket that morning. I'd heard of some lads who actually took drugs to get them through the boredom, but I never thought of that as a top idea. Neither was wanking. That was what I was doing on one of my unofficial nine o'clock breaks, when Foster, the boss, noticed I was missing from my bench in the stores. The first I knew about it was when I became aware of a pair of black, shiny shoes stopping outside the toilet cubicle in a position indicating that the owner was pressing his ear against the door.

'Peach, are you in there?'

'Yes,' I said, quietly folding up the Samantha Fox picture I'd got from that morning's *Sun* and shoving it back in my pocket.

'Are you ill?'

'No.'

'Then shift your arse out here, and get back to your bench. We're not paying you to crap.'

No, I thought, *you're paying me to wank.*

I flushed the chain, and did up my trousers. It was only after I'd fastened my green overall that I realised it was doing an impression of a magician performing that trick where a floating ball dances under his cloak.

'Martin,' called Foster, 'get yourself out of there... now.'

With my back to him I did this side-to-side crab walk to the sink.

'Just need to wash my hands, Mr. Foster. Health and safety and all.'When the primary school headmaster had given his boys only sex talk, he had recommended for ridding yourself of an unwanted erection (something which I had never experienced until this point) the act of washing your hands in cold water. It didn't work. I dried them on a paper towel as slowly as I could in order to buy time, but there was no change. I had to walk back through a load of sniggering circuit board assemblers, and if I had a penny for every shop floor worker who came to the hatch that afternoon complaining that I'd only issued them a two-inch knob, I'd never need to work again.

One of my teachers once wrote in my report that I had a natural sense of justice, although when I told Jo this she'd suggested it should have read ' a sense of natural justice.' Don't get me wrong, I'm not nasty, but I just can't stand it when people are and they don't get what they deserve. It's as if they've upset some sort of natural order of things that needs to be put right. A 'disturbance in the force.'

It came for Foster almost one year later.

At weekends Mrs. Foster liked nothing better than to be driven out to quaint country villages, eat in quaint country cafes, meet quaint country people, and insult them. So on the day that the travelling book salesman came, Foster had placed an order for the 'English Rural Scenes' calendar.

'This will give her some ideas' he said, admiring the picture of Matlock Bath on the cover.

Quite by coincidence, and in complete contrast, I had got hold of a calendar called 'Bitches in Leather.' Swapping them was easy, taking the stiff white envelope from Foster's desk and sliding one calendar out and the other in. The rest depended upon Foster not looking inside the envelope again, going home that night and saying, 'hello darling, I've got something for you; I thought it might give you some ideas.'

The next day, Foster said nothing, but I could tell by his bloodshot right eye and the bruising around it that my plan had worked. But the poisonous look I got told me that he had somehow worked out who the culprit was, and that my days at the factory were numbered.

*

And that's why I'm standing on a wet pavement outside an old folks' home in North London. I managed to get a bit of a kip on the train- long enough to miss the concrete cows at Milton Keynes- but I'm still knackered from last nights drinking marathon. A thick fog is creating small droplets on my glasses and distorting the glare of the yellow streetlights. I feel like the priest arriving in 'The Exorcist.'

'By the way,' said Jamie, as he dropped me off, 'When you meet Kevin, your new flatmate... don't ask.'

' Don't ask what?'

He said nothing, but gave me a wicked grin as he closed the dented door of his green mini and drove off.

Jamie wasn't what I'd expected at all. Most bosses I know wear ties, but Jamie was dressed like a hippy. I shook his hand anyway when he met me at the tube station, but as I did that a pile of underpants fell through the broken zip of my bag into a puddle. Saved the day though: cracked a joke about being 'care in the community.' I think that broke the ice.

Don't ask what?

What had once been the flat of the officer in charge at the 'Willows' old folks' home is now used as stopgap accommodation for

34

new Social Services staff moving from out of the area. The home is warm and smells of drying laundry and piss. I unzip my leather jacket, pull out a shirt flap and wipe my specs, then an old guy with tartan 'bootee' slippers and a Zimmer-frame leads me to a door marked 'staff only', next to which is a notice board with large black interchangeable letters which reads:

Today is: 25th of June 1986.
The weather is warm

Through the door, I find myself in a dark corridor, the only light being the dimmest of slits at the far end. As the first door slams

behind me I feel for a light switch, find it and press it, but nothing happens. Holding my bag out in front of me I shuffle along- I know it's irrational, but it just seems like the sort of place where you could stumble over a dead body- and all the time I'm telling myself:

This is not a tunnel, I am not enclosed, I can get out.

There's a clunk as my bag hits the door. And beyond the door there's somebody shouting.

'Well go and shove it up your arse, you motherfucker.'

Entering the dimly lit room, I notice a familiar smell: *Christmas. It smells like Christmas: Candles and alcohol.* As my eyes adjust I see a hunched figure sitting on a beanbag with his back to me, silhouetted in the light of a single tall white candle.

'Go screw yourself you Thatcherite bastard.'

Then I notice something gleaming in a line along the floor either side of him: knives, forks and spoons, all laid end to end. This must be something to do with drugs. I'd seen Bob Geldof in 'The Wall,' where he played a rock star who did that when he was going off his head. When there's a gap in the cursing I cough and the bloke turns round, the candlelight showing the outline of a blond beard. Half a beard. The guy had shaved off half his beard.

'Shit, you made me jump...who the fuck are you?'

I introduce myself and he gets up, my voice trailing off as I try to work out what it was exactly that Jamie had warned me not to ask. Was it 'why are you sitting on the floor shouting obscenities at a candle' or 'why have you only got half a beard?

TASTING THE WIND

The answer to the first question soon comes, as he gets me to help gather up his CB rig. There's the unit itself, masses of wires, and a tall aerial on a heavy metal base. I remember my mate Dave telling me how if an aerial's indoors it needs a 'ground plane', loads of metal objects extended from the base, before it can get a decent signal.

'I'm Kevin,' he shouts, as we fling everything into a cupboard. Then he blows out the candle, plunging the room into complete darkness, and a crack of yellow light appears as he opens a small gap between the curtains.

'Come and have a look at this if you want a laugh.'

I move over slowly, feeling how you must if you're being held hostage by a madman, where you have to comply with their requests as if they're perfectly reasonable in order to keep your earlobes out of tomorrow's post and the next day's papers. What we're actually looking out onto is the street. The foggy, dark, and empty street.

'What are we doing?'

'It's called 'bucketmouthing'.'

'Oh'.

A police car pulls up, and from the half-bearded Kevin comes a wheezy laugh, a bit like Muttley, the dog in the cartoon.

'Stupid bastards,' he whispers, 'now what are you going to do, raid the place?'

A copper winds down his window and shakes his head, turning to his unseen colleague to say something like 'this can't be right, its an old folks' home.' The police car remains there for a few minutes, and then slowly starts to inch along the length of the fence.

Just as it's about to head off down the road, the light in the room comes on. I spin round, and so does Kevin the half-bearded, and at the same time he lets off the loudest and most sickeningly ripe fart I have ever heard, an endearing feature of his which, he tells me later, he attributes to his constant diet of vegan curry.

'Turn the fucking light off.'

Before I can see who's there, the light goes off again and Kevin eases the curtain open slightly.

'It's all right, he says, in the tone of somebody on a reconnaissance mission at a Nazi H.Q., 'they've gone.'

The light clicks back on, and standing in the doorway is a lad who must be about my age, but has a sort of old-fashioned look about him: black, shiny, you- can- see- your- face- in- me shoes, amazingly thin legs in black drainpipe trousers with a sharp crease, a white shirt and plain navy blue tie. His dark hair is cut in a short back and sides, and looks like it's Brylcreamed. He has eyebrows that look like the type that a woman would spend hours drawing on, and wears on his tie one of those Christian fish badges that's supposed to be some sort of secret code to other happy-clappies.

'I'm Simeon' he says, shaking my hand firmly. I arrived earlier today.'

As Kevin checks the window again to see if the police really have gone, Simeon leans forward and whispers:

'Have you been into the bathroom yet?'

It strikes me that this sounds like some sort of proposition.

'No', I croak, 'I haven't,' as I reluctantly follow him out of the lounge.

'It's just that, well, I know we'll have to be tolerant if we're going to live together and all, but I don't think that this is reasonable.'

When he opens the bathroom door it feels like going into the tropical house at the zoo: the light is one of those with an enormous bulb, which doubles up as a heater, and it feels like it's been on all day. Simeon nods in the direction of the bath. It's half-filled with soil. From the soil there are small shoots that have started to develop distinctively shaped pointy leaves.

'Why on earth,' he says, getting quietly angry, 'would anyone want to grow tomatoes in the bath?'

On the way here, Jamie had mentioned how he eventually wanted to visit India.

'What for,' I'd asked, jokingly, 'to find yourself?'

'No, he answered, 'I found myself a long time ago, and I liked what I found so much I decided to treat him to a holiday...so why did you want to come to London?'

'To lose myself,' I'd said before I'd even thought about it, and Jamie had laughed. It was only after I'd said it that I realised I wasn't joking.

It occurs to me that in a very short time, and for no particularly good reason, by saying 'goodbye' to a nice flat, a steady job and a relationship and 'hello' to living in an old folks' home with Mork and Mindy, I've already gone a long way to achieving that goal.

TASTING THE WIND

'So where are you working?' asks Kevin, as we rejoin him in the lounge. I'm surprised, because I thought that we were all at the same place, but it turns out that only Simeon will be working with me. Kevin works in homes for the elderly, but reckons he could turn up on our team at any time, as he also gets placements through an agency.

When I tell him that I'm going to be working at Oulston Hospital his face falls.

'And you haven't done this sort of job before?'

'No... is there something wrong?'

'No, no, it's just that it's one of the most difficult ones. There were some big abuse investigations in the seventies which led to so much public outrage that it kicked off the hospital closure programme.

Oulston came top out of all of them. In fact its record for unexplained deaths led to its nickname: Hearse-town. Don't get me wrong man, it's a job that needs doing, and it's long overdue. But do yourself a favour: try not to turn too many stones. You never know what ugly stuff you'll find underneath them.

All you have to do is go in there, get the poor sods out...and do everything you can to make sure that the same mistakes aren't made again.

-Chapter 4-

Minutes of staff meeting.
Tue. 4th November 1986,
09.00a.m.
Present: Jamie (chair,) Colin, Jane (minutes,) Simeon, Martin.
Apologies: Ruth.

1.Jamie explained that he and Colin had been running things since the departure of the manager. A new manager had been appointed and would be starting before Christmas.

2. There would be no further additions to the furnishings and decor of the Bungalow. The new residents would be involved in choosing their own pictures and ornaments for their new home.

3.Jamie stressed that the Bungalow was a home and not a workplace, so all files, stationary etc. to be kept in a locked kitchen cupboard. The residents were to be helped to live normal lives, using the same things in the community that we use: the pubs, the clubs, the cafes, the doctors' the churches etc.

4. Colin explained the key-work system: all staff work with all residents, but everyone is allocated an individual for whom they are particularly responsible.

5. Jamie and Colin gave brief pictures of the people who had been offered places:

Rose Box. She enjoys music and dancing. She has no speech, but will smile if she likes something, completely blank you if she doesn't. She has severe epilepsy, and wears a helmet to stop her from causing herself too much damage when she has a drop fit. She can self-induce seizures through hyperventilating.

Michael Chang: A deep, infectious giggle. Slides around on his bottom most of the time. He often has unexplained bruises. This is thought to be because he is an easy target for some of the other patients.

Rita Spinks: Now thirty, been in the hospital half her life. Great character, but people who misunderstand her think she is aggressive. Has a severe speech impediment but has other ways of getting her meaning over.

Billy Kinkladsi: mid fifties. Great fun. Has a few words but mainly says 'hello.' He sounds quite childish, and this can be a problem if he's going to be treated as an adult. Some of the staff refer to him by his nickname of 'Frankie,' because he reminds them of someone who once lived there.

Andrew Wellman: Really nice lad. Uses a wheelchair. Has very good eye contact. Martin will be his key-worker.

Oscar Doyle: very able. Had proved to be elusive, and at present is refusing to come to the Bungalow. He will be approached again and given the chance, but if he declines he cannot be made to leave.

6.Martin said that he thought that the hospital was closing.

Jamie said that it was, but it would take ten years, based on a forecast of how many people would be resettled and how many would die in that time. The beds of the six people would be kept open until October '87, so that anyone it didn't work out for could return.

7.Jamie raised the subject of terminology. Previous labels had tended to stigmatise people and group them together. He said that it was offensive to call people 'the mentally handicapped', as it was a negative label. People are not mentally handicapped, they HAVE a mental handicap.

Jane asked how we should refer to people. Colin said that at his previous place of employment they were called clients, but this had connotations. Jamie said that 'users' was common, but that in his view this made them sound like drug addicts.

It was decided that the people who live in the Bungalow should be referred to as 'The People who live in the Bungalow.'

12.30. p.m.

'I thought I'd bring you here first,' says Jamie, ' so as not to scare you off. It's one of the better wards... honest. On this one they've actually managed to get rid of uniforms, the girls call the staff by their first names and they're trying to make it a bit more homely. You'll see what I mean.'

Small flecks of off-white paint fall from the peeling door of Marjoram ward like scaly patches of eczema as Jamie presses the jarring buzzer.

'This usually takes a while,' he says.

As we wait a disembodied chant comes to us from one of the corridors, although it is impossible to tell from which direction:

> *'Whose in the cupboard?*
> *Rang the bell,*
> *Kissed the nurse*
> *Made the noise,*
> *Naughty Mr. Hill.'*

'What's all that about?'

'Haven't a clue,' says Jamie.

The spy-hole darkens for a second, then a rusty bolt is drawn and the lower handle pressed down, followed by the one above head height, which signifies that this is the entrance to a secure ward.

Our tour guide is Julie, the staff nurse, five foot nothing in her white trainers, and there isn't a single thing about her appearance- from her blue jeans to her white blouse and wild brown hair- that says 'nurse.' In the day room, three old ladies sit in a horseshoe of armchairs, which are either threadbare, or covered in green vinyl. One of them is knitting, another rocking and talking to herself; the third stares at me as if she's seen some horrific vision of my death. The lino floor, which must originally have been something close to blood red, is now so scuffed that it looks like a mass of threatening purple clouds, occasionally obscured by discarded items of clothing and scattered women's magazines. Down one side of the room there are five large, high windows, paint overlapping from their metal frames onto the glass, all offering the same view of a flat, grey sky. Somebody had tried to make it look a bit friendlier by sticking transfers of butterflies, balloons and poppies in the windows, and at one a mobile of seagulls had been hung. The opposite wall is decorated with a mixture of modern art prints, but in spite of the effort there is no disguising what this is.

In a corner, under a poster of Dali's 'Swans Reflecting Elephants' is a green bean bag, on which a little girl lies face down, like a rag doll with thin limbs that are bent and pointing in unexpected directions. She looks like somebody whose parachute didn't open. Her hair is short and unevenly cut and when she looks up her face is red, as if it has been repeatedly slapped. Her dress, which must originally have been dark blue, is now blue-grey with faded yellow carnations. Suddenly feeling like I'm staring at an accident victim, I concentrate on the posters: assorted Dalis, Klees and Hockneys, and 'The Scream' by Edvard Munsch. I know a little bit about art. I suppose I got into it through collecting science fiction magazines, but it was Jo's idea that I do an 'A' level, during one of her many campaigns to get me to improve myself.

' I got most of these at a car boot sale,' says Julie, 'I thought they'd make the place a little less like a hospital ward: not because of any artistic value, but because they cover the big holes in the plaster.... Sue,' she calls to a freckly nurse who is popping her head round the dining room door, 'could you be a hero and get us three coffees.'

As we sit down, the chairs make a farting sound, setting one of the old ladies off cackling, then the other, and then the third. The little girl who had been lying floppy and lifeless on the beanbag springs up onto all fours, then squats cross-legged on the bag. She wears nothing but the thin floral dress, literally nothing, and her face remains impassive as her soiled fingers delve and pick at her inflamed fanny. An auxiliary who had been fishing behind a huge grey radiator with a window pole triumphantly pulls out a dried up jam rag and bows to the rapturous applause from the telly, where Mrs. Thatcher has just made a speech about how much the nation's quality of life has improved under her government.

'Maggie, stop that.'

Julie has sprinted over to the girl, pulling her hands from where they explore, and rearranging her dress to cover the angry wound between her legs.

'We've got visitors. Sorry about that...so is this your first time in a place like this then?' asks Julie, passing me a coffee from the tray that Sue has brought in.

'Yes,' I say, sipping the coffee, and wondering if she'd realised I'd nearly thrown up at what Maggie was doing. I notice that the mug is chipped in several places, and the surface of the drink is rippling because my hand is shaking.

'Is it what you expected?'

Before I can answer there's a shriek like nails down a blackboard. It's coming from Maggie, who's pulling her hair until chunks of it come out, and sounds like a perfect interpretation of Munch's painting: scared, empty, horrific.

'Just ignore her, she's only attention seeking. We've tried everything, now we're hoping that if we don't react she might stop. You'll get used to it. If you lived here you'd probably be pulling your hair out too.'

As Maggie carries on screaming it sounds like a riot's broken out in the next room. A deep female voice is shouting 'fa'off, fa'off, I hay yow,' followed by a repeated slapping sound. Julie and Jamie seem oblivious to it, so I suppose I have to follow suit.

'Is, er, Maggie one of the patients coming with us?'

'No,' says Jamie, 'there is one person coming from this ward, though. Sounds like she's in the dining room.'

'Just finishing her lunch.' says Julie, ' you'll like Rita. She's very...spirited.'

'Fa'in 'ell...fa' off you cow...fa'in Goolie.'

The voice is getting closer.

'I've had to put her on a diet. I didn't want to, but she has trouble with her walking.'

The sound of a fist being banged on a table is followed by that of chairs skidding across lino floors and hitting walls. Then the door to the dining room is flung open like something from a western saloon scene, and through it comes Rita, a short, stocky one-woman barroom brawl, charging across the room head down, like a limping bull, in tight slacks and an oversized navy blue cardigan.

'Rita,' says Julie, quietly. Rita stops and spins round, her clenched fists seeming to push out from her body with centrifugal force, her long fringe bouncing up to reveal eyes that bulge with anger:

'Want sex' she bellows, and for a moment I feel a cold shudder run down the length of my spine.

'You've had enough already,' says Julie, turning to me, 'one portion of the mush they serve up in here is enough for anyone, but Rita can always find room for seconds.'

Rita stomps, with an uneven gait, down the length of the day room, back to the dining area, waving her fists at anybody who's looking, then with the slam of a door she's gone as quickly as she came.

In Rita's aftermath, the place seems quiet. I say 'quiet', but it strikes me that there can never ever be silence here. Apart from the distant scraping of plates and the ever-present sound of the telly, there's the constant chatter, the moaning sounds of a tall pretty girl with long ginger hair, who constantly paces up and down, wringing her hands like Lady Macbeth, the cackling of the old ladies, and the sound of Sue trying to coax Maggie to the bathroom.

'How many women are there on this ward?'

'Twenty,' says Julie, her tongue searching her teeth for bits of ham, as time has moved onto an indistinguishable staff lunch break.

'There were twenty-five this time last year. Two died, three have been resettled. Rita will be the next to go, when she comes to you.'

I try to imagine Rita living in a normal house, in a normal town, and suddenly something that happened the other day makes sense. Des Machin, the area manager, had phoned me just before I left. He'd phoned to check if I was still coming, which I thought was a bit strange in itself, but as we finished speaking he'd said 'oh, by the way, you do realise that the people in the hospital aren't the cute little Down Syndrome types you're used to.'

'How long has Rita lived here?' I ask, desperately trying to sound relaxed.

'Since she was fifteen. She's thirty now. Maggie has been here for ten years. She started on the children's ward when she was five. Mother couldn't cope. Children's ward couldn't cope. Came here. Maisie over there, the one talking to the doll, she's eighty-two in December and has probably been here the best part of sixty years. Rumour has it she was perfectly all right before they put her in here for having a child out of wedlock.'

The shock of realising what I'm witnessing here feels like a dull blow to the back of my head, which refocuses the whole scene into a disorientating blur. Then I realise that I have actually received a dull blow to the back of my head, and that the ward has, in reality, become a blur. The scene has taken on an impressionistic quality of fuzzy shapes against a white background into which human forms have simply disappeared. I try to adjust my glasses by pushing them with one finger at the top of the frame, but only succeed in poking myself in the eye because the glasses aren't there. The other sensation I'm aware of is that of warm liquid seeping into my crotch, and spreading between my legs, between my buttocks.

Oh my God, I've wet myself. I'm in a mental hospital, I've had some sort of turn and I've wet myself.

'That was a bit drastic,' says Jamie, handing me my specs, 'I usually just tell them they make crap coffee; I've never had to pour it over my arse to make the point.'

As I wipe the red-brown smears from my glasses, and carefully bend one twisted arm back into place, I can hear Julie's voice, at the other end of the ward, telling Maggie off for snatching them from my face.

'So where are you off to next?' asks Julie, leading the now naked Maggie back to where she had dropped her dress.

' Time warp,' says Jamie.

'Time warp?'

'Oh that's what we call Thyme ward,' explains Julie. 'All of the wards on the west wing are named after herbs. The ones on the east are named after flowers. Thyme and Coriander are the male and female 'severe' wards.'

'We've three people coming from Time Warp,' says Jamie. 'One of them you will be key-working for, Martin: Andrew Wellman. You'll realise what we mean by 'Time Warp' when you see it.

As we leave Marjoram It's like the little bit of my brain that does logic is shouting urgently for my attention, but I can't quite make out what it's saying.

For some reason I'm thinking about one Christmas, sometime in the seventies, when the portable telly suddenly became the top present, and I discovered the 'Midnight Movie.' I realised that there was a lot of crap around, but there were quality films like 'The Fly,'

'The Incredible Shrinking man,' and 'War of the Worlds.' If it wasn't science fiction it would be a Hammer Horror. I never got nightmares because of horror films, but sometimes I'd find myself looking around nervously or *forgetting* to switch off the light. The ones that really got to me were the Edgar Alan Poe adaptations: 'The Pit and the Pendulum,' 'The Fall of the House of Usher,' and 'The Masque of the Red Death.' They prodded the same nerves as fairy tales had in the infants, leaving you feeling cold and wet, and aware of another world where there was only disease and cruelty. And that's how I feel now.

Then it comes through loud and clear: *You've just been to a place where you were attacked by a naked girl with shit and God-knows-what on her hands, then the nurse said something which indicated that it wasn't a 'severe' ward.*
No no no, Marjoram isn't a severe ward, but Thyme ward is.
And that's where I'm going next.

-Chapter 5-

4th November 1986
1.45 p.m.

A door to the outside opens, shedding winter light into the corridor, and with it the clearest and sweetest of voices, although I don't recognise the song. Through the white shaft an angel appears, the sudden waft of the open door causing dust to swirl and create a halo around her head, as she gently sweeps a golden tress from her eye. She seems to glide towards Jamie and me, her long cream-coloured raincoat flowing behind her like a robe.

'Oh you're in luck, Martin.' says Jamie.

You can say that again

' Ruth can take you to Thyme ward. She's been here for a week now and knows her way about; she's Rita's key-worker.'

The angel looks up. She'd seemed to be in a world of her own until she was right up to us, but now she smiles, and I forget where I am, my fear being overwhelmed by another basic instinct. When I'd left Marjoram ward I'd intended to ask Jamie there and then for a reference, one which said something like: *although Mr. Peach only worked with us for a relatively short time...*but now things are looking up. Maybe I'd better stay a bit longer, write to Jo and tell her how well I'd taken to my new job. Maybe send her a photograph. Of myself. And my new work-mates.

'I need to be somewhere else now,' says Jamie. 'Ruth, this is Martin, could you navigate for him?'

Now I had heard that London girls were a bit forward, what with this politically correct thing and all, and I think I'm open-minded, but what happens next shocks even me: Ruth holds my hand as we walk down the corridor.

'Where are you going?' she asks. She's a lot smaller than I first thought, and has to tilt her head to look at me.

'Thyme Ward.'

'Thyme? You can't live on Thyme, it's for...' she snatches her hand away like somebody who's accidentally delved into an old sack full of clinical waste.

'You're not...you're...staff, aren't you?'

I nod. She's looking me up and down, staring at my bent glasses with filthy lenses, my bloodshot eye, and the large brown stains on the front and back of my trousers. I suppose it's an easy mistake to make.

Thyme Ward's telly is fixed in a corner about ten foot above the floor. Although you can hear a daytime soap, the picture's a snowstorm of interference which rolls around in need of vertical hold adjustment, like a madman shaking a Christmas ornament. To the group of patients who had been positioned in their wheelchairs to face that direction It didn't seem to matter if there was a picture or not; they just sat there, feet strapped to metal footplates, grey blankets tucked tightly round their legs, like half a dozen guy Fawkes, or scarecrows whose pale heads droop in the heat. And it's not the fresh, outdoor heat of a summer's day, it's more like the warmth of an unwanted and restricting caress from an elderly aunt who smells of antiseptic and piss.

One screams. One cries. Another blows raspberries. Aggressively. I would never have thought that a room full of people who can't speak could make so much noise. Most of them rock backwards and forwards like metronomes, and at quieter moments, where a lull in the bedlam of the ward intersects a gap in the noise from the telly, there's a sound like the continuous winding of a large clock, or of a kid drawing a stick across fence posts.

'Teeth-grinding,' says Carl, the nurse who'd let Ruth and me onto the ward.

'Teeth-grinding? How do they do it so loud?'

'They get plenty of practice.'

Carl's a handsome black guy, not that I'd ever use the word 'handsome' about a bloke, but I suppose he must be by the way Ruth can't take her eyes off him. And even though I've only just met her I can tell that she's using what is obviously her 'special smile.' I am definitely *not* getting the 'special smile,' or anything resembling one, and I've got the definite impression that in a really short time I've somehow offended the beautiful Ruth, but for the life of me I can't think how.

As Carl reaches up to switch off the telly I can't help clenching my teeth together and grinding my molars, but all I manage is the pathetic squeak of tooth against filling.

'You need to get through the enamel first' says Carl, matter-of-factly.

A deep-throated giggle comes from somewhere over in the corner of the room, but I can't see who's making the noise for a man who wears a helmet and is strapped into what looks like an electric chair.

'That's Mickey's laugh' says Ruth, giggling,' infectious isn't it?'

'Have you come to see anyone in particular?' asks Carl.

'Yes, Martin will be key-worker for Andrew. Is he in today?'

'He's having a shower, 'says Carl, wiping the beginnings of a saliva stream from the chin of one of the rocking scarecrows, 'shouldn't be long if you want to hang on.'

The giggling turns to an excited squeal, as a small, oval, oriental face pops out from behind the man in the electric chair. Wearing a faded pink T-shirt and blue denim dungarees, Mickey shuffles towards us, pieces of shredded magazine pages and the ragged seat of his dungarees trailing behind him.

'Good morning Mr. Chang,' says Ruth, 'brought someone to see you. This is Martin. Martin: Mickey.'

Mickey babbles and sticks his thumb into his mouth as far as it will go, stroking the side of his face with his fingers.

On my induction day a bloke called Colin had told me about this thing they call 'normalisation.' Normalisation is to govern everything we do. It isn't, Colin had stressed, about trying to make people 'normal,' but about giving them normal life experiences and choices, the same as anybody in their age group. This means not living in a hospital, (because hospitals are for sick people,) going out to the same pubs and shops and restaurants as everybody else and, it seems

49

to me, having normal conversations with them that they can't possibly understand.

My ability to treat Mickey normally has hit a bit of a set back, as I wave   weakly, looking suspiciously at his hand, which I would have shaken if It hadn't been glistening with saliva.

'Ruth, you couldn't do me a favour could you?' asks Carl, who's standing behind her with an empty wheelchair, 'we're running a bit late, and Mickey needs to be over at I.T.U.'

Ruth squats down in front of Mickey, who grabs her round the neck with both hands, and is hoisted to his feet.

'Can I come with you?'

I know I've got the tone wrong. I know I wanted it to say *can I come with you because I would really like to see an I.T.U, whatever that is,* but it actually came out as *can I come with you because I'm shit-scared of staying here on my own.*

'It's OK.' she says, as she sets off with a gurgling Mickey 'you may as well hang on here and meet Andrew.'

As the door closes the man in the helmet starts to moan. He stares blindly through eyes that look like rotting frogspawn, as he struggles to lift his head. I can see now why Des Machin had warned me that they weren't the cute little Down Syndrome types I was used to at the club, and I find myself wondering how Neville's going on in his quest for a job and rampant sex. There was nobody like this at the 'Breakaways.'

The ward has two rows of beds, about twenty in all, each with grey counterpanes that look like cardboard, and a paper-white sheet .The wall at the far end consists completely of grey, built-in cupboards. This is where the identical men that are lined up in the day-room sleep, in identical beds, and no doubt their identical clothes are kept in the identical cupboards.   As Carl shows me the ward I keep having to remind myself what that Colin bloke said when he did my induction about how you must never forget that these people are human beings, and how they had been made to conform to the rules of the institution. Two of the beds are occupied: in one a kid who looks no more than two has tubes coming out of his nose. In another there's a huge head, almost as big as the mound of pillows it's propped on. You're torn between wanting to look away, and a strange fascination where you find yourself wondering how big a human head could possibly get, or if a head could burst, cartoon style. Yellow matter around the eyes brings back images from your childhood books of Humpty Dumpty, all propped up on the wall, then on the ground, bits of head scattered around, running with sticky yolk.   At the far end of the room there's a long, old-fashioned wheelchair, which looks more like an oversized pushchair. Its occupant rocks, not like the others, but with purpose, because his rocking's moving the chair down the room. He looks middle-aged, with black, greasy hair scraped in strands' across a balding head. Completely wrapped in a red blanket, you can't tell whether he's got any arms until he starts to struggle to free them.

'Ayo,' he calls out in a baby voice.

'Hello'

'Ayo.'

'This is Frankie...sorry, Billy,' says Carl, 'He's one of yours, but I wouldn't get too close to him.'

'Ayo.'

Billy's face crumples in a toothless expression of joy as he manages to get an arm free, elbow first, from the restricting blanket. Then I notice something I've never seen before: he's wearing a sock for a glove. A grey sock, secured at the wrist with sellotape.

'What's that for?'

'He's a grabber, says Carl, 'could give you a nasty nip without those on. They also discourage him from sticking his hand down his throat so that he can projectile vomit.'

I can do that, I think, but I don't say it, because it doesn't make you any friends. But I can, and I can even remember how I learned to do it. It was one summer's day when I was about ten years old and me and Dave were hunting frogs along the banks of the bright orange canal known locally as 'the dirty cut.' Dave threw a shard of glass at one, and a minute later, when its body rose through the orange clouds, it was cleanly decapitated. I ended up retching behind some bushes. The first time that Ricky, my friendly neighbourhood child psychologist and home-wrecker, locked me in the cubbyhole, I pictured the headless frog, and threw up all over his sheepskin jacket.

I must have been stepping back from Billy without realising, because I suddenly get this door handle sticking in my back. There seems to be a small square room in the corner of the ward that looks like it had been plonked there after everything else was finished.

'Do you want a look at the punishment room?' says Carl.

51

'The what?'

'Well, time out room we're meant to call it, but it's really a punishment room, despite what fancy jargon they use. Have a look.'

I open the door, and reluctantly step in, but as Carl clicks the light switch outside the room I shiver at what I see.

'Sometimes patients go ape, and get violent, and they're put in here to calm down. Not just patients on this ward- it's the only punishment room there is, so they'll be brought here from all over. The only problem is... oh shit. Someone must have used this last night and not cleaned up. The Sister'll kill me if she sees that. Just hang on and try it for size while I get a mop.'

With that he leaves, closing the door behind him. I try the handle but the door won't budge; the stupid bastard must have locked it, his idea of some sort of sick initiation into the feel of a real institution. Is it just me, or do you put out signals about the worst possible thing that could happen to you, which people pick up on and almost always get the opposite way round, thinking that you might actually enjoy it? You know, like if you've developed an ingrowing toenail, suddenly everybody wants to stand on your foot. For me it's the claustrophobia thing: more than a normal proportion of people seem to want to lock me in small rooms, or worse. Like when I worked at the factory and the lads got me drunk on my birthday. Problem was it was dinnertime, and we had to go back to work after half an hour of four pints with whisky chasers. They shoved me into a crate and put the top on, so when I came round I thought I'd been buried alive.

Now I'm locked in a room with a pile of human shit, which is probably the only thing stopping me from going into a foetal position and writhing around on the floor. The room is about six foot square, but as high as the ward, creating the feeling of being trapped in a mineshaft. A single light bulb, covered in cobwebs, dangles way above my head, dimly lighting the brick walls, which somebody, a long time before, had painted in a pale blue gloss. I'm starting to sweat now, the room seeming to constrict itself around me. As my eyes get more accustomed to the dim light I see where whoever was incarcerated in here the night before has smeared crap on the walls and door, and I want to retch.

'OK. Carl, I've got the feel of it now.'

I start to focus on other things: a thick clump of hair in the corner, like unwanted remains regurgitated by some beast that lives in here; as I start to bang on the door I notice that it is covered in scratch marks.

'Come on, enough is enough.'

I can feel the shakes starting. Next comes the blind panic. I raise both arms, and am about to beat on the door with clenched fists, when it opens. Ruth is standing there, and a brief expression of horror flashes across her face when she sees me looking like the Incredible Hulk, or some sort of crazy man, with my face all contorted and my fists ready to crash down on her. Carl appears behind her with a mop.

'What's wrong?'

'You...you...locked...door'

'Oh that, no it's just a bit stiff. Honest. Somebody peed on the hinges. It needs seeing to.'

'He's right, Martin,' says Ruth,' I just opened it when I heard you. There's no key in it, look... You OK?'

'Well, yeah,' I say, trying to act cool, pushing my hair back from where it sticks to my forehead.

A sudden noise behind Ruth and Carl causes me to look up from where I stand in the punishment room doorway. A thin youth in a wheelchair is having a violent fit, his eyes rolling up into his head as his body shakes like a pneumatic drill. For a brief moment he comes out of it and his deep blue eyes seem to be looking straight at me. Then they flicker and bulge, as he's racked by what looks like some sort of aftershock, which causes his body to arch and strain against the leather harness that holds him to his wheelchair. The boy wears a faded black tracksuit, which looks several sizes too big. An arm is held stiffly down his side, the other bent up like a dog begging for food. Both hands are twisted inwards so that his fingers, long and thin like a piano player's, press against his wrists. I follow Ruth's lead and speak to him just like you would a normal person but, just as I thought, there's nothing. He doesn't even know I'm here, and to be honest I expect no more response than from a dog or a baby. I touch his hand, not managing to shake it like Ruth had done, because I'm scared of snapping his thin white arms like sticks of chalk. As another fit starts to shake him his chest strains again at the leather harness and a river of saliva and blood runs down his chin onto his bib.

'It's all right,' whispers Ruth, who must have caught my expression. 'Tongues bleed and heal very quickly. Andrew's used to it.'

53

TASTING THE WIND

'Andrew?' I say, thinking that this must be the most handicapped person I have ever seen.

'Yes,' says Ruth, 'It's Andrew. Andrew Wellman. It's him you'll be key-working for.'

-Chapter 6-

Having a name like 'Vertue', and a degree in Biblical Theology, Jane had stopped being surprised when people assumed that she was either wishing to enter the ministry or heading for holy orders. Not that the former was an option, female ordination still being a heresy-hunter's stonesthrow away, but when asked if either vocation was her intention she would patiently point out that her interest in theology, although originally inspired by a faith she had long since abandoned (or had abandoned her, she wasn't quite sure which) had now become something she maintained purely 'for the love of it.'

The team had met up for a coffee at the 'Happy Owls,' and at one point Martin had made the mistake of asking Simeon what his 'Ichthus' badge meant. He went on about how Jesus was associated with fish, because he'd enabled the disciples to bring in a miraculous catch, and then he said it was a secret sign telling early Christians where to meet for their 'praise meetings' in the catacombs. Jane pointed out gently that 'praise meetings' was probably anachronistic, and suggested that if the early Christians did have them in the catacombs they would have been easily recognised by their persecutors because of the cricks in their necks. She was going to leave it at that, until Simeon intimated that because the pastor at his church had spoken about the ichthus sign on the previous Sunday, that what he said about it had to be true.

'I think you'll find,' she said, writing down the words in Greek, and passing the note to Simeon, 'that 'Ichthus' is an acronym for: Iesous christus theou huios soter.'

Although she was never comfortable with intellectual snobbery, she felt that on this occasion it was justified.

TASTING THE WIND

After attaining her Masters' degree at the University of Manchester, Jane had decided to take some time out in the 'real world.' No need to decipher symbolic language there, no ancient texts to translate or mysteries to unravel. Or so she thought. Jane had always had the knack for 'noticing things,' things that seemed to scream out to her when everyone else was totally oblivious- like the Masonic symbolism in the West window of her local Anglican church, like the fact that Martin- whom she had only just met- was besotted with Ruth, and the belief she shared with Jamie that there was more to the model village in the 'Happy Owls' than met the eye.

The 'village' took up the best part of a large ex-snooker table at the far end of the Social Club. It's papier-mâché hills were once bright green but had become dulled with dust and cobwebs. At its centre was a fairy-tale landscape with a fair, cottages, a gingerbread house and a town hall. Dotted around it were several figurines: Jack and Jill falling down from the well at the top of a hill; Little Bo Peep holding a crook, looking into the distance, as a dish and spoon frolic, hand in hand. The plaque above the model read:

Made and presented to the hospital by the friends of Oulston.
March 1955

Jane noticed how some of the figures were placed more centrally to give them greater significance and that some were slightly larger than others.

Hieratic scaling.

One of the largest was a grinning figure in a red and green suit, holding empty hands out to a man with a tray full of pies.

The Rosetta stone used to interpret the imagery of the model was its 'town hall,' which was clearly and unashamedly based on the main building of the hospital, even down to the clock with the year 1832 in gold figures on the face. Perched on top of its tower was Peter Pan, the largest character of all.

'So why do you think,' said Jamie, 'that Simple Simon should feature so prominently in a model at a mental handicap hospital?' Jane was about to speak, when he continued- 'It's an example of how we devalue people through images. We make them into jokes; we caricature them and turn them into cartoons. And once you've done that it's easier to marginalize them, to abuse or even kill them, because they're no longer human.'

'When you say 'kill'' said Simeon, 'you don't mean actual murder...do you?'

'Don't I? One of the reasons why the hospitals are closing is the number of abuse cases coming to light. And yes, in some instances, people died. Sometimes they died through negligence. Sometimes they'd been given the wrong drugs, or been restrained in the wrong way. But something happens before that, and that 'something' is a mindset that sees 'them' as less than 'us,' a mindset which portrays them as sub-human, or as quaint caricatures of us 'normal' folk.

Once you have that you can do what you want to them, and if that mindset permeates the whole institution, there won't even be a proper enquiry. I remember hearing about someone dying in this very hospital when I was a nursing student, and how after the so-called enquiry an auxiliary was bragging about how they'd got...'

Jamie was interrupted by an ancillary who screamed like a harpy as a man with a long, pockmarked chin stretched out to touch the Peter Pan figurine:

'Get your hands off that, you naughty boy.'

Naughty boy? thought Jane, *He must be at least as old as I am.*

Everyone's attention was focused upon the man, including that of 'hospital bully,' Don Maguire, a brawny man in a green jacket, who looked and swaggered like John Wayne. Don shouted a mixture of obscenities across the room from where he stood at the pool table:

'Cunting fucking nee naw arse...lesby homo Eddie Sparrow.'

His cronies laughed uncontrollably, then carried on with their game of pool, which seemed to consist of Don missing shots and waving his cue at the other player until it was agreed that he'd won. Oscar Doyle was lounging by the television, keeping his head down, with a cup of tea and two custard creams perched on his chest.

Eddie turned round and flashed a cheeky, toothy grin at Jane and the rest of the team. As he approached their table he swung a plastic carrier bag in one hand, as with the other he motioned for his invisible dog to follow.

'This,' announced Jamie, as if introducing a celebrity, 'is Eddie Sparrow. Unfortunately he won't be coming to the Bungalow, but he has a great gift for gate-crashing parties, so we'll doubtless be seeing lots of him before we up sticks.'

'I've got a dog at home,' said Eddie, to which Jane replied:

' Oh.... What's it called?'

'Pansy. And I've got a cat.'

'And what's the cat called?'

'Paul.'

'Paul the cat?'

'Yes.'

'Isn't that a strange name for a....'

'Eddie,' interrupted Jamie, who had been through the ritual several times before, 'would you like a drink?'

Colin offered a large bottle of 'Vittel' around, saying how he didn't trust anything out of the Happy Owls urns. Simeon accepted, but nearly choked as Colin told Jane of his forthcoming nudist holiday with his new partner, Derek. Jane understood why Colin felt as he did, because as clean as the cafe area looked it had a musty smell, as if poisonous fungi were growing in the wall cavities and beneath the brown tiles. She had taken an instant liking to Colin, who, although pushing fifty spoke like a children's television presenter, had the curliest blond hair and wore the brightest waistcoats she had ever seen.

'Six teas please' said Jamie to the sour-faced ancillary who had screamed at Eddie for touching the Peter Pan model. She stood with her hands on her hips behind the serving hatch, like a gunslinger at the door of a saloon bar, anticipating a shoot-out.

'How many staff, how many patients?'

'It doesn't matter,' said Jamie.

'Mr. Hill's gonna pull the cat's tail off,' called Eddie.

The woman looked at Jamie as if he should know better, then past him to Eddie, and said:

'So that'll be five staff and one patient.'

Jamie returned to the table with a tray holding six cups: five china, and one in thick, green, unbreakable plastic. The sixth cup had been poured from a different pot, to which milk and sugar had already been added.

'Anybody like very sweet milky tea?' Asked Jamie. 'No? In that case, I'll have that one.'

The ancillary watched through piggy little eyes as Jamie, grimacing, sipped the tea; then she focused on Eddie, who'd been given a china cup.

They were never given the real cups. *They* were likely to break them and cost the hospital so much money that some terrible crisis would befall. *They* hadn't got refined tastes, so preferred lots of milk and sugar; no Darjeeling or Earl Grey for *them*, oh no, it would be wasted. For staff a choice. For patients, it was sweet white tea only.

Eddie sat mumbling to himself and staring into his teacup as he swirled the dark liquid round.

'It's not tea,' he said, 'not tea. It's not.'

'It's O.K. Eddie,' said Jane, 'it is tea, look.'

She picked up a plastic milk portion, emptied it into Eddie's tea, and the miraculous transformation stilled the storm. Eddie put the cup to his mouth with both hands and in two gulps it was empty. Nobody was going to take that from him. He looked down to check that his carrier bag was still held tightly between his legs then, smacking his lips loudly, said:

'Ahhh... It looks good, it tastes good, and by golly it does you good.'

For a moment Eddie looked as if he was in a waking dream, then his eyes lit up in a look like recognition as he said:

'Mr. Hill is going to smash the cup.'

The woman behind the counter scowled, and started to raise her hand, her trigger finger beginning to uncurl into a reprimanding pointer, her mouth starting to form the words: *I told you this would happen.*

'Mr.Hill is going to smash the cup' repeated Eddie, laughing like a maniac as the cup, anticipating its disintegration, rattled in its saucer.

'Don't be a wally, Eddie,' said Jamie 'give us the cup.'

'Mr. Hill is going to smash the cup.'

The ancillary, unable to stand the tension any longer, lifted the counter and squeezed her grubby- aproned rump through the gap.

It was the slamming down of the counter that made Eddie jump. The jump caused the cup to fall over in the saucer, but Jane's mistimed grab knocked it onto the table; the cup bounced, Martin lunged for it, and missed, as it skidded over the edge and smashed on the brown tiled floor.

'Mr. Hill has broken the cup' trilled Eddie triumphantly.

TASTING THE WIND

'And he'll bloody well pay for it one way or another' screeched a voice which sounded like a vacuum cleaner being dragged over tiles.

'He didn't break it,' said Jane, calmly, 'I did.'

'Look on the bright side,' said Martin, 'you gave us a cup, we give you back a thirty piece set.'

The woman looked at them as if to say it was obvious to her, and should have been to everyone, that there was more than a broken cup at stake here.

'You shouldn't give them the best cups. There's not enough money in hospitals for them to have best cups.'

'Eddie didn't want sugar,' said Jamie, 'I did.'

'But they all have sugar.'

Not just a cup, but some eternal law had also been broken. All patients take sugar. Eddie is a patient, therefore Eddie takes sugar.

'Not any more they don't' said Jane. 'Anyway, like I said, I broke the cup, so I'll pay for it.'

Unable to cope, the woman stormed back to her little kingdom, slamming the counter down to reinstate the border between it and the badlands beyond.

'Whose in the cupboard?' chanted Eddie,
'Rang the bell,
Kissed the nurse,
Smashed the cup,
Naughty Mr Hill.'

The excitement over, Jane turned her attention back to the Nursery rhyme tableau. Something was just not adding up.

The prominence of Simple Simon is obvious, but what is Peter Pan doing on a nursery rhyme tableau when he's not a nursery rhyme character?

And not only was Peter Pan on the wrong tableau, she observed, but he was also the largest character.

Hieratic scaling. And Peter Pan represents... Of course: Within this model is a statement about an entire philosophy of care in which people do not think twice about calling a mature man a naughty boy, or disregarding his basic rights, including his right to choose to have milk and sugar in his tea or not.

'M- bloody 25,' ranted Colin, complaining about how long it had taken him to drive the mini-bus from the Bungalow to the hospital that morning. 'Thatcher only opened it a week ago, and already it's a car park.'

'The eternal child,' said Jane, interrupting Colin's flow.

'What was that, dear?'

'Sorry, I was just thinking out aloud...'

> 'Whose in the cupboard? ' Chanted Eddie,
> 'Rang the bell,
> Kissed the nurse,
> Smashed the cup,
> Naughty Mr Hill.'

'...I'd noticed that Peter Pan doesn't belong because he's not a nursery rhyme character, but as the town hall is really the hospital, whoever put the figure there is saying that the patients are like children who will never grow up.'

'But that's awful,' said Ruth. The people here are all adults...'

'Give the girl a gold star,' said Jamie, 'aren't you the bright one?'

'Not really,' said Jane, 'it's the theologian in me- you learn to make the most tenuous of links, and to pick up the smallest of nuances. Problem is, most of the time they don't exist.'

'I first saw this model about ten years ago, said Jamie, and apart from 'Simple Simon,' which is obvious, I never thought to ask if any of the other characters had significance. It just shows how you stop really looking at things when they're always there.'

In the same way, the nurses had long since ceased to listen to Eddie's chant, and the Bungalow staff were continuing in that tradition- it was just something that Eddie did, something that was always there which, like the babble of so many of his peers, had no meaning.

But occasionally, just occasionally, the words changed.

> 'Whose in the cupboard?' Chanted Eddie, as he skipped round the tables,

> 'Kissed the nurse,
> Tied the socks,
> Killed the man...'

But Eddie was a man with an invisible dog, and it was universally accepted that most of what he said was the raving of a harmless, though over-imaginative and damaged mind.

TASTING THE WIND

And as Jane smiled at her iconographic discovery, clues to a deeper, darker secret skipped past her and out through the door of the 'Happy Owls' social club.

-Chapter 7-

17th November 1986

My mate Dave (like he always said he would) drives lorries for a living now, and I (like my teachers always said I would) have ended up in an institution. Today Dave's on another long haul, so he's called in with some more of my stuff: my portable hi-fi, telly, and Spectrum computer. He's already pissing himself laughing about me living in an old folks' home, and when I tell him about my flatmates I know it'll be all round the pub tomorrow night.

'He Weed in the bath... So what's up with that?'

'No, Dave, no, he hadn't weed in the bath, he's growing weed in the bath, come and see for yourself...'

'And he's only got half a beard?'

'Yes.'

'Why?'

'We don't ask.'

'Oh. And this guy's looking after the mentally handicapped?'

'No. He's looking after older people. Only we don't say 'looking after,' we say, 'enabling,' and we don't say 'the mentally handicapped,' we say 'people with a mental handicap'. I've picked that up from things that Colin and Jamie have said, but although I'm impressed with it, Dave isn't. To Dave, political correctness is something politicians get at weekends from women dressed as schoolmistresses.

'Bovine excrement' he says, eating his last chip.

'Eh?'

TASTING THE WIND

'Only I usually say 'bullshit', 'cos shit's shit no matter what you call it. Do us a favour, Mart: when you get your senses back and return to the real world, dunner come back as a pretentious southern get will you?'

Dave always says things like that, but this time he sounds sort of sad. I look at him as he's about to leave, filling the doorway in his blue overall, not knowing whether to shake his hand or hug him, but settling for the absolutely no response which blokes use in the hope that it says something exact at the same time as upholding their masculinity. And I don't say, 'Have you seen Jo?' guessing from the fact that he says nothing, that he hasn't. What I do say is:

'Fuck off and put wood in th'ole then, us old folks are freezing us knackers off in here.'

As Dave's lorry disappears round the corner I wonder if I will ever find as good a mate down here. It certainly won't be Simeon or Kevin. Jamie seems all right, as does the beautiful Ruth, and the other girl, Jane. Jane's not unattractive, but she's probably a bit 'intellectual' for my tastes. O.K., so Ruth is no dunce, but if I was to choose between a girl who can argue from experience for the existence of the G-spot, and one who can quote five scholars who are for and five against... who would you choose?

The flat seems quiet now that Dave's gone. The lads are both out, so at least I've got space. Not one I can call my own, but at least it's somewhere I can escape to and do my own thing. And tonight the thing I'm planning to do is sit stark -bollock -naked (because the flat is old folks' home temperature) and play chess on my 'Spectrum' computer, in the dark, with a can of 'Special Brew' in my hand.

I nip out to the offie, and when I return Kev is back. If you can call it that. Several red candles flicker in the living room to the unmistakable sound of Floyd's 'Dark Side of the Moon' as Kevin, the half-bearded bard slumps cross-legged on the floor over a typewriter, which is spattered with fag ash. Although I've only been gone for about half an hour, an empty red wine bottle lies to his right, and to his left a pile of paper. Poems. The verse in the typewriter reads:

I didn't have a woman
So I made one out of poo,
She could do all of the things
That a woman ought to do

ALLAN MAYER

Apart from being a soul mate.
And I couldn't kiss her lips.
Just one more example of
A shit relationship.

No intelligent life here then.

Before I left Stoke I'd saved a half-finished chess game on my computer. This time I'm going to win, and go on to the dizzy heights of a level-two game. So, kit off, a foaming pint of brew in the silver tankard the lads at the factory had bought me as a leaving present, and I'm going to slaughter the bastard.

About twenty minutes later I've nearly finished my can, and for the first time ever I'm two moves away from Check Mate. I'm feeling a bit peckish, but decide to finish the job before celebrating with a portion of Kev's curry that's been maturing in the pan for three days.

Black to move. After a two second deliberation a knight takes one of my pawns and...

Fork.

It's called a fork, where one knight threatens the king and the queen at the same time. You can't leave your king in check, so you move it and kiss your queen's ass goodbye. So I do what I always do when this happens: I resign. I select 'New Game,' and all of the symbols are back on their starting squares.

At some point tonight, I'm aware of Kev falling into my room in a drunken stupor, then pulling himself up on the door handle and staring at my freckled body, which is lit only by the green light of the screen. He thinks he's stumbled across some sort of alien invasion. When I tell him I'm just playing on my 'Spectrum' he staggers out, apologising for interrupting my wank.

I carry on with the new game, knocking back the booze a bit quicker than I ever used to. Some of the images from the hospital won't go away, so I have to keep focused on something else, feeding and numbing my senses at the same time to stop them from going down roads I'd rather not travel. I'm about to get up and go to the kitchen for another drink when it happens again: the door opens behind me and there is a sound like somebody stumbling. But this time nobody falls in. I stand up, put on some underpants, and look out into the hall, expecting to see an inebriated flatmate, but the hall is empty. Kevin is still in the lounge, communing with his typewriter, and I have to shake him to bring him round.

'Kev, wake up. I think there's somebody in the flat.'

He follows me, eyes puffed from smoke, red wine and creativity, to Simeon's room, where the door is open, but before we get any further Simeon appears from the door to 'The Willows', clutching a Bible.

'What's going on, man?'

'Someone broke in,' Says Sim. 'The bathroom window must have been open. I was just having my quiet time with the Lord when I heard running and a bang from the bathroom.'

We examine the bathroom, and the window is wide open.

'Oh shit, man,' whines Kev, 'my weed.'

In his hurry to get away the would-be burglar had fallen into the bath, flattening Kevin's indoor garden. Pleas from Simeon and me had failed to restore the room to its rightful use, so we'd eventually got our baths by sneaking into 'The Willows' at off-peak times. We stand and watch as Kevin sorts through the shoots, trying to find any that are undamaged, and as he does so the realisation starts to dawn on me.

'Sim, where've you just been?'

'I was in my room reading...'

'No, after that.'

'I popped into the office to call the police.'

Kevin's silent obscenities are telepathed to both of us as he tears up the bruised weed and starts to feed it down the toilet.

'Sim, get rid of the soil.'

'How?'

'I don't care...wash it down the fucking plughole, just...'

'There's no need to swear, and I don't think we should be disturbing the soil- the burglar may have destroyed your tomato plants, but he's left a perfect...'

'They're not fucking tomato plants! Now get rid of the soil...Martin, the CB, the sodding CB; hide it in the cupboard or something.'

The two policemen, when they eventually turn up, explain that this is just one of many calls they get these days. More and more old folks' homes (or 'homes for retired people,' corrects Kevin) are being targeted for easy pickings. According to P.C. Plod, Ph.D., It is a time when 'nothing sacred' is spreading from the occasional to the usual, and when the 'honest criminal', if he ever existed, is disappearing like the red squirrel under the weight of numbers of his less attractive counterpart.

Lying in bed I can't drift off for wondering what the police officers' report looks like.

We responded to a call from 'The Willows' Old folks' home (or home for retired people), and were directed by the Officer in Charge to the flat that forms an annex to the above mentioned home. There we were met by the three occupants of the flat, Messrs Leach, Peach, and Costello, who are employees of Social Services. Mr. Peach was wearing a pair of purple Y-Fronts. Mr.Leach was wearing a bathrobe and carrying a Bible. Mr. Costello had half a beard. Mr. Leach and Mr. Peach said that they had heard an intruder in the flat at around midnight. Mr. Costello said that he had heard nothing because he was 'pissed out of his skull.'

I investigated the bathroom window, which was the suggested entry and exit route of the trespasser, and was surprised to find the bath full of mud. Mr Costello explained that he had earlier prepared the mud bath for Mr.Peach, as a treatment for his embarrassing freckly skin condition.

Remembering previous calls to this locality, I asked the three men if either of them had experience of Citizen Band radio. They said that they had not. Mr. Costello said that he had seen me looking around before, and that he would wave the next time he 'eyeballed' me.

When I eventually get to sleep my dreams are filled with burglars and scenes from the hospital. At some point a policeman escorts me to the dock of a court which is filled with nursery rhyme and cartoon characters. At the back of the darkened room I see what I think is a familiar silhouette. The voice that comes from it certainly is familiar, and as Jo steps out of the shadows she repeats one of the accusations I remember from THE BIG ROW:

TASTING THE WIND

You don't know the first thing about unconditional love...

I hadn't got a clue where that one had come from, but to be honest, she was right. I don't have a clue about it because I don't do it, because there's no such thing. There's no such thing because love, no matter how good it is, is always tainted with self-interest. Show me the bloke who will give his bird an orgasm because he loves her and never want one himself. Unconditional love is a myth in the same league as God, the Loch Ness Monster and happy ever after: they don't exist.

...Therefore you stand accused of...

But the words are drowned in a swell of cartoon babble.

'What...What am I accused of?'

You stand accused of....

Again the words disappear into chaos, as Andrew Wellman floats down the aisle in his wheelchair.

'What am I accused of?'

Imitation.

'Imitation. Of what?'

Of someone who gives a...

-Chapter 8-

18th November 1986
6 a.m.

...Shit. The overwhelming odour of Thyme ward this morning.
I'm starting to feel like each day is blending into the next, and the
feeling isn't helped by the fact that I hardly slept last night because of
burglars and bad dreams. And this would have to be the one where
Jamie's had the bright idea that we spend an entire day at the hospital,
just to get a better grasp of what life is really like for The People,
which is why I'm here on Thyme Ward at this Godforsaken hour.

'You can help a man by making his bed,' Jamie had said, 'but to
know a man you must share his bedroom.'

'Who said that?' Jane had asked.

'Me, just now,' said Jamie with a grin.

Angela, who does the same job that Julie does on Marjoram,
(with more efficiency and less humanity, reckons Jamie,) directs me to
the shower room where Carl is 'cleaning up' Andrew.

'Give us a hand then' says a disembodied voice.

'Just a minute, my glasses have steamed up.'

Outside it's one of those days they say is 'too cold to snow',
whatever that means. The room is like a sauna, and there's a sharp,
chemical smell, not like a bathtime smell, more like the acidic aroma
of some sort of industrial hand-wash. Over the top of my glasses I can
just make out Carl, leaning over a blue shower trolley with raised
sides, showerhead in hand. Next, I see a mop of wavy brown hair, then
Andrew, looking sort of alarmed, his eyes and mouth wide open. From
beyond Andrew comes a moaning which might be an attempt to make

a word, and as my vision clears I see a row of five men on trolleys, lined up like bodies in a mass grave. Only these skeletal figures are writhing, and crying out, and although the words aren't formed the tones are unmistakably of discomfort and protest. Andrew's chest rises and falls slowly, rasping air escaping as if from a deflating balloon. With each inhalation I wonder whether the white skin will be able to stretch again over that washboard of ribs without bursting, as Carl showers soap down each distinct rivulet.

'Here,' says Carl, chucking a sponge at me, 'you can do his back.'

I move round to the other side of the trolley.

' Andrew always has to lie half turned,' shouts Carl, over the din of the other men and the jets of water. 'He can never lie fully on his back because of the curve of his spine. Like elephant man.'

Andrew's spine is bent like a bow, and I can see how the skin is stretched tight over vertebrae that look as if at any time they could puncture the centre of each round, red sore. I dab his skin lightly, the soapy water running past the large red patch on his lower back, welling round his little-boy bottom and following his thin, concentration camp leg, to an outlet at the foot of the shower trolley.

'You've never done this before, have you?' Says Carl, smiling now.

'No, I…'

'Well we all had to start somewhere. Best to jump in at the deep end, and soon you'll be wondering what the problem was.'

Carl signals for me to come round to his side of the trolley, and hands me the showerhead.

'Here, you can finish him off for me, he's still got something stuck in his hair.'

I look at Andrew's head, but his hair seems clean.

'Not that hair you stupid git.'

Some of his pubes are matted. I wave the showerhead at them and watch the brown debris race over blue vinyl into the black hole.

'So what are you doing for Christmas?'

'What? Oh…' it was the socialising tactics of the hairdressers that threw me, a bit like small talk in a gas chamber. '…I'm going back up to Stoke.'

'Stoke Newington?'

'No, Stoke… where the mugs come from.'

70

'Family?'

'No, I don't really have one. I'll be staying on a mate's floor.'

Dave was on his own now in my ex-flat, his latest relationship having lasted less than two weeks, due to 'irreconcilable differences' caused by his fishing obsession. She had thought the shoal of cute little minnows in the bath were just an eccentricity, until Dave explained that they were live bait for a pike fishing expedition. But she got over that. She'd even got over finding a tin of maggots in the fridge. What finally did it was Dave reading that a good catch of big carp was guaranteed if you tied female pubic hair onto the hook.

I'm about to ask Carl what his plans are when I realise that my rhythmical waving of the showerhead has caused Andrew to have a hard-on. Carl notices it at the same time.

'Angela usually pours cold water over it,' he says, 'but if there's no rush I just let it die down naturally.'

I feel a blush playing 'join-the-dots' with my freckles as the thought shoots round my mind like some wild pinball, ringing bells and lighting up areas I never knew existed: people like Andrew can have erections. I remember how I'd been embarrassed when I'd walked through the factory with an obvious stiffy, and how, in a way, that had eventually led to me being here.

But at least I have some sort of choice. As for Andrew, there is bugger-all he can do about it.

***

Jane had spent the morning observing Rose in the 'sheltered workshop,' a characterless, rectangular room smelling of pine shavings, where people were sorting out a spaghetti of wool strands into their various colours and sending them to an adjacent room, where another group mixed them up again. The sheltered workshop supervisor had justified this by saying that it 'kept 'em occupied.'

Jane had also observed a behaviour management 'technique' known as 'pindown,' which, as the name suggests, consisted of several staff falling upon a patient who was perceived to be causing a problem and pinning them to the floor until they were subdued. She had found herself wondering if they realised how ugly with pleasure their faces were when they were carrying out this procedure.

Having witnessed as much as she could stand, she was retreating for lunch at the 'Happy Owls,' when she noticed something strange about an unmarked door next to Fuchsia ward. She had always assumed it to be a closet, only today it was not fully shut, there was a light on inside, and there were unexpected sounds coming from it . The first was like a cat purring. The second was a voice she recognised.

'What's that noise?'

'Hello,' she said, easing the door open.

'There's nobody in.'

'Is that you, Eddie?'

'Mr. Hill's gonna pull the cat's tail off.'

Worrying that she was about to witness some cruel act against a defenceless animal, Jane slowly opened the door, and as she did so the purring sound became that of a coin spinning and gradually winding down to a wobbly halt. The closet was empty, apart from Eddie, who was kneeling, his carrier bag between his knees, over a blue plastic dish, which Jane recognised as a 'Battling Tops' game similar to one she had had as a child. She entered the closet and closed the door, her eyes adjusting to the dim light as she squatted beside Eddie, who was carefully winding the string around two tops then setting them spinning in the blue arena. Clenching his fists as if witnessing a real fight, Eddie was wild-eyed and totally engrossed. Seemingly unaware of Jane's presence, he whooped with unabandoned joy as the yellow top flew into the air.

'Yeah yeah yeah, knocked him out of the ring. Floats like a butterfly. Floats like a butterfly. It's in the wrist action...'

 Eddie looked up and, staring Jane straight in the eye, said 'spinning things' before turning back to follow the progress of the victorious, but now staggering, red top. ' Like spinning things... Psychrist told me.'

'Can I have a game, Eddie?'

Eddie looked down, muttering something under his breath, then said 'No. Only two tops left.'

Only two tops left.

In Eddie's world it made sense: it was probably one for Eddie and one for Pansy. Jane didn't expect Eddie's invisible playmate to be Mr. Hill, whoever he was, because from what she had heard Mr. Hill had quite a different function in Eddie's life to that of his imaginary dog. Jamie had told her that there were two theories on this: Hill was either Eddie's alter ego or his imaginary 'friend'.

'When I say 'friend,'' Jamie had said, 'perhaps 'antagonist' would be closer to the truth.'

Sometimes Eddie would talk to Hill but at other times he would act as him, so both were probably true. One thing was certain: anything bad that happened around Eddie was either done or inspired by the unseen presence. Feeling that she was interrupting something private, Jane got up and quietly opened the closet door. But what Eddie said next was so unexpected that it stopped her in her tracks.

-Chapter 9-

As Eddie had left the ward that morning someone had shouted three innocent words: 'Christmas soon, Eddie,' and since then the images he associated with the word 'Christmas' had jostled in his head. One of them repeatedly struggled to resurface, calling out to him to tell someone about it: the image was that of a man tied to the rails of his bed with grey socks.

'I saw them,' he said, his eyes clear and fixed on Jane.

'Who did you see, love.'

'I saw them. They killed him.'

Jane felt like her heart had missed a beat. There was something very immediate about Eddie now, very aware, and she sensed a real feeling of urgency. Sliding down to crouch where she could meet his eye she said:

'Eddie, what did you see?'

'They stretched his arms out.'

'Who?'

In Eddie's mind the word 'Christmas' repeated again and again, and the images continued to mingle, as if the promenading actors of two opposing mystery plays were filling his vision: the infant Jesus, shepherds and Magi, Jesus carrying his cross, all flooding in and covering the picture he wished to retain.

'Whose arms did they stretch out, Eddie?'

'Jesus.'

'Oh. I see.'

Jane had felt certain that she had been about to hear evidence of some horrific crime. Now it appeared that to Eddie the suffering of

Christ could be as real as anything he had seen. Generations of Christian mystics had spent lifetimes trying to achieve that.

'They killed him at Christmas,' said Eddie.

'No Eddie,' said Jane, 'it was Easter. They killed Jesus at Easter.'

Eddie started to rock gently, then moved his attention back to the spinning game. As Jane quietly rose to her feet, he said:

'I'm special, very special.'

'Yes,' said Jane, 'I think you are.'

'Are you glad I'm alive?'

'Yes, Eddie...yes I am.'

***

What I really want to ask Angela is- do you pour cold water on every erection you see or is that just reserved for the poor sods in here who can't complain? Instead I place the Dictaphone on the desk between us, press 'record' and 'play' and start to read from the list of questions that Jamie has given me.

I would never have believed it possible, but today has been even more boring than a day at the factory. That's because all they do with Andrew all day is sit him in front of the telly, periodically interrupting him to feed him mush and tablets. The interview is short and not very sweet, a bit like Angela. Not that she's unattractive- she has Barbie Doll features, obviously spends a lot of time on her hair and make up, and there's an air about her which says that she is too good for nursing. According to Julie from Marjoram ward she is driven by a single, overriding medical ambition- to marry a doctor. From the lack of interest in her answers I get the distinct impression that Angela doesn't much care for Andrew or what happens to him in the future.

'How does Andrew communicate?' I ask, taking on the tone of some cub reporter.

'He doesn't,' says Angela, her bored tone offering a direct contrast to my efforts at enthusiasm '...there's nothing to communicate.'

'Oh...Do you have any photos of Andrew that we can take with him when he leaves?'

'No.'

'Er, right...'

Wondering what Michael Parkinson would do at this point I scratch my nose, and look down at my next question.

'Do you have any files on Andrew that we can take with him when he leaves?'

'I've only got the ones that cover the last few years in this ward.'

Silence.

That's it: I'd once heard that silence was an essential part of interview technique. Leave a gap, and they'll be obliged to fill it.

More silence.

'Er... where would I find the others?' I say, as Angela just sits staring at me.

'The early ones, including the one which has his admission document in it, aren't available. He was probably admitted onto a different ward for assessment, and the files never came over.'

'Oh...next question then: what are his likes and dislikes?'

'He likes everything.... No reason   to   think   he   dislikes anything. He   just has what he's given...'

She breaks off as if something's coming to mind- probably that she has a hairdresser's appointment tonight.

'...Oh yes, there might be one 'like,' if you can call it that, though I doubt it: Sister Claire says that when they first brought him in they noticed how his head could be rolling and when a bright red object was put in front of him he'd fix on it for a bit.'

'That's good, so we can say that Andrew likes red things.

'Maybe. Although I've never seen him do that myself.... It's probably just one of those rumours. Like the poppies...'

'Poppies?'

'Oh there are lots of spooky stories around a place like this. Particularly about what happens to some of them when it's a full moon. Now that is something I've seen for myself. I think it's something to do with the pull of the moon on the water in the body...'

'You were saying about Andrew and poppies.'

'Oh yes. It's just a story about Andrew. A few people saw it. Apparently, one Christmas a bunch of bright red poppies   appeared on his bed.'

' Poppies? You mean, as in the flower?'

'Yes. Bright red ones. Out of nowhere. They say it was the Christmas the year we'd had the big heatwave.'

'1976?'

'That's the one. And how do you explain that- poppies in the middle of winter. Makes you think doesn't it?'

***

It's late when we eventually pull onto the Bungalow's forecourt, and nobody is saying a word. Simeon rubs his arm where Billy has bitten him for no apparent reason, although I could understand it, as I'm starting to get irritated by the superior tone that he seems to have when speaking to the mentally handicapped and the unsaved (or should that be people with a mental handicap and the eternally challenged?) Having to wait for him to do the paperwork, followed by an hour's free parking on the M25, leads to us getting back a lot later than any of us had wanted to.

And the lights are on in the Bungalow.

As we enter, I wonder if I'll come face to face once more with the person who had broken into the flat, and if he'll recognise me with my clothes on. Everything's all right until we get to a small room at the front of the Bungalow, which was going to be used as a second lounge. The light's on, and the door's slightly ajar. Jamie calls 'is anyone there?' and when there's no reply he pushes it open.

'What the...'

I can't see past Jamie, but from his reaction I think that the room's been broken into and vandalised. When I look over his shoulder I see that what had been the second lounge has now been completely and effectively turned into an office. There's a desk facing the door, and on it an Amstrad computer and printer. Next to these are a Dictaphone, a desk tidy and a Walkman, all arranged with geometric precision. On each side of the desk are filing cabinets, and on the wall a year planner on which somebody has already placed black dots to represent their holidays for the coming year.

As we stand, speechless, outside the new office, a toilet flushes in the bathroom at the end of the corridor. The door opens and, preceded by wafts of shit, a huge woman comes out and walks toward us. At first I think she's wearing a nurse's uniform, but this is just the effect of the starchy white blouse and black trousers. As she holds out her meaty hand I notice the black down on her arms, then in a voice that is the deepest I have ever heard coming from a woman she says:

TASTING THE WIND
'Hello. I'm Della Belk, your new manager.'

-Chapter 10-

17th December 1986

Today, for the first time, all of The People are going to meet under one roof. For the last month we have done nothing but observe them and interview their staff, and I for one am glad for a change in the routine. The venue is the 'Happy Owls.' Jamie had chosen it because it's always deserted late afternoon, apart from Oscar, and as Oscar's refusing to come it was decided to take the mountain to Muhammad.

The 'introductory session' is being run by a small lady in a grey trouser suit with silvery hair tied back in a neat little bun, who introduces herself as 'Yolande Green, Speech Therapist.' Yolande has had the brilliant idea of having a small buffet set up to entice Oscar away from the Telly. Once they've all had their share of sandwiches, crisps and, in Andrew's case, yoghurt, Yolande gets us all to form a circle, which she stands in the middle of, holding a big blue ball.

'I'd like to welcome you to the first of what I've called 'getting to know you sessions..."

'Whose in the cupboard?' sings a voice from somewhere behind her.

'...The idea,' she continues, ignoring the interruption, 'is that you all get to know each other, starting with your names...'

'Rang the bell
Made the noise...'
'Who is that?'
'Naughty Mr.Hill.'

79

TASTING THE WIND

Aided by Colin, the Speech Therapist searches the room, until they locate the source of the voice, under the table with the nursery rhyme model. Shuffling out, Eddie sees the blue ball, and says: 'can I have a go?'

So The People who are, or might be going to live in the Bungalow, plus Eddie Sparrow, sit in a circle, around a woman with a blue ball. That is apart from Mickey, who keeps sliding down onto the floor, and Rose, who wants to walk around. Oscar, who is scowling at the fact that he has been conned, pacifies himself with fairy cakes which he's taken from the buffet and squashed into his pockets.

'Now,' announces Yolande, 'we're going to learn each others' names by passing this ball around and naming the person we're giving it to. So I'm going to give the ball to...Mickey. That's Mi-ckey.'

Mickey sits cross-legged on the floor, so the speech therapist places the ball between his knees. Giggling, he throws it over his head, and it narrowly misses a tray full of cups and saucers on the counter.

'Omigog.' shouts Rita.

'So Simeon has the ball now, doesn't he? That's Si-me-on.'

Si-me-on passes the ball to Oscar, who takes it grudgingly and gets butter-cream fingerprints all over it.

'Now Oscar has the ball. Os-car.'

'Why's she talking like that?' asks Oscar, throwing the ball to me. Pretending I hadn't heard him I pass it to Rose, thinking how glad I am that she's only got one syllable. Rose drops the ball, and it rolls to Mickey.

'Now Mickey, I want you to pass the ball to Eddie. Ed-die. Where is Ed-die?'

'Why is she talking like that?'

'Pass the ball to Eddie.'

Eddie gets up and, taking the ball from Mickey, walks over to Andrew.

'Well done. So who are you passing the ball to?'

'Eddie.'

'No, you're Eddie. You're passing the ball to Andrew. An-drew.'

Ruth lifts Andrew's arm, and rests it on the ball.

'Now Andrew is going to pass the ball to Frankie...er...I mean Billy. That's it Bil-ly.'

'Why is she talking like that?'

80

'Mr.Hill's a silly Billy, Mr.Hill's a silly Billy...'

'Omigog Eggie.'

Billy has trouble holding the ball because it's smeared with butter cream, and he's got socks on his hands, so he drops it, and it rolls to Yolande's feet.

'Thankyou, Billy. Who shall I give the ball to now? I know, I'll give the ball to...Rita. I am giving the ball to Ri-ta.'

Rita smiles broadly, licks the ball, then folds her arms around it.

'Now Rita, where is Rose?'

Rita nods in Rose's direction.

'Now Rita is going to pass the ball to Rose.'

Rita looks at the ball, then at Rose, then at Yolande and pouting, says:

'No'

'Why not?' asks Yolande with a sweet but forced smile.

'You say you gi' bow to me. It ma bow.'

'No no no,' says Yolande, approaching Rita, 'when I said I was giving you the ball, I didn't mean to keep. Please pass the ball to Rose.'

While this is going on, Rose is walking around the room oblivious. She has this sort of straight-legged walk that sways her from side to side, a bit like a sideways version of one of those birds which dip their beaks into a glass of water. At any minute I expect her to topple over, and looking at the bruise on her cheek, the scar over her right eyebrow, and the helmet that she always wears, that must be something that happens a lot.

Jamie hasn't said much all afternoon. He sits just outside the circle, looking from one person to another. In fact neither Jamie nor Colin have been themselves since the new manager started, which is understandable I suppose, as they've been used to running things. But I think there's more to it than that. They've been having meetings where only Della's voice can be heard through the office door, and they've come out each time looking really pissed off. And when she's not been meeting with Jamie and Colin, she's been on courses, or at Social Services Head office. One place she hasn't been to is the hospital.

Della did have one meeting with us all the morning after she arrived, where she told us a bit about her background. Apparently she'd been a nurse, and then had gone on to do something called a CQSW, which is a social work qualification. Before coming here she'd had a couple of jobs as deputy manager of care homes, which must have made her a prime candidate for this job.

But the moment I met Della I got what Han Solo would call 'a bad feeling.' It's not just that she looks and talks like a bloke, or the way that her and Simeon seem to hit it off, just because they both wear the same bible bashers' fish brooch. It's probably more to do with the way she smiles when she gives her orders out. I'm more used to proper bosses, whose faces match their words when they call you a wanker. And, surprise surprise, I've already claimed the position of public enemy number one.

It was something to do with the daft exercise that Della had us doing last week. She'd been going on about the fact that she thought that in the absence of a manager, Jamie and Colin should have done more work on budgets, instead of spending so much time at the hospital. Then she told me and Ruth to work out a menu for six people and staff for one week, write a shopping list for it, and price it up at the supermarket.

We'd started off at fresh fruit. By canned vegetables it was beginning to get tedious. We noticed that by the time we got to canned fish a man had been following us since rice and pasta. In pickles and sauces we were intercepted by the man, who was a store detective, and asked to go to the manager's office. It took a phone call to Della to convince them that we were neither casing the joint nor weighing up their prices on behalf of a competitor.

When we got back, she looked at us as if we were shit on her shoe, like the whole thing had been our fault. And I don't know why, but since that supermarket thing I've been feeling like a marked man. It reminds me of this war correspondent I saw being interviewed once about the first time he'd been on a battlefield. It had been a full-blown battle- guns blazing all round him and all sorts of shit flying over his head. Every time he moved a bullet ricocheted somewhere near him, so he turned to a soldier and said 'at the risk of sounding silly, I think someone's shooting at me.' The soldier explained how once a sniper gets you in his sights he'll not bother with anybody else until he's taken you out. And that's exactly how I feel.

'Penny for them?' says Ruth. I'm about to answer, when I realise that she's talking to Jamie.

'I'm just thinking,' he says, 'the closer we get to the moving date the more I wonder if they've got it right. If these people would really choose to live together.'

I slide my chair back, and ask a question which had never occurred to me before: 'so how were they chosen?'

'God knows,' says Jamie, 'Health authorities work in mysterious ways. They all have to come from the same borough, then a group were prioritised because certain wards were targeted for closure first; then it came down to alphabetical order. It just bothers me that choice and compatibility never came into it.'

I'm starting to wonder whether reality ever came into it, because if some of The People behave in the community like they do here it's going to make the job interesting to say the least. Take the situation that's developing now:

'Rita,' says Yolande, trying to sound firm, 'please pass the ball to Rose.'

Rita looks over her shoulder, a puzzled expression on her face, as if she has failed to see someone who she expected to be there.

'Where Gon?' she asks.

'Where's who gone, dear?' asks Yolande.

'No 'gone'...GON.'

'I'm sorry Rita, I don't understand...'

'I think,' offers Jane, 'that she means 'Don.' Is that who you mean, Rita, Don Maguire?'

'Yeah...'e ma boyfren.'

Jane   gives me a worried glance, but I take a bit longer to realise the implications of what Rita's just said, and it's not until Yolande begins to offer her explanation of why Don is not there that It really sinks in.

'No dear,' says the therapist, ' Don wasn't invited because this is just for the six people who are going to the new Bungalow...'

'Gon no go Bunlow?'

For some reason, no one had known that Rita had a boyfriend, let alone that it was the Don himself. When she was asked to go to the Bungalow she had assumed, like you would, that it was to live with him.

Her face red with anger, Rita looks up to the counter they serve the drinks from. The old bag who practices cup-apartheid isn't there, but there is the tray of china cups that Mickey's random throw of the ball had failed to hit. With a scream she launches the ball, which sails past Rose and scatters the entire tray full of cups, the china cups which patients aren't allowed to use because they're too expensive. As they crash onto the floor I wonder if this will lead to the downfall of the entire health service. There's a split second of silence as the one remaining intact saucer rolls to a halt, then all hell breaks loose: The noise causes Rose and Andrew to go into fits, Rose turning stiff as a board and falling where she stands. There's a high-pitched scream from the other end of the room, as Billy grabs Simeon by the balls, and Rita goes on the rampage, hurling several chairs before storming out of the room, shouting 'I no goin fa'in Bunlow.'

Cross-legged on the floor, Mickey giggles and slaps his hand on the tiles as the speech therapist, who seems to have developed a stutter, says:

'I th-think that that will be enough for today...'

*

As the others are taken back to their wards, Eddie and Oscar stay to raid what's left of the food. I'm about to leave with Andrew when Eddie heads towards us, swinging his carrier bag, his mouth bulging and a smear of mince on the front of his unevenly buttoned light blue shirt. As he gets closer I notice something that for some reason I hadn't picked up on all afternoon: Eddie has a black eye.

'Hello, Eddie,' he says, spitting out a shower of pastry.'

'No,' I say, 'you're Eddie. This is Andrew. I'm Martin. What happened to your eye?'

Eddie gazes into the distance, and then bursts into a chorus of 'two lovely black eyes.'

'Eddie,' I say, did somebody hurt you?'

Eddie's head goes down as he mutters 'Mr. Hill' and I realise that he will probably never be able to tell what happened. He could have walked into something. He could be being beaten by other patients, or even by staff, but as long as he inhabits the world of Mr. Hill he might never be able to string the words together to tell. And there's something else on Eddie I'd not noticed before: He's wearing a badge on the lapel of his shirt, a green four-leafed clover, with gold edging.

'What's that, Eddie?'

'Good luck,' he says, lifting the lapel, 'it belongs to Eddie, and some good it's done him.'

'Right... I could do with some of that.'

Eddie holds his carrier bag between his legs, slips the badge from the stud that holds it and then thrusts them both at me.

'No Eddie, that's really nice of you, but I just meant I could do with...'

Before I can take my hands from the handles of Andrew's wheelchair, Eddie slips the badge and stud into my pocket, saying 'Christmas present,' then runs off, slapping his thigh for Pansy the dog to follow.

We follow him, and for a long time I can still hear him chanting about 'Mr. Hill,' laughing and calling his dog, but it's difficult to tell in the maze of corridors just where the sound is coming from. I'm about to give up when a voice I recognise calls: 'hey, mister, you with the cripple.'

Oscar is out of breath, as if he's been running.

'I was hanging around waiting to talk to that Jamie, but he's disappeared. Can I ask you?'

'Ask me what, Oscar?'

'About this Bungalow.'

'Please do. What do you want to know?'

'Is *he* going?' he says, jabbing a finger toward Andrew.

'Yes.'

'And is that Don Maguire going?'

'No.'

'And that mad lad, Eddie Sparrow?'

'No, he's not one of ours' I say, and I can hear a tone of regret in my voice. ' Talking of Eddie, do you know where he would have gone to?'

Oscar, still panting, and starting to wheeze slightly, points down the corridor in the direction we're facing.

'That way... prob'ly safer that way. He doesn't want to go getting beaten up again.'

'What? Beaten up? Who by?'

'Oh Don Maguire and his gang. They rule round here. They keep beating him up for fun, holding him down and pissing on his face and stuff.'

'And what do the staff do?'

85

'The staff...' laughs Oscar. 'The staff don't see it. The staff think the hospital's one place when it's really another, know what I mean?'

I nod, suddenly seeing it all in a different light. I'd thought of it as a place of routines and institutional practices, with people being fitted into them like plaster into a mould. But they were human beings, and human beings, as my old biology teacher used to say, are nothing if not adaptable. Some adapted by drinking boiling hot cups of tea straight down, so that nobody could take it from them. Others clawed their way up the hierarchy, surviving by bullying and intimidating the weaker ones. Then there were the Oscars, having to keep on their toes to stay one step ahead or go under. I can see now that the hospital is a living community, with its own rules, its own politics and power struggles. The policies, rotas, and systems of the staff are nothing but symbols and contours on a map that could never hope to represent the real landscape.

'So, getting back to what I was saying,' says Oscar, 'did that Jamie tell you that he had invited me ever so nicely to come to the Bungalow?'

'Yes,' I say with a faint smile, remembering Jamie's account of Oscar's invitation.

'And did that Jamie tell you what I said in reply?'

'Yes, he did.'

'And is Don Maguire definitely not going to this Bungalow place?'

'No.'

'And do you have to sit in a circle and pass a ball round?'

'No,' I say, 'I think that's just a speech therapist thing.'

'Good,' he says, with an exaggerated nod, 'then can you ask that Jamie to count me in?'

-Chapter 11-

5th January 1987

Christmas came and went and, God knows why, but I'm back in London. O.K., so I'd secretly hoped to bump into Jo and get back with her, but when that didn't happen there was no reason why I couldn't have stayed and lived a wild bachelor life with Dave. Perhaps it's something to do with being too proud to hang around and watch Jo with another bloke. I don't know.

Last night I had one of those extended dreams which seems to go on all night, the type you can wake up from and go back to. I'd gone home for Christmas, and Jo came round to say that she'd made a mistake, and still loved me and wanted to marry me. I woke up in a sweat, reached out to where I knew I'd left a quarter portion of chow mein, finished it and went back to sleep. Then I saw this picture of domestic bliss: a cottage with kids and a garden. I woke up with a start, went to the toilet, splashed water on my face, and shuffled back to bed. I wondered if this was something I'd heard about where your subconscious mind tells you what you really want deep down. Next, I'm back at the cottage, and I get a call from Ruth, begging me to go back to London, as she can't live without me. I wake up, and then can't get to sleep for the rest of the night, because a line from a Neil Diamond song that my dad always used to play keeps going round and round in my head:

L.A.'s fine but it aint home,
New York's home but it aint mine no more.

Swap that for London and Stoke and you get the right sentiment. It makes a shit song, but it's the right sentiment.

TASTING THE WIND

So I'm here again, waiting outside Time Warp's door for the usual five minutes. It's like I'm starting to get familiar, in fact almost comfortable, with the hospital. Less than three months ago it was the thought of what lay beyond this door that made me shudder. Now it's just the icy wind that's channelled up the long corridor directly to my feet. And now I know my way round all of these long, samey-looking corridors, so much so that If they did 'The Knowledge' on the hospital the same as they do with the London cabbies I would have passed with honours by now.

Eventually the top lock of the door grates open, then the lower one, and Carl comes out, with a yellow plastic bag and a long face.

'I'm just taking this to the incinerator. Angela's on the ward.'

I find Angela in the nurse's station, removing bottles from the drugs' cabinet. Andrew's in his wheelchair at the side of his bed, his face looking as if it's finally taken its colour from his diet of mashed potato. But in all of the sameness he seems somehow different, somehow more still than I'd ever seen him. I hadn't realised how animated he usually is. Yes, he's wheelchair bound and stiff-limbed, but usually there's some movement: a roll of the head, a lick of the tongue or spasm of an arm or a leg; but today, stillness.

And something else is different, something more unexpected: there's obviously been some sort of reshuffle, as there's another patient In Billy's bed, a gurgling man-baby called Paul. He dribbles 'Weetabix' down the pink rabbit on the front of his pyjamas, his large head nodding, as bulbous eyes move lazily under their half closed lids.

'Hi, Martin, did you have a good Christmas?' With that, Angela has pulled back Paul's sheet, rolled him onto his side and proceeded to insert an enema.

'Er, no, not particularly...'

Not that I can remember most of it, and the bits I can remember, I don't really want to. Crashing out on Dave's floor among the socks and empty lager cans was always going to rate it way down the scale of 'best Christmases ever.' I remember a bit of Christmas night: Den left Angie on 'Eastenders' and Vince married Penny on 'Just Good Friends,' but I'm finding it difficult to recall anything from 'real life.'

As Angela inserts the enema (an operation I don't think should be interrupted by distracting chatter) I wrack my brains for any other memories of the Christmas I've just had. There's only one.

It was New Year's Eve, there was a fancy dress do at the pub, and the beer was cheaper if you wore a costume, so most of us joined in. Dave went as the Incredible Hulk. I went as Julius Caesar in a white sheet I'd borrowed from Dave. He'd insisted that the brown stains on it were tea or ale, and my 'Veni... Veni... Veni' joke went straight over his head. Some old bloke, dressed as Alf Garnet (or was he?) started telling me what a good job I did. Nothing wrong with that you might think. Then he went on to say how I must be very patient, looking after such poorly people. I told him that they weren't poorly, they'd just ended up in hospital, well, by mistake really, but that now they were coming out, and he would eventually have to get used to seeing people like them in his own pub.

I went to the bar and Gaynor pulled me a pint. Beautiful, bouncy Gaynor, who as a spotty, flat-chested school girl had had a crush on me for years, took up with another lad when I'd shown no interest, and her chest had developed faster than a Kodak instamatic.

If only I'd known how you'd turn out.

I'd felt briefly ashamed- partly because I wasn't sure if I'd actually said that out loud or just thought it, and partly because I get pissed off at being overlooked because I'm not exactly a grade one hunk, and I'm here seeing somebody in a totally different light because of a few inches of flesh.

Nice though, aren't they?

'Champagne glasses', I said.

'They don't 'ave 'em 'ere.' said Dave, who was standing next to me, his Hulk- green body-paint rubbing onto my toga. 'No demand.'

'Champagne glasses were designed by Napoleon, based on the shape of Josephine's tits.'

'Oh,' said Dave, as Gaynor pulled him a pint. 'Then give me the wife of the bloke who invented the pint pot every time.'

In the mirrored tiles behind the bar I could see Julius Caesar, out to conquer the world in spunk-stained toga. To my right, the incredible Hulk. To my left, Alf Garnet, flanked by Mr. Spock, Nurse Gladys Emmanuelle, and Frankenstein's monster. Behind me was the

Christmas fairy, Fred Flintstone, Popeye, a convict and a very convincing devil who, for some reason, winked at me.

This was that vague thing, that ideal thing: community. And we were soon to be bringing The People into it.

As Gaynor switched the radio on and turned up the volume for the chimes, I wondered what Ruth was doing. I wondered what Jo was doing. In that order. One step further away from the mistake I'd made with Gaynor, from the mistake I'd made with Jo, a giant leap toward my next mistake.

As Big Ben chimed I leaned over the bar and kissed Gaynor, kissed a female Hitler in a Maggie Thatcher wig, nearly snogged the Incredible Hulk, then turned to somebody who had come as a bag lady. I remember thinking how accurate her costume was. Too accurate, from the scuffed boots, to the second hand coat and tacky brooch, the fraying tartan scarf, to the gin-reeking breath, to the tear that ran down premature lines.

'Martin,' she said 'Isn't it time we made up?'

I tried to pull away, but felt Dave's meaty paw in my back. We stood for what seemed like minutes until I said:

'Happy New Year...Mum.'

And yes, we talked. I wouldn't have dared do anything else with the Incredible Hulk watching. I even bought her a drink. But this isn't a story about a miraculous reconciliation, it's about another thing altogether. This is just something that happened at the time, and when we parted we didn't arrange to meet again, and I don't suppose we ever will.

'Are you O.K.?' Asks Angela.

'Er, yes, I was just wondering where Billy was.'

Angela looks at me across the bed, holding her stained rubber-gloved hands in a half-shrug.

'The bloody communication in this place,' She says, shaking her head. 'Don't you know?'

'What?'

'Billy Died. Christmas day. That's why we've got Paul. We're more used to people like Paul here than they are on Fuchsia, and they're planning to close it before the other wards. You know: costs the same to keep one ward open with half the patients as it does full.'

'Died?'

'Yes. We lose a lot this time of year. Viruses. Choked on his own vomit apparently, which is a bit spooky really, because Sister Clare said that Frankie, the one who Billy was always getting mixed up with because of the socks and all, he died like that on a Christmas day. Makes you think doesn't it?'

It does. Like how Billy should never have been in this place, how close he was to getting out, and how he had known nothing else, and now never would.

'...So I come back on Boxing Day and we've got a spare bed.'

Billy died. Spare bed. They seem to mean the same thing here, each said with the same degree of emotion. Billy was a bed, and now that bed is called Paul, the same as Eddie's cat. That bed would need emptying, making, maintaining occasionally, and every so often it would change its name, as its contents were replaced and buried. Andrew had probably watched as his body was removed, with whatever belongings he had. I can't even think of anything that might have been called belongings, and when I ask Angela she says there had been a baby's rattle in the cabinet at the side of his bed, and a black and white photograph that she guessed was Billy's mum. Apart from that there was a pair of grey socks with sellotape around them. These were the accumulated treasures of a lifetime, bundled up with his clothes- no, not with his clothes, because somebody else was probably wearing them now- and taken out in a yellow plastic bag.

***

Della flashed up a screen on her computer with a list of names, and from it deleted Billy Kinkladsi.

In her view the 'Bungalow project,' as she called it, was not going well. Billy had died, and Rita was refusing to come, as she had found out that her boyfriend was not included in the invitation. Martin had reported that Oscar had had a change of heart just before Christmas. But Martin was inexperienced and naive- not the sort of person she would have employed if she had been involved in recruitment. He didn't know how well the likes of Oscar could string you along.

'Marvellous,' she muttered to herself, 'one dead, and two- the only two who can actually talk- having doubts about coming.'

Then there was Rose's mother, who was putting up a fierce battle against her moving, and was lobbying against the hospital being closed at all. And the moving day was now only a matter of weeks away.

Whoever interviewed Billy's replacement would have to be insistent and know how to offer the choice of moving in a way that was no choice at all. That ruled out Martin Peach. Martin had no idea about assertiveness, as he had demonstrated by his inability to obtain Andrew's early files, including the one that contained his admission documents, from the hospital. Because of Martin's ineptitude nothing was known about Andrew from before the age of eighteen. It was as if he had suddenly appeared from nowhere, a man with no past. Perhaps she should give the task of inducting the new patient to Simeon. This project not only had to work, it had to be the best of its kind, and no one was going to jeopardise that: not the woefully inadequate staff, or even the residents.

Della scrolled down the list to see who was next in line.

She read the name slowly, as if it was one she had known and was now discovering for the first time on a gravestone:

Eddie Sparrow.

And she had known him. He was only a boy then, but the feral look in his eyes as he attacked her was still clear in her mind, and wove its way into her each and every nightmare. Although it was now over ten years ago, the memory was never far from her: it was the night before Christmas, the night when a virus had almost brought the hospital to a standstill; the night she had had sex in the punishment room.

The night that Frankie Adams died.

-Chapter 12-

17th February 1987
1.05am.

'So how did you get into this game then?

Ruth was used to men addressing questions to her chest. It always happened. It had been happening since she grew it. At first she'd found it embarrassing, then slightly amusing as she began to realise it's potential as a passport to a whole new world. But on this occasion she was not impressed. She had felt uneasy with Martin from the moment they met when he had, she felt, deliberately misled her into thinking that he was a patient. Now she had to spend a night under the same roof with him on an induction sleep- in.

The idea of the induction programme was that the residents got to stay for the odd night at the Bungalow to help them get used to their new surroundings before the move. But it was not going well. The overnight stay that should have happened on the seventeenth of January had been called off because heavy snow had closed the roads around the hospital. This was the second attempt, and only Rita, Eddie, and Rose were able to come, as the others were battling a virus- the one to which Billy had succumbed. Eddie's involvement had been a cause of great celebration, as had Rita's. Ruth, and Julie the staff nurse, had negotiated with her very carefully, and eventually she had agreed to come for one night, on the condition that it was a one-off, a short break from which she could return to the ward with more than the average amount of kudos. Even as they talked, Ruth had heard the sadness in Julie's voice. Julie knew that once Rita had seen the Bungalow she would be saying goodbye to her forever.

TASTING THE WIND

The three had arrived in the early evening. Della had waited in order to greet them and to give Ruth and Martin a checklist of everything that needed to be done, which included at the bottom her home phone number and the phrase: *for use only in absolute emergencies.* Ruth had spent the afternoon cooking a lasagne, which was very popular with everyone, including Martin, who made a mental note that she was not just beautiful- she was also good in the kitchen.

The meal over, the rest of the evening was spent exploring the Bungalow and watching the TV. Eddie was the first to take himself off to bed. Of all of them his body-clock was the most attuned to 'institution time.' Bedtime at the hospital was never a question of personal choice- it was governed by the time at which the night staff came on, so staying up past ten was never an option. Rita, on the other hand, was determined to use her new-found freedom to stay up for as long as she possibly could: a real challenge, which she would win, no matter how hard it was to keep her fluttering eyelids open. For most of the evening Rose had wandered with her pendulum gait from the lounge, through the kitchen, down the corridor to her bedroom and back again, until Ruth directed her to the bathroom and then to bed. It was almost one o'clock before snoring could be heard from each bedroom.

'You're not a 'Pink Floyd' fan then?' said Ruth, as Martin switched the TV over, without any reference to her whatsoever, from a programme about one of her favourite groups.

'No. I like heavier stuff- Zeppelin, Sabbath. That sort of thing.'

'Yes, I'd got you down as a headbanger...'

'Oh. Do you...?'

'No... It's all right, I suppose, but I'd rather have prog rock and concept albums.'

Ruth was aware that the conversation was becoming stilted, but Jane hadn't helped matters by suggesting to her that Martin seemed to have a 'thing' about her. He reminded her of Norman, a boyfriend she'd had at the age of seventeen, and the harder she tried to repress it, the more vividly the picture of Norman's ginger pubes forced itself into her consciousness.

It was at this point that he turned to her and asked the question, in her mind predictable, in his pre-coital:

94

'So how did you get into this game then?'

'I suppose,' said Ruth, deciding that a brief period of self-revelation followed by a hasty retreat to bed was preferable to listening to Martin's autobiography, 'that I should start when I was seventeen. It was all to do with me having a good singing voice and something my mum was told by the local fortune-teller.'

'What?'

'I thought that would get your attention.' *At least away from my tits.* 'I'll explain: my mum had got it into her head that because I could sing a bit I was going to be rich and famous, so she took me to see Madam Delores, the local fortune-teller. She doesn't live far from here, but her flat is like entering another world. The place was dark, with shelves full of big black books, skulls and stuffed animals with shiny eyes. We sat at a table with a crystal ball, and Delores asked if I wanted any particular advice from the spirits. I was just about to ask if I'd cop off with the lad from the corner shop when my mum jumped in and asked what career the future had in store for me.'

'And what did she say?'

'Nothing like I expected. Basically she told my mum that one of her children would never have to work for a living.   Of course, my mum being my mum worked out that as my brother worked in a brewery it wasn't him, so it meant that I was going to be the next Debbie Harry. The first thing she did on the way home was stop at the newsagents, where she'd seen a sign that said: *local Band on the verge of fame requires female vocalist.'*

'So what happened?' asked Martin, 'I mean, how did that lead to you doing a job like this?'

'I'm coming to that. Now where was I? Oh yes, I was totally pissed off, but when I screamed at her she started to cry, so I decided there was nothing lost in giving it a go. And that was how I met Richard.'

'Richard?'

The name pricked Martin's fantasy like a pin, and there was an almost audible gasp as it deflated.

'My boyfriend. He'd got this band together. They didn't particularly need a female vocalist, but they thought it would be a good way to get the crumpet to come to them. I fitted the bill, so they gave me a place in the band, we did a few gigs, and that was that.'

'So you did have to work for a living?'

95

'Well, obviously I never became a pop millionaire. But I'm still with Richard. For some reason mum never liked him, and if that's not bad enough, she has to live with the fact that she introduced us.'

'But what about never having to work for a living?'

'Well I'm here, aren't I? Basically, we were crap. Richard's more into making money than making music, and that was the idea of the moment.'

Martin took a long drink from his can, which gave him an excuse to swallow hard.

'So Richard isn't in this, er, line of business then?'

'Oh no, he's 'something in the city,' as they say, something in stocks and shares. I don't really understand it.'

'So the prophecy was wrong?'

' Well no, not really. That was the thing. Yes, she faked a lot of it, but she had this knack of getting things right. It was just that they never happened how you expected. Bit like life, really.'

Ruth swirled the last drop of cold coffee around in her mug. Halfway through her account she had decided that she wanted to cut her story short, as she still found its ending painful to relate. Hopefully Martin wasn't a good enough listener to realise that she hadn't answered her question. Tiredness made her lashes flutter, and her black skirt rode up over her thigh.

'We'd better go to bed,' said Ruth, ignoring Martin's hopeful glance, 'we're both tired, and tomorrow morning will probably be shitty. Literally.'

'Yes,' said Martin, bending his head to his hand to stifle a yawn and to get a better view of Ruth's knickers, 'but you didn't tell me the end of your story. How could the Gypsy have been right?'

'The Gyp... Oh Delores.' Ruth trailed the tip of her middle finger from the corner of her eye, down her cheek, as if removing sleep. 'Well... the following year, Mum had a baby. It was about nine months after my audition for the band. I knew that she was on the pill, so I imagine that in all of the excitement of her daughter being tipped for pop stardom she forgot to take it. To cut a long story short, the baby...my brother, Sam... was born severely disabled. I helped her to look after him. Doing that you suddenly discover this huge subculture of people in the same boat; so that's how I got into 'this business.' He was the child who never had to work for his living. Shows what happens when you go to fortune-tellers, doesn't it?'

***

'Martin...Martin...wake up.

'What the...' as I come round I realise that despite our intentions to get to bed we must have both drifted off in the lounge. This is probably the closest I'll ever come to sleeping with Ruth.

'Martin, wake up, there's someone in the Bungalow.'

All I can hear is the sound of snoring. Ruth gets up quietly and opens the door fully. The lingering smell of the lasagne drifts in, competing with the fresh paint, like a promise that the new building will eventually be a real home.

'How do you know?' I ask, groggily.

'I heard a voice, Martin, and it wasn't Rita's or Eddie's.'

We creep out of the lounge into the kitchen/dining room. There's a corridor leading off to the left, to Rita and Rose's rooms, and another to the right past Della's office, which leads to Eddie's. Somewhere a clock chimes two. Then I hear it, and I feel the hair on the back of my neck stand on end:

'You shouldn't be here, no, no my lad you should not be here.'

The voice is that of an old man. If we're being burgled it is by a geriatric, a campaign by the residents of 'the Willows' to annexe the Bungalow.

'I know that voice.' says Ruth.

'What?'

'That voice, I know it. It's old Arthur from Fuchsia ward.'

'Yes.' I say, 'I know who you mean, but how can it be?'

'He must have stowed away in the minibus.'

'Stowed away? You mean when Colin went to pick them up an old codger sneaked past him, kept his head down in the back of the bus all the way from Oulston, then got past everybody and hid until now?'

'I know it sounds far-fetched, but that's old Arthur's voice. How else do you explain it?'

I have a bad feeling about this.

The door to Della's office is ajar, which is unusual, because she normally keeps it locked when she's not around. I'm standing there wondering what to do when Ruth stretches round me and pushes it fully open. I switch on the light then jump back like I'm deactivating a bomb. There's nobody in the office.

I can't help but notice the room's orderliness: the numbered files all neat and straight on the shelves, the books in alphabetical order. The items on Della's desk all seem to be laid out equidistant around her computer: a 'desk-tidy', a calculator, a Dictaphone and a portable electronic chess set with an uncompleted game.

' She's followed you boy, she's followed you here...' says the voice of old Arthur.'

The voice is coming from Eddie's room.

'...And now she's found you she'll probably kill you.'

As I open the bedroom door my hand shakes and slides sweatily on the handle. I wonder why, because the voice conjures up only the image of an old man, white-haired, stooped and frail... an old man with the concealment skills of a sniper, granted, but an old man just the same.

Eddie is sitting up in bed grinning, the ethereal glow of the corridor's emergency lighting shining on his half- moon face, twinkling in his eyes and on his front teeth.

'"Ello.'

'Hello Eddie.'

'Sorry to disturb you,' says Ruth.

I look around the room, check the wardrobe, test the window, which is closed, and look under the bed.

'Eddie,' I ask, 'was that old Arthur's voice we heard just now?'

'Yes', says Eddie, 'old Arthur.'

'Er, in that case, where is old Arthur now?'

'On Fuchsia ward,' says Eddie.

'Eddie,' asks Ruth, 'if Arthur is on Fuchsia ward, was someone else in your room?'

'Yes,' says Eddie shaking his head and looking at us as if to say the answer should be obvious to a child of three. He closes his eyes, and sinks back down under his duvet.

'Er...who?'

'Saw him tonight,' said Eddie, pulling the duvet over his head, 'followed me here.'

'Who, Eddie?' asks Ruth.

'Mr. Hill.'

'Oh, I say,' turning to go, 'him again.'

'Yes,' says the voice of old Arthur. And it causes my flesh to crawl, because this time it is coming from under Eddie's duvet. 'Yes...

Eddie thought he was escaping. But he's been followed here. Now no one is safe.'

-Chapter 13-

27th March 1987
3.15 p.m.

The People who were going to live at the Bungalow left the hospital, where some had lived for most of their lives, on a fresh Spring day, when birds sang from the clock tower against a backdrop of clear blue sky. In their tattered hand-me-downs they looked like a rag tag bunch of refugees, not running to freedom from the forces of a dictator, but from the concrete expression of one, older ideology, to that of a newer.

Most of them carried battered old cases and carrier bags. Only Rita had something that you might be proud to take with you on your holidays, as the nurses on her ward had collected for new luggage for the start of her new life. Her brief taste of living outside the hospital having succeeded, she trudged down the corridor in her kingfisher blue overcoat and dirty white trainers, her thick stockings wrinkling around her ankles, refusing any help with the case.

On Thyme ward, Andrew and Mickey had been sat facing the door, matching hospital blankets over their legs and two yellow bags marked 'clinical waste' dumped behind them.

'Oh, their clothes are in there,' said Angela. 'It was the best I could find.'

'Which is which?' Asked Jamie icily. It was obvious that she hadn't really thought, or even considered that it would make any difference.

'Er...this one's Andrew's,' she said, nudging one of them with her foot. 'I've just got to see to a few things on the ward. Please make sure that the door closes properly behind you.'

'Is that it?' Martin asked Jamie.

'Looks like it.... 'Sorry you're going. We couldn't manage a gold watch, so we've all chipped in for a clinical waste bag instead."

They opened the double-locked ward door just as a panting Carl arrived. He wasn't in uniform- his appearance in jeans and a scruffy duffle coat set him apart from the hospital, like someone suddenly divesting themselves of camouflage.

'Looks like I just made it,' he gasped, reaching into a carrier bag and taking out two parcels. He handed one to Mickey, who didn't notice the box of chocolates that fell out, as he shredded the blue wrapping paper with the rapture and single- mindedness of a true artist.

'You'll enjoy those later, Mick,' said Jamie, putting the present into one of the yellow bags.

'And that's for you, Andrew,' said Carl. Andrew's eyes followed the bright red package as it was placed into Martin's hands. 'Maybe someone will open it for you when you get to your new place.'

'Thanks, Carl,' said Jamie, 'I'm sure they both appreciate this.'

A sudden draught from the corridor created a small hurricane in the open door way which picked up Mickey's shredded wrapping paper, showering them all in the blue confetti that he had made. Mickey laughed uncontrollably, until he was left wheezing, his face wet with tears. Carl leaned over, kissed them both, then, to fill the silence said:

'Can I give you a hand?'

As Martin and Jamie wheeled Andrew and Mickey out, Carl followed with their 'belongings.' Shabbily dressed patients, some of them holding hands in chains passed by as they always had. The baggage trucks buzzed up and down the wide corridors with their quarry of yellow and red bags, containing soiled clothing, sheets, or the belongings of someone recently deceased.

Then the peeling door with the double locks slammed shut behind them for the last time.

TASTING THE WIND

On the bus, Ruth sat next to Rose, and was stroking her stiff hand as she hyperventilated, trying to bring on a seizure. Jamie showed Martin and Simeon how to get Mickey and Andrew onto the bus with the tail-lift, and how to clamp their wheelchairs in, before going back to look for Eddie. Martin managed to catch a finger in one of the clamps.

'Hold it up,' said Ruth, as Colin threw the first aid box to her. Martin's senses were suddenly concentrated into his hand: the throbbing pain, the trickle of blood, the softness of her small hand holding his, as he tried to read minute messages at the interface of their nerve-endings.

'Are you all right?' asked Ruth.

'Yes. Fine.'

'It's just that you were going a little...distant. You don't faint at the sight of blood, do you?'

'No, of course not.'

'Omigog.'

Rita was sitting at the front of the bus between Colin and Jane. The whole vehicle tremored as she changed her position, folding her arms tightly across her chest, her bottom lip jutting out in an exaggerated pout. At intervals of about one minute, Rita would turn to Colin and say 'we go now, man?' Colin tried to explain that the clock, which now said two-twenty, would probably have its big hand pointing right down by the time they left. Rita started to laugh.

' You no know tha' mean half pa' two? You menkal man.'

This caused a general ripple of laughter throughout the bus, which diffused some of the tension. Mickey joined in, as he always did, not sure why they were laughing.

'Do pardon me for being impatient...' said Oscar '...can I say patient now? I suppose I can until I get out of the gate, but I suppose it's a different patient isn't it? As I was saying, pardon me for being impatient, but what are we waiting for?'

By way of an answer there was uproar at the main door. Eddie's leave-taking was that of a celebrity: kissing the reception staff, waving to all and sundry and swinging his carrier bag as he passed through a corridor of patients, all chanting 'nee-naw nee naw.' Behind him came Jamie, uncharacteristically red-faced, carrying a large blue suitcase with a red balloon tied to the handle.

'Come on, Pansy, come on boy, we're escaping.'

102

'Eddie,' Jamie called as he approached the bus, 'I thought you'd agreed to leave Pansy behind?'

Eddie looked down, his eyes glazing. Then with a beam and a flicker of white tipped tooth he said 'Yes, Pansy, stay here boy, off you go,' as he pretended to throw an invisible stick and watch the dog race back into the hospital.

'Bye Pansy. Be a good dog.'

As Eddie squeezed into his seat he held his carrier bag to his chest and, staring at the hospital, muttered, 'mustn't forget Frankie. Must take Frankie with us.'

'But there isn't a Frankie,' said Ruth, 'or are you thinking about Billy?'

Eddie shook his head, as if she was misunderstanding what he was saying and there was no way that he could ever explain.

As Rita and Oscar started to cheer, signifying that the bus was setting off, Eddie stepped for a moment out of his private world and joined in, waving his bag as if it were a flag. With the other hand he was patting the air and talking out of the corner of his mouth: 'Hush boy,' he whispered, 'need you where I'm going, but bark like that and the screws will hear you.'

At the main gate, Don Maguire was leaning against the post. For once he was not wearing his green jacket. Instead he wore jeans and a T-shirt, and was pretending that he was too much of a man to feel the chill of the early spring breeze. Rita turned from him, rubbing her eye.

''E no ma boyfren no more.'

Colin stopped as a tractor went past, giving Oscar a chance to slide open a small window and give the Don his parting message:

'Bye Don. Will you miss me?'

'Fuck off.'

'Hey Don, when I was in the office I saw your records. They say you've got the biggest brain in the mental hospital...'

Don's chest puffed out as he shrugged as if to say 'isn't that obvious?'

'...And the smallest cock they've ever seen.'

As the bus started to pull out of the grounds, Oscar reached into the black bin bag at his feet and held up a green jacket, which he waved like a victor's banner. A study in rage, Don Maguire shouted obscenities and waved his fists; but there may as well have been an invisible field across the entrance, because he never once stepped out of the grounds. As Don's rage receded into silence, Colin looked in his mirror, watching the hospital grow smaller and smaller, until it disappeared.

They had left.

-Chapter 14-

27th March 1987
4.35 p.m.

Della's face beamed like a full-moon as she welcomed The People to their new home, their feet and wheels crunching across the wet gravel and over the welcome mat, leaving a criss-cross of patterned lines on the new dining room carpet and kitchen floor.

'Are you the cook, then?' asked Oscar.

'No' said Della, maintaining her smile, 'we don't have cooks here; you'll be helped to do your own meal preparation. I am the manager but just for today I have made something to welcome you to your new home: these are canapés. I can recommend the smoked trout mousse with caviar.'

'Ayo man.'

Della's face was eclipsed by a red shadow at Rita's greeting. She could cope with being mistaken for a cook, as she did have culinary pretensions, but not with doubt about her gender.

Eddie was investigating the fridge.

'Who's in the cupboard?

Rang the bell

105

Kissed the nurse

Made the noise
Breaks the bottle,
Naughty Mr.Hill.'

'I would like to welcome you all to your new home,' said Della, trying to ignore Eddie, as he picked up a full bottle of milk. 'I hope that you have many happy years here, and...'

'Mr Hill,' said Eddie, brandishing the milk bottle and pushing his face right up to Della's so that their noses were nearly touching. For a moment she froze, her face draining of colour, then as she raised her arms against what she perceived to be an attack, she accidentally knocked the bottle from Eddie's hand. Rita whooped with delight as Rose, who had gone into a seizure at the sudden sound of breaking glass, upended a table full of crockery and food, and Della's welcome party collapsed into chaos.

Andrew had already been taken to one of the bedrooms- not his own, but the one that had been allocated to Eddie and Oscar. Next to him was the yellow plastic bag with all of his belongings, and on top of that the unopened present from Carl. Simeon looked into the single room that should have been Andrew's, and found Oscar, his stocking feet up at the pillow end of the bed, hands clasped behind his head. At that moment, Jamie appeared from Mickey's room.

'Problem?'

Mickey could be heard giggling from behind his door, as Jane swept up the glass in the kitchen to the repeated mantra:

'Mr. Hill smashed the bottle, Mr. Hill smashed the bottle, Mr. Hill smashed the...'

'It's...It's just that...' stuttered Simeon,' I thought that this was Andrew's room.'

Oscar sprang up into a sitting position: 'No, no, this is fine thank you.'

It had been Della who had eventually decided who went where, under the guise of a 'consultative' meeting. Her reasoning was that Andrew had medical needs that could be better attended to in the privacy of his own room. Jamie had argued that Oscar would choose a single room; and so he had.

'You see,' said Oscar, lowering his voice and leaning towards them confidentially, 'it's not that I'm not used to sharing, it's just that I don't want to share with that Eddie.'

'Why not?' asked Jamie.

'Haven't you noticed?'
'Noticed what?'
'You're kidding aren't you? You have noticed, haven't you?'
'What do you mean Oscar? Noticed what?'
'That Eddie,' he said, looking around to see if anyone else was within earshot, 'he's pigging mental.'

In the double bedroom Colin, who had failed to secure Eddie's co-operation, unpacked his crumpled clothing. Inventories had to be written, and Della had stressed that these be 'precise and descriptive.' Eddie came in and sat at the foot of his bed, wringing his hands and singing into his wardrobe:

> 'Who's in the cupboard
>
> Rang the bell
>
> Made the noise
>
> Smashed the bottle
>
> Broke the cup
>
> Naughty Mr Hill.'

He rocked back and forth in time with his chant, and on each backward rock his frayed trouser legs raised to half-mast, revealing silvery skin above the tops of odd socks. The clothes that Colin was unpacking didn't look much better:

Inventory for Eddie Sparrow

1) Two previously red polo shirts with crocodile motif, hint of green.

2) Two previously green, as above, hint of red.

3) One blue anorak, Zip broken.

4) 21 assorted socks

5) 2 pairs shoes (1 black, 1 brown).

6) 5 long-sleeved shirts (with enough buttons for three)

7) 4 pairs trousers- short legged.

8)1 pair tracksuit bottoms

9) 2 frayed pullovers

10) 2 pairs red pyjamas

11) 7 pairs of underpants.

12) 1 Bathroom bag with assorted toiletries

13) 1 'Spinning Tops' game

14) 1 carrier bag (contents unknown)

The underpants were grey-white, with more than a hint of skid-mark. Not that that was Eddie's doing, as each pair had a different name on the label: John Holmes, Oscar Doyle, Timmy Weakman- a full cast list of Fuchsia ward, with the exception of Eddie Sparrow: first-up-best-dressed Eddie, Eddie with the 'split personality,' had one pair of randomly named underpants for each day of the week.

Andrew's unpacking had yet to begin, as Martin was still in the kitchen helping Jane clear up the broken glass and crockery.

'Let's see what you've got here.' Said Colin, opening the present from Carl. The package contained a bottle of aftershave and a pair of grey socks. He placed the socks on the bed and sprayed some aftershave onto Andrew's neck.

'What do you want to do with this?' he asked, untying the balloon from the handle of Eddie's suitcase. Some of the hospital staff had carefully written good luck messages on it in Biro. Eddie's eyes glazed over. For a moment his mind turned like a revolving stage, bringing another scene into view, and for that moment the scene was his only reality, with all of the sights and sounds and smells of a day long gone.

It was a summer's day, and he stood in the hospital carpark, watching a man in a red tanktop lift a thin boy from the back of a black Morris Minor.

As the man placed the boy in his large pushchair a blonde woman in a short skirt looked on distastefully.

'For God's sake hurry up, will you. I don't want to spend a moment longer here than I have to.'

As the man adjusted the boy's position and fastened his lapstrap, Eddie saw something shiny fall from the boy onto the ground.

'What's that?' Asked the young Eddie.

The woman spoke, but her voice was drowned by Colin's:

'You all right Eddie?'

As Eddie's mind began to return to the present, the last image of that day long ago was of his outstretched hand holding a badge that was in the shape of a four-leafed clover.

'Give the balloon to him,' said Eddie, pointing to Andrew. Give it to him for the badge. He likes red things. Don't give the balloon to Mr. Hill... Mr. Hill wants to burst it....'

Andrew likes red. How does Eddie know that? thought Colin. Maybe during their recent contact it had been mentioned, or perhaps their paths had crossed more often than had been supposed during their years in the hospital. Colin wedged the balloon between Andrew's leg and the arm of his wheelchair, and as he did so, Andrew's head, which had been lolling around incessantly since his arrival at the Bungalow, became still, his eyes focussing on the balloon.

From the corridor, Della's voice could be heard, explaining how, as her budget would not stretch to the real thing, she had committed the sacrilege of using fake caviar on her canapés.

'Come on Eddie,' said Colin 'help me put your clothes away.'

'Clothes away. Eddie Sparrow, put your clothes away or I'll punch you in the face.'

'We'll have none of that here,' boomed Della, from where she stood in the doorway. Turning to Andrew she said: 'I'll help you unpack, as no one seems to have got around to it yet. You won't be wanting this, will you?'

As she took the balloon from where it rested and squeezed it into the litter basket, Andrew's head started to roll around again, his eyes flickered and his tongue was pushed repeatedly out then drawn back into his mouth in what Colin felt was a gesture of protest.

' Eddie gave that to Andrew, Della,' said Colin, with a challenging edge to his voice. 'He likes red things.'

'That,' said Della, without meeting his stare, 'is a matter of conjecture. Besides, it's hardly age-appropriate for adults to play with balloons.'

'Ayo man,' said Rita, as she barged her way into the already crowded room. She was closely followed by Ruth, who held a pair of large white knickers and was clearly failing to get Rita to unpack her own clothes.

'Can we have anyone who does not belong in this room out straight away,' said Della, ignoring Rita and looking straight at Ruth. Her voice had raised an octave, either from exasperation or as a statement of gender for Rita's benefit.

Ruth was about to turn away but suddenly noticed what was happening behind Della.

'Andrew…you poor thing. What's the matter?'

Everyone turned to Andrew. Large tears rolled down his face, his arms were in spasm and his head turned. His eyes seemed to be fixed on the bed. On the pair of grey socks.

'Have you been spraying something?' asked Della, sniffing the air.

'Just this,' said Colin, 'it's Andrew's aftershave.'

'Well that will have to go,' she said, snatching the bottle, 'he's obviously allergic to it. It's all right not using animal products, but some of these cheap scents just aren't good for us.'

She tossed the bottle towards the bin, where it bounced off the balloon and onto the floor, then exited, followed by Rita who mimicked her haughty posture. Ruth, not convinced with Della's explanation of Andrew's distress, took him to the garden for some fresh air, leaving Colin alone with Eddie.

Picking up the aftershave, Colin sniffed the bottle, then placed it in the drawer of Andrew's bedside cabinet. The balloon could not be rescued. It had started to deflate and wrinkle, the greetings from the hospital shrinking to illegibility.

Eddie sat on his bed, rocking and muttering to himself. he had been agitated from the moment he arrived at the Bungalow. That, Colin knew, was to be expected. Moving home can be traumatic for anyone, but moving from what you have known for years when you don't have the mental ability to brace yourself for the shock of change would doubtless cause some feelings of unease and even lead to what was now being euphemistically called 'challenging behaviour.'

But added to that, Eddie seemed particularly ill at ease with Della. Even when he had come for the overnight stay, Colin had noticed a change in his demeanour when he met her, probably brought on by her authoritarian aura.

Probably...

'Excuse me Eddie mate,' said Colin, as he took a jotter and pen from his back pocket and scribbled some hurried notes.

'Who's in the cupboard?

Rang the bell

Made the noise...'

For a moment Colin paused, his concentration on what he was writing broken by something he thought Eddie had said, but which he felt certain that he had misheard. Surely the 'Mr. Hill' chant had taken the usual formula, with its mention of a cupboard, a bell, and a noise. What he thought he heard was:

> *Who's in the cupboard?*
> *Rang the bell*
> *Made the noise*
> *Tied the socks*
> *Killed the man*
> *Naughty Mr. Hill.*

It was only when Colin ran through the usual chant in his mind that he realised that the word he must have misheard was 'kissed.'

'What's all this about kissing men?' asked Colin, ' I thought you only kissed nurses?'

TASTING THE WIND

Eddie was silent, obviously travelling again in his own private world. Colin looked on and wondered what events in his past had created the necessity for this escape, and where the animals and people that populated Eddie's speech came from. He had recently attended a lecture by a leading expert in communication with people with mental handicap and mental health issues. The lecture was entitled 'Everything Means Something.' According to the theory being expounded, nothing in the speech of someone like Eddie was meaningless. Everything had significance if it was important enough for the speaker to want to put it into words.

But how do we connect it to his past without having been there?

'The thin boy with the four leafed clover...' said Eddie from his trance, '...he saw what happened...'

Everything means something, thought Colin, *every single thing. The only problem is.... how do we find the key?*

-Chapter 15-

27th march 1987

10.15 p.m.

Across the road from the Bungalow is the Cat and Lobster, where a designer-stubbled youth in baggy denims threatens a slot machine and, perched on barstools In a cloud of smoke, two women in shoulder pads giggle at a group of teenagers in bright suits as they swig lager and talk about their futures in futures.

'How do you think it went?' asks Jamie, placing a pint of bitter on the table in front of me. In my private re-run of the day I'd just got to the part where Eddie has fooled Jamie into seeing an invisible dog bound off into the sunset as the real invisible dog creeps onto the bus.

'Martin?'

'Sorry?'

'How do you think the move went?'

'Oh, OK...I think it went well'

I take a gulp from my pint, glad for the company but not wanting to get into a conversation about The People for fear that Jamie will see how far out of my depth I am.

'Ee by gum lad, is it that bad?' Says Ruth.

Ruth, beautiful Ruth; All that beauty and drinks pints and rolls her own fags. Not only a tasty piece and a good cook, but a cheap night out.

'Is what bad?' I ask.

'Southern beer? Weak as gnat's piss, no head, and no ferret down t'trousers, 'appen.'

'Sounds interesting,' says Jamie, who is sitting across from us with Jane, 'so what's the verdict?'

'It's not that bad, but yes it does cost more, and I do miss a nice creamy head, if you know what I mean.'

'Not the beer- the move. The fact that it's finally happened.'

Shit. 'Well... I thought it went quite smoothly.' I take another swig.

'And wasn't the send off from the hospital spectacular?' says Jane, holding her hands up, 'the fireworks, the brass band. It was nice of Julie to pop down, though.'

Julie, the nurse I'd met on Marjoram ward, had called in later in the evening, just to see how Rita was settling, and to make some arrangement with Jamie, which he still hasn't stopped grinning about.

'And how do you think Andrew will like it?' Asks Jamie.

'Andrew?' I say, wondering what sort of answer he's after, 'he seems fine...yes I think he'll be fine here.'

In reality, I don't think that Andrew even knows that he *is* here, or that he's anywhere different to where he's been for the last umpteen years of his life.

'Oscar,' I say, changing the subject 'now he should do well in the community- there's no reason why he can't live as normal a life as you or me.'

Well said, the man who is living in an old folks' home with a religious nut and a guy with half a beard who grows weed in his bath.

'Are you sure?' asks Ruth

'What?'

'Are you sure about Andrew. You say he's all right, but he was crying.'

'Yes, I heard about that,' I say, 'but didn't Della think he was reacting to the aftershave?'

'He might have been. He might also have been reacting to the move- it doesn't matter how grotty we think the hospital is. It was Andrew's home.'

Whatever they say, I'd still rather believe that nothing is going on in Andrew's head. Surely that would be better for him? Better than knowing that he's got no choice, no control? I remember my Dad lying in that hospital bed, my mum telling me to speak to him because he could probably still hear, and me hoping that he couldn't, because I couldn't stand the thought that he might have known what was happening to him.

A draught sweeps across the floor of the bar as a very odd looking couple enter. Fur coated, she's typical of the Maggie clones who are springing up throughout card-carrying conservatism: solid blonde perm, granite smile and lethal handbag, she is just one step away from the operation which will finally transform her into her leader. With her is a weedy, old-fashioned looking man with a neat moustache who reminds me of Arthur Pewty, Monty Python's boring accountant. Instead of choosing a table or going to the bar they split up and approach each of the tables in turn.

I thought that the job was difficult enough to start with. Looking at the emerging situation I realise that it's about to get worse.

***

Outside the Cat and Lobster a small man in a pinstriped suit, and a woman in a fur-coat with a clipboard had almost knocked Oscar over as they barged in front of him to open the door to the bar. It turned out to be a fortuitous piece of rudeness for Oscar, because as the pair passed through the door he caught a glimpse of a group of staff from the Bungalow, and decided to try another pub. Not that he had any problems with drinking in the same place as staff- they had to drink somewhere, and had as much right to be out as him- but they would probably cramp his style.

A little further along Moonfield Road is the entrance to the park. Although it was now dark, the gates were still open, and in the distance Oscar could see the glittering lights of the town. Fixing on the lights, he set off through the darkness. After years of wandering around the hospital grounds at night he had a complete disregard for any danger that might wait in the shadows, and habitually listened for the sounds of couples having sex, like the ones he occasionally used to trip over. The night was clear, a cool wind whistled in the branches of the trees, and an owl screeched at the moon. Oscar felt alive and free.

Emerging on the other side of the park, Oscar stood outside the Salvation Army meeting room and, looking down the high street, counted about five public houses. The first was full of leather-clad bikers, and its steamy windows vibrated with heavy rock; not at all what Oscar was looking for. At the second pub, the 'Black Horse,' there were a few middle aged and older couples, sipping from half-pint glasses. Oscar went in and walked up to the bar. No music, just quiet chat. Perfect.

'A pint of beer please, barman.'

Oscar slurred his words, trying to copy Tony, one of the patients on Fuchsia Ward; as the barman pulled his pint, he leaned over the bar, and with a big grin said:

'I've got a dog at home.'

'Oh. That's nice.'

The conversations were dwindling, as the couples in the room began to turn their attention to the strange newcomer, measuring him against their scales of normality. Down the ages there have always been classifications of people. People have been assessed as idiots, imbeciles, low grade, severe, profound and so on. 'Experts' have formulated tests to determine mental age or I.Q. but all of these classifications have come after the event: before the professionals or the wise ones have put their mark on someone, they have long since been judged by common consensus. Common consensus says: 'everything starts with 'us.' 'Us' is at the centre of the circle, and within the circle is 'cleverer than us' and 'thicker than us.' Anything outside of the circle is 'not us.' The patrons of the Black Horse pub were searching their collective unconscious to decide if Oscar was just 'thicker than us' or 'not us.' There is also an unwritten rule that If you are 'not us', then you must have 'come from somewhere' and on that point Oscar left them in no doubt.

'I'm from the home you know.'

'Are you?'

Around the room several people were nodding, their assessment confirmed. The barman handed the pint to Oscar, who felt in his left pocket for his wallet, which he knew contained the five pound note he had picked up at the last hospital gala day. Digging into his right pocket, he scooped out a handful of copper coins.

'You'll have to count it out for me. I'm not good at money.'

The barman counted out thirty-seven pence.

'Sorry, mate, there's not enough there. Have you got any more?'

'No,' he lied, 'that's all they gave me. I'm mentally handicapped you know.   He pushed the pint back, sniffed pathetically and turned to leave.

'Hang on,' said a white-haired man behind him, 'I'll buy you a pint.'

Bingo.

Oscar spent the rest of the night going from table to table, spinning yarns of hospital life, and timing the end of each pint exactly with those of the other drinkers. He had found what he wanted, and his money could be saved for more important things.

***

At the Cat and Lobster things have definitely taken a turn for the worst.

'Sign the petition, sir?'

'What?'

'The petition.'

Arthur Pewty hands me a leaflet as Cruella Deville approaches with her clipboard.

'How dare you spread this libellous crap around here?' It's Jane's voice, up several octaves, angry, but on the verge of tears. I've never heard her swear before. When I look at the leaflet I understand why. It's on sticky, light-sensitive paper, and reads:

Residents of Moonfield Road and its environs.

Say <u>No</u> to Mental Patients in our Community.

'No no, my dear,' says the woman through a small, tight smile, as if instructing a child who is not grasping a universally held truth:

'you see, the community is not the right place for these people. They should be being looked after properly.'

'Kept away from normal people, you mean, like your self?'

Jamie gently places his glass on the table, puts his hand on Jane's arm, then calmly asks the woman:

'Have you ever lived in an institution?'

'Certainly not.'

'Then I'd like to invite you to visit one with me, so that you can have a more informed opinion. How about tomorrow morning? Nine o'clock not too early for you?'

Behind the humanoid mask the phrase 'does not compute' repeats to oblivion. When words fail to emerge she pirouettes to the next table like a clumsy dancing bear, leaving a small cloud of dust.

We watch as people sign the petition. A bloke in a wheelchair proclaims that he is glad that he hadn't been born a 'cabbage' and thrust out into the world without proper care. Jane wants to follow the campaigners around the room to put anybody else off from signing.

'No,' says Jamie, 'the trick is to learn ways of calling members of the public ignorant bastards without losing your job. When they sign that petition they're signing against a stereotype. They aren't saying 'we don't want you Andrew, Mickey, Rita,' they haven't met them... Yet.'

Taking a long drink from his pint, Jamie sits back, his eyes following the odd couple around the room.

'It's no use getting wound up about that. It's too late for petitions. The revolution's already started.'

From the pub window I can see the lights of the Bungalow. A carriage lamp illuminates the porch, and through the frosted glass of the front door I see a light from the kitchen. Another one comes on, creating an orange glow through the curtains of one of the bedrooms. Mickey's bedroom. That would be Della and Sim putting him to bed. They were all there: Mickey, Rose, Andrew, Oscar, Eddie and Rita, settling down in their new home, oblivious to the 'community' with its strangers and petitions, unaware that the issue of where they live their lives is so politically and emotionally charged.

'Tomorrow night,' Jamie says, 'we'll bring The People over here. This is their local now.'

-Chapter 16-

28th March 1987
4.30 p.m.

Della's eyes were heavy and bloodshot at the shift handover as she recounted the happenings of the first night. Simeon sat upright, unblinking, like some pious sectarian who had overdosed on prayer and fasting.

'Mickey,' began Della drowsily, 'was up all night, shuffling up and down the corridors, banging on all the doors. He resisted every effort to get him into bed. We haven't slept a wink. Mickey is now fast asleep on the floor of his bedroom.'

'Don't you just love him?' said Colin, who was met with a withering look from Della. 'So how did the others do?'

'Rose hasn't slept. Mickey's banging around set off a series of minor seizures.'

'Rita,' added Simeon, talking like a sleepwalker, 'was a bit excitable. She managed to flood the bathroom and emptied the contents of her drawers all over the bedroom floor looking for her nightdress. When Mickey started rampaging she joined in, but by about three o'clock she was out like a light and slept through the rest of it. We blocked the other corridor with a kitchen table, so that at least Oscar, Andrew and Eddie could get a good night's sleep.'

Eddie had done exactly the same as on the one night trial stay: at ten on the dot he was up and off to bed. It was half way through a film on BBC1, so the 'News at Ten' chimes could be ruled out as a prompt. But there were no strange voices from Eddie's room that night, so Della and Simeon had totally dismissed what Ruth and Martin had reported after the first stay. Oscar had waited until Della and Simeon had taken Andrew to bed before he walked out of the Bungalow.

'I wasn't worried,' said Della, 'and there's nothing we can do because Oscar is free to go where he wants. When he came back at eleven thirty I did explain to him that it might have been good manners to let us know where he was going.'

'So where had he been?' asked Ruth.

'To the pub, obviously.'

'He wasn't in the Lobster.'

'He must be choosy about who he drinks with,' added Colin.

'He'd been to another pub,' said Della, 'he was stinking of alcohol.'

'But what can we do about that?' asked Jane, 'Oscar isn't able to make an informed choice about drink.'

'So what makes you more able?' asked Della. ' You see, Oscar is free to do what he wants to now. He is as free to go out and get drunk as the rest of us. That is 'Care in the Community' working.'

8.30 p.m.

'Hi... Andrew. Can I call you Andy?'

Andrew sits at the side of his bed in his wheelchair, looking nowhere in particular, but definitely not at me.

'What do you want to do tonight?'

I can feel myself blushing as I look around to see if anybody's standing behind me, like I've just realised I've been talking to myself.

'I was wondering if you want to go to the pub.'

No answer. Of course there's no answer. He can't talk. The others, the ones who had done this sort of thing before, seem to have a way of talking to people who can't talk back and making it seem natural. I haven't, and can't even see the point of it. I don't even know

120

if he knows what a pub is. Andrew's head starts to move from side to side. I know this doesn't mean 'no' though; it's what Della calls 'involuntary movement.'

'Or maybe you'd like to stay in and watch some telly?'

Great idea that. You ask somebody who can't speak a question, and when they don't answer you ask another just to fill the silence. Andrew's head continues to move from side-to-side, and his tongue sticks out. I sit on the corner of his bed, at a loss about what to do next, wondering what would happen if one day he suddenly did shake his head and mean 'no.' We'd probably still think it was 'involuntary movement.'

The room is over-warm and smells of fresh paint and new carpet. Perhaps if we went to the pub we could grab a snack there, the evening meal having been such a disappointment. I had planned to cook burgers, until I discovered that during his nocturnal rampage, Mickey had left a perfect dental impression on every burger in the freezer. My attempt at a curry lacked whatever Kevin's gained over several days of maturation, and was mostly binned when Rita pronounced it 'cack.'

'The pub it is then,' I say, no longer able to stand the silence.

I take Andrew's coat from the wardrobe- when I say Andrew's, I mean the one he was sent with, a shabby old blue parka with an orange lining and the name 'Frankie Adams' indelibly inked on the label- and contemplate how the hell I'm going to get it onto him. The giant step into the community will be delayed for a while as I work out how to get a coat onto a stiff-armed man strapped into a wheelchair.

'You'll need this,' I say, holding the coat up like a matador, 'It's cold out.'

I put the coat down and start to unfasten the leather harness that strains across Andrew's chest. It's like cutting the tethers of a mediaeval catapult, as Andrew's body arches, his top half springing forward then hanging over the right arm of his chair, and his feet coming out of his slippers, which are left strapped to the footplates.

'Oh shit...OK...don't move.'

Don't move? I don't know where I think he's going to go exactly. At least he's still held into his chair by a seatbelt, but I have visions of his thin body snapping under the pressure. A tremor starts in his leg, which gradually moves up his whole length.

He's going to go into a huge fit, and it's my fault.

'Do you want a hand?'

I don't know how long Ruth's been watching from the door, but she's got one of those one-sided smiles like she's come to the aid of a particularly stupid kid and is desperately trying not to upset him by laughing.

'Yes please,' I say in a small dry voice.

Ruth picks up the coat, concertinas a sleeve and, pushing her hand through the hole, takes Andrew's wrist and pulls it through. Easing Andrew's back away from the chair with one hand she passes the coat round him, then puts the other arm through the sleeve in the same way. Going round the back of his wheelchair she puts the brakes on and leans it back on two wheels so it's resting on her. As she eases Andrew back into a sitting position she gets me to gradually tighten his harness.

'Easy,' she says, 'when you know how.'

*

The Cat and Lobster is quiet as the grave, apart from the noise made by the slot machine man, who's there again, trying to get his money back from the night before. In a corner an old couple sit, not talking, but sipping from their half-glasses of stout in complete unison. Me, Jamie and Ruth are out with Rita Andrew and Eddie. Eddie sits upright, looking at his half pint of Guinness with narrow eyes and a half smile, chanting:

'Shaken, not Shtirred, shaken not shtirred.'

Every time a man enters the bar, Rita grabs Ruth's arm and buries her face in her shoulder, giggling like a schoolgirl. Her first 'Irish cream' has taken four seconds to down, so she sits running her finger around the inside of her glass, recovering the remaining coffee coloured film.

'More?'

'You'll have to wait until we've all finished,' says Ruth, ' you'll be sick'

122

'Omigog.'

With that, Rita taps her chest twice with her finger, announcing in sign language that she's going to the toilet, then stomps off with a pout that she could almost trip over. She passes a white-haired party of four who had just come in and were heading towards the table next to us.

'Hello,' says Eddie, 'I've got a dog at home.'

Suddenly, agreeing that the corner is a lot draughtier than it looks, they go to the far end of the bar, each of them smiling apologetically as they pass.

'Draughty?' I say, looking at the floor, as if trying to see the draught, because I sure as hell can't feel it.

'You'll get used to this,' says Jamie, 'areas that are draughty, or too warm, or don't have a good enough view.'

So this is integration. Welcome to the community- sorry, the community can't be with you at the moment, it just popped out to lunch. Don't call us, we'll call you.

'Martin,' says Ruth, waving a plastic beaker at me, 'I think Andrew wants a drink.'

'How can you tell?'

'Well his mouth is watering. Apart from that, you've not given him one yet. It's not rocket science...'

I half fill his red beaker with still orange. A sticking plaster covers the Mickey Mouse picture on the side, Jamie's suggestion until we can find something more 'age- appropriate.' I push on the spouted top and, holding a wad of tissues under his chin, begin to trickle the drink into the side of his mouth. Jamie had explained how Andrew had something called a 'bite reflex,' some instinct a baby has to clamp its gums round the nipple, which some severely handicapped people never lose. You avoid triggering it by giving food and drink into the cheek. I'd seen staff at the hospital hold his nose and call him a naughty boy when he wouldn't- couldn't- let go of the spoon. And every time they did that they were putting him though hell for something he couldn't understand.

If 'The Community' was finding our corner a little bit too draughty before, it would think there was a hurricane brewing now, as strings of orange saliva streak Andrew's chin, dyeing the tissues I'm holding under it. As the rest of the pub begins to fill up, the noise level rises and a smoky haze descends, causing Jamie to take a puff on his asthma inhaler. Eddie has sensed that it is nearly his bedtime, so Jamie goes back with him to the Bungalow. Just as Ruth is about to go in search of Rita, who has gone to the toilet for the third time, she appears, carrying a drink.

'Rita, where did you get that?'

'Man.'

'You shouldn't be asking strange men for drinks.'

'Why?'

'Because... they'll think you're stupid or childish, and you don't want that do you?'

Rita looks at her free Irish cream and grins at Ruth, who is failing to understand 'Ritanomics.' A free drink is a free drink, and there are very few things that can make that in any way wrong. She knocks it back, clears the glass with her finger, and says:

'More?'

Without a word passing between us, we decide that this would be a good time to bring our first forage into the community to an end. At first, Rita clings to her seat, but as we begin to disappear round the bar she springs up, and stomps after us with a scowl. But just as we get to the door, it happens, and there's nothing we can do to stop it.

As she is about to pass the bar, Rita stops and grabs a pint from where it sits in front of a small bald guy and takes a swig. Then she storms off out of the pub, followed by Ruth with Andrew, leaving me to explain things. At the hospital you knew that the more able patients would steal drinks off the others without a thought. It happened every day. But this is not the hospital. It comes as a surprise that the guy is *at first* very understanding, and refuses to let me buy him another drink. But there's something I haven't mentioned about Rita. In fact there's a whole side to this job I haven't really gone into yet, and it concerns some of the things that The People brought with them from the hospital: like Rose's 'institutionalised bowel,' which is caused by regularly eating food which has been cooked in a central kitchen, placed in a heated trolley where it is left to keep warm then, when all of the goodness has gone out of it, is wheeled to the ward; like Eddie's scabies, little black things that burrow into your skin, which we had to get rid of by standing him in a bath and covering him from head to toe in gunk, using a large paintbrush; like Mickey's threadworm, friendly little creatures that lay eggs in your arse, which travel under your fingernails to the incubator, which is your throat. These were some of the hidden extras of care in a Mental Handicap Hospital. And Rita? Rita was a Hepatitis B carrier. I wasn't certain if it could be passed on through sharing a drink, but I sure as hell didn't want to find out.

'It really is O.K.' says the bald guy, lifting his pint, 'she didn't drink much.'

'No... It's not O.K.' I say, grabbing the glass and spilling some of it down his shirt, 'it's just that she's...' *Jamie and Colin had drilled a word into me: 'confidentiality.'* 'It's just that she...she's got something.'

'What, like AIDS you mean', says the guy, as the pub becomes silent and the barman looks with horror at the pint pot. As he pours the beer away and bins the 'contaminated' glass I can see all of our plans to integrate The People going the same way.

'So what then?' says the bloke, who's getting a bit shirty now, 'has she got the clap or something?'

'NO... something like that...no, nothing like that...I just can't...'

'That's all right then,' says the barman, laughing, 'If she's got the clap she'll fit in well round here.'

As he laughs at his own joke the regulars start to join in, and gradually turn back to their own conversations. I can feel my face burning, and as I turn, Ruth is there, trying hard not to wet herself. She's taken Rita and Andrew to the Bungalow, then come back to see where I am.

'So...' she says, '...I see that went well.'

*

At about eleven thirty, Oscar staggers in through the front door with a foolish grin on his face. We're sitting with mugs of drinking chocolate at the kitchen table, where Ruth has spent the last hour trying to convince me that I haven't completely jeopardised the future of the Bungalow.

As Oscar raises his hand to say 'hello' a wad of paper falls from his pocket.

'Hey, guess what,' he slurs, 'I've been in a pub tonight, the 'Black Horse' I think it was called, and a nice man and woman came in and asked me if I was local. I said that I was now, so they asked me to sign a thing called 'say no to mental patients in our community petition', so I said 'no, I'm afraid I can't do that.'

'Well done, Oscar,' we say in unison.

'No, don't get me wrong. What I mean is, I'm pretty good with numbers and money and stuff, but not with writing, so I can't sign, although I bloody well agree with what they're saying. I told 'em I didn't want mental people on my street either, and that I know what I'm talking about because I've spent most of my life living with 'em. They laughed at that. So anyway, I ended up helping to give out some leaflets, and guess what? They bought me a pint for doing it'.

If accepting its values and working with its members towards a common cause is any measure of his success, then Oscar Doyle could certainly claim that this was the night when he had begun the process of integrating himself into the community.

-Chapter 17-

15th April 1987

Della rearranged the items on her desk into size order, then flicked up a screen on her computer with the title 'strategic plan,' which listed all of the steps towards her vision for the Bungalow for the coming year.

Item 9: All residents to have a day placement within one month of move.

Della typed 'completed' against the item, as everyone had already started to attend the local day centre. Everyone, that is, apart from Oscar, who had learned the frustration of receiving a token payment for monotonous employment in the hospital's sheltered workshop. So far, Oscar's days had been spent either in his bedroom, in front of the television, or wandering the town. But Oscar's Individual Programme Plan meeting was due, and Della was confident that he could be persuaded to spend his time more usefully.

Item 10: All residents to have an Individual Programme Plan (IPP) within the first month of the move.

Mickey's Individual plan had one major priority: to get him walking again. The Physio had confirmed that there was no reason at

127

all why Mickey shouldn't walk, so once new shoes and callipers had been obtained the sky was the limit. If not the sky, at least Mickey would be able to reach the food cupboards and not rely on frozen burgers for his midnight feasts.

At Rita's IPP meeting her parents had said that more home visits would be possible now that she lived closer to them. Despite Jamie's misgivings around the grouping together of people with disabilities it was agreed that Rita, at her own request, should attend the 'Gateway Club' where she had been a member before she moved to the hospital. She was also to get a long weekend in Blackpool- the family holiday venue of her childhood- before the end of the year.

Eddie's plan for the year included joining Rita on her holiday, improving his self-care skills and- as he had been an avid attendee of the hospital chapel- finding a church.

Not that Eddie will still be at the Bungalow one year from now.

Eddie's presence brought back too many bad memories for Della, and she was already devising her own Individual Plan for him, one which would ensure his return to the hospital, or somewhere very much like it, within the next six months.

Against Eddie's name in bold print she typed '**October '87.**' His bed was being kept open until that date. That would be her target; and she was good at hitting targets.

Further down the page, in a subsection to item ten, was a list of residents with the names of their key-workers and a record of how far their IPP was progressing. Against Rita's name, Della typed the word 'completed.' Of the other five, two had happened within the last month and two had been set.

Only one remained.

Typing an asterisk after Andrew's name, she glared at the screen, feeling a vein in her neck writhe like a netted serpent.

Martin Peach

This was typical of him, she thought, typical of his 'laid back' attitude and inability to take anything seriously, an attitude which made him the total antithesis to her ordered and efficient approach. It also infuriated her that Martin failed to listen properly to her instructions, but hung onto every word from Ruth, as if she were some sort of incarnate goddess. She picked out Ruth's name on her strategic plan, and against it typed one word in bold print:

whore.

Her blond hair, her generous breasts and conventional beauty even turned Simeon's head.

Whore...Whore...Whore.

But Ruth was not the real problem. Della felt a familiar tremor beginning in her hands. Clenching her jaw, she jabbed at a single key repeatedly as if carrying out a frenzied attack, her agitation possessing her, quickly transforming into a fit of all-consuming fury. When she eventually emerged from her silent rage she felt her blouse sticking to her back. The tip of her index finger was sore. She had broken a fingernail on the keyboard. On the monitor a string of bold question marks followed the name of Martin Peach. Looking at her hands she could see that the tremor was beginning to still, indicating that the episode was over.

But *they* were still there: *The voices...*

She had first heard them one Christmas in the mid nineteen seventies. Since that time, whenever she was stressed, they jostled to be heard, a hurricane of sounds of which she was the epicentre. Mostly they were indistinguishable, but occasionally individual phrases would rise above the cacophony. Sometimes they were taunts from the playground, but they would usually be those of her mother or father, questioning her school grades, criticising her choice of career or partner. But one voice chilled her more than any other, even though she had never known to whom it belonged to or what it meant. She heard it at times when her mind was in its deepest and darkest disarray. She even had a name for it:

Nemesis

She had first heard the voice of her Nemesis at the hospital. It was the voice of a woman with an Irish accent, and, for reasons she could never understand, it said:

Their heads are green and their hands are blue.

Della unlocked a drawer to her desk. Over the years, she had found only one sure way of stilling the voices, and restoring focus to her mind. Next to a small pile of pills lay a gleaming scalpel.

Hitching up her skirt, her hand still shaking, she guided the point of the knife to the vast expanse of thigh. Choosing a place where earlier scars had healed sufficiently to tolerate further incision, she jabbed the instrument into her flesh and drew it along in a straight line. Repeating the process until three perfectly spaced red lines of identical length decorated her skin, she used the index finger of her left hand to form a dam for the trickling tributaries of blood. Holding out her hand she watched a droplet form at the tip of her finger.

He's not good enough for you...
Nursing? You should be going into management...
Their heads were...

The voices gradually reduced in number and began to fade as if a volume knob was being turned, and then they stopped, the sweet pain focussing her mind, allowing her to think with clarity.

This is what we need, she thought, *a bloodletting.*

It had already become clear to her that if her Bungalow project was to work, if it was to be that perfect thing, beyond the criticism of any other mortal, she would have to make sacrifices.

A drop of blood from her outstretched finger splashed onto the desk.

Edward Sparrow.

A second droplet formed and fell alongside the first.

Martin Peach.

From her meditative state Della was suddenly aware that someone was knocking on the office door and, looking up, she was shocked to realise from the position of the key that she had forgotten to lock it. Pulling down her skirt she grabbed a tissue, wiped the droplets of blood from the desk then wrapped the scalpel in the tissue and deposited it back in the drawer.

'Come in.'

It was Simeon.

'I'm just making a cup of tea,' he said, 'would you like one?'

'Yes,' said Della, who was now smiling serenely, 'I've hidden some Lapsang Souchong behind the recipe books on the top shelf.'

Simeon nodded.

'And Simeon...'

'Yes?'

'I've had quite a few important things to do this morning, but it gets a little lonely here in the 'throne room.' Would you care to join me?'

As Simeon left to make the tea, Della searched for a packet of antiseptic wipes that she kept in her briefcase. She dabbed the scarred thigh and rubbed at the stained finger until all signs that she had been bleeding had gone, depositing the used wipes in her brief case just as Simeon returned.

It would not do for him to realise that she had blood on her hands.

-Chapter 18-

29th April 1987

To help us, that is those of us who are Individual Programme Planning virgins, Jamie had got Oscar's permission to video his IPP meeting for staff training. But, for a reason that was never made clear, the video was never used. In fact Jamie had meant to wipe it clean, but Colin managed to save it and, billing it as 'unmissable,' had invited me to the premiere the next time we were on a sleep-in. So far I've managed to put off doing Andrew's IPP, and I've got a good excuse: to do an IPP you should have members of the person's family there, and even though Jamie has now taken on nagging the hospital to find Andrew's file it still hasn't turned up, so we don't even know if he has a family. For my part, I wonder how on earth I can be expected to plan somebody else's life when I've made such a poor job of planning my own.

Once everybody's settled, Colin gets a brown leather hip-flask from his pocket and offers me a swig.

'It's the one they named after me' he says, 'the 'Macallan.' Mellow and sweet because it's spent half it's life maturing in sherry casks- a feature which I also resemble.'

I know that there's a rule about drinking on duty, but as Colin's senior to me I suppose it's all right as long as we don't get totally pissed. I soon realise, the way he's guzzling it, that there's not much chance of me getting so much as another sniff.

'This you have got to see,' says Colin, setting the video going.

The first view is of Oscar, grinning at the camera.

Jamie: (off camera) Welcome to the IPP of Mr. Oscar Doyle. I am Jamie Heffer, Senior Residential Social Worker.'

(The camera pans around the lounge)

'I am Colin Macallan, Senior Residential Social Worker, and Oscar's key-worker.'

'Della Belk: Manager of the Bungalow'

'Ida Dolittle: Social Worker.'

'Mr. Pinkerton: Supported Employment, whom Ida, ahem, has taken the liberty of inviting for my contribution.'

'Oscar Doyle: Star of the show.'

Colin: To kick off, I'd like to thank Oscar for his last minute decision to attend, as this is his meeting and its very important that he tells us what he wants from the service.

Colin was wearing his serious professional head for the meeting. At the age of forty- eight he had worked for Social Services since leaving school, at first in children's' homes, more recently in mental handicap, and usually gives the impression that he's seen so many trends and changes come and go that anything beyond the nitty-gritty real world of caring isn't worth getting excited about. But in this setting, Colin could play the game as well as anybody.

Jamie: As I didn't have time to talk to you about what you wanted, Oscar, I have a list of suggestions that you might want to consider. The first is to do with your accommodation, where you live. How would you feel about eventually moving from the Bungalow to live more independently, perhaps in your own flat?

Oscar: But I've only just moved here.

Jamie: We're not talking about moving immediately, more in the long term. You should think of this as a bridge between the hospital and something more normalised. You can learn some of the skills that you need here, then, say in perhaps a year from now, you could start looking for a flat, with someone to look in on you from time to time.

Oscar: Who would cook?

Jamie: We'll discuss that one nearer the time.

Colin: You have to agree, Oscar, nice as the Bungalow is, it isn't the perfect home for you…

Oscar: It's not bad, apart from that bloody noisy woman. Couldn't you get rid of her instead?

(The T.V. screen momentarily fills with snow.)

'It's not Rita we need to get rid of lad' says the real Colin, as if thinking out loud.

'You what?'

'Oh, nothing. Just venting my spleen with regards to our glorious leader.'

'Oh her,' I say, surprised that Colin, who usually plays his cards close to his chest, so obviously wants to talk about his problems with Della. I'm thinking it's something to do with   the whisky he's just knocked back, but as Colin has a reputation as an experienced drinker I wonder if he's had something earlier.

'So what do you think of her' he asks.'

'Well I used to work in a factory…before I got my art degree…and I thought the bosses there were bastards. When I came here and met you and Jamie I thought it was great that you were human. But Della…'

'So,' says Colin, pausing to sprinkle the last few drops of whisky onto his tongue 'you think that Della's a bad manager, do you?'

'Yes…'

'Well you're wrong.'

'What?'

'You're wrong. She's much worse than that.'

'What do you mean?'

Colin slides down in his chair and puts his hands behind his head.

'Hang on a minute...this is a good bit...'

Colin: So it's agreed, then, Oscar, that now you're more familiar with the town   you might want to do a few shopping trips on your own. Now, employment- do you have any ideas about what sort of job you might want to do?

Oscar: Well, Colin, (Oscar leans back with his hands clasped behind his head) to be honest I don't really want to do a job. I had a bad experience in the hospital, so no.

Della: I think you should give it serious consideration, Oscar; it is part of living a normal life in the community.

Oscar: Let me tell you about my experience in the hospital: I used to work in the workshop. We used to put plastic bits onto plastic tubes, letters into envelopes, that sort of thing- easy jobs, even for mental lads. It was boring, but it wasn't the boredom that put me off. Then there were the people. There were some very nice men, but there were some buggers like Don Maguire. There were fights, but I stayed out of them, although I did once get a cup of tea poured over my privates. And some of the lads used to try to fiddle with you, but I kept away from them. But it wasn't that that put me off. Do you want to know what really put me off? It was getting to the end of the week and being given a brown envelope with a quid in it. So I started asking a few questions and found out that when I put a full week in I was getting five pence an hour. I could find more than that in two seconds if I looked round the grounds after Gala Day. And when I didn't put a full week in they'd knock money off. Sodding cheek, I thought, so I packed it in.

Mr. Pinkerton: If I may interrupt you, er, Oscar, I do have several people who have worked whilst receiving a small allowance,

135

and have used their work experience to find real employment. There is a local supermarket where you could learn shelf stacking. Who knows what that might eventually lead to?

Oscar: That's very kind of you, but I do have an idea of what I want to do.

Ida: What's that, Oscar?

Oscar: Well, I got to watch a lot of telly in the Happy Owls, and I listened a lot to Mrs. Thatcher. What do you think of Mrs. Thatcher? Well, I think she's a nice lady, and she said that anybody could have their own house and have their own business. So that's what I want to do.

Della: What?

Oscar: Start my own business. Mrs. Thatcher says anybody can do it, and I'm anybody.

Della: Do you think it's realistic?

Oscar: No, it's just my little joke, but I got you going there, didn't I? How could I set up a business, mental lad like me?

Ida: (Leaning forward) Mr. Doyle, would you mind if we use the term 'person with a mental handicap?'

Oscar: Why?

Ida: Because it's what people with mental handicaps prefer to be called.

Oscar: But I've got a... well anyway, as I was saying, I would prefer to be idle.

Della: I don't think, Oscar, that we can put that down on you Individual Programme Plan, can we? You see, you are meant to be getting a better quality of life now that you are living in the community, and having a job will be part of that.

'Can you see what Oscar's doing?' asks Colin, with a broad grin.

'How do you mean?'

'I mean how he's meant to be the one with the mental handicap and they're the ones with the qualifications, yet he's completely taken over the meeting. And Della hates it. It may be about Oscar's life, but she so desperately wants to be in charge. Just look at her face'

I watch as the 'Oscar show' unfolds, but I'm waiting desperately for Colin to tell me what he meant when he said that Della was worse than a bad manager.

'You were saying something about Della.' I say, trying not to sound too eager.

Colin stares at the screen, where Della is grandstanding, and says:

'Whatever you do, don't repeat this, because I've no proof. in fact, it would be impossible to prove... but you tell me: what do you think about Della's relationship with Eddie?'

'Well,' I say, not entirely sure where this is leading, 'it's crap, isn't it, just like Della's relationships with everybody else...'

'And is that all?'

'What, like the fact that Eddie's always agitated when Della's around?'

'And how does Della feel about Eddie?'

'I've never really thought about it, but... she's scared of Eddie, isn't she?'

'Yes she is, petrified. And why should she be? Everybody likes Eddie. He's the joker in the pack.'

Colin is smiling at me like a teacher trying to tease an obvious answer out of a pupil in the 'slow learners' group.

'Do you know, Colin,' I say, ' when I was a kid I could projectile vomit at will when I got angry or frustrated. And I can remember how to do it, so spill the beans...before I do.'

'O.K.,' he says, ' here goes: I think that Eddie and Della the fella have met before.'

Not sure what to make of that, I think through comments that Della has made about Eddie, and about the nature of their encounters in the Bungalow. It occurs to me that these are few, that when they happen they are negative, but for the most part Della does seem to avoid him.

'But how do you know? And why hasn't she told us?'

'She hasn't told us because she has told us only the absolute minimum about what she did before she came here. And no, I can't be sure, but there was something strange about both of their reactions the first time Eddie came here.'

'What, when he moved in and smashed the milk bottle?'

'No. Before that. It was when he came for the trial stay. I drove the mini bus, and when we arrived, Della was here to meet them. Eddie marched straight up to her, said 'Mr. Hill,' and she nearly lost it.'

'And that makes you think they knew each other?'

'I know it doesn't sound much. I can't explain it. You would have to have been there and seen the look.'

I turn back to the video, where Oscar is addressing his audience.

Oscar: Well, like I said, I watched a lot of telly in the hospital, and according to that there are millions of normal people who are idle: there's all the miners, and now there's the mental lads, like me.

Della: What we will do then, is ask Mr. Pinkerton to find an appropriate place for you, and then you can go and give it a try…

Oscar: er…

Della: Next item, Colin.

Colin: How would you feel about taking a holiday this year, Oscar?

Oscar: That would be great, as long as you don't expect me to go with that bloody noisy… (The screen is filled with lines, and then clears.)

Ida: So before we finish, Mr. Doyle, is there anything that you would like to do this year that we haven't discussed.

Oscar: Well yes, actually, there is something that is very important to me, and was actually one of my main reasons for deciding to leave the hospital.

Ida: Yes?

Oscar: Well, it's just that there wasn't much to choose from in the hospital, so I thought I'd have more of a chance out here.

Ida: Yes, go on.

Oscar: Well, I'd really like...how do you say it? You know, I'd really like to... shag a tart...'

(Lines, snow, and when the picture returns it is accompanied by the theme tune to 'Eastenders.')

'Did you see that?' asks Colin, and although I'm nearly wetting myself at what I've just seen he's looking completely serious.

'See what?'

'Look,' says Colin, winding the tape back, and stopping it just after Oscar's proclamation. Although the picture is lined and flickering, you can clearly see that the camera had swung round and momentarily caught Della's expression. Her ugly, hateful, expression.

'Do you see that?' asks Colin. 'That is Della with her guard down. I was there, and everyone else was suppressing laughter, maybe some of them were mildly embarrassed. But that is Della's reaction.'

Although the picture is far from clear, Della's lip can be seen, momentarily curled into a snarl, her eyes bulge and a vein stands out from her neck.

'O.K., says Colin, 'so maybe Eddie hasn't met Della before. Maybe he's like me. When you've been around 'carers' as long as we have you develop an antennae when you meet one.'

'One what?'

'An abuser lad. An abuser. And this old antenna has never twitched so much.'

-Chapter 19-

2nd May 1987
11.50 p.m.

Jane sat reading the local paper in the sleep-in room, propped up on three pillows. She sighed and shook her head as she read the head- line again:

Residents fear influx of mental patients.

There was a picture of a lady called Mrs Busby, looking mournfully at her large Edwardian house on Moonfield Road. The attached article told of how she had been visiting local groups and pubs with her petition. She was quoted as saying that it was cruel for these people to be dumped in a home on a busy road, and that she had heard loud screams from the Bungalow, and didn't feel safe. Almost as an afterthought, she mentioned the falling value of her house.

The article contained an interview with the local MP, Dan Kerr, who at a time when he thought his party would rule forever had, like many of his peers, allowed his guard to slip and spoken freely. He had, he explained, no problem with the closure of the Victorian institutions, but felt that patients would be better placed near to the local council estate.

The manager of the unit has refused to comment.

Jane could not sleep. Voices had been raised that day at the staff meeting when Jamie had asked if waking night staff could be employed, as some of the residents had life-threatening nighttime seizures that could not be responded to by staff on sleep-in duty. Della had insisted that there was no money for this because the Bungalow had originally been funded for more able people. The mood in the Bungalow that night had been tense. Jane wasn't sure whether Della had the greatest antipathy toward Martin or Eddie, but when she was around either of them it was as if she were spinning a dark, tangible web, or creating a black hole that was dragging everyone down into it.

But now, all was quiet, apart from Rita's snoring, which reverberated down the corridor. Mickey slept peacefully, as he did every night since Jamie had developed a programme to encourage him to stay in his bed. Each time he emerged from his door, two staff had gently lifted him back, offered him a mug of drinking chocolate, then sat and talked to him for five minutes. After three nights Mickey was taken to bed and stayed.

Jane looked at the vacancies pages in the newspaper. Some of them had been ringed, or cut out. She had started to feel that the idea of the Bungalow as a stable home environment was going to be difficult to realise. Most of the staff seemed to be just 'passing through,' and she wondered if within a year The People would have to get used to a whole new set. Colin wanted to be a writer. Ruth, although she would never admit it, still hankered after a singing career. Even Jamie talked about eventually packing everything up and travelling. Martin didn't seem to know what he wanted. She knew that he was finding things difficult. Only Simeon seemed to see it as a long-term career, but Jane did not think that this was a good thing.

She herself would eventually go into teaching or lecturing in theology. This was a stopgap, a chance to answer a 'calling' she had had years before, which had never gone away, although she now doubted if the owner of the voice even existed. She put down the paper, and picked up a second-hand copy of 'The Myth of God Incarnate' from the bedside table. She had been leaving it there in the hope that it would either enlighten or annoy Simeon when he was sleeping in. For months she had avoided talking religion with him, then one night earlier that week he had decided, uncharacteristically, to join her and Martin at the Lobster after a late shift. As soon as Martin went to the bar, Simeon had leaned over.

'I hope you don't think I'm being cheeky, Jane,' he said, conspiratorially, 'but how did you lose your faith?'

141

Jane did not know whether to laugh or scream at him. Suddenly it became clear- he had wanted to drink with them tonight because he saw her as a lost sheep to bring back to the fold, another notch on his belt of salvation.

She looked him in the eye and said: 'I didn't lose it.'

Simeon glanced at the floor, then back at Jane. 'I thought I'd heard you say something once about how you used to go to church, and since then the spirit has been laying it upon me to....'

'I didn't lose my faith,' she snapped, 'if anything, I found it. I've found my real faith, as opposed to the second-hand one my parents gave me.'

Martin returned from the bar, carrying a tray with a pint of beer, a dry white wine, and an orange juice.

'You're not taking her on at religion are you Sim? Don't you know she wrote a book on it?'
Jane blushed.
'Oh. What did you write?' asked Simeon, feigning interest.
' It wasn't a book, it was a thesis.'

Jane remembered mentioning it to Martin some time ago. He'd got this thing in his head about everyone at the Bungalow being a graduate, and had been asking her what their disciplines were. She didn't mind talking to Martin about her theological background, but the last thing she wanted were Simeon's ill-informed fundamentalist views.

'So what was the subject?' asked Simeon, clasping his hands together on the table, his head cocked to one side, as if he were a priest about to hear a confession.
Jane took a deep breath.

'I was trying to answer one of the trickiest questions in New Testament criticism,' she said with a sigh, like someone who had spent years unsuccessfully trying to track down a lost love.

'Which is?'

'Who wrote John's Gospel?'

'But… isn't it John?' asked Martin. Simeon nodded his head, and Martin shot an apologetic glance at Jane, unhappy to find himself in agreement with his flatmate.'

'No, it isn't. Well at least I don't think so. It's a long argument. Sixty thousand words long in my case. Simply, there is no complete ascription of the Fourth Gospel to the Apostle John until a hundred years after the most likely date of writing; the writer is more familiar with Jerusalem than Galilee, and...'

'It's O.K., I'll take your word for it,' said Martin, 'he should have signed the bloody thing, shouldn't he?'

'So,' said Simeon, a superior smile spreading across his face, 'you don't accept that the Gospel has apostolic authority?'

Jane wriggled down the bed, grimacing at her memory of the conversation. She had simply said 'no' and changed the subject. At one time she would have argued, but successive encounters had made her realise that arguments with the likes of Simeon were pointless. At one time she would have held very similar views to his- but that was a long time ago. When Jane first went to University she had joined the Christian Union and attended her home church on each weekend visit to her parents. At first, the theology had informed the practice, and the practice had kept the theology living. She could quite easily accept that there were apparent contradictions in the scriptures, but put this down to her lack of understanding.

During the holidays, Jane would return to her home church and attend the weekly Bible study. It wasn't until the end of her second year at University that she realised from the elders' answers to her questions that, imperceptibly, a great gulf had been fixed. On the third week she was taken to one side after the study and asked not to raise certain questions, as these were damaging to those who were 'young in the faith.' She had felt her heart sink – she still saw herself as young, as questioning and in need of answers. Now she was cast in the role of the serpent in the garden, raising doubts about the very words of God. She knew then that she had to get back to University, and that the home and church where she had grown up were now part of her history. That year she applied for the Master's course: better to gorge yourself on food offered to idols than starve on a pinch of bread and a sip of wine.

TASTING THE WIND

Saint Simeon's first evangelistic voyage to the Cat and Lobster having failed, he had finished his orange juice and retreated to his flat for prayer and fasting.

'It's just typical,' said Jane, relating to Martin what Simeon had said to her. 'He didn't want to join us for our company- he just wanted to preach to me. He doesn't want to know what I think, just to get me to see things his way. He doesn't care about what I believe.'

Martin took a long drink. 'So you do believe something then?'

'Well, yes, but it's a bit unformed, a sort of faith by process of elimination I suppose. I systematically went through it all, starting with the infallibility of scripture and eventually ending up with the atonement- all the things I'd been told to believe. I gradually argued the lot out of existence. I was left with two things. God- I couldn't get beyond a belief in a creator, but I still have to adapt that one. I'd been taught a small God for so long it's easy to lapse back into that way of thinking.'

'God and what?'

'What?'

'You said two things. God, and…?'

'Oh yes, the other one is synchronicity.'

'What?'

'Synchronicity. It's when things happen by coincidence, but too often, or too much 'on cue' to be accidental. For instance, thinking about someone you haven't seen for years, then you meet them or they ring. It can be an object or a symbol that keeps on turning up, or appears in an unusual place. In fact big events, like death, seem to set them off- clusters of synchronicities. Someone dies, and that December a butterfly enters the garden of a loved one….'

'Or poppies appear on somebody's pillow on Christmas day?'

Jane had heard about Andrew's poppies, and despite her natural scepticism, hoped that there was some truth in it.

' Yes. That sort of thing. Synchronicity may be the echoes in creation that demonstrate its unity, the glimpses of pattern that are part of nature and force themselves through what we perceive as chaos. It is a chain that is infinite. God and synchronicity: the great cause and the great symptom. It has had some sort of academic respectability since Jung used it.'

'Jimmy Young?'

'I'm being serious.'

'So am I.... anyway, John's Gospel: did you ever find out who wrote it?"

'No. The question isn't that simple.'

'So you wrote sixty-thousand words, and you didn't answer the question?'

'I discussed the question. I came up with a hypothesis. I knew more when I'd finished than when I started. When I started I thought I didn't know who wrote it. When I'd finished, I knew that I didn't know. That's Higher Education for you.'

Jane snuggled down, smiling as her eyes fluttered to a close. Martin always made her smile. As she drifted off she thought she heard a voice. It was a woman with an Irish accent, saying:

'Their heads are green, and their hands are blue,
And they went to sea in a sieve.'

The Jumblies, she thought, *Edward Lear.* She began to pull back from sleep, but another voice, that of her ebbing, conscious mind, said:

'*The doors are locked. There's no one else here. You've already started dreaming...*'

-Chapter 20-

5th May 1987

'Who's in the cupboard?
Rang the bell
Made the noise
Smashed the bottle
Broke the cup
Played the game
Naughty Mr. Hill.'

'Edward,' said Della, 'I thought we'd agreed that you were too old for that game?'

Eddie glanced up, red-eyed, from where he sat on the floor, then down at the spinning tops game. He bent over it so that it filled his field of vision, making it his whole world, a world that was endlessly blue, where he looked down, god-like, and had something resembling control.

'So shall we put it away and have breakfast? You'll be late for the day centre.'

Eddie gave an almost imperceptible shake of his head.

'You did agree,' said Della, easing the game away from him, causing the spinning tops to wobble, lose momentum and rattle to a halt. She slid the game into its box, tearing one of the flaps, and took it to her office. It would have been unethical to throw away the game without Eddie's consent, but it was, she explained, her duty to stop him from playing it. Della smiled triumphantly: a small step towards the 'normalisation' of Eddie Sparrow. Or If not that, it would be the first step towards pushing him over the edge and initiating his return to the hospital.

'Spinning game,' said Eddie. He bent closer to the floor, so that his nose was almost touching it, as if analysing the weave of the carpet, then started to rock rhythmically, like a martial arts master about to smash an imaginary pile of bricks with his forehead.

'What's 'agreed'?' He muttered to himself, his rocking growing more and more frenetic.

Later that day, Eddie returned from the day centre with a note to say that his behaviour had been very disturbed. Ruth gathered from him that he had sat on orange chairs at grey tables with wooden puzzles and a boy with red hair and a green nose had tried to take his carrier bag. Later in the day Mr. Hill had made an appearance and Eddie had run screaming down the corridors. At some point in his rambling explanation it had come out that the spinning game had been taken.

'You see, the real problem,' said Della, as she got up to leave that night, 'Is that Eddie's placement here is inappropriate. Eddie comes more under 'mental illness' than 'mental handicap,' and if I'd been around when the list was being drawn up for the Bungalow he would never have been on it.

'But why shouldn't Eddie play the spinning game?' said Ruth, tentatively, 'It relaxes him, makes him happy.'

Della stopped by the door, and turned round slowly, smiling as if addressing a child.

'Eddie is an adult. If he plays with children's toys he will be treated like a child.'

'But,' said Ruth, 'should it all happen at once? Can't we do it a bit more gradually and leave him with things that give him a sense of security?'

'There is a policy,' said Della, 'a borough-wide policy, that we practice normalisation. I think you should familiarise yourself with it. Besides, you ought to be sorting out your own client and leave Eddie's programme to Simeon. I will see you tomorrow.'

Her slam of the door caused Andrew to jolt into a short but violent seizure. His eyes rolled up into his head as his mouth stretched into the false smile of a ventriloquist's dummy. Then his head slumped, and a thin trail of saliva, streaked with blood, ran from his tongue and dribbled down his chin. Ruth wiped it, dropped the crumpled tissue onto his empty plate, then bent to retrieve a baked bean from the floor. She looked up at Simeon, who had been silently pretending to read a report throughout the encounter. There was a tear in her eye.

'She had no right to take that game from Eddie.'

Simeon looked up from his report. ' I think you'll find that she had every right.'

'What do you mean?'

'I mean that Della is the manager. She runs the Bungalow. If she makes a decision it is based on years of experience...'

'Della runs the Bungalow? Sorry, but I thought the Bungalow was someone's home.'

'That is not what I meant,' spat Simeon, gathering up the papers he had been reading and retreating to the sleep-in room.

For the first time, Ruth found herself wishing that Martin was there. She was going to follow Simeon and have it out with him, but that thought stopped her in her tracks. She was warming to Martin. At this point he would have made a quip or shot her a glance which would lighten things a little.

Ruth had realised for some time that allegiances were forming: There was Della and Simeon, and there was herself, Jane, and Martin. Jamie, she knew, was part of that grouping, but he was always professional, and although it was obvious that his views were often diametrically opposed to Della's, he never allowed personal differences to spill over. Colin was one on his own- good company, but cynical and aloof, as if he stood outside of the whole scenario.

But for some reason sides were being taken, camps formed, and battle lines drawn. Somehow Ruth had found herself on the same side as Martin, but the more she thought about it the more she realised that she not only didn't mind, but was actually quite happy with the fact.

-Chapter 21-

9th May 1987
12.30 p.m.

Ruth is trying to get Rita to gradually replace everything that she had brought with her from the hospital, and choose more 'appropriate' clothing. Well at least that's the theory. For 'appropriate' read: anything that isn't red sandals, white ankle socks, and flowery middle-aged skirts and blouses. Oh, and elasticated slacks.

I suppose I've broken some sort of normalisation rule by not taking Andrew with me when I'm buying clothes for him, but we're stuck for transport, and there's no way of negotiating the tube system with somebody in a wheelchair. As far as I can see we've reached the mid-eighties in supposedly the most enlightened century yet, and the only acknowledgement of access difficulties on the London Underground system is the Wizard of Oz telling us to 'MIND THE GAP' every few minutes. I'd thought that going with Eddie and not Andrew would be the easier option, but the idea of taking somebody who might at any moment strike up a conversation with anybody or thing that moves or spins, or chase his invisible dog along the platform, and all of this without being able to hold his hand, will give me material for my nightmares for a long time to come.

'Tarzan. 'Says Eddie, as we pass through Russell Square station.

'Tarzan?'

'Tarzan. Tarzan made Cheetah in a pie.' Eddie bursts into manic laughter at his own surreal joke.

'Tarzan made Cheetah In a pie?'

Maybe I should be worried, but sometimes I think I'm getting onto Eddie's wavelength. For tea last night he'd had cheese and onion pie. Cheetah in a pie. I'm smiling at making the connection until I realise that Eddie is half way down the carriage, swinging on the straps and making a Tarzan call. The people on the train stare out at the fascinating tunnel wall, and you'd have thought they hadn't even noticed Eddie, if their reflected expressions didn't look so uniformly shit-scared.

We get Andrew's clothes first but, after about half an hour, male shopping lethargy has set in. I do try not to be a stereotype. Jo had always gone on about this, and now that I'm here in the heart of p.c.-dom I'm making an effort to blend in. Only I feel a bit like the guy at the end of 'Invasion of the Body Snatchers,' trying not to let any of the normal feelings show, just in case the alien beings that have sprung from the pods realise that I'm not one of them. But there's no fooling Ruth. After two women's clothes shops, Eddie and me are relegated to the bench outside Dorothy Perkins. Now I'm all for equality, and the same money for the same job and all that, but at the end of the day you have to acknowledge that there are built in differences between the sexes and that we would be tampering with nature if we tried to change them. One of these is shopping. How many blokes, asked what they want to do on a Saturday afternoon, would say 'I'm really looking forward to going in and out of clothes shops'? We do other things.

'You've been doing what?' says Ruth, holding a Dorothy Perkins bag and looking at me accusingly. She'd asked Eddie what we'd been up to while they'd been in the shop. Eddie had replied:

'Playing 'bosom of the day."

I can tell that she doesn't believe that this had been Eddie's idea. That was the last time we were allowed to wait outside.

'So did you find a winner?' asks Ruth.

'Winner?'

'Bosom of the day.'

'No. I was stuck between two...'

'In your dreams...'

'You're smiling.'

'No I'm not.'

The shopping allowance exhausted, Ruth has found Rita jeans, T-shirts, skirts, blouses, shoes and underwear, all of the type that would not shame any self-respecting thirty- something. Well, perhaps not the underwear, as Rita does, regardless of any advice from Ruth, still have a thing for big bloomers. But at least that isn't likely to socially stigmatise her- unlike when she went to the till at the first shop, hitched up her skirt and extracted her purse from said big bloomers.

We're about to leave for home, when Rita spots an electrical goods shop, and with a scream of delight, ploughs through the door. Ruth rushes after her, followed by me, tugging Eddie by his coat-sleeve, as we thread between hundreds of bag-laden shoppers who Rita had nearly toppled like ninepins.

Inside the shop a trail of carrier bags, their contents spilling, leads to Rita, who jabs a finger at a glass-fronted display.

'Mee-ee?' she sings to a young sales assistant who, to his credit, is trying to respond like he's been trained to:

'Are you interested in that particular model, madam?'

'Mee-ee?' she says, louder this time and thumping her chest, as if to say 'isn't it obvious?'

'I'm sorry, I'll just ask Mr...'

'Oh fa' off man.'

Then she's round the back of the display cabinet, looking for a way to open it. She had seen children all day with their Walkmans (Walkmen? Perhaps around here *Walkpersons*) and, riding the high of her spending spree, wants the slickest looking and most expensive one in the shop.

'Rita,' says Ruth, touching her elbow, 'you can't afford one of those today- you've spent up. Maybe you could save up and get one next time we come?'

The sales assistant smiles and nods at Rita, then jumps back, raising his hands as she lets out a scream and drops, bum first, onto the green carpet.

'Mr. Hill is going to break the glass box.'

'No Eddie, that really is not a good idea.'

The once-bustling shop has taken on the appearance of a snapshot, then half of the would-be customers suddenly realise that what they really want is garden furniture, as dismayed assistants watch pounds and pounds worth of commission walk through the door. The half that remain pretend that they aren't in the least interested in the outcome. They must be the sort of people who creep along the motorway when there's been an accident on the other side, taking in every last detail so they can be the first to tell their drinking mates what they'll read in tomorrow's paper. I could hear them reciting it to their families over tea, and to their friends in numerous Cat and Lobsters all over London:

'Two kids came in with a couple of mentally handicapped. One of 'em, a big girl she was, wanted a radio. Well, they wouldn't let her have one, so she sat on the floor, screaming. Bloody disgraceful, I thought. They should 'ave more control over 'em than that, and besides, the girl only wanted a radio. Anyway, you'll never guess what happened next. This ginger lad, one of the house parents I would guess, well he looked as if he knew what he was doing'

…I'm thinking 'oh shit, what do we do now?' and trying to look in control because we we're out in public now. This isn't the hospital with its punishment room or chemical cosh- we're showing that there's a better way. It's also time that Ruth saw that I can actually handle things, and that she doesn't have to keep coming to my rescue…

'...So he went over to her, bent down to get her up and, blow me, she lashed out at him an' broke his specs'

'Oh fuck'

'...He shouted, so I'm reporting him to the authorities. Bloody disgraceful, if you ask me'

'Martin,' says Ruth, handing me the left arm of my glasses, 'can you see enough to get Eddie out?'

I tell her I can, although what I'm seeing is the impressionist masterpiece, Monet's 'shopping centre at Giverny.' I grab Eddie's arm and wait for the next part of the plan. Ruth whispers something to the shop assistant, then turns to Rita.

'We haven't time for this, Rita. We're going home for dinner. You'll have to find your own way back.'

At that she picks up the shopping bags, and leaves, with me and Eddie in tow. Outside I rub my sore nose and realise that it's been bleeding where the glasses had banged into the bridge before snapping.

'What did you say to the assistant?'

'I told him to ignore her. It's simple psychology. Watch.'

Eddie's arm in one hand, my glasses held up to my eyes with the other, I watch Rita through the gap between two Sinclair computer adverts. She's still sitting on the floor, but looking round and obviously beginning to feel foolish as shopping returns to normal and a Walkman is not forthcoming. With another scream she scrambles to her feet and stomps out of the shop. At Ruth's prompt, the three of us have already started to walk before Rita emerges from the shop. As we head out of the centre we can hear the familiar irregular footsteps behind us, and the occasional muttering of 'fa'in cow, fa'in ma'in.'

On the tube going back, Rita sits several seats away from us, still chuntering about the Walkman.

'Ruth,' I say, 'how did you know that it would work, and that she wouldn't just trash the shop to get us back?'

'I didn't,' she says, and she's smiling, but as soon as she turns away her reflection in the window is drained of colour, and she has the expression of somebody who has just narrowly missed falling under the train.

-Chapter 22-

9th May 1987
5.15 p.m.

The steel spoon chinked against the enamel of Andrew's incisors, as Della tried to cram another spoonful of pureed shepherd's pie into his mouth.

Where the fuck are they?

The shoppers were later getting back than she'd expected, leaving her with the time-consuming job of feeding Andrew. So far, he had taken in one mouthful, then had clamped his teeth shut, denying the spoon any further access. The pie had been made previously and frozen, and the act of heating it up had seriously offended Della's culinary sensibilities and nose, the cloying aroma of cheap minced meat bringing back bad memories of the hospital. At least, she reminded herself, she didn't have to eat it. For her own meal she had fried up some chicken livers, with garlic and fresh red chillies, which she had brought in for such an emergency.

'Come on Andy Pandy, open wide. That Jamie thinks he's so clever doesn't he? Bite reflex indeed. I know what a bite reflex is. There was a patient at the hospital- it might even have been you- who was meant to have a bite reflex. But I knew what to do. Bite reflex? You are just a naughty boy, that's all. Now open your mouth.'

Andrew flinched as the spoon again hit his teeth, and Della took his jaw in her meaty hand, squeezing the hinge until his mouth was forced open.

'There's a good boy, now here's some more food for you.'

As she packed the grey sludge into his mouth, Andrew's teeth clamped shut on the spoon.

'See what I mean? You're doing that on purpose. Now let go.'

Della wrapped her fist around the handle and pulled, scraping the metal against Andrew's teeth, but failing to remove the bowl of the spoon.

'If I remove the spoon from your teeth, do I become the Queen of England? Or should I just remove your teeth?'

She laughed, at first quietly to herself at her analogy, then out loud, a deep snigger as she pictured a toothless Andrew. From the lounge she could hear Mickey giggling in response to her laughter. At least he wasn't attempting to enter the kitchen. Neither was Rose. The specialised lounge chair in which Rose sat had Velcro on its arms, which helped to secure a tray. Although the tray was intended to promote good posture, Della had learned another use during her time at the hospital: for someone with Rose's lack of muscle tone it was an effective restraint, especially if her arms were placed under it.

'Now Andrew, for the last time: OPEN YOUR MOUTH.'

On the last word she tugged hard on the spoon, jerking Andrew's head forward. What would have been a loud scream of pain emerged through his clenched jaw and full mouth as a muffled hum. Della looked at the clock.

'Where the fuck are they?'

She would have words with Ruth and Martin when they eventually returned. She had more important things to do than this, but there was no way that she could leave the residents to their own devices.

It suddenly occurred to Della that if Martin and Ruth arrived now and saw a metal spoon protruding from Andrew's mouth- and not the plastic bite reflex spoon- they would use the fact to try to crucify her. There had been a meeting where they had ganged up with Jane and Jamie and demanded that Andrew be fed with a special spoon, one that would not damage his teeth, into the side of his mouth. She had let that one pass. Sometimes, she knew, it was good practice to allow the staff to think that their ideas and suggestions were valuable, but she now felt that this one act of kindness could very soon backfire on her.

Pushing her face right up to Andrew's she said: 'Come on Andrew, one more chance, then I will have no option.'

Della jumped as she heard a rattling noise behind her. There was someone at the door. It could have been Oscar, returning from town, or it could be the shoppers. A trickle of sweat ran down her back. She tried to lever Andrew's jaw open by twisting the spoon, but still it remained firm. Della fancied that she heard a fluttering sound at the door, as if a bird was flapping its wings, trying in vain to escape a snare. She gave a sigh of relief as she realised that the sound was the paperboy, shredding the front page of the local paper as he struggled to get it through the letterbox.

'Right. I warned you,' Still holding the handle of the spoon, Della pinched Andrew's nostrils together between her thumb and forefinger. Andrew's chest heaved as he struggled for air, his senses filled and overwhelmed by Della: Della's voice in his ear, her round, sweating face filling his vision, the smell of garlic from her meal sealed inside him with his last breath, and the sting of the red chilli oil from her fingers causing tears to spill down his cheeks. Not even questioning their cause, Della traced the progress of the tears from his bright blue eyes, down the fair, flawless skin of his cheeks, and felt a pang of jealousy.

'Such beauty,' she said, aware that she had never noticed it before 'and you will never feel a lover's touch.'

Della found herself pondering how Andrew saw her. Maybe he only thought in images, having no words to describe his day-to-day experiences. Maybe he saw only random shapes that his brain could not put together into anything resembling her reality.

'Maybe,' she said, 'just maybe, you see me as someone infinitely more able, more intelligent and more powerful than yourself. Maybe you see me as a god, one who could take your life with the same ease and impunity as snuffing out a candle.'

Della felt a surge of excitement at the realisation of the power that she held over the man who writhed before her.

' Not that I could allow you to die, of course. Not that I would euthanase anyone in my care. Not intentionally. You see there is only one person who has the power of life and death, and that is the Lord your God. I may look at you and think you would be better off in the heavenly kingdom, but I cannot act on that. I am waiting for a sign. Until then...'

The spoon loosened, and slid, gratingly, from between Andrew's teeth.

'Now there's a good boy. You know, I was beginning to worry that you wouldn't let go, and what would have happened then?

Although Della now had the spoon she had continued to hold Andrew's nose, and the palm of her hand had slid down to cover his mouth. As she released it Andrew sucked in a long, rattling breath, then coughed out a stream of cottage pie and saliva.

'What was it that that imbecile Peach was on about the other day? Oh yes, something about how every decision we make creates a different universe.'

She raised her hand slowly and covered Andrew's mouth and nose again. Her grip was gentle, but as Andrew thrashed his head around to try to shake it she allowed her hand to follow his movement.

'I've just had a really funny thought,' she said, her voice trancelike, 'it occurs to me that I make a difference, that if I was not here the world would be a different place. But you...it makes no difference if you are here or not.'

Della removed her hand and again Andrew drew a long painful breath into his aching lungs.

'This choice,' she said, covering his nose and mouth again, 'is the Universe without Andrew Wellman... or... the Universe with...with...without...with...without...'

And if Andrew died, what then? There would be another one, another name from the list in the endless parade, another twisted person, and another and another. If she wasn't careful, Della thought, this endless caravan of need, this great wall of water, would sweep her away. She had seen it happen to lesser people. But it would not happen to her. There was more to her than that, in fact much more than anyone realised.

It was only when Andrew's lips began to turn blue that Della decided that she would let chance decide on his survival. Soon, Martin and Ruth would return to find her in tears, an ambulance at the door, and paramedics fighting to keep Andrew alive.

When it comes to making decisions about which way to split the Universe, she thought, *everyone, even a god, has times when they need to step back and leave things to fate.*

-Chapter 23-

27th May 1987

The lounge, a blank drawing board until now, is starting to display The People's signatures: small scraps of paper under the settee, all that's left of a magazine that Mickey had yesterday; a faint purple stain where Rita had chucked a glass of blackcurrant squash; an indentation in the cushion of the chair where Oscar spends most of his days watching the telly. But Oscar's not here today, because today, Andrew Wellman, this is your IPP.

Della had finally insisted that I go ahead with it, and Jamie had offered to lead the meeting, to show me how it's done. He'd explained to me beforehand that because Andrew's not the sort of person who is valued by society, and is surrounded by so many 'negative associations,' it's a good idea to start the IPP by getting everybody to throw together a list of positive things about him. These are then written on a flipchart, which makes all the difference.

Andrew is at the meeting, the idea being that decisions about his life should only be made when he is present. I'd put him in a new tracksuit, which I'd got for him on the infamous shopping trip, and made sure that his hair was clean and nicely combed, like a kid going for his first interview.

First, we do the introduction thing, like I'd seen on the video of Oscar's IPP. There's Andrew, me, Jamie, Della, Andrew's Social worker (Miss Dolittle, who I recognise as Oscar's), and two people from the day centre. One of them is a woman of about forty in one of

158

those flowing, flowery skirts which she wears as some sort of a statement that she's a 'child of nature' or 'earth mother' or something. She has a bit of a Mediterranean look about her: wavy red/brown hair, big brown eyes and olive skin, and introduces herself as Zuska, Andrew's occupational therapist. The second wears dungarees, a tie-dyed T-shirt, and Doc Marten's boots. Her hair is like a white shaving brush which has been radically trimmed, and her small round glasses emphasise her eyes. I find myself thinking about the mural on the wall of the 'Sinister Owls.'

'Hello, I am Ms....'

For no apparent reason, Andrew has gone into a short but noisy fit. When he recovers, she tries again:

'Hello, I am Ms...'

I don't catch it that time either. She'll just have to make do with 'Ms.' and looking at her I don't think she'll be much bothered.

Jamie starts off by writing positive things down about Andrew on a sheet of the flipchart. Then, my worst nightmare: he asks us all to add something. And he wants us to answer in clockwise order, which means that I have to go first. I look at Andrew, his pale skin and large blue eyes with lashes that even Ruth says she could kill for, and say the first thing that comes into my head:

'Well... he's a good looking lad, isn't he?'

'Good. Excellent' says Jamie, like a teacher trying to encourage the 'special needs' kid, 'You're a good looking young lad Andrew, and you always dress well.'

He writes 'attractive' on the sheet.

We end up with about ten things, including 'potential' from Ms. and 'positive aura' from Zuska. Jamie just writes this as 'positive', at which Della lets out a large sigh.

Zuska smiles at her: 'Glad to hear you're getting rid of negative energies, Della.'

'To carry on,' says Jamie, 'We now look at Andrew's needs and commit ourselves to assisting him to achieve his potential over the next year.'

Zuska talks about Andrew's need to stand in a frame every day at the day centre, so that's written on the flip chart. Ms., who you can tell has been preparing herself all meeting for some grand proposal, takes a deep breath and, clearing her throat, says 'I think that some sort of work experience would be a good idea.'

159

I focus on the world outside, feeling not for the first time that I'm losing my grip on reality. Although heavy, the rain seems to be falling slowly, large droplets running down the patio doors, making it look as if the world outside is splitting up and melting away.

'That's a wonderful idea' says Miss Dolittle, excitedly, 'What would you suggest?'

'I was thinking perhaps that Andrew might like to sit in an office, soak up the atmosphere and become a part of things. Maybe Social Services head office. His presence would remind some of the pen-pushers what their job is really about.'

At the last comment, the enthusiasm seems to drain from Ida, who sits back in her chair. But Ms. is on a roll now.

'Maybe,' she goes on ' we will find that Andrew has an undiscovered talent, and that he could contribute to the actual work of the place.'

'Yes,' I say, trying to be positive, 'they could use his tongue to wet stamps on.'

Silence.

All eyes turn to me. All minds try to work out if I really am trying to get into the spirit of things, or if I'm just taking the piss. Zuska smiles at me, and then turns to Ms.

'I think you have a very positive philosophy, but do you think that a work environment is appropriate to Andrew?'

Andrew begins to cough, his chest straining against his harness. Jamie moves to his side to wipe away the expelled phlegm.

' I'm not saying he never will be able to do that,' continues Zuska, 'just that for now, as Andrew has recently had the massive trauma of coming out of familiar surroundings, I think we should be concentrating upon more immediate needs: his physical programme, stimulation of the senses in as many ways as possible, and encouragement of gross motor skills.'

'Such as?' asks Della.

It's as if Darth Vader's stepped out of the shadows with his light sabre, ready to do battle with Luke Skywalker. Della and Zuska obviously have a history that I know nothing about. Perhaps Della had been Zuska's mother (or father) before the dark side turned her into something ugly and half- human.

'At the moment,' says Zuska, 'I'm working on a programme of physical stimulation including the use of a ball pool, rubbing Andrew's

160

body with different textures, and using full-body massage. Perhaps, Martin, you'd like to come over to the centre next week and see Andrew in the ball pool.'

'And what is your long term aim?' asks Della.

'There is a long term aim, but I think it's more important that in the short term Andrew is doing things that he enjoys.'

'And the long term aim?'

'The long-term aim is that Andrew achieves more independence of movement. When he lies in the ball pool he sometimes tries to turn over. I am encouraging this so that he can learn to change his own position in bed, and so reduce pressure sores. Does Andrew have cot sides on his bed?'

'No,' says Della, Abruptly, 'Why should he?'

'It would be a good idea, just in case he suddenly started to turn over at night.'

'No, no, no. You see, cot sides belong to hospitals, not to people's homes. They would make the place look like an institution. And I'm not going to spend good money on something that we've no proof that we'll need.'

'So it's all about money, is it?'

I hadn't seen anybody stand up to Della like Zuska did. It's like watching a debate in Parliament- for the rest of the meeting you know that anything one says, the other will just disagree with.

It takes Hurricane Eddie to break it up. Returning from the day centre, he bursts into the lounge, chanting his Mr. Hill thing, then reaches into his pocket and pulls out a packet of white chocolate buttons. Handing each person an individual button, he makes the sign of the cross and says: 'the body of Christ.' Then he gently takes hold of Della's hand and pulls her to standing, repositions the chair- *his favourite chair*- and says:' Go in peace to love and serve the Lord,' before slumping down and kicking his shoes off.

Everybody uses eating the chocolate as an excuse to cover their mouths and stop themselves from laughing at the bright red Della, who looks more like she's just been dragged into Hell rather than from a chair, and doesn't seem to be seeing the funny side of it. We wait for her to say something, but instead there's this awkward silence, which is only broken by Eddie, singing:

'Who's in the cupboard

161

TASTING THE WIND
Rang the Bell
Made the noise
Kissed the nurse
Tied the socks
Naughty Mr. Hill.'

I look around at Della, for no other reason than to enjoy her discomfort, but she is nowhere to be seen.

*

In her office Della shook with silent rage.

He had said it hadn't he? It wasn't my imagination, I wasn't making connections where none exist: Eddie had said 'tied the socks,' and it was a direct reference to the man who had died at the hospital.

It was now clearer than ever that Eddie had to go. Of course, no one else at the Bungalow would know what he meant, but what if he made other, more direct references?

And what about Jamie?

Jamie had been a nursing student at the hospital, and he once told her he thought they'd met before. She had cursed herself for even allowing the staff to know that she had once been a nurse, but managed to put Jamie off by telling him that she worked in a hospital in the north west at the time he would have seen her at Oulston.

But why oh why should that one event, after all these years, emerge and threaten to spoil things now?

At her conversion she was told that Jesus had washed away all of her sins. For a long time she doubted if this included what had happened that Christmas Eve, but the doubt was tempered by a feeling that because of the man's condition what she did may, by some, be considered a merciful thing.

But still the doubt gnawed at her, to the point where, feeling that she was on the edge of madness, she went to see a 'spiritual counsellor' at her church, 'the Church of the Whole Truth.' Telling him that she had to make a big decision about something that would drastically change the course of her life, he laid his hands on her head, prayed and spoke in tongues, until a word of prophecy arrived from the Lord. And that word was: *wait upon the Lord. Do not act yet, for*

162

the time is not right. The Lord will send you a sign, and when he does it will be clear to you.

The sign had not arrived. Not yet. But Della had recently begun to feel that it was imminent, and that when it came it would free her mind of its fetters. And together with this certainty came another: she sensed that it would also, in some way that had not yet been revealed to her, be essential to what she had to do with The People who lived in her Bungalow. But that was for the future. For now it was imperative that something was done about Eddie. The simple act of removing his spinning game, the possession that comforted and grounded him, had created some disturbance in his behaviour, but it was not enough. Re-organising the stationery and gadgetry on her desk, Della knew instantly what her next move was to be. It would be easy to carry out, completely undetectable by the staff, and utterly devastating to Eddie. Soon, that already fragmented mind would lie in a million pieces at her feet.

Or, more accurately, on the floor of a punishment room in the corner of a familiar hospital ward.

-Chapter 24-

1st of June 1987

'I'm really sorry', says Zuska 'but you're not going to get to see what you came for.'

Standing in the foyer of the day centre, next to a display case full of oddly shaped pots, Zuska looks uncomfortably over her shoulder, then back to me with an embarrassed shrug.

'What's wrong?'

'Well, nothing's wrong exactly. It's just that it's Zena's birthday.'

'And is that a... tragic thing?' I say, wondering if it's the birthday of somebody who'd died. Before she has a chance to answer, Jesus steps out of the office opposite. At least he looks like Jesus in every respect apart from the 'Motorhead' T-shirt and the earring.

'How do you do,' he says, in a Dorset accent, as he holds out an incredibly long-fingered hand, 'I'm Reginald Molehusband.'

Something tells me that he's used to hearing a giggle or a joke at this point, but although I recognise the name I can't for the life of me think where I've heard it before.

'This is Martin Peach,' says Zuska. ' He's Andrew's key-worker at the Bungalow. Reggie is the day centre manager.'

I look at Zuska, then at Reggie, but there's no indication that this is a wind up. We shake hands, and he takes on the same constipated, apologetic look that Zuska has.

'I think you'd better step into the office.'

'See you later,' says Zuska, as I follow Reg and ready myself for some sort of bollocking, which, in my experience, is the only reason why a manager ever calls you to an office.

Reggie's office has a desk facing a wall, which is piled up with papers. To the right a plastic tray marked 'out' is just visible under the pile. I guess that somewhere to the left there's another one marked 'in'. On a corner of the desk, which is the only space, there's an empty 'Vittel' bottle, a Cox's apple, and a half-eaten sandwich, which had now begun to curl at the edges.

'Please sit down' says Reg, removing a pile of files from a chair and dropping them on the floor. He asks me about Andrew, the Bungalow, and myself, before telling me about the day centre.

'The original building is Victorian,' he says, gazing out of the window at a vast lawn, 'It was a convalescent home for the gentry. It underwent some modernisation in the sixties when a special care unit was added. Until a couple of years ago the Health Authority ran the centre, then Social Services took it over. We try to provide age-appropriate services in keeping with the precepts of normalisation. This came as a bit of a shock to some of the older staff, and to our 'friends' association. They raise funds for us. Since I came here as manager I've succeeded in changing quite a lot of things, but as you can imagine, after being run for so long with a completely different philosophy, certain practices still linger. Which brings me to fuck face...'

I had started to drift off until that point.

'Who?'

' Sorry. Did I say fuckface? So sorry, that was a slip. I meant Frederick. That's it. His name is Fred... anyway... Fred Cheeseman is the chairman of our friends' society. When I first took over here he used to come to Christmas parties every year as Santa Claus. He would give presents from the friends' society to all of the 'boys and girls' as he calls them.'

Reggie takes a sip from his water bottle, and as he does this I notice that he has a slight tremor, and a tic in his left eye.

'But I put a stop to that. It wasn't easy, but I did.'

'Well done...Reginald Molehusband' I say encouragingly, wondering where all of this is leading.

'But there's something else he's always done. Something he's doing today. He plays the ukulele.'

'Ukulele?'

'Yes... Badly... very badly. Whenever we have a birthday party he comes along and sings childish songs. And it's absolutely dire. He used to come to every single party. We have fifty-two people attending, which means that on average he would be here once a week. I've managed to get him to come to about half of them. I just wanted you to know that I don't approve of it. It's just that at the moment the friends are fund-raising for a hydrotherapy pool...if you see what I mean.'

There are thirty-odd people in the large rectangular lounge, all with varying degrees of disability. Some of them sit in a circle of green plastic armchairs. Others, including Eddie, sit on the floor. Andrew and another man are standing, supported by wooden frames. Andrew is strapped to the contraption at his feet, hips, and chest, and his arms are resting on a large tray, which juts out in front of him. They are all looking at a bald man with a white moustache, who is just about to launch into another ukulele-accompanied classic.

'Let's start with the birthday girl....

Zena Woodrow, Zena Woodrow,

Where are you?

Here I am

There you are

How do you do?'

I stand by Ms., who I didn't recognise at first because she's now got bright red hair, and she's making no attempt to hide her contempt for Mr. Cheeseman.

'Fuckin' shit isn't it?' '

'Surely it's worth it though,' I say, 'for a hydrotherapy pool?'

' No it is not. Some things cannot be compromised.' Ms. nods reverentially toward a board that's labelled 'current events.' It's covered in pictures of Nelson Mandela, and there's a running total of 'days in captivity.'

'And let's not forget the new boys...

'Andrew Wellman,

Andrew Wellman,

Where are you...?'

'Fuck me, does he do a verse for every single person here?'

'Yes,' says Ms., looking at the ceiling, 'Thatcherite git...'

'Eddie Sparrow, Eddie Sparrow,

Where are you...?'

'Had enough yet?' asks Zuska, who I hadn't realised had joined us.

'Here I am

There you are...'

Eddie is rocking backwards and forwards, muttering to himself. He has that look like he's engaging with a totally different world to ours, but occasionally he looks over his shoulder, his eyes wild with fear. For the first time I think that there's something wrong with Eddie. Very wrong.

'I'm sorry you haven't seen much today,' says Zuska, as we enter her room. 'Next time you come I'd like to show you what Andrew does in the ball pool. Oh, and if you can make it on a Thursday you could come along to Papaver.'

'Papaver?'

'It's a riding stable; we're going to try Andrew out with horse riding.'

Zuska's therapy room is sunshine yellow, rag-rolled with peach, and smells like a tarts boudoir. She offers me a choice of herbal teas, and I settle for raspberry and ginseng, which tastes like medicine.

'I thought we could probably talk about Andrew's progress.'

Progress isn't a word I associate with Andrew. I can't really see how he could progress after leaving the hospital, unless you count having a better chance of wearing his own underwear.

'I would usually include him,' says Zuska, adding a spoonful of honey to her tea, 'but sometimes it may be better that he doesn't hear everything. I need to talk to you about what Andrew is doing in the ball pool. Della didn't want to know, but I think she's underestimating its importance. Do you know what I mean by a ball pool?'

'Er...no, not exactly.'

'Well it's a padded pit full of coloured plastic balls. I lie Andrew in it, and it moulds itself to Andrew's body, giving him a whole new medium to work in. Like I said at his IPP, he's tried to turn himself over.'

'But how?'

'I think it's to do with the stimulation he gets from lying on the balls. He can feel where his body is in space, and you need that before you can perform any gross motor movement.'

'Can I just ask you something Zuska?'

She nods.

'Don't get me wrong, it's just that you talk as if Andrew understands things, that he...' I take a sip of tea and try not to grimace, 'that he thinks like we do. Do you really think he does?'

Smiling, she takes a large swig from her tea then swirls the last bit around in her cup like a fortune-teller.

'I don't know. I suspect. But I don't know.'

The strains of Mr. Cheeseman singing 'for he's a jolly good fellow' can be heard in the distance.

'Whether he does or not, I always try to give him the benefit of the doubt. Just in case.'

'But you suspect that he does understand things?'

'Yes'

'Why?'

We're leaning towards each other now, speaking very quietly, as if uncovering some treasure unseen for thousands of years.

'He has a really powerful aura. Can't you see it?'

We are distracted by a sudden commotion outside. Somebody is running, banging on doors and shouting:

'I'm escaping.'

I recognise the voice as Eddie's, but not Eddie the imp, the Lord of Misrule: he's scared, running for his life. Something thuds against Zuska's door. The handle squeaks as it's pressed, then the door swings open and Eddie staggers in. He heads for a corner of the room, then collapses into a crouching position, from which he stares like a hunted animal. Zuska is immediately there beside him, gesturing to the door:

'Close it, and pass me the basket from under the desk.'

I pass her the basket, which is full of brown bottles, like those on the shelf, but bigger.

'He's after me...after me...' screams Eddie.

'Who's after you, darling' whispers Zuska, her arms round him as he shakes in terror. He opens his mouth, but nothing comes out. Zuska rummages in the basket of bottles and, choosing one, unscrews it, and pours a little of the oil into her hand. The odours of the room are suddenly dominated by its sweet then spicy scent. Zuska gently rubs her palms together...

'He's gone to our Lord...'

'Who, Eddie?'

'...I'm going to set my dog on you.'

Zuska massages Eddie's temples with the oil, talking to him quietly, reassuring him.

'He's after me...'

'Who's after you Eddie?'

Eddie slowly turns and looks at the door. Although his face is glistening with sweat he shivers as he says: 'The Devil.'

Within ten minutes, Eddie is cuddling into Zuska's bosom and sleeping. I kneel on the floor, trying to get my head round the scene. I know that I should report this, but Della has been making no secret of the fact that she thinks Eddie shouldn't be at the Bungalow and will just use it as an excuse to get rid of him.

Before I go, Zuska gives me a bottle that's labelled 'Andrew.' She says that if I massage his feet with it it'll help his circulation and instil a feeling of deep relaxation.

'So what was in the one you used on Eddie?'

'Oh that's just a mixture of calming oils that's been used for centuries,' she says. It has relaxing qualities, but it was originally used by tribesmen in the rain forests. Today we would call it calming, relaxing. We would say it creates 'inner balance' and stops us from being fearful. Back then they said they were using it to ward off evil.'

-Chapter 25-

6th June 1987

Evenings at the Bungalow are starting to settle into a familiar pattern. Oscar goes out at about eight o'clock; Eddie springs up at ten- *time for bed for Eddie.* Rita is still enjoying her newfound freedom, and whenever it's suggested that she might need to go to bed she does a door-slamming circuit of the Bungalow, before falling asleep in the lounge.

Mickey's bedtime routine always begins with him being encouraged to pull himself up out of his wheelchair and to hang onto the sink while his face is washed. The physio who visits the day centre is encouraging us to do this as the beginnings of a walking programme. Once it's been mastered, Mickey will be encouraged to balance independently, then to take a step, then to walk. But for now, the next part of the routine is to brush Mickey's teeth, which is not easy. Jamie puts this down to the heavy-handed way in which the hospital staff had carried it out when faced with a great line of mouths. At some point Mickey's fraenulum had been broken. The fraenulum, Jamie explained, was the piece of skin that you can feel with your tongue between your top lip and gum. It is not to be mistaken for the fraenum, which is something quite different and could only be damaged with a toothbrush if you were engaged in some sort of perverse sexual act.

And Mickey's not the only one to be picking up new and useful skills. I've started to develop a real talent for working out rotas before

170

Della distributes them. Jamie had joked that it was a sign of autism, when he found that I could tell him the dates of his sleep-in duties over the next two months.

'You're like the people they call 'idiots savants,' detached from the real world but with a talent bordering upon genius in one specific area.'

I wasn't sure if that was a compliment or not. The only reason I can do it is that I like to work out when I'm on sleep-ins with Ruth, which I look forward to, and when I'm on with Sim, so I can take my days off. Tonight I'm on with Ruth.

Eddie has been in bed about an hour when we hear him start to scream. The nightmares had been happening every night over the last couple of weeks. By the time I get to his room it's over. Andrew lies on his right side, the only way that he can lie, facing Eddie. His eyes are wide open, but he has this really calm smile on his face.

'It's O.K. Andrew,' I say, 'It's just Eddie having a bad dream.' But I don't think my words are needed. Eddie is lying on his side looking at Andrew, and he's got the same smile.

'Sleep well, Eddie,' I say, 'you're going to church tomorrow.'

Because Eddie had always attended the hospital chapel, it had been suggested that joining a church might help to settle him. But it's always a problem trying to work out what he really wants, because he can be talking normally one minute, then on a satellite link from planet surreal the next. And if we can't know what Eddie wants, what chance have we got with Andrew? I've had a few dreams where The People can talk, and tell you what they think about things. I even had one where Mickey had a physics degree and Andrew was writing a book. Both Jane and Ruth say they've had dreams like that. Jane reckons it's wish fulfilment, coming from our insecurities from not knowing what The People are thinking. Ruth thinks it's similar to what people's parents get, wondering what they would have been like if they hadn't been born handicapped.   Anyway, I'm looking at Andrew looking at Eddie, and if I didn't know better I would have sworn that I'd just walked in on a conversation where Andrew's saying 'it's all right mate, you've just had a bad dream.'

TASTING THE WIND

At about 11.30 we hear Oscar returning. He spends several minutes trying to get his key into the door. Speech problems, a strange gait, and the inability to think straight. They all become more acceptable when accompanied by the smell of alcohol, what Colin calls 'the great equivocator.' Once Oscar has slurred 'goodnight' and staggered to his room we settle down again to watch the telly. Even Rita has opted for an early night and I'd made a good job of convincing Ruth of the merits of 'Planet of the Apes', which is the late film.

'It's full of amazing social comment' I'd argued.

'But it's so obvious they're rubber masks,' says Ruth, who carries on reading her magazine, pretending not to take any notice of the film. 'So how are you getting on with Andrew then?'

'He can talk.'

'Who, Andrew?' says Ruth, looking up with a grin. 'You have done well in a short time.'

'What? No, I mean Taylor, the man- he can talk, but the chimp doesn't realise. Just watch this bit.'

'I said, ' how are you getting on with Andrew?''

'Oh, I went to see him at the day centre. He was being strapped to a frame and sentenced to death by ukulele. And some mad Occupational Therapist was telling me of the benefits of lying him on his balls.'

Through the wall that separates us from Oscar's bedroom we hear the first round of snores. When I was a kid I lived just a few miles from a Ministry of Defence testing range. I had forgotten the sound of the repeated 'dumdumdum' until I first heard Oscar snore. It's a good job he'd wangled a single room.

'Do you know Zuska,' I say, 'the O.T.'

'Yes.'

'Well she seems to think that Andrew is, well, that it isn't necessary that he has a mental handicap. That he thinks like we do.'

'Has she any proof?'

'Not really. She says he's got a strong aura.'

Ruth rolls her eyes. 'It wouldn't stand up in a court of law would it? She takes a swig from an almost cold cup of coffee, and puts the mug back on the floor. 'It's not impossible though.'

'But there's not much of a chance of that is there? I mean, they had psychiatrists and all sorts of people at the hospital, and none of them ever thought that did they?'

Ruth puts down her magazine and looks me straight in the eye.

'Have you met the psycho at the hospital?'

'Briefly.'

'Dr. Parmar sees everyone in there as a cause for sedation, whether he's met them or not. I don't think he's capable of having a thought that would in any way connect him to another human being.'

I'm starting to get tired, but Ruth seems to want to talk about this, just as the film is building to its big turning point...

'What happens if we start at the other end?'

'It's not legal in this country...'

'Martin, I'm being serious. Answer me a question: How do you know that Andrew can't reason?'

'He's got a severe mental handicap.'

'How do you know?'

Apart from hearing the words applied to Andrew by other people, I don't know, do I? How do you know how another mind is working? Something occurs to me:

'He doesn't make eye-contact.' I say, suddenly becoming aware of Ruth's eyes.

'So,' says Ruth, looking away, 'He might not be able to control his eyes. He might have sight problems.'

'O.K. then: he doesn't communicate anything to us.'

'How do you know?'

'What?'

'How do you know? He makes sounds, he sticks his tongue out, he moves. He might be communicating to us all of the time. It may just be that we can't interpret what he's saying, or we might be blinded by our assumptions.'

'Do you think that's the case?'

'No. That is I hope not. I'm just saying that we've no proof either way.'

I sit silently, trying to focus on the T.V. screen, but unable to get out of my mind the feelings I associate with enclosed spaces. What if Andrew does have an active mind? What if he understands his situation and everything that has ever happened to him, but can't make his body do anything?

On the screen, Charlton Heston is struggling to get his words out, as the chimp patronises him for mimicking the actions of the more intelligent species.

Then the man speaks.

Then all hell breaks loose in the Bungalow. A raucous bell rings, as Rita runs screaming up and down the corridor in her nightie.

'Ruth, what's happening?'

'Fire alarm. We need to evacuate.'

'But there's no fire.'

'We still have to evacuate.'

A naked Mickey appears, shuffling across the floor, bawling. I dash to his room and grab a pair of trousers as Ruth goes to get Rose.

'Shit, Martin, she's fitting. I can't move her.'

'We'll get the others out first.' I push Mickey so that he's lying down, then unceremoniously slip the trousers on him. Both feet have gone into the same trouser leg, so I pull them off, take a deep breath, then put them on properly. A bead of sweat runs down my forehead into my eye as I help Mickey into his wheelchair. Sniffing for smoke, I look round at the kitchen, but find no sign of fire.

'What's going on? I thought it was somebody's alarm clock, but...'

'Oscar, it's a fire alarm, take Mickey out.'

Oscar, in his big blue bathrobe, wheels Mickey out into the forecourt, as Ruth emerges with a wobbly Rose, wrapped in a blanket.

'She's come round, but she's dazed, poor thing.'

'I can't see any sign of fire,' I shout, 'do we have to do this?'

'Unfortunately, yes. The alarms here are linked to the local fire station, and we have to follow procedure.'

We sit Rose on the bench by the door, leaving the semi-sober Oscar to prop her up.

'Just like the bloody hospital this,' he mutters, 'somebody was always setting alarms off.'

We're about to go back for Andrew and Eddie, when a sound I'd not heard for a long time drifts across the forecourt:

'Neenawneenawneenaw.'

Eddie runs backwards and forwards at the front fence. He wears only his red pyjamas, and waves his carrier bag like a flag. In the distance the sound is echoed by a real siren.

'We need to get Andrew out,' says Ruth.

I pause at the door. 'Do we have to? I mean, there's no fire, and if there was they say you shouldn't go back in to a burning building.'

Ruth looks at me, then into the Bungalow. 'If this was real, and there was just Andrew in there, would you leave him?'

Wrapped in his duvet, with just his head visible, we wheel Andrew out of the building. Without his harness he slumps sideways in his chair. Flashes of blue light spasmodically light the scene outside. Rose sleeps on Oscar. Rita carries on screaming, until she sees two uniformed firemen approaching and hides behind me. Mickey looks pale and petrified, his face soaked with tears. Only Eddie seems to be relishing the moment, skipping around in the gravel, singing:

'Whose in the cupboard?

Rang the bell,

Made the noise,

Smashed the glass,

Naughty Mr.Hill.'

Smiling broadly, Eddie skips up to Andrew.

'You like red things,' he says, pointing at the fire engine. 'Got you this.'

One of the largest red objects you could find, something to fill the senses, and Eddie has got it for the room mate who sees him through his nightmares. But Andrew isn't smiling. His eyes are wide with fear and the flashing light of the fire engine picks out a shiny trail of tears on his cheek as his whole body begins to convulse. At first I think it's a fit; then I realise what I'm seeing: Andrew is sobbing.

-Chapter 26-

8th June 1987

'As you're going into town, Oscar,' Jamie had said, 'Could you pick up half a dozen eggs from the supermarket?'

Oscar bristled as he walked through the park because only the week before Simeon had asked him to do exactly the same thing. As it turned out on that occasion he hadn't bothered getting the eggs, and timed his return to coincide with the arrival of the evening shift, so that he didn't see Simeon and pocketed the money instead.

'They don't really need eggs,' he said to himself. 'They didn't last week, and they don't today. Eggs are bought on Saturdays when the big supermarket shop's done.'

Oscar had developed a way of sorting things out in his mind by talking to himself on his frequent walks around the hospital grounds, but he was always careful to do it a long way away from other people. Only a certain type talked to themselves, and he didn't want to be classed with them.

'This is probably a trick to make me do my own jobs, then before I know what's happening they'd be saying 'Oscar Doyle, you're a clever man, you've now proven you can look after yourself,' and I'll be so clever that I'll be out on my ear, living alone in a dirty flat and doing all my own shopping and cooking and washing.'

Shaking his head, he pushed his hands deep in his pockets, where he found a piece of toast he'd saved from his breakfast. It occurred to him for the first time that there may be something a little strange about this. It was a habit from his hospital days, when things had to be hoarded and hidden, or carried around in bags in order to preserve any sense of ownership. He ate the toast anyway, but these days it didn't taste quite as good as it had.

There hadn't always been a hospital. He remembered a time when he lived with a family- his mother and lots of children, although he could only recall the name of one of them, Jimmy, because it was Jimmy who shared his bed. There was also a social worker, who seemed to be there more than his mum was, who was always annoyed about the dog making a mess on the carpet and it not being cleaned up. Then one day two social workers came instead of one, and that was that.

'Maybe it's not to prove I can live on my own,' said Oscar, remembering how the social workers had tested him before he went into the hospital, 'maybe it's just to see how clever I am so they can give me a grading. Ahh... I see. If I don't get the eggs this time they'll probably put me down as low grade and send me to a day centre where I just pass a ball round all day. Well if that's the case then Oscar, you clever lad, you'd better get the eggs and show 'em. I'm not having them labelling me 'severe.' '

One hour later, Oscar arrived back at the Bungalow empty handed, his mission having failed, despite his new resolve. He had hoped that Jamie would have left, so that he could have pocketed the cash, but there was some sort of meeting going on around the dining room table, and all of the staff were there.

'It wasn't entirely successful,' said Jane, speaking about Eddie's first experience of church, 'but if you're asking if it's raised his spirits, then yes...'

Simeon did a stage cough and said: 'Er, excuse me, but do you think we should be discussing this in front of Oscar?'

'Why not?' said Oscar.

'Yes, why not?' said Jane, 'it's not exactly confidential. There's no reason why Oscar shouldn't hear what his housemate's been up to. This is his home.'

'Yeah,' said Oscar, sitting at the table and taking a drink from what had been Simeon's cup of coffee.

177

'So where was I?' continued Jane, 'Oh yes, it did raise his spirits, only for the wrong reasons. It was all a bit serious and stuffy really- bells and smells and ladies in flowery hats. Eddie enjoyed joining in with the singing, and he was suitably quiet during the prayers. Then we had to offer a sign of peace. Everyone was shaking hands and, as you can imagine, Eddie got a bit carried away. He went all down the line as if he was meeting the performers after a Royal Variety Show. I couldn't get to him, then before I knew what was happening he was kissing the organist.'

'He snogged the organist?' blurted Oscar, almost spraying everyone with coffee.

'Kissed. I said kissed. You know, a peck on the cheek. He was moving onto the vicar when I caught up with him, but he was in 'Mr. Hill' mode by then. I managed to get him back to his pew, but it was time for communion. He knew exactly what to do, kneeling at the altar, genuflecting. He ate a wafer, then the cup came to us. I took a sip. The vicar put his hands on Eddie's head- he must have thought Eddie didn't take communion.'

'Typical', said Jamie, 'he was treating him like a child.'

Jane tried to continue, but was finding it difficult to repress her giggles.

'So what happened?' asked Colin.

Jane took a deep breath.

'Eddie said 'I lay my hands upon your head, behold ten thousand bugs are dead,' then he took the cup off me and swigged the whole lot back. It threw the vicar right off. He sort of looked around like he'd suddenly forgotten where he was, then had to go and bless some more wine.'

'On the way out the curate asked us where we were visiting from. When I said we weren't visiting, but were here to stay, his jaw did a bungee jump.'

'Do you think he should go again?' Asked Ruth.

'No. I don't think it's fair on Eddie,' said Jane, shaking her head, 'he didn't get much of a welcome and I don't think he'd get one next time either.'

'Don't you think,' said Jamie, 'that Eddie's presence there would be educational for other people?'

'I'm sorry, Jamie,' said Jane, 'but that wouldn't be integrating Eddie- it would be exploiting him. We've got to find him somewhere he will get something from, and eventually give something to. He's not here to educate a bunch of po-faced old hypocrites.'

Jamie nodded. Simeon cleared his throat, and said:

'May I suggest that next time he goes somewhere a little more... lively.'

'Yes, said Jane 'I think you're right, but I don't think we'd be acting responsibly if we took him somewhere where they were speaking in tongues and falling over- he's got enough problems.'

Seeing Simeon taking a deep breath and preparing to shoot an angry retort at Jane, Jamie jumped in with: 'so we're ruling out happy-clappies and bells and smells. Where does that leave us?'

'What about the Salvation Army? There's one on the other side of the park.'

'Brilliant,' said Jamie, smiling broadly, not just because he felt that it would fit the bill, but at the fact that the idea had come from Oscar.

As the meeting began to break up, Jamie took Oscar to one side, and after thanking him for his contribution said, 'By the way, did you get the eggs?'

Oscar's face fell. 'No I didn't. Bloody place doesn't bloody sell 'em does it?' With that he stormed into his bedroom and slammed the door.

'How bloody stupid is that?' said Oscar as he threw himself onto his bed, 'bloody supermarket that doesn't sell bloody eggs.'

It wasn't as if Oscar hadn't tried. He wanted to prove that he could do it and that he knew that half a dozen meant six. Apart from that, he wanted to do it for Jamie. It was Jamie who had tried to find Oscar's family for him, and when he came back saying that they had disappeared from the face of the earth, Oscar could tell that he was really upset. Not that he was surprised about his family, because when Jamie said what he did it all came flooding back how his mum was always on about seeing spaceships and had pictures of oval-faced aliens all over the place.

In his mind, Oscar went back over what had happened at the supermarket. He had walked up and down each aisle three times. There were no eggs with the dairy produce. There were no eggs with the fresh things, like fruit and vegetables. He looked on the meat counter, hoping that they had been paired with bacon, but they weren't there. He even checked to see if they were next to tinned goods, or with cleaning materials but, as he had expected, no eggs. Eventually he approached a spotty shelf-stacker, who pointed him in the direction of a pile of grey boxes.

'Are you taking the piss?' He'd asked, before storming out.

As Oscar lay on his bed he felt the coins jangle in his pocket. He had been genuinely annoyed at failing to get the eggs, but at the same time it occurred to him that if he stormed off, Rita style, it might make Jamie forget to ask for the money. His mood lightening more and more, he shook his head at the incompetence of the young shelf-stacker, and smiled as he visualised eggs in boxes. He knew that they didn't come in boxes. Eggs, those white discs with a yellow dome, came in trays on a pool of grease.

'Try putting them in boxes' he said to himself, 'and just think what a mess that would make.'

Picturing the gormless looking shelf-stacker, Oscar wondered if getting paid employment was a much easier thing than he'd imagined.

'Just goes to prove,' he said, 'they're not all inside as should be.'

-Chapter 27-

11th June 1987
2.15 p.m.

After heading out into the countryside for so long that I'm thinking we will end up back at the hospital, the bus turns down a narrow lane and into the 'Papaver Riding School'. The entrance is framed by a horseshoe shaped arch, the appearance of the stables and buildings beyond giving the deliberate impression of a western ranch. A field had been set aside for parking, but recent rain had caused it to be ploughed into furrows by the wheels of cars and buses.

'There is a proper car park,' says Ms. as she wrestles with the steering wheel, 'but the reactionary bitch who owns the stable won't let us use it. She is quite happy to take our money, but doesn't really want us near to her house. Thatcherite cow.'

Ms. has a mean, Schwarzenegger sort of expression, and looks like she'd gladly swap horse riding for petrol bombing. She's spent most of the journey explaining how she doesn't mind driving, but that she has misgivings about assisting with riding, as she feels that horses are a separate species from whom we had stolen their freedom, in the same way that we had stolen milk from cows (worse- from the mouths of their calves) and honey from bees. I wonder if, taken to its logical conclusion, her restriction should stretch to vehicles powered by the juices of insects, no matter how long ago they were crushed. I decide not to get into that one, as it's a long way to walk back even if you aren't pushing somebody in a wheelchair.

As well as Ms. and Andrew there was Pete, a well-built bloke with a strong northern accent and unruly blond hair, Mickey, and

Eamon, who is my worst nightmare. Eamon looks a lot like Andrew-strapped into a wheelchair with all sorts of gadgets and add-ons to accommodate his twisted frame. He lives at home with his parents, and there's something about him, not just in his dress but also in his full face and healthy skin, which shows that he has been loved and looked after. But there's something else about Eamon, and it scares me shitless: he's aware. Not just aware, but aware in a way that nobody I had met at the hospital, in the 'severes' ward, was. His eyes meet yours and hold them and he laughs in all the right places. Ask him a question and his head strains forward as a rasping breath escapes from his throat, through a mouth that can't form words because it's fixed open.

Zuska had told me that it was widely felt that Eamon had nothing resembling a mental handicap, but that there was nowhere else for him to go. Tests to find out exactly how much he understood had failed, as had attempts to teach him to communicate by pointing to pictures with a stick attached to his head. But this was probably the result of involuntary movements and delayed responses, not mental retardation. His mother had developed her own system of communication with him, and everybody who knew Eamon knew that there was more to him. I look at him and feel like I'm being buried alive.

While Ms. sits with Eamon and Mickey, a girl from the stable helps me and Pete to choose Andrew a riding hat and shows us how to get him onto a docile bay horse called Rodney. Rodney is led down a ramp into a concrete trench. We park Andrew in his wheelchair on a platform next to the horse, whose back is now level with the cushion of the chair. To my surprise there's no saddle. Next, Andrew is unstrapped, and with me behind him, holding his arms into his body as best I can, Pete takes his legs and we lift him.

'Er...now what.'

'Turn him over,' calls the girl from the other side of the horse. 'Lay him on his stomach across Rodney's back.'

I look at Pete, who smiles and nods, then we turn Andrew over and, assisted by the girl pulling from the other side, put him over the horse, saddle-bag fashion.

The horse is led into an indoor arena. Pete, who has obviously done this before, uncurls Andrew's fingers and helps him to stroke the animal. I had half expected Andrew to be tense, even to go into a fit, but there's a stillness about him that I hadn't seen before. He can touch and smell the shiny coat and, as the horse walks slowly around, he feels the rippling movement of its muscles. Probably for the first time in his life, Andrew is higher than everybody around him. When I swap sides with Pete I can see that a smile has spread across Andrew's face- not the exaggerated one he sometimes has before a fit, but a smile of pleasure, and I find myself smiling back.

When it comes to Mickey's turn, I can understand why such a placid, easygoing beast as Rodney is chosen for these sessions, as Mickey, with an almost orgasmic expression of glee, laughs like a machine gun and pats the horse heavily with both hands.

Not that I have anything against Ms., but not fancying another rant against all of the un-vegan practices of farming/horse riding folk I decide to take Andrew exploring. Ruth had explained to me the importance of giving people who could be 'locked into themselves' as many different sensory experiences as possible to connect them to the world. I had drifted into my own inner world at the time, dreaming of the possibility of connecting to Ruth, and the great sensory experience that would be, but the principle wasn't completely lost on me.

'As children we explore everything,' she had said, 'looking, listening, smelling, touching, tasting, putting things in our mouth that we probably shouldn't, but in this way we build up a catalogue of what things are like. Andrew has not had a chance to do that. Unable to explore, to reach out, he can only experience what is directly presented to him.'

Whereas Jane knows all about the different syndromes, and all of the ethical debates, Ruth seems to know more of the practical things, which I suppose comes from helping bring up her handicapped brother. Coming from that angle you're going to be more bothered about the day-to-day things like what he's going to do and where the money's coming from than the latest ideas of professor whatshisface.

Behind the stables the road passes a paddock where a group from a special school are having a lesson, then out through open fields. In the distance I can see a large white house, and beyond it a lake.

'Let's check this out.'

Although it's a warm, still day, as we pass by the stables Andrew's tongue comes out as if he's feeling the wind on it.

I watch the tiny children as we pass by. A couple of them have Down Syndrome and most are in wheelchairs. One of them looks like a mini version of Andrew. I suppose he's been lucky to be born now, as whatever his future holds, he won't be going to the hospital.

As we get closer to the house a woman on a black horse trots up to us.

'Where are you taking that child?' she demands. She looks to be in her late forties. There are grey strands in the black hair, which is scraped back under her riding hat. The heavy lines on each side of her lips look like they've been etched there by her permanent scowl. She glares down her long nose at Andrew with what looks like a mixture of disgust and fear.

'We were just exploring...'

'Well I am the owner, and I am telling you that you are out of bounds here.'

If only Ms. were with me. This could have marked the beginning of a revolution. We would have dragged the bitch from her horse, set the creature free, and turned the big white ranch into a commune. Instead I just spin Andrew round and turn back, mumbling *'ok.... but he's not a child.'*

-Chapter 28-

20th July 1987

There were more voices now. Voices and faces, not many familiar, not many friendly. Someone was after him. It was sometimes Don Maguire, or Mr. Hill, and sometimes the Devil. Eddie would sit in corners, mumbling, and when Pansy licked his face he would try to kick him, but always missed. He would rasp curses at Mr. Hill and sit rocking in a way that became more and more frenetic with each passing day.

'Mr. Hill's in the cupboard again, Mr. Hill is naughty, Mr. Hill...Mr. Hill...Mr. Hill'

At the last chant of the name he raised his fist and banged so hard on the table that a cup fell over and smashed. The bang caused Rose to fall from her chair in a seizure, to Rita's cry of 'Omigog,' but Eddie, who before would have made a song up around the event , just clenched his fists and shook, as if in an icy draught that no one else could feel.

That night, Eddie climbed out of his bedroom window and ran away. Fortunately, Jamie had heard his feet crunching on the gravel drive, and found him cowering at the gate. All that he could make out in the nervous torrent of words was 'He's found me...he's found me... the devil has found me.'

At the staff meeting the next afternoon, Della suggested that a doctor be consulted, with a view to finding a medical solution to Eddie's problem. This, she emphasised, was to be an interim measure, leading to his eventual return to the hospital.

'No,' said Jamie, his eyes flashing, 'that's too easy. He's already on high doses of anti-psychotics. There must be another answer. We're letting him down somewhere.'

'We will be letting him down,' growled Della, 'if we do not allow him the benefits of modern medicine, and advocate for him to be in the proper environment for his needs.'

'Maybe,' said Simeon tentatively,' we should be trying harder to address his spiritual needs. He hasn't been back to a Church since the first failed attempt, and there was a suggestion that he went to the Salvation Army.'

Della smiled uneasily, wanting to encourage Simeon, who she saw as something of a protégée, but at the same time conveying that they were not singing from the same hymn sheet.

But, she thought, *all of this has no bearing. I'm already beginning to see the results of my new strategy. Eddie's behaviour is going off the scale, and not one of them suspects... If things continue this way, it won't matter what they try.*

'All right,' said Della, 'as a believer myself I must agree with the...efficacy of the Church. But we would be failing Eddie if we did not also go down a medical route. He's running off at night, he's acting aggressively, he's breaking fire alarms. What next? The nearest specialist is based at the hospital, so I have already arranged an appointment with Dr. Parmar, who will be coming to assess him tomorrow. '

'Not the Marzipan Man?' blurted Jane.

'Dr. Parmar is a respected psychiatrist, and I would ask you never to use that nickname again.'

Jane sank down in her chair. She had come across Dr. Parmar at the hospital, where he prescribed Carbamazapine as enthusiastically as if he were a shareholder. Its usefulness for both epilepsy and behavioural disorders served to make it a popular prescription in a place like the hospital, where Dr. Parmar would dish out the pills like sweets, regardless of whether or not he had actually met the patients.

From the first time she saw the hospital, Jane had pictured it as a sluggish, many-eyed monster, and when The People left she believed that they had escaped its clutches for good. It appeared to her now to be a beast with long tentacles. Long enough to reach even to the Bungalow.

-Chapter 29-

The ball pool is like any you might see in an indoor play area, only this one has a ceiling track hoist fitted above it. The thin boy is suspended in its canvas sling, his head moving from side to side as the hoist buzzes until it stops over the middle of the pool, and lowers him into it.

The sensation of being suspended in air changes to that of plastic balls pressing against his back. He feels them spread out under him as they are displaced, the shape of the mass moulding itself around him. Two people wade noisily to each side of him, remove the sling, and then climb back out. Above him, a butterfly mobile shimmers in multi-coloured lights.

'What do we do now?'

'We give verbal prompts. Andrew's beyond the physical prompt stage. Say with me: 'I turn my body over."

'What?'

'I turn my body over. You say it in the first person, so that Andrew will get it in his own head and tell his muscles to work. It's like when athletes talk to themselves to improve their performance.'

Through the hazy mixture of colours, the boy hears them chanting ' I turn my body over.' There is a pause. They repeat: 'I turn my body over,' a note of impatience creeping into Martin's voice.

'It's not working, is it?'

'I've seen him do it, Martin. He just needs time. It's a very hard thing for Andrew to do, and there may be a delay between his brain giving the order and his body responding.

They repeat the mantra: 'I turn my body over,' pause, then say it again...

'I'm sorry, Zuska, I'm going to have to get back to the Bungalow.'

From the ball pool, the thin boy can hear the muffled conversation continue in the corridor outside the room.

'You don't believe me do you?'

In the boy's mind, the phrase continues to repeat: I turn my body over. I turn my body over. I turn my body over.

'No, I do believe you,' says Martin, 'and I'd love nothing better than to go back and tell Della that I'd seen it happen. But I haven't. Maybe another time?'

The pull on his side, when it comes, is painful. He turns his head as far to the left as he can, and feels a burning sensation in his neck muscles. His body arches, but this time not in spasm, and he begins slowly to turn. With each inch of movement the coloured balls slip in behind him, supporting him. His face is now becoming submerged in them, turning his view into a mass of colour, as he hears the music of the spheres, and the sound of Zuska bidding Martin farewell from the corridor.

***

21st July 1987

I've been getting letters from the accommodation officer, reminding me that the flat is only temporary accommodation for people moving into the area. Kev reassures me that I won't get chucked out on the street, because he's lived there for over two years and just ignored the letters. But as the idea of spending the rest of my life with Kev and Sim is far from appealing, I decide it's time to attend to my own personal IPP. Item one: find somewhere else to live

Next to the tube station there's a shop that's either a pawn shop- these have re-emerged in Thatcher's Britain- or a porn shop. It's called 'Tit-for-Tat,' so I can never quite tell. Above it there's an accommodation agency run by a baby-faced gangster. Padded shoulders, stripy tie, tiepin and cufflinks, hair like a bed of nails on a tiny head, Cockney accent- Jim Davidson, but uncouth. I imagine that there's a little boy underneath that lot, standing on the swivel chair.

' So what can I do yer for?'
Never spoken with greater sincerity.

He asks what sort of price range I'm looking for, what I do for a living, and where I want to live - in that order. The data's processed, then with a big smile he picks up his phone and dials.

'Perfect place for you. I'll just give the old bird a bell.... oh, hello love. It's Gordon Blue Accommodation Agency here. Your studio flat- got a lovely bloke for yer, single bloke, mental nurse, yeah, and he'd like to come round to see the place.'

He looks up at me:
'Six o'clock tomorrow all right?'
'Er, no, I'm on a two-ten shift.'
'He's on a shift, being a nurse and all...how about 10 a.m.?'
'Well, yes, but where is it?'

He lifts a piece of paper from a red tray marked 'urgent' and hands it to me.

'And how are Albert and Victoria, Mrs. B?... really?...you ought to get them to the vet's then.'

The house on the sheet is 13, Moonfield Road, a massive Victorian building at the posh end of the street.

'Lovely residence, big posh house, but hey, why not talk to her yourself?'

He hands me the phone with the smug look of somebody who is not only going to take a large part of my wages, but is getting me to do his job in order to achieve the transaction. The voice is posh, Tory-voting, red hat and no knickers, more tea vicar, send them back, save the hunt and bring back hanging. From her tone I can tell that she has similarly made a snap judgment about me, and probably has me down as a lager swilling by 'eck ferret breeding northern yob.

'Well it is rather a large flat- it used to be our billiard room, but it is fully converted to suit someone like yourself. It has a shower facility and a kitchen in a recess. Are you married?'

'No. Why?'

I'm getting the strangest feeling that I've heard her voice before.

'Well it would be suitable for a newly married couple. Oh, and I have strict rules about visitors. I would ask you not to have people staying, if you get my meaning.'

'How much?'

'£90 per week.'

'*How much?*'

'£90 per week, but you will get a pound of that back if you pay up on time.'

'Oh, I'll make sure that I do, then I'll be able to eat as well.'

Yuppie boy is leaning back in his chair working out his fee. The equivalent of one month's rent from me and the same from Mrs. B. equals seven hundred and twenty pounds for the privilege of using his phone.

But it's not going to happen, because I'm starting to match a face to the voice. I have a flashback to a night in the Cat and Lobster when a fur-clad witch came to our table with a petition against The People. She's the woman who was in the paper standing next to this very house. This could be fun.

'So where is it exactly?'

'The far end of Moonfield Road, backing onto the park.'

'Oh really? Is there any negotiation on the price?'

'No, not at all. It's a very competitive price for a luxury flat.'

'But I've heard things about that area- that some of its residents aren't what one might call desirable neighbours.'

Silence, apart from an almost audible quickening of the pulse coming down the line, then a nervous twitter:

'Oh, I see- well there are some, er, unfortunates who have been... poorly. They live in a house at the other end of Moonfield Road. But it is a long road, so we don't really see them.'

I savour the gap, then:

'Oh no, I don't mean The People who live in the Bungalow. No, there's talk of Moonfield Rd. being the centre of Fascist activity.'

'Fascist...'

'Oh yes, and there's some mad woman going around preaching eugenics, is that right?

'I don't know what you're talking about young man, but I think you've got the wrong road.'

'No, I don't think so. And this lad here has told me that your house is riddled with damp and cockroaches.'

The yuppie nearly falls off his chair. 'What?'

And in my left ear: 'Hand him the phone, I wish to talk to him.'

'I just have one more question. When you asked me if I was married it was because you didn't want me co-habiting wasn't it? Well could you tell me if a verbal agreement's all right, or do you want me to sign a no-shagging clause?'

The little businessman almost shoots out of his suit as he lunges across his desk.

'Give me that phone, you crazy bastard.'

'Tut tut, not in front of the lady.'

As I leave I can hear him pleading, 'No no, I never said it was damp, no I never said that Mrs. B... Mrs. B?'

***

My next option, a flat-share advertised in the window of the newsagent's, is on the other side of town, about thirty minutes walk from the Bungalow. I'd expected to see a student or Yuppie open the door. Instead it's an old woman with dyed jet-black hair, a red headscarf, and make-up just this side of Barbara Cartland. As she ushers me into the small hallway, a cat brushes past me as it runs out into the street. Drawing a curtain to one side she leads me up a narrow staircase.

'It's not a large room, but it will suit one person, and it's very cheap compared with London prices.'

We stand on a landing with three identical doors.

'This is the bathroom.'

On the windowsill, and along two shelves, are several pots overgrown with herbs, which are in need of watering and hang like cobwebs.

'I'm a herbologist,' she says, 'amongst other things. Only there are so many herbs in the world that I'm running out of space. You don't mind, do you?'

'Oh no. I've seen worse things growing in a bathroom.'

She nods wisely. 'What do you do for a living? No... Don't tell me,' she says, grabbing my hand. 'You work in a factory.'

'No... no. I did. Now I work in care... with people. Which one is the bedroom?'

Slowly letting go of my hand she opens the door to the right, and we both step in to the room. The bed is small, and has a blanket with a zoo animal pattern. She switches on the pink bedside lamp, disturbing a layer of dust. On the shelves are books- 'Blue Peter' annuals, 'Famous Five,' 'Pippi Longstocking' and 'Stig of the Dump'. Under the bed I can see a pile of games- 'Cluedo,' 'Frustration,' 'Magic Robot,' things I hadn't clocked since I was a kid. In a corner is a pile of 'Look-in' and 'Jackie' magazines.

'This was a child's room. She hasn't slept here for some time. She says she doesn't mind things being moved. Times are hard.'

More than anything in the world I want to make a fast escape, but I am nothing if not polite to my elders, even if they are nutty as fruitcakes. I follow her downstairs into the 'lounge.' What I see makes me step back, the hair on the back of my neck standing on end.

'What are you sensing?'

'I don't know. I just feel like I've been here before.'

The room is dark, with a crystal ball on a central table, shelves full of old books, stuffed animals, statues of idols and a human skull. When I was a kid I would have killed for a room like this, the sort of thing that professors of the occult had in Hammer Horror films. Then it strikes me where I must be: this is the home of the fortune-teller that Ruth visited all those years ago.

'Are you Madame Delores?'

It was her turn to look shocked. 'Do you have the gift?'

'Er, no, I've just heard of you. I don't really go for that sort of thing.'

'Oh. What would it take to convince you.'

'Don't know,' I shrug, 'couple of horses at 100-1?'

Madame Delores sits behind the table, her face distorted and upside-down in the crystal ball. 'Please sit down, I'll do you a psychometric reading... free of charge. I have the ability to tell things about a person from the vibrations of objects they own. Now, show me what you have got in your pockets.'

I think hard, just in case there's anything embarrassing in there, like a massively out of date condom. I dig into my left pocket, and come out with a handful of mixed change.

'What's that?' she asks excitedly.

193

I have this habit of changing trousers and just transferring the contents from the pockets of one to the next. Sticking out of the handful of coins is a badge: the four leafed clover that Eddie had given me at Christmas.

'This,' she says, picking out the badge, 'is a powerful talisman.'

'That,' I say 'is something you get out of a plastic egg.'

'No, no, no,' she says, stroking the badge and holding it up to her eye as if examining a precious stone, 'the object is not important- it's the spirit vibration from a previous owner.'

'Go on.'

She closes her eyes. 'I feel a pure mind, someone who is close to his creator...but he has suffered deeply.'

She looks at me for agreement, but I try to keep my face in neutral. I know how these people work.

'This person...this person has...' Delores lets out a gasp, and spreads out her red-nailed fingers, letting the badge fall onto the table. 'This person... has witnessed murder...'

'Er, no, I don't think...'

'I'm getting something else... the name of the person who first owned the badge... it's... it's... Andy?'

I can't believe how disappointed I am- there's part of me that really wants to believe there's something in this tripe.

'Not bad,' I say, 'It was Eddie actually, but Andy/Eddie, pretty close. Anyway, I've got to go...'

'But the room?'

'I'll let you know...'

As I open the front door the cat, which is waiting to come back in, spits at me.

'Martin, my spirit guide tells me that although you can only see your piece of the story, you are actually part of a bigger one. Much bigger. Open your eyes.'

'Yeah...right.'

I step out of the door, but Delores grabs my wrist.

'You don't even notice them, do you?'

'What?'

Her bony fingers tighten, and I'm amazed at the strength of her grip but when I look at her expression she seems to have gone into some kind of trance.

'The straws in the wind. They blow past you, and you don't even notice them because they seem so small, insignificant and unconnected. But why are there so many?'

I try to pull away, but her bright scarlet nails press into my skin.

'Observe them, Martin,' she pleads, as her grip lessens, 'observe them and take note of the direction in which they fly.'

I walk back to 'the Willows' feeling more than a little spooked, and decide that my search for a new home should probably be put on hold again. If the experience has taught me anything, it's that there are actually worse places to live in London than in an old folks' home with Sim and Kev. Thinking over what Delores said about murder and straws in the wind I decide that it's either a load of made up gobbledegook, or somewhere she's got her ethereal wires crossed and has given me somebody else's message.

But how did she know my name?

I must have told her. Of course I'd told her. I just forgot that I had, that's all.

-Chapter 30-

22nd July 1987

So cometh the Marzipan Man. Dr. Parmar had agreed to do a home visit, as he was in the area, so Eddie took the day off from the centre. The morning was spent sitting on the floor in the lounge with Ruth, watching videos and playing the Bungalow's growing CD collection. To Ruth's surprise, Eddie had been picking out words that he recognised from their covers.

At about two-thirty a black Mercedes pulled up outside.

'Psychrist here,' announced Eddie.

Ruth was about to open the door when a small, dapper, middle-aged man stepped in. He carried a slim briefcase, and wore a black suit with a tightly knotted grey tie.

'Er...Dr. Parmar?'

'Mr. Parmar.'

'Oh. Hello, I'm...'

The 'Mr.' breezed past her and, sitting next to Eddie, placed his shiny briefcase on the table. He took a file from the case and, glancing briefly at his patient, scribbled a few illegible notes.

'Would you like a cup of tea?' asked Ruth.

'No. I cannot stay long. I have to assess the level of Edward's deterioration.'

'Deterioration?'

'If I may have a little silence...'

Parmar leaned towards Eddie, and waved his hand in front of his face. Eddie froze, thinking he was about to be attacked.

'Can you see me, Edward?'

Eddie smiled, realising that this was not an attack, but a game.

'Mr. Hill smashed the bottle.'

Mr. Parmar made a note in the file, and Ruth heard him mutter 'deteriorating.'

Excuse me Dr... er...Mr.,' said Ruth, her growing sense of outrage fuelling her confidence, 'but Eddie doesn't have any problems with his sight, does he?'

'No no no. This is not a sight test. I am testing Edward's grip on the real world, and as you see, the delay in answering and the inappropriate response is proof of his deterioration. Now Edward, what did you have for your lunch today?'

'Potatoes.'

'You see. I have known Edward for twenty years, and he always answers 'potatoes.''

'But he has had potatoes...he had lamb chops, potatoes and...'

'No no no. You don't understand. His answer was parrot-fashion; it's what he always says. I can understand you wishing him better than he is, young lady, but in my job you have to be realistic. Eddie's condition is deteriorating. He used to be able to read a few words, but now...'

'But he still does that.'

'No, he does not. He lost that skill many years ago.'

'But I saw him only this morning...'

'And how can you tell that he wasn't just guessing from the context, from pictures, or perhaps your own unconscious prompts? Anyway, I will leave this.'

Mr. Palmar quickly scribbled a prescription and tore it from his pad, handing it to Ruth.

'Please give this to a senior member of staff- I think Nurse Cahill works here now, yes?'

'Who?'

'Your Officer in charge?

'Our manager is Della Belk...

'Yes yes yes, anyway, if you could just pass this on, there's a good girl.'

With that, he bustled through the door, leaving Ruth with angry tears welling in her eyes. She turned to Eddie, who had sat silently throughout most of the 'consultation.'

'So how much do you suppose he gets paid for that?'

Eddie smiled, and then laughed in a way that told Ruth that Pansy had just entered.

'I'm detearatin'.'

'No you're not,' said Ruth, 'you've just got things on your mind. Like the rest of us.'

She squeezed Eddie's hand. In the other she held the prescription, which creased in her shaking grip. She knew that Diazepam was another name for Valium, but the other item would only make sense to a pharmacist. It would doubtless be yet another chemical cosh. Eventually the answer to Eddie's occasional outbursts would be the total suppression of his personality. And this had come from a stranger, who hadn't even conversed properly with his patient.

Deep down Ruth felt shame, that she should have said more. She looked at the prescription and thought about crumpling it up, throwing it away, and telling Della that Parmar had prescribed nothing new. But Della would find out. And who was she to do that? Maybe Eddie did need the drugs. Maybe he would feel better with them.

'What's that noise?'

The washing machine had clicked onto the spin cycle, and Eddie rushed over to it, dropping to his knees and laughing riotously.

So why am I getting so upset about this?

As she watched Eddie, a discussion with her old school friend, Bridget, came to mind. Bridget had lived for six years in Germany, where she had worked with people with mental handicaps, before returning to England after a messy divorce. According to Bridget, services there were not as developed because the learning disabled population was comparatively far smaller. The conversation moved on to the old ladies who had spent almost their entire lives in the hospital, and Ruth had asked how people of retirement age were treated in Germany.

'Dumbkopf,' Bridget had replied, 'they don't have services for the elderly mentally handicapped, because basically there's not much call for it. In fact most of the people in their institutions tend to have been born after 1945, yes?'

Ruth remembered something that Jane had told her about the holocaust, how as well as the Jews, other groups, including people with disabilities, were slaughtered in their thousands because they did not match the Arian ideal. Jane had also told her of a group of rabbis in a nazi concentration camp, who put God on trial for what was happening to them, and found him guilty.

'I have always felt that there is something so right about that level of honesty,' Jane had said, knowing that Simeon was in earshot. 'It must be healthier to challenge God rather than just lie down and take what you're given. Especially when you've got the moral high ground.'

The last part she had said with a wry smile, and her eyes half closed, as if she had expected a storm of righteous indignation to crash down upon her head.

Picking up the prescription, Ruth felt again the chill that had passed through her when she first realised the significance of what Bridget had told her.

A stranger with authority, a questionable theory, and a rushed signature changes Eddie's life, perhaps forever.

She placed the piece of paper flat on the table and smoothed it out. What would Jane do? But Jane wasn't there, and Ruth knew that she could never view the world like Jane, because she wasn't Jane, with her moral precision and gnat-straining philosophies. This was, quite simply, not her decision to make. It was between people who were paid far more than she ever would be. All she had to do was play her part and pass it on.

-Chapter 31-

24th July 1987

Della's on holiday, so there's a more relaxed feel about the place. Jane, with a glance at the ceiling, tells me that Simeon's off sick. Even though we share a flat I don't see that much of him, as he tends to spend most of his time on what he calls 'church business.' I smile in anticipation of what Ruth would say about Della and Simeon being off at the same time. We had invented a game: 'position of the week', imagining sex positions, not for us unfortunately, but for the gruesome twosome. Well it made us smile.

Pulling Andrew's sheet back, there's the usual sign of a dark pool on the crotch of his red pyjamas where wee has seeped from his full pad. Jane helps me to lift him into his wheelchair- *One...two...three...lift-* and fastens his belt while I strip the sheets and wipe the plastic mattress cover. No time to insert the pommel between his legs, so I'm off with a half-lying Andrew to the bathroom.

Whoever designed this bathroom hadn't planned for somebody like Andrew. All there is a white plastic chair, which you strap a person into, crank up, swing over, and then crank down into the water. And bathing Andrew takes two of us- one to support him, one to bathe him. But at least the rows of writing bodies have gone. And that has to be better.

Shaving's a good game, trying to chase Andrew's chin round without causing too much bloodshed, and brushing his teeth is something that needs the skill of a surgeon. On mornings when he isn't soiled, we sit Andrew on a commode, where he's held by a harness, which means that he can be left to do his business in private while we get Rose up.

Andrew and Rose are always started on their breakfast first, as it takes them so long, then it's time to wake Mickey. Once he's up and bathed, we carry on with his pre-walking programme, getting him to support himself on the sink as his teeth are brushed. He's getting less and less afraid of the toothbrush, the only trick now being to brush his teeth before he sucks all of the paste off.

And then there's Eddie. He's still going to bed early, the same internal body clock telling him to get up at six, only now that there are no nurses dressing him and telling him what to do he sits on the edge of his bed and waits. Jamie had come up with the idea of leaving a set of clothes on his bedside chair. His attempts to dress himself are improving day by day- O.K., some mornings we go in to his room and he's wearing one sock, or his underpants are over his pyjama trousers, but he is making an effort.

Last night, Jane had commented on how much calmer Eddie is when Della's not around.

'He's not the only one,' I'd said.

'Seriously, Martin, I wouldn't say this to anyone else, but I've been starting to wonder if she's doing things to him.'

'Like what?'

'I don't know. It's just that she seemed to think his behaviour was a problem before any of us had seen anything, and now...well he's giving her all the ammunition she needs to get rid of him.'

My only problem with Jane's idea is that ever since Colin said what he did about Eddie and Della's relationship I've been watching them, and it's obvious that, wherever she can, she avoids him. So I can't see how she can be doing anything to wind him up. Having said that, there is a big difference in the Eddie we've seen over the past few weeks, and the one who now sits calmly shovelling corn flakes. A big difference.

TASTING THE WIND

Oscar and Rita both like to lie in as long as they can. Once he hears the clanking of breakfast dishes, Oscar comes in and takes a tray back to his room. Della had once tried to stand in his way and make him eat with the others, until he said calmly that if she made him eat in the middle of this 'bloody zoo' he would report her to his MP for infringement of his human rights.

Rita waits until the very last minute, and after several calls rolls reluctantly out of bed to stomp around the kitchen, swearing at the staff because the toast is cold. At about nine o'clock the ambulance arrives to take The People to the day centre. When Jamie's there he invariably tuts, shakes his head, and says 'aren't ambulances meant to be for sick people?'

Then the door closes and everything seems incredibly quiet, apart from the clanking of plates and the sound of the washing machine.

Before leaving this morning, for a reason known only to himself, Eddie had poured a load of washing powder down the toilet, creating a volcano of shitty suds, so I have to pop out for a new packet. When I get back, Jamie and Oscar are sitting at the kitchen table, sharing an enormous grin.

'Don't tell me- the Joker's poisoned the Gotham City water supply again?'

'The postman's just been,' says Jamie. 'Brilliant news; two lots in fact. Tell him yours Oscar.'

Smiling, Oscar draws himself up in his chair, his uneven teeth like randomly scattered dominoes, and says:

'I've got a job.'

I sit down next to him, allowing my mood to be swept along with his and Jamie's, until I realise that this is Oscar, who had sat for years in the Happy Owls with his feet up, and had dedicated his life to idleness. So what had changed?

'I saw reason,' he says, ' I went to the supermarket the other week, the one which doesn't sell eggs, and there was a lad there doing a job who was a bit simple. Since then I've been thinking 'Oscar, if somebody like him can do a job and earn real money, then so could you. Then, believe it or not, Mr. Pinkerton came to see me the other day and said that there was a job at the supermarket which was right up my street. I was a bit confused at first because I live on Moonfield

Road and there is a garage at the end of it, but no supermarket. Then he explained that it was the supermarket I'd been to on the other side of the park, in the row of shops across from the Salvation Army church. So, out of the blue I hear this voice saying 'why not?' and I'm imagining what I can do with my money, and now this letter says it's really happening. I'm going to be like that bloke on the telly, whatsis name....' Oscar gets up, waving his letter in the air, 'that's it: LOADSAMONEY!'

'No,' says Jamie, as Oscar disappears into the lounge, 'I don't understand the U-turn either. He said he wasn't managing to save enough for his 'special project,' but he wouldn't say any more. I think he might want a portable telly for his bedroom or something. Anyway, look at this.'

Jamie picks up a battered brown envelope and drops it on the table in front of me.

'It's the information from the hospital on Andrew,'

Inside are a form and a wad of papers held together in one corner with green string. The form contains details on the front like full name, date of birth, and address. Inside is information about his condition, his medication, and a whole list of things he can't do. The other sheets are notes about Andrew's early days at the hospital on Fuchsia and Thyme wards.

'Julie found these. They've moved the final few people from Fuchsia ward into Thyme to save on the heating bills. She was helping to empty the office and came across this. Not much, but it fills in a few gaps. It looks like Andrew was on Fuchsia for assessment, moved to Thyme, and then in 1977 was back in Fuchsia for a few months, although I can't find any reason why. This file never went back to Thyme with him.

As I glance down the sheets a word jumps out at regular intervals:

Screaming

I could never imagine Andrew screaming.

'But why was he screaming? He didn't know what was happening did he?'

Jamie points to a scribbled note that says 'urgent admission-both parents recently deceased.'

'Both parents died at the same time,' says Jamie, ' and while you're going through all of that loss you're put in a hellhole. You don't need an intellectual response to scream at that.'

The admission date was 25th August 1971. His parents' names are there: James and Miriam Wellman. They must have died in some sort of accident, but there's no hint as to what it was. The word 'screaming' appears throughout the notes for the whole of that year. The word 'bruise' appears as frequently:

> *Bruise to right eye*
> *Bruise to jaw*
> *Bleeding from nose, eyes blackened.*

With the introduction of medication 'to help Andrew sleep' the incidence of screaming lessened.

'Look at this.' I point to the entry for December 25th, 1976.
Somebody had placed poppies on Andrew's bed.

'I dunno what that is,' says Jamie, 'Poppies' was probably a cuddly toy. A teddy bear or something.'

'No. I remember the nurse saying something about a story that went around the hospital about there being poppies on Andrew's pillow on Christmas day.'

'And where would you find poppies in December? It's probably another example,' says Jamie, 'of an 'urban myth.' A 'hospital myth.' You always get them around places like that; they reinforce prejudices that people in them are somehow different, a bit spooky. Have you heard the story about the decapitated driver? And there's loads about things that happen in institutions when there's a full moon.'

Thinking that Jamie probably has a point, I turn my attention to the front of the form. It looks like somebody had actually got Andrew's name wrong originally, as a word's been totally obliterated just in front of it.

'Somebody made a mistake.'

'I'm surprised they bothered to correct it,' says Jamie. ' People's names don't usually mean much in there. And look at this- Andrew's date of birth is November 11th.'

'Poppy day?'

'Yes... O.K.... and we were at the hospital at that time, but there was never any mention of a birthday. This year we'll have to celebrate big style... hang on.'

Jamie's finger goes to the contact address.

'All right, Mart,' he says, shaking his head, 'I know what I said, but this is a bit of a co-incidence, isn't it?'

We look at each other, back at the sheet, then at each other again, shaking our heads, neither of us knowing what to make of the fact that Andrew's home address, the place where he was born and brought up before going to the hospital, is a place called 'Poppyfield Farm.'

-Chapter **32**-

26th July 1987,
6.20 p.m.

If only my mates could see me now. I'm walking through the park with Eddie, who's in the middle of a conversation with himself- or Mr. Hill- on the way to the local Sally Army. I could just hear Dave singing 'Bringing in the Sheaves' and doing the does-Jesus-save- wicked-women-well-tell-him-to-save-one-for-me gags. A ray of sunlight appears through a break in the white clouds, illuminating the leaves of a great oak. Eddie looks up and, waggling the fingers of one hand says 'Hello God,' as if he's just spotted a friend at a supermarket. I find myself looking up too. So Eddie thinks he's seen God. He might have done; who am I to say? I've been in this job long enough now for nothing to surprise me.

On the theme of 'unsurprising,' I should have known better than to think that once Andrew's files turned up it would have gotten Della off my back. Oh no, first thing she does when she gets back from her holiday is give me grief about the fact that I haven't traced any of his family yet, which is rich, considering how Simeon went to Eddie's mum's, didn't get an answer, and never went back. And is she making a fuss about that? Is she hell. Not that I'm allowing any of it to get to me. Today it's just me, Eddie, and Pansy the invisible dog; it's a sunny day, and all's right with the world.

On the other side of the park there's a small row of shops and pubs, a tube station and the Sally Army meeting place, what the locals call 'the tin tabernacle' owing to its corrugated iron roof. When Eddie sees it, his face lights up like Moses seeing the Promised Land. I feel more like Damien in 'The Omen'. Not that I've anything against religion. Deep down it's probably something we all need- a bit like sex- but both are things I think are too private to be announced over a megaphone in the main street.

The church has grilles at the windows, and is surrounded by black railings, but the prison-like darkness is lightened by a well-kept garden. Not that I know anything about gardening. There are some roses, but beyond that I would have to say there are blue things, purple things and, of course, some more red things. But I can tell that the garden is well kept, as can Eddie, who shows his appreciation by getting down on all fours and smelling the flowers.

In the doorway a large woman in a blue uniform with a wide smile that seems to echo in her chins, gives Eddie and me a hymnbook each. One of us nods and says thanks. The other one says 'Hello Mummy' and plants a smacker on her enormous cheek. She doesn't seem to mind. Probably doesn't get kissed much.

It's a very plain church- dark brown pews and pulpit and faded red carpet. The windows are frosted, no stained glass, just the shadow of the outside grille. Two rows of chairs with music stands face the pews. To one side is what looks like an organ under a black cover. The walls are cream, and in an arch- shaped recess at the front are the words 'Jesus said, I am the Way, the Truth and the Life.' It doesn't look like any church I've ever seen (and I had seen one when I was christened, and at my dad's funeral) but it is a church, because it smells like one, with its combination of wood, varnish, and old books. The scene is given colour by a container of mixed flowers at the end of each pew.

Eddie walks quietly down to the front and crosses himself, which is probably the first time anybody has ever done that in this building. We've sat for about ten minutes when a side door opens and in troops a mixed bunch of uniformed Sally Army types, most of them carrying instruments. They fill the chairs at the front. The rest of the congregation consists mostly of old ladies in hats, but there are more uniforms dotted around- one of them right in front of us.

'Hello soldier boy' says Eddie, tapping him on the shoulder, 'I'm Eddie.'

'Hello Eddie.'

There's a pause as Eddie grins at the lad.

'I've got a dog at home.'

'Oh have you?'

Wait *for it...one, two, three:*
'What's its name?'
'Pansy'
The lad smiles back at Eddie.
'I've got a cat as well.'
'Oh, right. And what's the cat's name?'
'Paul.'
'Right.'

I decide to thumb through the hymnbook and let the conversation take its course. The small room is getting quite full, and there's an excited babble. We seem to be attracting some attention as eyes sweep across us then look away. I suppose that most of the people here have been born into it and have been coming here all of their lives, so any new faces would stand out a mile.

'...That's an unusual name for a cat.'
'Is it?'

When I look up a uniformed woman is in the pulpit- she has black-rimmed glasses, her hair scraped under her cap, and insignia to show that she's a Captain or something. Looking straight at us she welcomes all newcomers, and says that this is a special service to dedicate the new organ to the service of the Lord.

Accompanied by the band we sing a song I don't know, about your anchor holding. I don't think Eddie knows it either, but it doesn't stop him from joining in. Nobody seems to mind, and as I watch him sing I can see that he's happy, ecstatic even, and oblivious to everything else. I wonder when the last time was that I felt like that, and realise I probably never have. I was going to hate telling Simeon, but he was right: this is what Eddie needs.

'Let us pray,' says the Captain.

Eddie leans forward so that his face is between the 'soldier boy' and the middle-aged woman next to him.

'Where's Harry?'
'Eddie,' I say, pulling him back, 'we're praying now.'
'But where's Harry?'
'Harry who?'
'Harry Secombe?'

The soldier boy's padded shoulders begin to vibrate.

'He doesn't come here' I say, putting a finger to my lips, 'now shh!'

'Why? Is it a secret?'

The soldier boy can't hold it in any longer, the laugh forcing itself out through compressed lips like a machine gun. The Captain, interrupted mid-prayer, gives him a look that says 'you'll be saving souls in Siberia next week sonny,' and then carries on with her intercessions for world peace.

The fat woman who had been giving the hymnbooks out reads something from the Bible, then after another hymn the Captain does a sermon about the gifts of God. Eddie sits remarkably still and listens well, occasionally whispering 'Shush now, Pansy.'

'And now,' announces the Captain, 'to the main business of the evening. Mervin, would you come to the front.'

A uniformed man with a round, sweaty face, and hair combed from the back of his head to form a fringe, steps out. I wonder what he's done, and if he'll be having his badges torn off and his drumsticks broken.

Eddie leans over and whispers in my ear:

'Is that the Bishop?'

'No, Eddie. I don't think they have them here.'

In a solemn voice, the Captain says

'Mervin, remove the cover.'

I suddenly see her as a leather-clad dominatrix:

Mervin, remove my bra.

Pause.

Mervin, remove my panties.

Pause.

Mervin, don't let me catch you wearing them again!

Maybe not. Mervin uncovers the new organ, and the Captain instructs him to demonstrate its range. Well It's hardly Rick Wakeman, but old Mervin gives a rendition of 'The Old Rugged Cross' that's good enough to bring tears to the eyes of half a dozen old ladies. Then there's a prayer to 'dedicate' the organ. I look around, and remember the feeling I'd got when I first stepped off the tube train back in October, and the first day at the hospital: a stranger in a strange land.

Somewhere outside, I think, they *must be erecting a huge wicker man.*

TASTING THE WIND

I had hoped to escape at the end, but the Captain herself swoops on us and asks us to stay for tea and biscuits. I look at my watch, and am conjuring up my most convincingly apologetic face when I realise that Eddie is already doing his royal tour of handshakes and kisses. The Captain has just started to interrogate me about Eddie's life story when Eddie, standing on his toes at the other end of the building, laughs and shouts: 'it's a clown, it's a clown.'

A man with a tanned bald head, a bulbous nose, and a Wyatt Earp moustache is singing deeply as he puts the cover back on the new organ. He wears thick glasses, which magnify his eyes, and a red checked shirt, sleeves rolled up to show a large anchor tattoo.

'Hello. I'm Eddie.'

'Hello Eddie, my name's Eric, pleased to meet you,' he booms in a broad northern accent.

'I've got a dog at home.'

Here we go again

'Have you. What's its name?'

'Pansy.'

'Oh. So it's a bitch is it.'

'No,' says Eddie, tilting his head and raising his eyebrows, 'a dog.'

Then something different happens. And I don't know if it's because it's the right time, place, person, or if it's just that nobody ever asked the right questions before, but the pattern changes.

'Pansy,' says Eric, 'Why is he called Pansy?'

'Because' beams Eddie, ' Joey says he's built like a Pansy tank... and I've got a cat.'

'That's nothing pal,' says Eric, with a grin, not knowing the significance of this conversation, 'I've got a cat too.'

'What's his name?'

' Ceefer.'

'That's a funny name,' laughs Eddie.

'No it isn't' says Eric with mock defensiveness, 'It's Ceefer Cat, Deefer dog, and if I had a bull I would call it Beefer, which is even more appropriate. If I had a goat it would be called...'

'Old Arthur.'

'Er, yes...So what's your cat called?'

'Paul.'

'Paul?'

210

'Yes.'

'Why Paul?'

Eddie looks at Eric as if he's asking a really daft question with an obvious answer.

'Paul...Paul the cat.... pull the cat's tail off.'

O.K., I should have guessed, but nobody else had. I suppose we'd just assumed that there were no reasons behind the names, like we just assume a lot of things about Eddie and The People that we probably shouldn't.

'And who's this?' says Eric, nodding in my direction.

'Martin.'

'Hello Martin.'

Eric has one of those finger-bursting handshakes, and Sherlock Holmes wouldn't have been exerting his logical powers too much to deduce that these calloused, meaty paws belong to somebody who's used to hard work. He looks so out of place but at the same time seems so at home among the old ladies and churchy types.

'Are you...'? I can't think of the word for it, 'one of these?'

'A Salvationist? No, not of the uniformed variety, anyway. They helped me out when I went through a bad time. I'm a sort of caretaker and gardener.'

'Roses,' says Eddie.

'That's right. All my own work- well, with a little help from the almighty.'

So I'm piggy-in-the-middle between one bloke who thinks he can see God, and another who talks about him as if he's with him on work experience.

'So where are you from, Eddie' asks Eric.

'Mental hospital.'

'Er, Eddie came from an institution' I interrupt, 'he used to live around here when he was a kid.'

Institution. How nice. How sterile. The place was a shit-hole asylum where people sat in shit, ate shit, and were treated like shit. They were drugged, beaten and isolated into conformity, had their identities robbed to the extent that they didn't even have their own clothes, and I use the word institution, which sounds more like a bunch of old duffers drinking port than an NHS concentration camp. And all because I'm the one that's embarrassed by what Eddie calls it.

'I liked the hospital,' says Eddie, in answer to a question I'd not heard, and any feelings of pride about Eddie's improved quality of life and my part in it are squashed.

'What did you like about it?' asks Eric.

Eddie's eyes glaze over.

'Home. Big fields for Pansy. Happy Owls with Timmy. Mr Cornes called me a good boy and gave me chocolate.'

Once more I am some oik who's conned handicapped people out of their safe, familiar surroundings, and placed them in danger. But maybe it's not that bad. I look around at the people in the hall as they chat, drink coffee and buy things from a charity stall. There are smiling, friendly faces, and lots of laughter. Maybe Eddie will find acceptance here and make a better life than he's been used to.

Maybe...

'Mr. Hill smashed the bottle.' says Eddie, but there's something new in his tone which brings me rapidly back from my train of thought, a manic, robotic quality which makes me think that things are beginning to slide and that this would be a good time for us to leave.

'Did he?' says Eric. 'Who's Mr. Hill?'

But Eddie doesn't answer. His eyes are watering, his breathing becoming rapid, and his knuckles whitening as he clenches his fist round the handle of his carrier bag. His stare seems to go beyond the floor, deep into the earth as if he's looking desperately for somebody who might be buried there. He begins to rock slowly, quietly chanting, the only recognisable words being 'Mr. Hill.'

What happens next is my fault. I'm so desperate to get Eddie out of here that I crowd him, and as I try to take his arm he lashes out with his fist, hitting me painfully on the thigh.

Della had warned us that in taking on Eddie we were sitting on what she called a 'behavioural time bomb.'

And I think it's about to go off.

***

The man at the door had a starved look, a gaunt face with black thinning hair. He wore a cream overcoat and his brown, pleading eyes, and the slight turn to each corner of his mouth gave him the look of a Labrador puppy who, despite poor treatment, still retained a desire to please and to find a friend.

'I'm Edward's uncle,' he said, 'Uncle Ray.'

Jane was surprised, both at this sudden appearance, and at the unexpectedly cultured accent of someone who looked so impoverished and was related to Eddie. As she invited the man in she had to stifle a laugh when she noticed the bulging carrier bag. *This must,* she thought, *be some sort of family trait.*

'I'm afraid that Eddie is out at the moment,' she said 'he's gone to church with one of the staff.'

'That's O.K. I just wanted to deliver some belongings of his. Although it would be nice to see him some time.'

Uncle Ray looked around the dining room and kitchen.

'This is so much nicer than where he was before.'

Mickey shuffled from under the table, where Rose sat, still chewing the last mouthful of her evening meal. From the lounge came the sound of Rita laughing at a 'Tom and Jerry' cartoon.

Jane was about to ask the man how he had managed to find Eddie when the call button sounded from the bathroom.

'Excuse me' said Jane, in a flawlessly calm and professional manner, 'there's an emergency. Please help yourself to a tea or coffee.'

Andrew was in the bath, in the middle of a violent seizure. Simeon stood clutching his own right hand, with a look of terror and pain, a tear running down his cheek. Normally two staff would bath Andrew, but Simeon had insisted that he could do it on his own.

'What are you doing?'

'My hand, I...'

Andrew's face was above the level of the water, but each convulsion banged his head violently against the bath. Jane pulled the plug, rolled up a towel and, placing it under his head, turned him onto his side.

'I tried to hold his head when it started. Got my knuckles banged. I can't feel anything in my fingers.'

'I'll carry on here. Can you go and entertain our visitor? Eddie's uncle has just turned up.'

Although Jane had always been more aware of her antipathy to Simeon's theology than to his working practices, she had recently begun to agree with Martin and Ruth that finding yourself on a shift with him was to get the short straw. Things happened when Simeon was around: there was always a far higher chance of Rita lashing out,

Mickey would refuse to settle down, Rose's mother would make a complaint. These may have been co-incidences, Simeon may just have been unlucky, but there was a growing feeling that situations were made that much worse by his handling of them. He was also getting a reputation for regularly being on sick leave, leaving the other staff to juggle their shifts or to have to do sleep-in duties alone. Despite all of this, and adding to the growing resentment, was the fact that Della so obviously favoured him.

Once Andrew's seizure had subsided, Jane hoisted him out of the bath, dried and dressed him, then headed back to the dining room. Rose still sat at the table. Mickey had raided the fridge, his face bright orange from a bowl of baked beans he had found there. On the kitchen table was Uncle Ray's carrier bag, and a note:

Dear Jane,

Eddie's Uncle couldn't stay, has left these. I have had to go home due to my injury. Sorry to let you down with the sleep-in,

Sim.

'Well fuck you,' she swore under her breath, surprising herself. She wondered if some of Martin was brushing off. Surely Martin and Eddie would be back soon. Simeon was meant to be sleeping in. Perhaps Martin would stay.

It wasn't until after she had washed the dishes and cleaned Mickey up that she remembered the carrier bag. Looking inside, she saw that it contained a pile of hard-backed books, diaries, each labelled in ornate calligraphy. Ten in all, the diaries were dated from 1962 to 1971. Flipping open the first one, Jane read the entry for New Year's Day:

Edward is less than a year old, yet already I could describe to you the life that is mapped out for him...

***

'Eddie,' I say quietly, 'shall we go home now?'

I look around at the people who are happily drinking their coffee and eating their custard creams, trying to pick out an escape route.

'Fuchsia Ward?'

'You like fuchsias do you, Eddie? asks Eric, misunderstanding Eddie's reference, but for a moment Eddie stops and looks at the man, as if there's something about his voice or appearance that fascinates him.

'Whose in the cupboard,
Rang the bell,
Made the noise,
Burst the balloon,
Smashed the cup,
Naughty Mr. Hill.'

'Eddie,' I whisper, 'Calm down mate.'

'What's that?' Eddie is looking at what seems to be a trapdoor in the uncarpeted floorboards at the front of the building.

'It's a baptistery,' says Eric. 'We don't use it. This used to be a Gospel Hall.'

'It's the tomb,' muttered Eddie,' his face and forehead now covered in small droplets of sweat,' the tomb of our Lord. They killed him, tied him to the cross with his socks.'

'Eddie,' says Eric, 'What do you think of the new organ?'

Eddie looks up and, as if snapping out of a trance, says 'Can I have a go?'

Jo had once conned me into going to a thing where 'local poets' recited their work, because there was really cheap beer. The recital also included something called 'Free Jazz.' 'Free Jazz' turned out to be a bunch of spaced out students randomly blowing and pounding on instruments they had never mastered, or even picked up. Eddie would have been at home there. But what the hell, it worked.

*

Rubbing what must be a monster of a purple bruise on my thigh I walk back through the park with Eddie, realising for the first time how much this change in his behaviour, with all of its implications, is really beginning to get to me. Correction: everything about my life at the moment is beginning to get to me. Things like

Della's attitude. Like that I'm spending every waking hour thinking about Ruth, but nothing is happening. Like the fact that I've asked everybody at the Bungalow if they know where 'Poppyfield Farm' is, and no one has ever heard of it. I know it's a long shot, but it might be that Andrew had brothers or sisters who inherited the farm. But where the hell is it? I've not been able to find it anywhere in the A to Z. I've gone through the telephone directory, and I've found and phoned three Wellmans, but none of them recognised the names of Andrew and his family.

And my domestic situation isn't helping my mood. Half-bearded Kevin has given up on CB radio as a form of communication and is now trying a Ouija board and tarot cards. I got back one night to find Simeon pressing both hands against a wall and praying for the flat to be blessed and delivered from evil. He told me that his constant illnesses were probably due to contact with unclean spirits brought into the flat by Kevin's Ouija board. I said that I thought it was more likely to be due to the unclean kitchen with its pot of everlasting vegetable curry.

Like they used to say in one of my favourite childhood shows: there's one thing I've gotta get- outta this business.

'Who's in the cupboard...?'

I stop and take Eddie by the arm.

'Eddie, listen to me.'

He leans forward as if he's giving me his full attention.

'It's about what you said to Eric about the hospital. Look, I know it was your home and everything, but you can't go back there.'

'Can't go back...'

'No. It's no way to live, and what about Don Maguire? He was beating you up. If you went back he could kill you.'

'Kill you... He's gone to our Lord...they killed him.'

'No Eddie, they didn't kill anybody, I meant if you went back they'd hurt you again.'

He shakes his head, then as he sees the Bungalow coming into view he seems to just close me out, as if he's wearing headphones, listening to something which to him is so real that it is deafeningly loud, but can never be heard outside of his own head.

And I think I've got problems. I wonder if we ever found a way into that head what we would find there, and having found it, how we would cope with Eddie's reality.

And I think I already know the answer to that one.

-Chapter 33-

August 4th, 1987,
7.30 p.m.

Rita's attempts to go to the Gateway club had, until now, been thwarted because the hall that was used was being refurbished. Tonight was the first chance she'd had to return.

She had giggled with excitement when she set off, remembering how, as a little girl, she had gone to the 'gayway' club, where there were games, and discos, and so many parties. Some of her school friends went there, and most of the adults were kind, gentle souls, who were easily manipulated by a pout or the first sign of a tear.

Rita remembered her last Christmas party. She had been the first child there, before anyone else, her uneven steps echoing on the floorboards. The only light was that from the Christmas tree, the fairy's silver dress casting a magical pattern onto the ceiling. From the kitchen came the smell of egg sandwiches, fresh cucumber, and fruitcake, and the sound of ladies chatting. And tonight she was going back to that.

The first thing Rita realised when she arrived was that the room was smaller than she'd remembered. Then she noticed that the wooden chairs had been replaced by plastic, and walls that had been flower-patterned were now painted a pastel blue. There were no familiar faces, and most of the members were younger than her and didn't want to talk. No matter how many doors she opened she saw nothing she recognised, could not find the ladies, the school friends, or the room with the Christmas tree.

When they had told her at the hospital that she was going back she thought that it was back to what she had left, to the people and places she had known before. They had lied. She had not gone back. She could never go back.

And plastic chairs did not splinter like wooden ones.

9.15 p.m.

'What're you reading, J?'

'Not telling you if you call me that,' said Jane with a mock petulance. In a recent conversation with Martin she had told him that she didn't like names being shortened and was glad, as a Jane, that she had a name that could in no way be reduced to a diminutive.

'Oh go on,' he said, 'What is it?'

'What this, or these?' she said, ignoring his teasing and pointing firstly to a notice in large dot-matrix letters, then to a pile of diaries.

Martin picked up the sheet. 'She must be bloody joking.'

It was a general invitation to the staff at the Bungalow to a meal at Della's flat.

'Well,' he said, 'I would have told her I'm washing my hair, but as it happens I'll be working. On a sleep-in. I bet that's why she's chosen that date.'

'Who else is on that night?' asked Jane, just to test a hypothesis.

'Ruth...I think.'

She was right. Martin had been looking ahead, working it out. He always seemed to know when he was on a shift with Ruth... the same way that Jane knew when she was working with him.

'Are you going?' he asked.

'No. Not if you and Ruth aren't.'

'So what are these?'

' These are the diaries that Eddie's uncle left. They're absolutely fascinating. Eddie's mum wrote them. I've only been dipping in, but I can tell from what I've read so far that she was one smart cookie. Simeon says they're blasphemous, so that must make them required reading.'

219

'Blasphemous? How can diaries be blasphemous.'

Jane turned the diary toward Martin.

'It's just that she's a bit scathing about God. It's understandable. She's bringing up a kid with a severe handicap, and she's asking why, if God is so good, do some people get such an unfair deal in life'.

'And does she come up with any answers?'

'If she did these would be a goldmine. She's obviously studied theology at some point. She writes some of the stuff in Hebrew, and even I'm struggling with some of her references. This one I recognise: she's writing of how in spite of his disability Eddie has the 'Ruach' of God.

'The what?'

'Ruach. It's a Hebrew word that means both wind and spirit. In Genesis when God breathes life into Adam he breathes Ruach.'

'So she thought that Eddie was God?' said Martin, shaking his head.

'I don't think she really thought that. It's just an exploration of a theme. It's all got such a depressed tone about it though. At one point she rails against God, and says that he didn't really experience human suffering when he came as Jesus, giving her son as a better example of suffering divinity. It's quite thought provoking, don't you think?'

'Hea-vy,' said Martin. 'It's a bit like that joke about how you can tell Jesus was Jewish. No? It's because his mum thought he was God and he thought she was a virgin...'

'Martin! Just put your serious head on for a minute. There's something else about the diaries which is quite fascinating- look at this.'   Martin took the diary from Jane and read the passage to which she was pointing:

Edward was born on a windy night, alight with mulberry tastes and sounds of butterscotch, harsh fingernails of hail tapping on the window.

The pain was almost sweet to me, but the sweetness of glycerine and sharp toffee apple on an exposed nerve; his first cries invoked swathes of imperial purple, sprinkled with misty violet.

'What the fuck is that about?'

'Promise me,' said Jane, 'that you won't take up a career in literary or Biblical criticism. Don't you think it's interesting that she seems to write as if her senses were somehow integrated, as if she could taste colours, see sounds? Here's another bit:

220

'We took Edward to St. James' Park. The billowing leaves were a symphony, chords of golden light glancing through them.

I took some bread to feed the birds. Holding my hand out, a sparrow hovered in front of it, flapping its wings frantically like a humming bird, before it stepped lightly onto my fingertips and pecked at the crumbs.

So light, so delicate, like my sparrow child.

After the sparrow had gone, I stretched out Edward's hand, gently uncurling his fingers and wiping his hot palm with a tissue before placing bread in it.

The sparrow returned. It alighted on Edward's hand, and he giggled. It was a reaction to the touch of the sparrow, to something more fragile than he, but filled with the same life force, trusting itself to him. He giggled, and it was orange sun and lavender scented.

Martin gave a wry smile. 'What was she on when she wrote that?'

'I'm not sure,' said Jane, flicking through the diary, 'but it lapses into this all the way through. I once heard of something where a person's senses are not separated in the same way as yours or mine are. They experience a taste when they see a colour, or hear the sound of a smell.'

'I've often heard the sound of a smell myself.'

'Martin, I'm being serious. What I aim to do now is read all of the diaries in order, just to see if there is any more genuine biographical material about Eddie. I can't really make much sense of them by just dipping in like this.'

'All this tight fingers and stuff,' said Martin, pointing to a line in the passage he had just read, 'does it mean that Eddie used to be even more disabled than he is now?'

'I wondered about that. Sometimes people develop a lot slower, take longer to reach their milestones. Eddie was about five then, he still couldn't talk and it looks like he was starting to stiffen up, a bit like Andrew. His mother must have put a hell of a lot of work in.'

Jane had already shed tears over some of these passages. The picture of Eddie living in a normal home, being loved and nurtured, was somehow sadder to her than imagining him as always being in the hospital. He had known something else and lost it, perhaps without

221

ever fully understanding why, but with no less a sense of bereavement and yearning than anyone else.

They were still looking at the diaries when Rita arrived. She stormed in, her face red and streaked with tears as she screamed 'No Gayway, no Gayway.' Jane slipped the diaries into a kitchen cupboard out of harm's way, as Rita overturned chairs and smashed cups, and Martin was left searching myopically for his twisted glasses.

*

Later that night, as Jane lay in bed in the sleep-in room, she tried to focus on the first diary, but two hours of attempting to calm Rita at the same time as ensuring everyone else's safety had left her physically and emotionally exhausted. Over and over, Rita had repeated the words 'no Gayway,' and Ruth eventually had concluded that she must have gone to the wrong place. Jane herself had taken her to register in the foyer of the club only the week before, but tonight she had gone for the first time on her own because It had been suggested at her IPP meeting that to give her some independence she should walk there, at least on light nights, unescorted. For some reason, Jane felt, she had become confused and walked into the wrong building, but her offer to go with Rita the following week had been met with an adamant insistence that she never wanted to go there again.

As the words on the page in front of her blurred, Jane realised that her systematic reading of the diaries would have to wait until another time. She was pleased, however, to have discovered something that her first cursory investigations had missed: a frontispiece stuck inside the cover. She had quickly realised that the short paragraphs were a much later addition- the ink was less faded than anywhere else in the document and its calligraphic style had more in common with that of the covers of the last three diaries. She hazarded a guess that it was written at a time when the author felt that a unifying theme had emerged in her writing. It read:

It is not at the greatest level, the cosmic and the eternal, that mankind is divided, but at the level of the microscopic and transient.

What unites man can be measured in universes and aeons because each and every one is made of the same stardust, given a spark of the same divine nature and a place in the same eternal pattern...

This, thought Jane, *fits in so well with my beliefs about synchronicity... whoever you were, I would have liked you.*

As Jane wearily placed the diary on her bedside cabinet she heard someone shout.

Eddie... nightmare again.

She was about to get out of bed when she realised that Martin was there, helping Andrew to settle after the disturbed evening.

'They killed him...' shouted Eddie,'...they killed him at Christmas...crucified him...they crucified...'

But the end of Eddie's sentence was drowned by the sound of a passing car.

That's odd, she thought.

She tried to replay in her head the word that Eddie had used, to disentangle it from the sound of the car and see if she had made some mistake. But if pressed she would have sworn that Eddie's last word had been 'Frankie.'

-Chapter 34-

August 4th, 1987
11.15 p.m.

'Who was Frankie?' I ask, but Eddie is fast asleep. I remember that 'Frankie' was a nickname for Billy, and wonder if Billy's death last Christmas is haunting him. Since he's been having these disturbed episodes, Eddie seems to be obsessed with crucifixion and murder. It's as if things he's heard in church and seen on films are crowding his mind and scaring the hell out of him.

For no apparent reason, Rita had come back from her club in a strop, twatted me and trashed the place. It took two hours for Jane to calm her down and persuade her to go to bed.

Eddie has obviously been disturbed, and even Andrew has picked up on the tense atmosphere, and had a series of small fits. As I settle him down in his bed, I notice on a shelf the large brown bottle of oil that Zuska had sent for him.

'Massage,' she had said, 'is more than just a physical exercise. When done properly it is a communication between two people.'

Bollocks I'm thinking, as I peel back the bottom of Andrew's duvet, to expose his feet. *It might help him relax though.*

I open the bottle, and pour oil into my cupped hand. I can smell the Valerian that Zuska warned me about. Even though she had tried to disguise it with rose oil there's still the odd whiff like sweaty socks. Sitting on the end of the bed, I begin to rub Andrew's feet.

'They went to sea in a sieve,' says the voice of a young woman. It's Eddie, who's still fast asleep. The voice, whoever it belonged to, is undeniably female, Irish, and probably an exact impression of whoever he'd copied it from. I wonder if it might even be the writer of the diaries, speaking to us across the years from God knows where.

Andrew's feet are completely smooth. He's never walked so there's no hard skin, no calluses. I cup them in my hands, and they feel icy cold, the pale flesh having a blue tinge, and the whole room is filled with the aroma. Closing my eyes, I see myself as a child opening a drawer, taking out a lavender bag, and pressing it to my nose to inhale its perfume. As I carry on, I can feel the tension begin to leave his body, as the tremors slow, and then stop. It seems for a moment that the sun has come out from behind a cloud, as through my closed eyelids I am aware of a bright, red light. I imagine, in fact I am pretty sure, that if I open my eyes I will be staring at a field of poppies.

No. I'm in Andrew's room. It's just the sun through the window and the blood in my eyelids.

Then I remember that it is night-time and open my eyes to find that the room is still only dimly lit, and that Andrew is lying perfectly still, smiling serenely.

*

Even as I lie in bed tonight, thinking over what's happened, I still feel so peaceful, as if I'm floating. I can smell the oil, see the gentle red light in my mind's eye, and feel the rigid muscles easing.

I see myself running along a country lane, hurrying to a dark building in the distance. It's a hospital. Not *the* hospital, but something representative of every out-of-the-way institution that ever existed. A hospital but with a Hammer Horror overlay, a gothic haunted house. And it's in black and white. I pass through the rusted gates, and approach the building along a drive. Heavy, swirling clouds provide the backdrop, but as I get closer I see that against the clouds are palls of grey smoke, coming from almost every window. Only one thing has colour, but in contrast to the rest of the monochrome scene, the vast expanse of green lawn looks gaudy.

As I draw closer I see that the lawn is covered with twisted metal, melted plastic and wheels with bent spokes. Mingled with the wheelchairs and almost indistinguishable from them, are bodies with twisted limbs, charred skin and pale eyes. It is obvious what has happened: there's been a fire in the back wards, the wards full of 'severes', and every single patient has died horrifically. As the wind blows, a cloud of ash rises from the bodies, stinging my eyes and filling my nose with the odour of dead flesh. I feel warm tears on my cheeks, something I haven't felt since I was a child, but as well as sorrow there's a competing emotion, telling me that they are released now, no longer suffering a living death.

They're better off dead.

On a hill behind the building an enormous cloaked figure nods approvingly. Then, in the midst of the charnel house, something moves... Apart from that one focus of life, the scene freezes. In that brief moment I know that I have to choose: to save this person I thought better off dead, or to leave him.

If I just walk away now, death will not be long. If I save him, it will be for this life I've already judged as worthless.

I hear Ruth's voice from the night that Eddie set off the fire alarm:

'If this was real, and there was just Andrew left in there, would you leave him?'

I wake up thrashing around, my sheets tangled and drenched with sweat. There's a crack of light in the curtains, the smell of rainy pavements drifting through the partially opened window, and I can hear the first notes of the dawn chorus.

Something has changed, something inside, and I've not worked for it to happen or invited it, but somehow I'm not the person I was. I remember having dreams about Jo, dreams that I could never tell her about, where she'd died. They say it's common when you love somebody and don't want to lose them. Now, it seems like I'm putting the same sort of value on Andrew's life.

And it's not just that I've realised how much I care for this person who not so many months ago I thought better off dead, it's that the whole of my life is now so different to what I knew before. And I'm feeling something that I thought had died a long time ago: a sense of family. And this is something that I want to keep, that I need, that I would fight for. Something that I would even die for.

-Chapter 35-

15th August 1987

Simeon stood outside the shiny red door of the St. John's Wood flat, nervously clearing his throat and checking that his zip was fastened. He wore a white shirt and a plain dark blue tie, black trousers and intensely polished shoes. His hair was unfashionably short, and he had such a broad white smile that had he not been alone, you could have been forgiven for mistaking him for a Mormon missionary.

What at first looked like a bible in his hand was, on closer inspection, a box of chocolates. At the sweet shop he had stood back, whispered to himself 'what would Jesus do?' and decided against buying 'Black Magic.'

Yet another example, he had thought, *of the thin end of a wedge that leads to the acceptance of evil concepts as normal, and eventually to demonic possession.*

Milk Tray. No danger there.

Simeon rapped with the shiny knocker, and had hardly withdrawn his hand when the door was flung open, revealing Della, in a tight black skirt and white blouse. Simeon thought that there was something unusual about her, and concluded that it was the fact that he had never seen her in a skirt before. He was totally unaware of the deeply repressed thought that she looked like a man in drag.

'Come in, come in,' effused Della, as she shuffled along the corridor in the restrictive skirt. Simeon froze on the doormat at the sight of the thick white carpet that ran through the flat.

'Shall I... take my shoes off?'

'No no,' said Della, giggling uncharacteristically. ' Just give them a good wipe.'

There is perhaps nothing guaranteed to make a visitor more ill at ease than a perfect white carpet. Add to that Della's white leather suite, and glass tables, and you have the recipe for a night of uncomfortable hospitality.

The T.V. screen was the largest that Simeon had ever seen. In the centre of the room was a table with a crisp white linen cloth, at which two places were set.

'Am I the first?' asked Simeon.

'First...and last,' said Della, lifting a large glass of red wine, 'alpha, and omega... Can I offer you a drink?'

'I'll have a fruit juice please, something non-alcoholic.'

'Oh yes, you don't drink do you? Do you mind if I do?'

'Oh no, not at all.'

Della rustled through the door leading to the kitchen, releasing a rich aroma, which seemed to be a mixture of chicken, seafood and garlic. Simeon was momentarily startled when, with a whirr and a click, the video recorder switched on, as his hostess returned with a glass of red grape juice, and sat next to him, the white leather cushion farting as she sank into it.

'The idea,' said Della, taking a long draught of her wine, 'was that I got to know all of my staff informally. Ruth and Martin are... 'working' tonight. Jamie, it would appear, is doing shifts for an agency at weekends in order to fund some trip to India that he has planned. Colin said that he had a long-standing engagement, although I suspect he is a little anti-social. Jane accepted, then said that something had come up- probably when she realised that her partners in crime weren't coming. But don't worry. It's quality that counts.'

The hors d'oeuvres, which Simeon took at first to be a stack of chicken wings in tomato sauce, were frogs' legs with a sun-dried tomato and truffle oil jou. He pulled back the skin on each with his knife and, ignoring the musky smell of the oil, which he singularly failed to identify, slid out the flesh with his fork, to be pleasantly surprised by the ambiguity of it's fish-fowl taste and texture. He had heard that Della was something of a gourmet. Martin had, in his typically cynical fashion, pointed out that only Della had said this, but Simeon could now put him right on the matter.

'Please,' said Della, wiping sauce from her chin, 'feel free to use your fingers.'

The first course finished, Della invited Simeon to sit back on the settee. She put on the 'Brothers in Arms' CD, explaining how she had always been a lover of gadgets, and had bought a CD player as soon as they had become available.

'Do you have any vices?' she asked, sliding closer, the white leather settee creaking under her weight.

Simeon had to think hard. As far as he knew he only had one besetting sin, which, no matter how many hours of fervent prayer he engaged in and how many cold showers he took, would always defeat him.

'I don't know,' he said hoarsely, ' I suppose I am rather too partial to Maltesers.'

Della giggled girlishly again, swirling her wine round it's voluminous glass so that stripes of sediment stretched like spider legs down its side.

'You know Sim... can I call you Sim?'

'Yes...'

'You know Sim- and I know I can trust you not to say anything outside of these walls- I'm glad the others didn't come. I think we have things in common that it might be considered unprofessional to talk about in the work place.'

Simeon slid an inch to his right, pressing up to the high arm of the settee.

'You mean...'

'Well, the fact that we are both believers; that we have values that none of the others share.'

'Oh, I see.'

'I knew you would.'

Della closed the gap between them. As she turned to face him, Simeon noticed how her blouse strained. He tried not to stare at the gap between the first and second button, but did a double take when he noticed black hair poking from her cleavage.

'There was something I wanted to mention,' she said, leaning across him to place her glass on the table. 'I shouldn't really be telling you this, because they told me in confidence, but both Colin and Jamie will probably have left by the end of the year.'

Simeon placed his glass beside Della's, a smile flickering across his lips as he felt he knew where this was leading.

'It's just that this will mean at least one senior post will be available, and I'd like to see you go for it.'

'Do you think,' he said, in the humblest tone he could manage, 'that I would be up to it?'

'Up to it? Of course you would. I don't want to...to say anything negative about Jamie and Colin, or any of the staff, but I think you will walk into one of those jobs. You see, I wasn't involved in the recruitment of anyone in the current team, and I'm finding, how shall I say this...I want to take the project, the Bungalow, in a particular direction, to make it the best of its kind in the country, but I don't think that many of the staff share my vision.'

The entree was an assortment of sushi. Simeon had never eaten raw fish before, but out of politeness cleared his plate, with the help of regular gulps of red grape juice to take away the taste.

'Delightful, isn't it?' enthused Della, a piece of pink sushi on her tooth. Simeon nodded, and took another drink. 'It's as fresh and natural a way of eating fish as you will find, although I did once see a documentary about Japan, where they filleted a live fish at the table, dipped the flesh into a piquant sauce, and ate it. I would love to try that...So what do you think of Martin?'

Simeon felt himself blush at the directness of the question, which was related to nothing that had gone before. For some reason, his newly filled glass began to shake.

'Honest?'

'Honest. It won't go any further.'

'Well to be totally truthful,' he said, drawing himself up, ' I don't think he is suited to this kind of work at all. I find him unprofessional, boorish and crude.'

With that he took a long drink. Only when his mouth was full did he realise that he was drinking wine.

'Oh I agree completely,' said Della, 'and if I get my way, which I intend to, we will be saying goodbye to Mr. Peach sooner rather than later.'

Simeon held the wine in his mouth. It made the inside of his cheeks feel dry, tingled in his throat and created a growing nausea. He didn't want to spit it back into the glass, and had visions of getting it all over the white carpet, giving the impression that a lamb had been messily sacrificed, and seriously endangering his newly offered chance of promotion. He swallowed hard, and felt almost immediately light-headed.

'I think,' he coughed, 'I got wine that time.'

'I'm so sorry,' said Della, 'I must have got the bottles mixed up. But you might as well finish it now. I won't tell.'

'Does your church allow drinking then?' asked Simeon.

'No. It is generally frowned upon. But because I work with handicapped people they think I'm some sort of angel, so overlook my minor peccadilloes. In fact I could get away with murder.'

Enjoying this new feeling of lowered inhibition, it occurred to Simeon that this might be a good time, in view of the promise of preferment, to further demonstrate his loyalty to Della by revealing some information about Martin that she might find useful.

'Have you heard...' Aware that there was a slight slur to his speech, Simeon concentrated on forming his words, and started again, 'have you heard the rumour about Martin's qualifications?'

Della sat up, and it was as if a shadow passed over her face as her expression became suddenly steely.

'No. Do tell.'

'It's just that I came across Ruth and Jane laughing one day- it was when we were at the hospital- they were sitting on the settees at the 'Happy Owls' and didn't realise that I was behind them. Jane said something about having proof that Martin didn't have a degree, and that if he'd got a certificate he must have faked it.'

Della smiled darkly. She had never thought to use Martin's application in her growing case for his removal, but knew that if she could find any evidence there of misrepresentation she could dismiss him instantly, without having to go through the charade of the three stage disciplinary process.

When Della went to the kitchen to check the main course, Simeon noticed that there was a spring in her step, but as he rose to investigate her book collection he found that his progress was not as smooth, as the room seemed to be moving in a way which was totally unfamiliar. He knew that to the likes of Martin and his beer- swilling kind a glass of wine would be nothing, but he had never let one sip of alcohol pass his lips before. The church he grew up in had long since decided that even the use of wine for communion could place temptation in the way of the weak willed, and had no problem with representing the blood of their saviour with 'Vimto.'

Finding his feet, Simeon made his way to Della's bookcase. He started to find the new sensation almost pleasurable, and felt glad that he had taken the drink by accident, so that it would not be considered a sin by the almighty. The shelves were neatly stacked, and the books were all in obvious categories. There was a large section on nursing, and almost as many on management. Below these were novels, with a clear preference for those of Barbara Cartland and Geoffrey Archer. The bottom two shelves were mainly Christian Theology. He was pleased to see the 'Lion Handbook to the Bible,' which he himself considered a classic. Simeon plucked out a Bible. It had silver writing on the cover and spine, which was creased through constant opening, and the blue cover was a network of scratches. Obviously a used Bible. Delicately flicking through it, he noticed that several pages had passages underlined in red:

Behold the Lamb of God, who takes away the sins of the world. The words 'takes away' were doubly underlined.

Be sure your sins will find you out. For some reason this was not underlined, but had beside it an asterisk and a large red question mark.

Like many of the underlinings, which appeared throughout, all in passages dealing with judgment and forgiveness, the question mark had been added with so much pressure that the paper had started to tear. Simeon found himself wondering if this was evidence of someone who had had a difficult life, and still carried some great burden.

'You can tell a lot about a person from their bookshelves,' said Della, as she entered.

'Yes...' said Simeon, closing the book and sliding it back between 'Paradise Lost' and 'The Screwtape Letters.' 'I like to see a well read Bible.'

Della had placed a covered platter on the table. She gestured for Simeon to return to his seat.

'Now I know that purists would say that you shouldn't follow fish with fish, but I think I could be forgiven for this: my piece de resistance.'

With a flourish she removed the silver cover from the platter to reveal a whole lobster, sitting on a pile of Mediterranean vegetables, glistening with a buttery sauce.

After this came the crème brulee, then the cheese and biscuits, then the coffee and chocolate mints. As Simeon sank back into the leather sofa with his coffee cup he noticed that it was approaching midnight.

'So tell me,' said Della, 'how did you become a Christian?'

'Well,' said Simeon, 'it was probably a lot easier for me than most. My family were Christians, and my dad is pastor of a large church. The mistake a lot of people make is to think that that makes them safe, that they are somehow born Christians. From the moment I was born my family prayed for me, but it wasn't until I was twelve years of age that I got down on my knees and asked the Lord to come into my life at a Christian summer camp. That's it really. How about you?'

Della looked down and brushed a sliver of caramel from the crème brulee off her white blouse.

'Not quite the same. In fact not at all the same. I didn't have christian parents. Not even loving parents.'

Her voice faltered, and Simeon thought he saw a tear forming in her eye.

'I've not been a good person, Sim.'

'None of us have. The Bible says that all have...'

'No, let me explain. I was quite a lot older than you when I found the Lord. When I was younger I was...promiscuous.'

Simeon finished his coffee and put down his cup. He was not expecting this. He had been used to hearing the tearful confessions of members of the church youth fellowship, but never from a woman of Della's age and experience. He leaned towards her, tilted his head to one side and adopted his counselling voice.

'You do know that when you became a Christian, God forgave all of your sins?'

'Yes,' she sighed, ' I know that, but there are things that still weigh me down. Like I say, I was promiscuous. But it wasn't just that...'

'The Lord is all-forgiving, Della.'

'I know, it's just that my promiscuity lead to something... something that affected the rest of my life...'

TASTING THE WIND

A phone rang in the kitchen. Red-faced, with beads of sweat on her forehead, Della rose and went to answer it. Simeon wandered again to the bookcase. Della's voice sounded agitated, but although he strained to hear what was being said he could not make anything out.

Della was suffering. She kept up a professional front at the Bungalow, behind which was a woman who carried a burden. For this reason the Lord had arranged that Simeon would be alone with her tonight, therefore the Lord would surely show him where to find the comfort she was looking for. He flicked through the pages of the Bible. When he stopped, he opened it out flat then, holding it in one hand, placed the index finger of the other on the page. Looking down, he found that he was pointing to Genesis chapter thirty-eight, verse nine:

But Onan knew that the offspring would not be his; so whenever he lay with his brother's wife, he spilled his semen in the ground to keep from producing offspring for his brother.

It didn't always work, of course. There was a joke at his church about a man who did the same and found that the verse was 'and Judas hanged himself.' There was no message here that he could see, for either Della or himself.

Then it started to come to him. He knew this passage well, but in his favoured, and to his mind more tasteful, Authorised Version, where the phrase was *spilling the seed*. That could mean something other than the obvious. it could mean losing a child, or... Della had said that her promiscuity had lead to something terrible. *She must,* thought Simeon, *have had an abortion.*

'Yes, I might have said that before...' Della was now shouting at the person on the phone, '...but that was when we started. I had expected you to have developed some level of competence by now.'

About a month before, the church that Simeon now attended had hosted a series of 'advanced teaching lectures' from a Texan pastor, who had outraged the anti-abortion lobby by arguing the case for abortion from the Bible. The timing of the talk, so closely followed by Della's revelation, now made perfect sense.

When Della returned she looked angry, and sat down with her lips pursed and her hands on her lap, as if she were trying to calm herself.

'What's wrong?'

'Wrong? Oh nothing. I just can't believe that I'm here in good company, having such a nice time, and then that place impinges on it. That was Martin. He said that I'd told him to phone any time, day or night if there was a crisis.'

'What's happened?'

'Apparently Andrew's had a seizure and gone into status epilepticus. The ambulance had just arrived. But I don't want to think about that until tomorrow.'

Della jumped up and began to clear the table. Simeon followed her into the kitchen with the dinner plates.

'What were we talking about,' said Della, 'before we were interrupted?'

'You were telling me about...'

'How I became a Christian. Yes... of course... Like I said, I lived badly. I tried to find the answer in drink. It didn't help. I even got married, but that failed. Then one night I wandered, stone drunk, into an evangelist's marquee. I sat at the back, and heard for the first time how my sins could be completely washed away because Jesus died for me. At the end they called for people to come to the front, and I found myself getting up with the whole row.'

'That's fantastic,' beamed Simeon, as he stacked the dishwasher. 'You must come up to my dad's church some time and give your testimony.'

*

As Simeon stood in the hallway, Della took his hand. 'You don't have to go you know'

'What?'

'You can stay.'

'That's very kind of you, but it won't take me long on the night bus, and I'm not in work until tomorrow evening.'

She smiled at his innocence, and then felt sadly envious. Perhaps she would arrange another evening. Soon.

'Before I go,' said Simeon, 'I think I may have a word for you from the Lord.'

'Yes?'

'Yes. It's something a visiting teacher passed on to me. He said: 'You have not taken a human life, if that life has not yet become human.'

'What?' Della felt the meal and wine lurch in her stomach, the hair on her arms stiffen and a wave of heat pass over her face as if her brulee torch had suddenly been turned on her.

'Does that mean anything to you?'

'Yes, but how...'

'He proved it from Genesis. God made Adam, but it wasn't until he breathed into him that he became human. He told us that the Hebrew word for breath and wind is 'Ruach,' which is the same word as spirit. So you can have a human body, but without the spirit of God breathed into you, you are of no more value than the animals.'

When Simeon had gone, Della opened another bottle of wine. Where voices had collided in her head there was now a silence and a feeling that something that had long been lodged inside had now unclogged and floated from her.

Simeon walked away with a stiff neck from Della's overenthusiastic hug, but with a broad smile as he whispered a prayer of thanks. The Lord had put him in the right place at the right time, and the obvious freeing of Della's mind would now enable her to see more clearly her vision for The People, and enable her to make the Bungalow what she wanted it to be.

Half way down her bottle of wine it was clear to Della that the difficult births experienced by many of The People had not only starved them of oxygen, but also of a God-breathed human soul. This 'Word of the Lord' through Simeon was the sign for which she had been waiting for so many years.

As she scraped the dregs from the coffee pot into the bin, they peppered the remains of the lobster. It had not been human. It was not a sentient creature, aware of its fate or its pain in the same way that we are. Its apparent scream and struggle to get out of the boiling water meant nothing. She still couldn't explain the thrilling shudder she felt when boiling a live animal, and why her mind should throw up pictures of a body writhing in a hospital bed as she tied the hands to side rails. But neither were human, as she now knew, so it didn't really matter.

-Chapter 36-

22nd August 1987,
10.20 a.m.

'HGT...AVF... LKM...'

Eddie rhymes off the letters of the registration plates to the rattle of a stick between railings. He always finds a stick in the park for Pansy, but never actually throws it. I wonder if part of him knows that the stick won't come back.

It's a nice day to be out: sunny, but with a breeze, perfect for lifting the mood. I've been worrying for a while about Andrew, who's been in and out of hospital with a series of bloody horrendous fits, but he seems fine now, so today it's me, Eddie and Pansy, out for a walk, and all's right with the world.

When we reach the tin tabernacle, Eddie comes to an abrupt halt, and leans on the stick like Charlie Chaplain.

'It's Eric.'

'Who?'

'Eric.'

Then I hear the voice, booming from somewhere in the small garden. It comes from a lavateria bush, which is threatening to sprawl out and engulf the path to the front entrance.

'All things bright and beautiful...'

'La la God maiden all...'

At the sound of Eddie's contribution the first voice stops, and Eric's bald head rises like the sun from out of the bush.

'Well if it's not me old mate Eddie.'

238

'Me old mate Eddie...'

Eric steps out from the bush. His vigorous pruning has covered his shoulders in lilac confetti.

'Can I have a go?' asks Eddie.

Eric looks at the secateurs in his hand, then to me as I shake my head. Nothing against Eddie, but I wonder what would happen if Mr. Hill got hold of them.

'I've finished this job now, Eddie,' says Eric, 'but there is something else you can help me with, if you've got time, that is.'

Eric leads us to a large urn at the side of the door which is bulging with what he tells us is white Alyssum.

'There's too much in that pot, so I thought I'd start some off over there,' he says, gesturing to a space in a border.

Cutting out a large clump of Alyssum, he hands it to Eddie.

'There you go, cup your hands and try to keep it together so that the roots don't break. Now bring it over here.'

Eddie follows Eric slowly, holding the plant as if it's a delicate chick he's returning to a nest. Eric makes a large well in the compost, and drenches it with his watering can.

'A half-crown hole for a sixpenny plant, that's what my old man used to say. Now place it in the hole.'

Kneeling down as if he's going to pray, Eddie presses the roots into their new home then, unprompted, draws compost from around the plant to cover the roots and stands up, pressing it down firmly but gently with his foot.

'Well done, Eddie,' says Eric, genuinely impressed, 'you're a natural gardener. Now you can water it in.'

Eric hands the watering can to Eddie, who sprinkles it round and over the newly established plant.

The lavateria waves in a warm breeze. Eddie smiles broadly and breathes deeply, as if drinking a long, satisfying draught of ale.

'..And The Lord God planted a garden...'

It's Eddie speaking, but the voice is a perfect impression of Father Quinn, the mad priest at the hospital.

'Bugger me,' says Eric, 'sorry Lord, I mean...who was that?'

'Oh just a priest that Eddie used to know.'

'How does he do that?'

'Oh it's just something he does, but it's usually only in his sleep. You're honoured. Half the staff at the Bungalow still don't believe he can do it. It's probably why Father Quinn thought he was possessed by demons.'

As the breeze continues to blow, a large white cloud begins to slowly sail from where it had blocked the sun. Eddie looks up, squinting.

'Hello God.'

'Not demons lad,' says Eric, 'just the opposite I'd say.'

I recognise the look on Eric's face- that pious look that Simeon has when he's about to slip in a sermon about how good God is and how he speaks through innocents like Eddie. Eric knows nothing of what went on at the hospital- the cruelty of some of the staff and of people like Don Maguire, and the sheer hard-bitten worldly-wiseness of so many of them who had lived on their wits for years. I wait, but fortunately he doesn't come out with any of that 'God's special children' crap.

Jane often talks of the offensiveness of the picture of people with mental handicaps as holy innocents. 'It's just as bad,' she says, 'as portraying them as depraved and violent. They are human beings like we are, with the same passions, the same aspirations and the same faults. To paint them as totally sinless is a denial of their full, rounded selves, a denial of their humanity.'

Religion has never played much of a part in my life, so most of what Jane and Simeon talk about goes over my head. I'm second generation lapsed catholic. My dad had set the example when I was six. I still remember the day the priest's car pulled up outside the house. It was large and black and looked like a hearse, and Dave used to say the screaming brakes were tormented souls in hell. Anybody else connected with St. Jude's seeing that car would begin to shake, to sweat, and to get a dry throat, and all the symptoms that I associate with claustrophobia. Not my dad. He invited the priest in, offered him a whiskey (which he accepted) and sat across from him, sleeves rolled up, puffing on his pipe, expressionless as a poker player.

'I'll get straight to the point, John,' said the priest.

'I'd be glad if you did, Patrick,' he'd said, cool as a cucumber, 'there's a race I want to watch at half past two.'

The priest pulled himself up in his chair and put the whiskey glass down next to a coaster on the coffee table between them.

'I would prefer 'Father O'Connor'.'

'Then I would prefer 'Mr. Peach.' Now what was the point you were getting to?'

'The point is,' said the priest, 'that I haven't seen you in church for the last six weeks.'

'Oh.'

Dad picked up the whiskey glass and placed it on the coaster, then sat back in his chair and relit his pipe. 'I wish you'd said sooner. There's a simple reason why you haven't seen me.'

He slowly puffed on his pipe as I viewed the whole thing from behind the settee, the same position from which I watched the Daleks.

'The reason why you haven't seen me...is because I haven't been there. Now fuck off.'

I seem to have multiple memories of how the priest left the house, and no longer know which is the most accurate: in one, I can actually see my dad physically ejecting him. In another, which I favour, Father O'Connor sits in stunned silence for what seemed like several minutes, then rises silently and, looking small and stooped, asks for his coat, and shuffles, unescorted, from the house.

But exactly how the Father left the house could not have matched the impact of what had gone before. It didn't matter how he left. It mattered that dad had said 'fuck' to a priest. In that moment I realised that there is a type of authority that is only in the mind, and could be exposed in the time it takes to say 'fuck off.' Not all authority, but pompous, inept, self-seeking authority. Which is most, I suppose. Yes, you would probably call the experience 'formative.'

'Pansy, look.'

Eddie's pointing to something, a patch of bright red that had gone unnoticed until it was illuminated by the emerging sun. We follow Eddie to the large red poppies, which sway delicately in the breeze.

'One of my favourite flowers,' says Eric.

I'd always thought of poppies as somehow sinister, other worldly. The first time I'd seen them was when dad had taken down a rotting old shed, and within a few weeks poppies had suddenly appeared where it had been- blood red with a black centre and stalks like thick, hairy spider's legs.

'Do you know much about poppies?' I ask Eric.

'A little,' says Eric, breaking the seed head off one that had lost its last petals in the wind, and placing it in his pocket.

'Do they ever flower in December?'

'Not that I've ever seen,' says Eric, looking at me as if I'm acting strangely, 'I don't think they would survive that. It's the seeds that are the great survivors. They can lie dormant for years, and then when the ground is disturbed you will get poppies appearing. That's why we have poppies on remembrance day- out of the churned up battle field at Flanders came hundreds and hundreds of beautiful red poppies. To me they're God's way of reminding us that the worst situation may still contain the seed of something quite beautiful. Yes, remarkable survivors, the Papaver family.'

'What did you say?'

'Remarkable survivors.'

'No, after that.'

'The Papaver family. Papaver Is the Latin name for poppy.'

As the full circle of the sun emerges from behind the cloud the poppies wave slowly from side to side- Poppy/Papaver/Poppy/Papaver. I don't know why I hadn't asked what it meant before. Surely Jane, with her interest in religion would have known a bit of Latin. But no one had realised, not until now, when it's blindingly obvious: Poppyfield Farm/Papaver Riding Stable. Andrew's home. I'd not only found it- I'd already been there.

-Chapter 37-

3rd September 1987
2.30 p.m.

There had been a dry spell, and it's a bumpy ride over the tractor tracks for Andrew, both in the van and in his wheelchair, as we go up to the big house at Papaver Riding Stable. Most of the buildings look fairly recent, and if I'm right about Poppyfield Farm being here it had either been destroyed or renovated beyond recognition.

The place where Andrew grew up.

Thinking back now to our first visit, am I reading things in or was there something different about him that day, some excitement, something to indicate that he recognised where he was? Even if Andrew's relatives haven't inherited it, I'm hoping that the owners might have bought it from them and be able to give a lead as to where they are.

As there's this huge flight of white steps up to the front door, I have to leave Andrew at the bottom while I stride up them and ring the bell. An upstairs curtain twitches, but nobody comes, so I start pounding with the heavy brass knocker. There's still no answer. I continue rapping on the door, count to ten, do it again, and am about to move away when I hear the sound of a large bolt being drawn. The door is flung open by the woman I'd seen on the horse the first time we came. She stares at me as if I've just vomited on her marble steps, then down at Andrew with a look of even greater disgust.

'Why do you keep bringing him here?'

'He comes to ride your horses,' I reply, not quite knowing what to say,' he happens to be a paying customer. I also think he might have lived here at some time. I was wondering if this used to be Poppyfield Farm, and if you knew what happened to the Wellman family.'

'I thought so' she says, in an exaggeratedly calm manner. Then her eyes well up, more angry than upset, and she pushes towards me, forcing me back down the steps.

'This was my brother- in -law's house,' she screams.

I'm on the verge of screaming as well, because I almost lose my footing on the smooth steps as she bears down on me. 'It's his fault they're not here now,' she says, thrusting a finger at Andrew, 'he should have died in their place- what use is he to anyone? Take him away and never come back- he doesn't belong here.'

Saying that she storms back up the steps, and as she reaches the door I notice the upstairs curtain move again. I wonder if she's got some mad old relative locked in there. With the slamming of the door there is a muffled cry, and Andrew goes into a violent fit which, fortunately, is short lived, but causes him to bite the tip of his tongue.

So that's it. I've found Poppyfield Farm. I've found living relatives. But after that reception I think that the trail ends here.

'Sorry Andrew,' I say, as I wheel him away from the house, ' I am so sorry... they don't know what they're missing.'

3rd September 1987
4.30 p.m.

Simeon is learning to drive. Not with just any old driving school, but with a friend he had met at church who is a driving instructor.

As the red car pulls onto the gravel forecourt of the Bungalow I notice that It's got one of those fish-shapes on its sign, and the words 'Ichthus School of Driving- Master the Narrow Road.' The car judders to a stop, and Simeon and his instructor get out.

It's a warm afternoon, and that, added to the fact that Della is inside, gives me a good excuse to sit outside with Andrew and Mickey. Andrew had been disturbed since the visit to his old home- writhing around in his chair and moaning- but he seems to be calming now as we watch Eddie kicking a ball against the wall of the Bungalow, chanting a little bit of Stokese that I'd taught him:

'Cost kick a bow agen a woe an yed it til it's bosted? Cost kick a bow agen a woe an yed it til it's bosted?'

'Nice one Eddie,' I shout, trying to ignore Simeon's arrival.

'Hi, Martin, this is my friend from church, Matthew. He's a driving instructor.'

'You don't say?'

Matthew has obviously been on some sort of hand-shaking course, or he could just be one of those guys who shakes your hand at the door in happy-clappy churches and smiles, knowing that you're going to Hell.

'Della said it would be O.K. for Matthew to have a look round the Bungalow.'

'Oh,' I say, 'is that O.K. with you, Eddie?'

'O.K.' says Eddie, as he stares vacantly at the car. Andrew is similarly mesmerised by the sudden appearance of the red object.

'Well, I suppose that's all right then', I say, casually kicking Eddie's ball as they go in without knocking.

Eddie has gone up to the car to look through the driver's window. The keys are still in the ignition.

'Can I have a go?'

'Er, no Eddie, I don't think so.'

'Why not?'

This is one of Jamie's favourite phrases in meetings when anybody questions The People doing an activity that the rest of us would take for granted.

'Rose at a riding stable so that she can wear a non-stigmatising helmet?'

'Why not?'

'Rita sharing a flat with non-handicapped people of her own age?'

'Why not?'

Some of Jamie's 'why nots' were more realistic than others. But what would he say now? I look at Eddie, then at the bunch of keys.

'Why not?'

*

245

'That one there,' I say, still questioning my judgment, ' is the accelerator.'

'Sellotaper.'

'It's all you need concern yourself with- that and the steering wheel.'

Leaning over, my feet on the clutch and brake of the dual controls, I turn the key in the ignition.

'Now Eddie, put both hands on the wheel, like this. Now press your foot down... no, no, stop.'

I've got the clutch pushed right down, so I'm not worried about the car racing off into the fence, but if Simeon hears the revs the lesson will come to an abrupt end.

'Eddie,' I say, as if a lightbulb has suddenly lit above my head, 'remember when you were helping Eric to plant flowers?'

Eddie nods.

'Well press your foot down like you're pressing the earth around a plant- firm but gentle. That's it, now hold it right there.'

The car purrs. With a quick look towards the Bungalow, I put it into first gear, then slowly bring up the clutch. It sets off smoothly along the gravel forecourt.

'Now steer...no, gently, that's it.'

One slow lap of the forecourt, then another, and after about five, Eddie needs no directions, but is driving around with a look of glee like I'd never seen before. Both hands on the wheel, the carrier bag is forgotten at his feet. He may only be circling round in first gear, but I can tell from his expression that in his own mind he's doing something great and significant: He is a formula one driver, an astronaut on the lunar rover, Ben Hur in his chariot, the demons that have tormented him left far behind. Andrew, perfectly still, follows the car with his eyes as Mickey chuckles and claps. Eddie is king of the road.

The first thing I hear is the screaming, followed by the slamming of a door. Then Della is standing in front of us, waving her arms in the air, but it happens so quickly that I'm lucky to stop the car just short of her.

'What do you think you are doing?' she bellows.

'I was going to ask you the same thing?' I say as I get out of the passenger side. ' We weren't doing any harm.'

'No harm? You were putting lives at risk. You had also stolen this vehicle.'

As Eddie gets out of the car, Simeon and Matthew emerge from the Bungalow.

'What's going on?' asks Simeon.

Before Della can answer, Eddie approaches her, waving his fists.

'I'm going to set my dog on you.'

Della pales, and for a moment looks wide-eyed with fear. 'Get him off me. Get him off.'

Simeon is apologising to Matthew, telling him how this sort of thing happened with people like this, but it didn't mean they were always aggressive. Matthew nods understandingly, as he quietly gets into his car and drives off. But I'm only vaguely aware of all of this, and of Mickey beginning to cry, because my eyes are drawn to Andrew. Andrew, who had been watching the car so intently, is now staring at Della with something that looks like hatred.

'Martin, get him away from me.'

'NO. He's joking with you, you stupid...'

'Come on Eddie,' says Simeon, taking him by the elbow. Della grabs Eddie roughly by the other arm, and together they frogmarch him into the Bungalow.

'Where are you taking him?'

'In the absence of a time-out room,' yells Della, ' it will have to be his bedroom- he needs a little time out to calm down.'

'Him calm down? It's not him that needs....' but they've gone.

-Chapter 38-

Minutes of staff meeting. 6th September 1987
Present: Martin, Jamie, Ruth, Colin, Simeon, Della (Chair) Jane (minutes)

1.   Della said that she had been auditing stocks. In the last period, ten packs of toilet rolls were used, and ten packs of paper towels. This was far too many, and if staff were not more frugal with supplies she would have to start to ration them.

Martin said that he thought it was reassuring that as many hands were being washed as bottoms were being wiped.

Della said that this was a serious issue, and that Martin should not be so flippant.

2.   Della reported that there would be an official opening of the Bungalow on Saturday, 19th September.

Simeon asked who would be opening it. Della replied that it would be Dan Kerr, the local MP.

Jamie asked what on earth we were doing having an 'official opening.' Not only had the Bungalow been 'unofficially open' for several months, but this surely went against every principle of normalisation.

Della said that she was aware that some people might see a conflict, but that there was a trade off to produce a greater good.

248

Because of negative publicity she thought it would be a good thing to have a 'housewarming' so that the locals would see that there was no harm in The People. Della asked if anyone had any idea where the rumour had come from that the Bungalow was a hostel for AIDS sufferers, but no one knew. She added that it might be a good idea if someone took Eddie and Rita out for the day, and asked Jane not to minute that.

Colin asked if Dan Kerr was the same MP who had come out recently in favour of foxhunting and in opposition to homosexuality. Della said that he was.

Della said that it was not necessary for Jane to minute absolutely everything that was said at the meeting. Colin said that it was.

Colin asked if Dan Kerr was the same MP who had suggested that people with AIDS be placed in out of town hostels (which had probably been the origin of the rumour) and their names kept on special registers. Della said that it was, and that if Colin felt strongly about it he didn't have to come to the opening.

Colin said that he wouldn't miss it for the world.

3.   Della reported that there had been a complaint from a Mrs Yealand at the Papaver riding school, saying that one of the staff- one with a Northern accent- was rude to her. Martin said that he had not been rude to her, but now wishes that he had been, as she had physically attacked him.

4.   Ruth confirmed that she had booked a holiday in Blackpool in October for Rita, Eddie and Mickey. The staff who had volunteered to go were Martin, Jamie and Ruth.

5.   Jamie said that Oscar's job, stacking shelves at the local supermarket, was going well apart from one small detail. Oscar had been approaching customers and saying 'are you a nice man?' A meeting had been called at which Oscar's social worker and a psychologist were present, and Mr. Pinkerton from supported employment, who was chosen to tell Oscar that this sort of behaviour was not conducive to his acceptance by society. When Mr. Pinkerton suggested that speaking to strangers wasn't such a good idea, Oscar had replied 'oh that's all right. I don't know any.'

Oscar eventually agreed that he would stop doing what he had been accused of. The following day, the supermarket manager reported that Oscar had approached a woman and asked 'is your husband a nice man?'

6.   Rita's behaviour was still a concern. She had been lashing out and throwing furniture. Almost every kitchen chair had had to be replaced, and the TV hire shop had complained about the number of sets that had been damaged.

7.   Andrew's seizures were on the increase again, and his neurologist was taking another look at his medication levels.

8. Simeon said that Rose's mother had walked into the Bungalow the previous evening and started to rummage through the freezer. Then she demanded to know what Rose had had for her evening meal, and complained that frozen lasagne wasn't adequate for her daughter. Colin questioned if she'd thought that the food in the hospital had been 'adequate' and asked what right she had to enter without knocking, as there were more than just her daughter living here.

9. Della said that in the light of recent events she had been in discussion with Des Machin, the area manager. Des had assured her that if there was one more episode of Eddie putting himself or others in danger, or absconding from the Bungalow, he would be returned to the safe environs of the hospital.

*

As Della gets up to leave, there is a stunned silence around the table. She had saved the bombshell until last. She is about to enter her office when she seems to have an afterthought:

'Oh, Martin,' she says, handing me a brown envelope from her briefcase, 'I nearly forgot.'

I remove the letter, which is on Social Services headed notepaper, and begin to read:

Dear Mr.Peach,

I am writing to request your attendance at a meeting on 14.9.87. at 4.30pm, in my office, with reference to stage one of the borough's disciplinary procedure. This is to discuss the events of 3rd Sept 1987, when you encouraged a patient in a hazardous activity with a stolen vehicle...

*

Della locked the office door behind her. It was important that no one disturbed her now. She was expecting Martin Peach to hammer at her door at any moment, but if he did, she would choose to ignore him. Soon, he would no longer be a problem to her. As yet, she had not managed to obtain proof of irregularities in his job application and reference- they were now in the hands of a graphologist- but the stunt with the car had been a gift, one which gave her no choice but to instigate the disciplinary process immediately.

Sitting at her desk, Della picked up her Dictaphone and said: 'note to self...speak to Dr. Parmar...complete Zuclopenthixol article...stock up with Bollinger, ready for the celebration.'

She switched off the machine and placed it back in line with the other items on the desk, and leant back in her reclining swivel chair, her hands behind her head, revealing dark sweat patches the size of saucers on the light blue blouse. She was never quite sure which was the most vexatious to her, Martin or Eddie, but she found that she could smile now when she thought of them, because she had got everything in hand. Martin had never been right for the job, and although within her scheme she felt that there was room for some individuality, he was too far beyond her boundaries. And Eddie? Well Eddie just brought back unhappy memories. She failed to understand why when people like Jamie and Martin spoke about Eddie it was as if he was some sort of god-like being. They couldn't see the danger in him. But they soon would.

Della reached into her trouser pocket, and pulled out a clear plastic container. It was about the length and thickness of her chubby index finger, and held in one of its four compartments a large white tablet, two smaller pink pills, and two capsules, half black and half a garish red. It wasn't fair, she felt, that what Eddie was capable of should be masked. Of course she had to be seen to be going through the motions of referring him to Mr. Parmar, and advocating for an increase in medication, but whether or not Eddie got it was her choice. She wasn't always around in the morning when the drugs were given out, but when she was she insisted on taking them to his room with a glass of water. The fluctuating levels were producing the desired effect on his behaviour, and soon he would be gone.

Della unlocked the bottom drawer of her desk, and opened it, revealing a growing pile of tablets and capsules, to which she added those from the container. Leaning over, she dipped a finger into the pile and stirred it round. She knew that there was a possibility of absorbing some of the cocktail through her skin, and had occasionally been tempted to try them herself as an aid to her research.

Why not just flush them away?

She wondered briefly if she had a desire to be caught, but instantly dismissed this and chastised herself for considering such a stock concept of amateur psychology. Besides, getting caught was something that happened to the wrong doer, and what she was doing was justified. She was the instrument of the Lord in the lives of his special children. Eddie was dangerous to himself, to the other patients (as Della still preferred to think of them) and to the public. It would be better for everyone if he went back.

Or died.

The thought was not a new one, and it in no way disturbed her. After all, God had now revealed to her through Simeon's word of prophecy that the patients were not quite human. And she had seen patients die before. It was just something they did. She remembered how, when Frankie had died at the hospital, and a woman called Faye in her last job, she had felt such a warm glow from those around her who supported her and realised how hard it must be to have someone die in your care.

Della saw a rain-soaked coffin being lowered into a muddy grave. Weeping into her handkerchief she is suddenly aware of a hand on her shoulder then, as she buries her head in his chest, Simeon is whispering comforting words.

Eddie's behaviour was spiralling out of control. Anything could happen, even that scenario, and as she smiled and wept simultaneously she knew that it was a realistic, indeed exciting, option.

-Chapter 39-

14th September 1987.
4.30 pm.

Della: Firstly, Martin, I have to ask if you object to me recording this meeting on my Dictaphone. It will help when I am writing up the minutes.

Martin: Whatever.

Della: You have chosen not to bring a representative.

Martin: Yes.

Della: So Martin, I have to inform you that you are accused of putting at risk the safety of a patient... resident... on the third of September, by encouraging him to drive a motor vehicle. Not only that, but other people were put at risk. What do you have to say for yourself.

Martin: Does it matter? We both know the outcome of this, don't we?

Della: You have the right to put forward your version of events, and to defend your actions. But I must warn you that your tone is not appropriate. So what do you have to say?

Martin: O.K., yes, I did encourage Eddie to drive the car, but he had asked to do it, and I thought we were meant to be giving people choices and normal life experiences.

Della: Not when they endanger people's lives.

Martin: But the car had dual controls, and we never got out of first gear.

Della: And did you ask permission of the owner?

Martin: Well, no. I suppose I should have done, but it was all a bit
　　　spur of the moment.

Della: So you are admitting to what you did?

Martin: Yes, I...

Della: Then I have to inform you that you are in receipt of a verbal
　　　warning, which will stay on your record for one year. If during
　　　that year you are guilty of any other misconduct, you will
　　　receive a written warning, and if you receive a third and final
　　　warning your contract will be terminated. Do you understand?

Martin: Perfectly. And what are my chances of staying here for a
　　　year? I'm thinking of setting up a sweepstake... (Click)

Della pushes her Dictaphone back into its allotted position on
the desk, between her desk-tidy and calculator, and leans forward, her
face so close to mine that I can smell the garlic on her breath.

'Now listen to me you little shit.'

Her face is suddenly bright red, as if she's torn off a heavy
mask that she can no longer stand or be bothered to wear. Even her
voice has changed, and has a definite cockney twang, instead of the
bass version of Maggie Thatcher that she usually puts on. 'It's up to
you,' she snarls, 'you can leave, or you can give me the pleasure of
getting rid of you.'

I stand and make for the door, and as I turn to close it behind
me I see Della, now back to her usual colour, smiling at me almost
sweetly. Afterwards I will think of all sorts of smart-arsed things I
should have said, but here and now I know that if I open my mouth,
for once nothing will come out. It's a sort of paralysis, like at that point
in the film where the characters realise that the one with the anti-social
behaviour is not purely the product of a bad up-bringing, or of a
traumatic experience, but is actually possessed by a demon.

*

4.45 pm

When I emerge from Della's office the Bungalow seems
deserted. I go out into the garden to get some air because I'm finding it

difficult to breathe, and for some reason the thought comes into my head about what a lonely death drowning must be. I'm beginning to think that I'm on my own, until I see Jane, sitting at a table, reading one of Eddie's diaries.

'So how's it going?' I ask. She's so engrossed that she hasn't seen me approach.

'Oh hi, Martin...how's what going?'

'The memoirs of the mad woman.'

'Slowly,' she says, scowling at me. 'How did you go on with Della?'

'I don't want to talk about it... tell me about the diaries... please.'

Jane had told me how successful biblical scholarship relied more than anything on obsessive personalities, and her need to decipher the diaries seems to be bringing out that side of her.

' She doesn't write in a straightforward chronological way,' says Jane, giving me a really worried look. 'There are long passages where the overlapping sensory material is hard to work out, and occasionally she lapses into Hebrew. Apart from that, it's easy peasy. Oh, and she also claimed to have prophetic visions.'

'What?'

' Look at this one.'

And what does the future hold for Edward...I see owls...not in flight but dragging broken wings as they limp towards a hospital which screams greyness.

'The sinister owls...' I say, '...Oulston hospital...do you think she had a vision of the hospital so many years before Eddie went in?'

'I would...if I wasn't a born cynic, trained in pure cynicism by the greatest cynics of our time...no, it wouldn't take psychic ability to foresee the possibility of Eddie's future being in a hospital. There was no other option at the time. And yes it would be Oulston because living round here he'd be in its catchment area.'

As I flick through the diaries I can't understand half of what I'm reading, but I can see what Jane means about their bitter tone:

TASTING THE WIND

So Jesus washed his disciples' feet. Big deal. I'd be more impressed if he'd wiped their arses...

What are we going to leave behind as our ultimate monument?

We breathe in the air and breathe out carbon dioxide. We breathe in the dust of the earth and make snot. We drink pure water and make piss. We eat the plants and animals and turn them into shit.

One day, aliens will find a planet whose air is unbreathable carbon dioxide, whose rocks are piles of snot, whose seas are piss, and whose land masses are stinking deserts of shit, and they will marvel at what man has done....

We sit and read the diaries until The People arrive. As it's a pleasant evening, Jane suggests a walk round the park after tea, which we achieve with me pushing Andrew, Jane pushing Mickey, and Rita walking hand in hand with Rose. Oscar, of course, opts out of the walk, whereas Eddie uses it to give Pansy some exercise. Yes, I'm starting to think the dog is real.

Jane comes the closest ever to falling out with me because I refuse to talk about the verbal warning I got from Della. I just don't know yet how to put into words what happened, or if it did happen like I think. What I do know is that all I need to do is keep my nose clean for a few months and it'll be off my record. Della might want to get rid of me, but even she has to go by the rules, and when it comes to self-preservation I can out-Simeon Simeon when it comes to doing the right thing, saying the right words and licking the right arses.

We call at the Lobster on the way back, and by the time we arrive at the Bungalow everyone is tired out on fresh air, and even Rita opts for an early night.

Mickey's bedtime routine is carried on the same every night, and starts with him hanging on to the sink while his face is washed and teeth brushed. After a bit you start to do things automatically, one night running into another, like somebody who drives a familiar route every day but forgets the precise details of each journey. You wheel Mickey up to the washbasin and help him to stand, guiding his hands to the side of the basin to support himself. Then you pull down his trousers, remove his Inco-Pad and put it in the san-bin. Next, sit him down to remove his shoes, socks and trousers, put his pyjama trousers on, but just around his ankles, remove his shirt and put on his pyjama jacket, then get Mickey to stand again, wash his face and brush his teeth (as well as you can when all he wants to do is suck off the toothpaste from the brush,) give his bits a wipe with a flannel if his pad's wet, put on a fresh pad and pull up his trousers. Finally, you open the bathroom door, take Mickey's hands, and encourage him to walk through it.

Each night, Mickey would simply sink to his knees until his wheelchair was brought to him. But tonight is different. Mickey is standing at the washbasin, but as I open the door I can hear Jane calling for help. I try to wheel Mickey's chair to him, but his lap strap has tangled in one of the wheels.

'Mickey, don't move.'

I rush to Rose and Rita's room, to find Jane kneeling and Rose lying on her side, the after- tremors of a fit rippling through her body.

'She's nearly finished, poor love,' says Jane, but she'll be worn out. I'll just need a hand to get her into bed.'

Rose's breathing is starting to calm, and to turn into a snore. Propping her up against my chest, I draw her stiff arms into her body. Jane takes her legs, and on a count of three we lift her into bed.

It's funny, I've seen so many fits now, and although it doesn't scare me anymore I still find that seeing somebody going through it leaves me feeling tired, as if I've somehow shared it.

And I can't get that last staff meeting out of my head: Rita's behaviour is worse than it was in the hospital, Andrew is having more seizures, and people, not always the ones you would expect, are going under. I've actually begun to get worried about Colin. He seems to spend a lot of time in his own world, and more than one person has noticed that he's become obsessed with record keeping and note taking. I have a hunch that he's keeping records on Della for a Social Services enquiry, but Ruth just thinks he's losing it. On top of all of this, Eddie is going back. We have failed.

As I come out of Rose's room a low giggle from the other end of the corridor causes me to look up. I see Mickey standing outside the bathroom door, holding on to the handle. *Surely, it must be better here? It has to be better, doesn't it?* I wonder what it says about us, about people, human beings, that so many things that start off good seem to just turn rotten, like the world of excrement in the diary, where everything we touch turns to shit. Like the hospital, where people were meant to be looked after, to be safe. Like the Bungalow.

Then Mickey totters forward. He stands, swaying like a tightrope walker in a sudden breeze, raising his hands, ready to fall to the ground. But he doesn't fall. This time he walks... five paces, ten... fifteen, almost the full length of the corridor. I walk towards him, both of us laughing uncontrollably, until he collapses, giggling, into my arms. And I don't know why, but a picture comes into my mind of something I'd heard about a guy who'd been held hostage for years in a small, dull room. For days, weeks, months, he was given a bland diet, not only bland but colourless: rice pudding, dry bread, maybe an egg. Then one day on his tray there was an orange. And he couldn't eat it. Not because there was anything wrong with it, but because it was the only thing of colour in his life and he didn't want it to end. In the middle of the dark, tense world that Della has created something beautiful has appeared, and the feeling is electric, like there are waves of joy sweeping over me. There has been so much crap recently, so much gloom, but in the middle of it all I feel like I've witnessed a miracle: Mickey has walked. And I was there.

-Chapter 40-

19th September 1987

Saturday came, and so did the visitors: Dan Kerr MP, with a group of men in grey suits and ladies in hats. Della had brought in a caterer, and the local press were out in force for the 'official opening' of the Bungalow.

Ruth spent the afternoon praying that Rita would not remember where she had seen Dan Kerr before, and vise versa, and that she wouldn't recall what she'd overheard of Colin's interpretation of the M.P.'s name as rhyming slang. Earlier that year, just prior to the Tory landslide victory in the General Election, Dan had been touring his borough in a big, blue, open topped 'battle bus.' Ruth and Martin had been out shopping with Rita and Andrew, when they saw the bus coming down the high street, festooned with blue rosettes.

'Why?' Rita had asked.

Faced with the task of explaining to Rita the intricacies of British politics, Martin had decided on a basic rendering, which wasn't that far from his own meagre understanding of things:

'Well he's from the government. The government are Tories, and have blue flowers. There's another man who wears red flowers. He's Labour. You have to vote for the one you think makes the best decisions for you. Now, not that I want to tell you what to think, but you know how you get a pound a week from the day centre?'

'Yeah.'

'And you know how you save fifty pence and have fifty to spend?'

'Yeah?'

'Well the blue party want to take it all off you to spend on themselves.'

It took a few seconds for the implications to sink in, but as the 'battle bus' passed by, Dan Kerr's benign smile faltered for a second as Rita held up two fingers and bellowed: 'Fa' off you man.'

Fortunately, Dan did not seem to recognise them; in fact all was going well, until the MP had completed his speech about what a fine job the staff were doing, and how patient they must be. It was then that Colin stepped forward.

'Excuse me,' he said, 'but I would like, if I may, to reply.'

Dan Kerr, unaware of the panic on Della's face, nodded and smiled paternally.

'I would like to say,' said Colin, 'that I am in full agreement with what Mr. Kerr said about the closure of long-stay hospitals, because, let's face it, these places are shit holes that you wouldn't want your dog to live in.'

Beginning to sense a story, the gentlemen of the press raised their pens and cameras.

'I hope my language doesn't offend. If it does, then does it offend you more than the way in which people- the people here today- have had to live? I hope not.'

'Has he been drinking?' Della whispered to Jamie.

'No,' said Colin, 'but I will be later, if anyone would care to join me. Let me get to my point. Mr. Kerr has told us how his caring government has pushed through 'care in the community' because it gives people better lives. And it does. Or at least it should. But do you want me to tell you why Dan is really so keen on 'Care in the Community? He thinks it's cheaper, that's why.'

As Colin spoke, he had started to undo his shirt, then let it fall to the ground.

'He's having some sort of breakdown,' said Della.

'Oh no he isn't,' said Colin, 'he has seen the truth. And that's what these people need.'

Colin kicked off his shoes, then pulled off both socks.

'They need services stripped bare of political ideology and pretension, services run by people, for people.'

Colin dropped his trousers to gasps from everyone apart from Rita, who screamed with laughter.

'And it's nothing to do with vote catching, Dan, or getting your picture in the paper, Della. These people should be at the centre of all that happens. Does anyone else here think it's inconsistent that Dan here was in the paper not so many months ago saying that the Bungalow should have been on the council estate, the one that Social Workers affectionately refer to as Beirut? Now that the campaign led by his voters has failed, now that he knows that the Bungalow is here to stay, he's realised that a picture with the 'ex-mental patients' might even boost his ratings.'

Della tried to grab Colin by the arm, but decided not to as the cameras flashed repeatedly. Instead Colin took Della's arm and, leaning towards her, said:

'I know what you did.'

Della felt as if the entire room had disappeared, leaving her alone with the near-naked Colin.

'But...but you couldn't...there were no witnesses and...'

It was the look of shock on Colin's face that stopped her from going further.

'You know nothing, do you?'

'No,' said Colin, his voice faltering, 'at least...I didn't until now.'

Light and sound returned to Della's world, in the form of flashing cameras and screams from Rita. Looking round, she felt certain, given how closely Colin had pressed his face to hers, and the level of noise in the room, that no one would have heard their exchange.

'Colin, take it from me,' she snarled, 'you are...'

'What? Sacked? It's too late. I resign. I don't need this any more.'

Fixing Della as if he were engaging her in an intimate dance or some form of martial arts demonstration, he circled her as the cameras continued to flash then, standing in front of her, allowed his underpants to drop to the floor, before walking in absolute silence through the door which led to the forecourt.

Once in his car, Colin put on the bathrobe he had left on the seat, and drove home, where his suitcase was waiting. He had half an hour to get to the airport.

From the moment he had heard that the Bungalow opening was to be performed by the homophobic Dan Kerr, Colin had planned his leave-taking. He had several reasons for exiting in such a manner, and he had achieved all of them. Yes, he had wanted publicity, and it would not be long before his ex-colleagues understood why he had left so dramatically; but he had also wanted to make a statement about The People. Dropping his underpants on the floor in front of the obsessively clean manager had been his idea of a symbolic gesture. He had left in the way he had wished, and had ruined Della's day.

But despite achieving all of these objectives, the much anticipated experience had been tainted beyond anything he could have imagined. No, not tainted, something more. Something of much greater importance than he could ever have anticipated had now thrust itself into his consciousness, meaning that he could not make his break as cleanly as he had wished. He would be spending some time out of the country, but he was now taking with him something unexpected- a burden to warn the Bungalow staff of what he had seen in the eyes of their manager.

What he had said to Della had been a bluff, something to test out a hunch that she had guilty secrets in her past. But her response, the degree of panic and reference to witnesses pointed to something more specific. He now knew that his suspicions about Della were not only well-founded, but her reaction had alerted him to the fact that there was something about her which was far more disturbing, far more dangerous, than he had ever imagined.

-Chapter 41-

29th September 1987
7.15 p.m.

The steak pudding had taken on the consistency of wallpaper paste when it was liquidised, but Jane could tell that Andrew was enjoying the taste by the way his Adam's apple bobbed up and down as his tongue worked rhythmically to convey the food to the back of his mouth.

One of the diaries lay open on the table and as Andrew took a break from the strenuous act of eating, Jane glanced down the open page.

No wonder Simeon thought they were blasphemous.

Christian apologists have often talked about the 'reasonableness' of Christianity. There's one argument that runs: Jesus was either mad, bad, or God. Since that woolly thinking first emerged, man has grasped more of the complexity of the human mind, and is now aware that some forms of madness can be specific. A man may live a normal life in all respects, hold down a job, (be a carpenter, for instance) but believe fervently that he is in touch with spirit beings from the planet Venus.

So why couldn't Jesus have been mad?

Look at the evidence:
Days without food where he believes that he can fly.
Look at the evidence:

The arrogance of a so-called religious leader who thinks it's all right that expensive perfume is poured over his feet when people are begging in the streets.

Look at the evidence:

He goes berserk with a whip on the most holy site in Judaism.

Look at the evidence:

If the Church is his family, then how can one family produce so many psychopaths, so many mad men, so many despots, and so many perverts, without it casting serious doubt upon the mental health of their progenitor?

Because of passages like this both Simeon and Della had refused to read the diaries. Colin had shown some interest in them, but he had now disappeared. Jamie had phoned him several times to no avail, and eventually went round to his flat to find it deserted.

'You don't think he's done something... foolish, do you? Ruth had asked on Jamie's return. It was obvious from the silence in the room that Ruth was not the only one to have had this thought.

Jane continued to feed Andrew, until the front door opened and a man she had never seen before entered. 'I'm sorry,' she said, 'I didn't hear you ring the bell.'

'Bell?' said the man. He was dressed in a suit with a pink shirt and tie. He would have been described as a yuppie, if not for the fact that he was too old, although he was holding the twin badges of that role: the Filofax and the mobile phone. He was conventionally handsome, with wavy black hair and a craggy face, but Jane was unaware of this, due to his haughty attitude and fixed sneer.

'This is a private house,' said Jane, 'you should ring before bursting in here. What do you want?'

Before he could answer, Ruth appeared from the corridor.

'Richard, what are you doing here?'

'As I was about to say,' drawled Richard, 'this is my partner's place of work. I was just passing by, and thought I'd drop in to kiss her goodbye before she goes off to Blackpool. And you are...?'

'I am Jane, and this is Andrew. This is his home,' she said, continuing to give Andrew his food.

Richard looked on in horror as Andrew pushed out a spoonful of brown gloop with his tongue, leaving a slug like trail of gravy and saliva down his chin and apron.

'Er, perhaps we could go outside,' he said, taking Ruth by the hand.

As the door closed, Jane offered Andrew another spoonful, which he ate with relish, without spilling a drop.

'Andrew Wellman,' she laughed, ' I do believe you did that on purpose. If only we could get rid of Della as easily as that.'

Get rid of Della. Get rid of Della. It wasn't until she had said those words that she realised the extent of her contempt, as she imagined how much happier and lighter a place the Bungalow would be. She wondered if anyone else had noticed how The People had started to recognise the distinctive sound of Della's diesel-engined car pulling into the forecourt, and how it had the effect of creating silence and casting gloom over the Bungalow. The People were supposed to be 'mentally handicapped,' but they were the first to pick up that cue. And now Della had upset Martin. He was trying to put on a brave face about what had happened at the disciplinary meeting, but seemed withdrawn, even depressed.

Jane's eye fell again on the diary.

Still the delayed milestones... still Eddie can neither walk nor talk. So what happened?

Jane found herself fighting off an uncharacteristic urge to jump to the end of the final diary and work back. She smiled at a recent conversation she'd had with Martin, where she'd said that she would read the entire first page of a novel before deciding to buy it, and he'd said he always read the last page.

'But what if the last page reveals who the murderer is? You'd know 'whodunnit' before you knew 'whodunwhat.''

'Even better,' he'd said, 'that way you can appreciate how clever the clues are without having to re-read the book.'

She found that she could almost appreciate the strange logic in that, but no matter how tempted she was she knew it went completely against the grain to jump to the end.

And she could never have guessed that one day it would be a decision which she would deeply regret.

-Chapter 42-

1st October 1987

The apartment is on a side road off the main promenade at the North Shore end of Blackpool, in a street consisting entirely of hotels, guesthouses, and the odd self-catering apartment. Ours has three bedrooms, a bathroom, a lounge, and kitchen. Jamie had whispered an obscenity when he saw the sign outside which read:

'Caremore Apartments: holiday homes for the disabled holidaymaker.'

Despite all of her talk of normalisation and her use of it as a weapon with which to beat her staff about the head, Della had insisted that we use an adapted facility. Jamie had argued that a chance for integration was being missed, but for once I found myself agreeing with Della, when she asked how we would handle Rita or Eddie if they had an outburst in a hotel, and what would happen if the place wasn't completely accessible for Mickey who, although he was regularly walking the length of the corridor, was still mostly dependent on his wheelchair for mobility.

Jamie had driven round for about an hour trying to find a parking space near to the apartment that was big enough for the van and the tail-lift. Eventually he stopped in the middle of the road, unloaded, and set off to find a space, leaving Ruth, Eddie, Rita, Mickey, and me with a pile of cases and packets of 'inco-pads.'

As soon as we've unpacked we set off for the promenade.

'Which way now?' says Ruth, as we cross at the traffic lights.

'Of course, you're all southern softies aren't you? Well if you go left there's a lot to see, and you eventually end up at the Pleasure Beach. But it is a hell of a walk. If you go right there are tableaux on the rocks at Bispham- and that might be just enough for our first evening.'

Mickey howls with delight at the illuminated tableaux. Eddie is fascinated by a massive fibreglass mock up of ancient Egypt, complete with a gormless-looking mummy, which rises periodically from its sarcophagus. Only Rita doesn't seem to be enjoying it, as she holds herself, stamping her feet and complaining about the cold.

'Spaceship,' cries Eddie, 'spaceship.'

'Omigog!'

A rocket-shaped tram, decorated with hundreds of coloured lights cruises along the road between the tableaux and the guesthouses.

'Can I have a go?'

'Why not?' says Jamie.

'Er, I think we may be better doing that tomorrow night,' I say, in the voice of somebody wise and experienced. ' There's never any room on them. You have to go down to where the line begins and queue for ages.'

Ruth smiles. 'We'll go with the native guide- he obviously knows the territory.'

All around are families, children with candyfloss, and street sellers with various torches, and illuminated toys. It looks like glowing red devil skulls are the popular buy this year. *Nearly a whole year since the Happy Owls was decorated for Halloween. Nearly twelve months since I first went to the hospital.*

Rita isn't impressed but I think it's brilliant this- the lights, the noise, the gangs of pissed lads and girls on hen and stag-nights, still dressed as if it's the middle of summer. Blackpool is the line where the completely naff verges over into genius, and it doesn't just stick two fingers up to the weather, it sticks three piers out into it, and says *we will not give in.*

Rita soon perks up when we offer her a chance of a drink at the nearest bar, but It's not until we get into the bar that I realise it's karaoke night. What with that and the lights it's crammed full. We're about to leave when a party of pensioners signals to us, saying that if they squash up there will be room at their table. I wonder how close this is to the ideal that we're striving for of integration into the 'ordinary' community: a group of people making room for us so that we too can sit and hear a load of drunken, off-key singing.

As singers of varying quality come and go, I look around at The People: Rita is obviously enjoying it. Since leaving Moonfield Road there hasn't been a single example of 'challenging behaviour,' just Rita being her usual fun-loving, moody, flirtatious self. Even Eddie, who we'd wondered right up to the last minute about the wisdom of bringing, is relaxed and up for it. Mickey's laughing, not showing the least bit interest in the karaoke, but looking from one person to the next and getting high on the holiday atmosphere. Jamie's engrossed in conversation with a white haired man who looks like the guy at Kentucky Fried Chicken. They're each having to shout in the other's ear hole to be heard and although I can't catch a word of it I know that Jamie will be saying something to the effect of: *they're not children, and no, we're not from a home, we're just friends on holiday together.*

A man and woman singing 'Please Release me' follow an Elvis impersonator, then a leather clad biker does the whole of 'Bat out of Hell.' Ruth has gone to the bar. Eddie sits next to Mickey.... correction: Eddie had been sitting next to Mickey. His seat, like his Guinness glass, is empty. I look to the bar, where Ruth is still waiting to be served, but no Eddie. I can feel my heart starting to pound. I look under the table, unable to work out how Eddie has got out, as I'm completely hemmed in. I try to signal to Jamie, who can't hear me for the applause for a grandmother from Chorley's rendition of 'Sex and Drugs and Rock and Roll', and to Ruth, but she's on her tiptoes trying to get seen by the bar staff.

Just as I'm about to climb onto the table, a familiar voice at the microphone says:

'Can I have a go?'

It's as if everything's gone into slow motion, as Mickey, Jamie, Rita, Ruth and me all turn to the stage, where the M.C. is holding up a mike to Eddie. There are giggles, and from the pensioners a resounding 'aah' when they realise who Eddie is. And neither Jamie, Ruth, nor myself can get to him.

'And what is your name, young sir?' says the M.C., who's wearing large pink glasses and a red sequinned jacket.

'Eddie.'

Aah.

'And what are you going to sing for us, Eddie?'

'I've got a dog at home.'

'I don't know that one. Unless it's a hound-dog, crying all the time.'

The M.C. starts looking round to see if anybody's going to claim Eddie. Ruth has started to push her way toward the stage, but is having problems getting through a many-tentacled stag night.

'So what songs do you know?'

Eddie glazes over, then smiles and says

'Queen.'

'You know some Queen? So do I, there are loads of them in Blackpool...but seriously, do you know 'We are the Champions?'

'Yes.'

'Well you don't hear that said much in Blackpool...but seriously, tonight Eddie will be...' he signals to a young man behind the karaoke machine,'...Freddie Mercury.'

Despite the prompt, the backing track doesn't begin straight away, but Eddie takes up a pose and puts on a hooded eyed, pout lipped, arrogant rock star face. Then it occurs to me what I might be about to see. Jamie had once described to me something called 'idiots savantes.' It was what they called it when somebody has a mental handicap and can't do simple things, but is an absolute genius at something else like maths or art. I had heard Eddie's impressions. We were about to witness the birth of an amazing new career.

The first notes begin, Eddie takes a deep breath, and from his lips there comes what I can only describe as tuneless gibberish. Part of the audience is beginning to dissolve into laughter. A smaller element are complaining that they did not pay for a night out to sit and listen to this din, and the pensioners, as one, are saying 'aah, bless him.' The M.C. is signing to his oblivious assistant to unplug the mike, when Ruth calmly walks across the stage to Eddie. Holding the microphone with him she joins in, prompting the audience to do the same. Soon little pockets of holiday makers are singing, then standing up and waving their arms in the air as the song reaches it's crescendo. Eddie Mercury bows, struts, and blows kisses to the standing ovation, then the crowds part, as he makes his way back to his seat.

But Ruth is not going to escape that easily.

'Hang on a minute little lady.' says the M.C., grabbing her by the hand, 'I do believe that I detected a voice there, yes?'

'Er, no...'

I have never seen Ruth blush before.

'Well I'm sure the ladies and gentlemen would like to hear more from you, wouldn't you ladies and gentlemen?'

A great cheer goes up, as the M.C. shows Ruth the song list.

From the first line, the chatter stops, as everybody focuses on the source of the clear but sensuous sound. From the limited list, Ruth had chosen 'Secret Love.' And as she sings it she's looking straight at me. The place is absolutely packed, and there's not one of them who realises as she sings over their heads, that this song is mine and mine alone. And not one of them sees me blowing her a kiss as she finishes. I'd started to think that all those months of wanting her were coming to nothing. But I know now, in this one precious and unforgettable moment, that she feels the same way.

-Chapter 43-

1st October 1987
11.10pm

The key, Richard had once said to Ruth at the beginning of their short career as a band, is to make every man in the room think you're singing just for him. This was something that she had learned to do when she was doing the club circuits, and the attention she got at the end of the night was flattering, although Richard was always close by.

As the pensioners started to disappear the stag party took their seats. Most of them were totally insensible, but a lean man with thick black hair and large blue eyes engaged Ruth in conversation. After five minutes she was laughing, oblivious to anyone else, leaning towards the man, taking in every word. After ten minutes she made the first touch, a quick but gentle forefinger on his wrist, which was returned, and then another.

'Ruth.' called Martin, but she hadn't heard him.

'Ruth!' He leaned over, tapping her elbow. 'Jamie's taken Mickey back, and I think it's time for us to go.'

Ruth looked at her watch, then to Eddie who had put on a pair of sunglasses and was doing his 'cool' frown, then to Rita, who was watching someone putting money into a slot machine.

'We're OK for a bit, surely?' she said, turning back to her conversation.

'A bit' became nearly an hour. The bar staff were beginning to stack the chairs, all but one of the stag party had moved on to a nightclub, and Rita was still watching the same man feed the slot machine. Ruth had taken time out to introduce Martin to 'Mark', before returning to her conversation, which was now about their mutual love of seventies concept albums.

'Ruth was in a band once, weren't you Ruth?'

'Er, yes... but whatever you say about 'Tales from Topographic Oceans,' surely 'The Wall' was the ultimate album...'

'With her boyfriend, Richard, wasn't it?'

Ruth's lips pursed,' my ex-boyfriend, Richard, now where were we...'

Martin looked away, not quite sure what his face was doing in reaction to her revelation.   He removed an empty pint glass from Eddie, who had been spinning it on the table, and handed it to one of the wary looking bar staff, then retrieved his and Eddie's coats from under the table. Ruth was saying something like *no, I'm working,* when Mark gave her a piece of paper with his phone number on it, before kissing her and leaving to catch up with his friends.

'What do you think you're playing at?' hissed Ruth.

'What do you mean?'

'Mentioning Richard like that.'

'I was just trying to get in on the conversation. Anyway, I didn't know you and Richard were finished.'

Ruth looked awkward. 'Well we're not...well sort of...we had a big argument the other day about something he did when he came around to the Bungalow. He... Martin?'

'What?'

'Rita.'

Martin looked over to Rita, who now had her head on the shoulder of the man at the slot machine. The man was wiry with a sallow complexion and deep-set eyes with dark rings under them. He wore faded denims and a silver dragon tooth pendant on his sparsely haired chest.

'Shit.' What do we do now? Should I go over and stop it?'

'Stop what?'

'It. Rita being chatted up.'

'Do we have a right to?'

Martin paused, trying to take in what Ruth was saying. She smiled when she saw his puzzled expression, and continued:

'Do we have a right to go up to single woman in a bar and tell her she can't talk to who she wants to?'

Martin looked at Ruth incredulously, then to Rita, who had kissed the man on his cheek and had the kiss returned, then back to Ruth.'

'Can't you see what's happening? If we can't stop him talking to her, then we can't stop him shagging her, then we can't stop her having a baby and...'

Ruth was laughing. 'I'm winding you up. But go on, what do we do?'

As Martin, Ruth and Eddie approached Rita, it seemed like the problem was resolving itself, as the man kissed her again and left.

'Who was that, Rita?'

'Gay'am'

'Graham?'

'Yeah. Ma boyf'end.'

'Oh,' said Martin 'Well we've all had a good night, so let's get off to bed, eh?'

Rita folded her arms and pouted. 'No. Gay'am say way 'ere.'

Ruth looked startled. 'So where has he gone?'

Rita made two quick strokes on her chest, signing *toilet.*

'Whose in the cupboard...' sang Eddie, who up until that moment had been quietly basking in the newfound glow of rock stardom,

'Rang the bell
Made the noise,
Broke the cup
Burst the balloon,
Tied the socks
Naughty Mr. Hill.'

'I'm just going to waiter me oss,' said Martin, as he headed for the door.

'What?'

'It's an old Stoke saying.'

Before Ruth had worked it out, Martin had gone.

He returned about two minutes later.

'That feels better. Rita, I saw Graham, and he said he was sorry but he had to dash. He left you this.'

Rita was filling her lungs in preparation for a scream, when she saw the dragon tooth necklace.

*

The first thing that Graham was aware of when he came round was a throbbing pain in his right cheek. The next thing was that his right arm was soaking wet and stank of urine. Groaning, he sat up and removed his arm from the urinal.

What the fuck...

He remembered getting hold of some good gear earlier in the day, with the money he'd got for a full jewellery box he'd lifted the night before. Taking off his denim jacket he rang the sleeve out onto the floor.

One of the bar staff came in to check the toilets.

'Time you weren't here mate.'

'Oh fuck o...' Graham threw up in the urinal. As he was frogmarched out he remembered how he had been at the bar getting slowly- well, quickly- out of his skull. A woman had been hanging onto him at the slot machine.

Some mental bird, but so what, she'd got tits and the same equipment as anybody else.

Sitting on the pavement outside the bar, oblivious to the cold wet tarmac, Graham tried to piece together the events of the last few minutes. He had gone for a slash. He had told her to wait for him. Although his bladder was killing him he found it difficult to wee with a semi-erection. Then he was tapped on the shoulder. Someone had said 'she's with me.'

Then the lights went out.

-Chapter 44-

2nd October 1987
8.15 a.m.

I'm coming round from a troubled sleep, where Della is stalking me with a chainsaw. I can hear   Simeon's voice:
'What's going on?'
I wish he'd shut the fuck up, I think, turning my back on the source of the question and trying to get back to sleep.
'I'm going to set my dog on you,' says Eddie
'O.K., but I'm trying to sleep.'
'Martin, get him away from me.'
Della! What the fuck is she doing here. I jump up into sitting and look around. There's nobody else there, apart from Eddie, asleep in the next bed.
A bright glint of autumn light cuts through a crack at the top of the heavy curtains, the luminous face of my travel alarm reading 8.15.
Last night I'd had a sort of argument with Ruth, firstly about the man she'd met at the bar, then about my method of dealing with Rita's 'Graham.' Jamie and Mickey were fast asleep in their room when we'd returned. Eddie went straight to bed, as did Rita, in floods of tears, clutching Graham's necklace. My fantasy of domestic bliss which emerged whenever I was on sleep-ins with Ruth had now moved onto the stage where the honeymoon is over and arguments are hissed to avoid waking the children. The last words she said to me were 'control freak.'

'I'm going to set my dog on you.'

275

TASTING THE WIND

It was Eddie. I look over at him. His eyes are closed, his duvet rising and falling steadily.

The next voice shocks me even more than Della's had: it's my own.

'NO. He's joking with you, you stupid...'

I jump up, almost falling out of bed.

'Jamie...Jamie...God you make me die you do.'

The fact that Eddie's lips aren't moving eventually leads me to conclude that it's actually Ruth who is speaking. The sound of her laughter comes from outside, followed by hammering, which disturbs Eddie from his slumber

'What's that noise?'

Reaching for my specs, I peer out through the crack in the curtains. Ruth sits on the wall, rocking with laughter, and Jamie is standing on it, wearing one shoe. With the other he is hammering drawing pins into a piece of cardboard to cover up part of the sign outside the apartment.

'We -re-fuse-to-be-la-belled.'

*

This is it: our only full day in Blackpool, so I'm determined that they get the full experience- the Golden Mile with its stalls and arcades, the promenade, all three piers, fish and chips from newspaper, sea food, fresh doughnuts and candyfloss.

The wax works is a big hit with Eddie and Rita. Rita giggles or hides, and Eddie strikes up conversations with several of the dummies. At the pleasure beach Mickey laughs uncontrollably at the clatter of the big dipper trucks, and Eddie shows such great interest in everything that we take it in turns to go on the rides with him, until the fish and chips, the doughnuts, the sea food and candy floss show signs of making a comeback. Eddie, however, just laughs, skips, jumps, and swings his carrier bag around like a Ferris wheel.

Earlier, Eddie had seen a rock stall and, pointing to a huge humbug, had asked to buy it. It occurred to me that it was the first time I'd seen him put anything into his carrier bag. He still slept with the bag, and took it everywhere with him. When the original one had developed a hole a few weeks ago, he had requested another 'for me gear', taken it off to his room and privately emptied into it the contents of the old one. As the bag opened briefly he said 'keepsake,' as he dropped the humbug in, and for the first time I glimpsed one of the objects he carries, which is a hard backed book. I wondered if this was yet another diary.

*

At one point we're walking along and I swear I hear somebody call my name out. I look round, and there's a hen party of about ten girls, all dressed in red with devil horns.

' Martin,' calls one of the girls, 'It's me, Gill.'

' Sorry... Oh, Gill. How the hell are you? I didn't recognise your voice.'

It was Gill, who had intercepted my reference request from Moonfield Road, and sent out my own version on headed notepaper. As she was Foster's secretary she had easily reproduced his signature, then sent it through the office mail system.

'Didn't recognise my voice? No wonder. You're already talking like a southerner. This is a spooky coincidence- I was only talking about you this morning.'

Now anybody else would probably think it was more than a co-incidence that on one of the days I'm up from London I bump into somebody I used to work with in Stoke, but when you realise that half the population of the potteries must find their way to Blackpool at some point during the year, I'm not convinced there's anything particularly 'spooky' about it. That is until she tells me what they were talking about, and that does make my flesh crawl. 'Now listen very carefully....'

'I shall say this only once...'

'Martin, this is serious. It's just that there is something you need to know: someone has been after you.'

'After me? Who?'

'He didn't say. He had a London accent and said that he was having to check up on your job application.'

'But I applied nearly a year ago. Did he say anything else?'

'Well, yes. When I said that Mr. Foster wasn't available but that I was his personal assistant and could take a message, he said that he just wanted to confirm your University and qualifications.'

'Shit. And you've no Idea who it was?'

'No. Except he had quite a deep voice, but occasionally said something that made me think it was a woman...'

-Chapter 45-

We watch the sun go down into a cool dark sea as the illuminations come on. I zip up Mickey's thick coat, then my own, and we decide to walk through the lights and find a watering hole- one in a different part of town to last night's pub. All day Ruth has been distant, speaking only when she had to, always staying on the other side of our group, and It's difficult to tell whether it's her or Rita who's the most disappointed not to be going back to the karaoke bar. I'm beginning to wonder if her serenading me over the heads of all those people really happened, or if it was just the product of a deranged mind.

The 'pub' we eventually end up in is a large bar at the end of one of the piers. We're keeping a very close eye on Rita as she again watches at the slot machine, but this time the man looks old enough to be her granddad. Mickey is dozing off after a day of fresh air and walking. A large part of the time he had actually walked, either tottering along unaided or holding onto his own wheelchair. Eddie has gone with Jamie for a ride on the illuminated rocket tram he'd seen the night before, leaving me and Ruth to sit in silence.

'All right, what's wrong then?' she says.

'Nothing.'

'What do you mean, nothing? You've hardly spoken to me all day...'

'I've hardly spoken to you? It's more the other way round...anyway, it doesn't matter, because I'm not going to be around much longer.'

'Why?'

'It might have escaped your attention, but Della's trying to get rid of me. I've had a formal warning.'

'What about?'

'Oh the thing with Eddie and the car. Have you ever heard anything so ridiculous?'

'Well I suppose it was a stolen car... and driving without a licence, and....'

'Thanks.'

' But it's only a verbal warning. All that you have to do is keep your nose clean, and after a year it'll be off your record.'

I take a drink. 'Problem is she's already onto the next one.'

'What?'

'There's something I've been keeping secret since I started here. I faked my reference to get the job. I thought I'd long since got away with it, but Gill- the girl I bumped into earlier, says someone's been asking about it. And I think that someone is Della.' I take another swig. ' And while I'm at it: I faked my qualifications. I said I was a graduate so I could get the job.'

Ruth has a faint smile on her face as she wipes a thin trail of coke-streaked saliva from the sleeping Mickey's chin.

'That's not exactly a secret, Martin.'

'What?'

We are interrupted by Jamie and Eddie returning from their jaunt. Eddie looks sullen, and sits muttering, his head down, not seeming to notice the pint of Guinness placed in front of him.

'Jamie,' says Ruth, shuffling to the edge of her seat, 'you know that Martin hasn't got a degree, don't you?'

'Ruth...' I can hardly speak, feeling my face turning suddenly hot, 'what the f...'

'Oh yeah,' says Jamie, slipping the change into a pocket of his combat jacket. 'Course I do... well have we had an interesting evening, or what?'

'Just a minute,' I hear myself saying, feeling like this isn't really happening, 'can we just go back to the last conversation. How did you know?'

Ruth and Jamie look at each other, then splutter into laughter.

'So what's so funny?'

'It's just that it doesn't matter,' says Jamie, ' as long as Della doesn't find out.'

'But I think she has found out. She's been phoning my old work place. Next she'll be phoning UMIST...what's so funny?'

Tears roll down Ruth's face and Eddie is joining in as everybody in the bar starts to turn to see what's going on.

'We worked it out ages ago,' she says, 'shall I tell him?'

Jamie nods.

'Tell me what?'

'It was Jane who pointed it out. You're supposed to have a degree in art: UMIST does science and technology.'

'Oh shit. It was the only degree certificate I could get hold of. My mate Dave, his brother went to university, and Dave nicked his certificate, doctored it up and made a copy. The stupid git.'

'Anyway, says Jamie,' I was going to tell you about our rocket trip.'

'Oh,' says Ruth, 'you got on it then?'

'Got on it? We queued for about an hour to get on it. Ordinary trams came and went, a Mississippi steamboat came, and a western steam train, but no, it had to be the rocket. So it came, and we got on it. It set off, and Eddie says 'where's the rocket then?' Of course, inside it's like an ordinary tram, so he's whinged all the way from Bispham to Starr Gate. '

I'm aware that I'm now flapping my hands, and how it must look, but I can't think of any other way to get their attention.

'Sorry to interrupt, but can you tell me what I do now?

' It's O.K.,' says Ruth. Haven't you noticed that we're not all graduates? It's not really a graduate job, but there weren't enough replies to the first advert, so Des Machin, the area manager had the idea that if he put the word 'Graduate' in big letters it might attract people who hadn't applied previously. So I wouldn't worry about it.'

'There is a problem though,' says Jamie, now looking very serious. 'It is a sackable offence to forge qualifications. Are you sure Della knows?'

Rita whoops as her sugar daddy drops the jackpot.

'Does Simeon know?' I ask.

There's a silence as Jamie and Ruth take a drink.

'Then she does know.'

-Chapter 46-

It's getting towards midnight as we approach Gynn Square on our final walk along the front. A few cars are still passing through the lights, but it's quieter now, so that where an endless black expanse lies beyond the sea wall you can hear the sea lapping. There is a chilly wind, and I imagine how, if Andrew had been with us, his tongue would have relished it. Jamie had offered to take Mickey back. I'd put up an argument, but he insisted, and winked as he left. I'm not surprised after tonight's revelation that yet another of my amazingly well kept secrets- namely, my feelings for Ruth- is also public knowledge.

'What are those lights?' asks Ruth sleepily.

'The Illuminations. Didn't you know?'

'Not those' she squeals, slapping me on the arm, 'those' pointing to glimmering lights out at sea, which are off shore oilrigs. Things are starting to warm up between us. Maybe the timing is right. Richard's off the scene, I'm free and single, so tonight I make my move.

Eddie and Rita are slightly in front of us. Eddie starts singing his 'Mr. Hill' song, and Rita joins in. It was Jamie who had pointed out that even after all this time The People rarely communicated with each other. They all related to staff (even Andrew, who could spit out food he didn't like) but that was a survival thing, learned at the hospital to keep in with the people who gave you what you needed. And that was a million miles away from friendly, give and take relationships. So we were encouraging communication between The People. It was happening more with Rita and Eddie than anybody else- she had made him a cup of tea a few weeks before the holiday and he'd kissed her.

Although she had turned bright red and run around shrieking for the rest of the evening, it was significant.

'Who's in the cupboard?'
'Who in va cabba?'
'Ruth?'
'Yes, Martin?' says Ruth, straightening up and mimicking my suddenly formal tone.
'Rang the bell...'
'Ran da beow...'
'I just wanted to say...well surely, you must know...'
'Made the noise...'
' May da noy...'
'Know what?'
'Smashed the cup...'
'Sma da cab...'
'Right. I'm obviously not expressing myself.'

I know that this is an understatement. In fact I knew from the moment I'd started that it was a mistake and that if I ever got to the end of it I already knew what the answer would be. I remember how I'd had this trouble asking Jo out, and that eventually she'd asked me.

'Burst the balloon...'
'Bur balloo...'
'Climbed the wall...'
'O.K....let me get to the point. I need to let you know how I f...
'Climb a wow...'
'How I f... FUCK!'

A new line has been added to Eddie's chant, and it is being sung from somewhere above. I look up to see him balancing on the sea wall against an ink black backdrop, his arms held out like wings, the carrier bag flapping in the wind, his head tipped back as he howls at the unseen moon. The twinkling illuminations reflect on the wall, which is wet with rain and sea-spray. If Eddie slips, he will at first slide down the sloping structure, but eventually he will land either on hard, skull-cracking rock or in the dark, freezing sea.

Eddie flaps his arms, shouting: 'I can fly.'

Rita is first to have an idea. Folding her arms she shouts: 'Eggie, I no your frien' an' more,' then storms off the way we had come. She knows that this is the way we had got her to follow us so many times. It works for Rita, but not for Eddie, who calls out again, 'I can fly.'

Ruth is about to make a move when I put my hand on her arm and say 'I can handle it.' I move slowly toward Eddie, talking calmly.

'Eddie, come down, you could fall and hurt yourself.'

'No, I can fly, I'm Peter Pan'

'Eddie, Pansy is tired, we need to get him to bed.'

'Silly Martin sees things. Pansy isn't here.'

I move a little closer. 'O.K. How about us going back and seeing if we can find some fish and chips?'

'...Shandchips...' Eddie looks at me and smiles.

Then the lights go off.

There is a shout of surprise, the sound of denim sliding against stone, a dull thud, then silence, apart from the lapping of waves in the dark, cold expanse.

-Chapter 47-

1st October 1987

The day that the group left for Blackpool, Jane had waved them off, wondering how the subtext to the holiday would work out. She had seen the glances that Martin gave to Ruth when he thought that no one was looking, how his eyes drifted over her bottle-blond hair as if he were discovering the Golden Fleece. She wondered which version of Ruth Martin had fallen for. Probably *poor me*, who was neglected by the man she loved, the man who had never even told her he loved her, and was probably screwing every woman within his orbit. Martin would never recognise the Ruth that Jane had come to know- the one who was well aware of the affect she had on almost every man she met, and who hadn't been exactly chaste herself with respect to the delightful Richard. She swallowed hard at the thought of Martin getting hurt.

Looking up, Jane focussed on the parcel that had arrived from Colin that morning, and her frown was replaced by a broad smile. On the day that Colin had left so dramatically both Della and the staff were, for the first time in the history of the Bungalow, unanimous in their belief: Colin had had a break down. He had done it in style, telling the truth and spoiling Della's big day, yet nevertheless it was a breakdown.

But this morning all was made clear when a large parcel arrived, containing several signed copies of a novel called 'Integrating Arthur,' by Colin Macallan. In it a care worker writes a best selling book based on his experiences, and as a publicity stunt does a public strip.

That explains it, thought Jane. *That's why he was taking notes all the time. We were his raw material.*

Flicking through one of the copies, Jane had ascertained that it was about a group of people moving out of hospital. One of the stars was a man with Down Syndrome, who had an invisible hamster. There was a recognisable assortment of residents and staff, and they were all terrorised by their manager, a small man with an unusually high voice. She had wondered about reading it Martin style by starting at the last page, but again resisted the temptation.

I wonder if Martin knows how much of him has rubbed off on me?

Knowing how Colin felt about Della she was certain that the manager in Colin's book would come to a very sticky end, one which Martin would enjoy, but would read well before he knew why it was deserved.

The photographer from the local newspaper had taken quite a few snaps of the real event of Colin's leave-taking, knowing that there were tabloid-sized earnings to be had from them. Jane now realised what Colin was doing: the story in the 'News of the World,' together with that of the Tory MP's attempt to have him arrested for indecent exposure, would assure huge sales of his book, enough to provide him with an ample pension.

Colin had sent a signed copy for everyone. Jamie's had an envelope taped inside the front cover; Della's had the message:

> *To Della,*
> *Shove this up your arse, but read it first, as it has a lot of insights about what it is like to be truly human. Hope you get all you deserve from life,*
>
> > *Colin*

Putting the book aside, Jane picked up one of Eddie's mum's diaries -1970- and flicked to where she had left off:

How can I prove that this child, whose mind seems locked away from the world, can love? Better start with the fact that love is one of the building blocks of the universe, as essential as atoms, and that nothing can exist without it. Then say: prove to me that he cannot love.

Surprised at the sudden change in tone from what had gone before in the diaries, she read the passage again and realised that she had mistakenly resumed her reading at the fifteenth of July, instead of the fifteenth of June.

So what happened? Love is one of the building blocks of the universe? I thought this woman hated the universe for what it had done to her son...

Jane turned the pages back, then read on, until she arrived at the entry for the twentieth of June:

Last night I had a dream in which Edward was running around with a red balloon on a string...he was laughing and talking to me. When I asked him what the balloon meant, he said: 'the balloon is colourful and causes smiles and laughter wherever it goes. Although it is little more than air, we ascribe to it value. I suppose that's the nature of balloons. As is their fragility, their transience. Look upon it and learn of me.'
When I awoke I wept, and it felt as if the years of bitterness, the mental anguish and spiritual yearning for my lost faith were flowing from me. I looked at Edward and remembered how he appeared in the dream, and it came to me that this was no fancy, but a mother's intuition, which had connected me with his inner self, his Ruach. And I knew that from that moment it was my life's task to find a way to bring him out of his silence.

Jane felt a sudden surge of excitement, knowing that soon she would find the secret of how Eddie's communication skills and physical abilities were accelerated. But who could she tell? Martin would not be back for a couple of days, and Simeon and Della, who were due to arrive at any moment, had piously refused to have anything to do with the diaries.

The last time that Jane had worked with Simeon he had tried, again, to engage her in a theological debate. She knew that his motive was never to have a discussion, but to point out the error of her ways and convert her back to the truth- his truth, his unanalytical, interpretational, intellectually insulting, truth. She had once made the mistake of referring to 'St. Paul', resulting in a long diatribe about how all believers were saints.

'Including you?' She had asked.

'Including me.'

287

When she related this to Martin, he had asked what Simeon was the saint of, eventually suggesting that it should be 'St. Simeon the Wanker.'

Simeon And Della arrived together. Simeon was just concluding the punch line to a joke about Catholics, and both of them were in an unusually jocular mood.

'This way, this way,' said Della, in a singsong voice. Two men in overalls followed her. One of them carried a fold-up bed, still packed in cardboard and cellophane.

'Jane, could you unpack this?'

Jane took a sharp knife from the kitchen drawer, and started to cut the wrapping, wondering about the destination of the folding bed. The two men came out of the sleep-in room carrying a mattress and when they returned they took the base of the bed, which they squeezed out of the door, and into the back of a Social Services van.

'Della,' asked Jane quietly, 'what's this bed for?'

'Sleep-ins' snapped Della, as if no other explanation were needed.

Throughout the afternoon there were sawing and hammering sounds from the room. At one point the men took in a large board. They left just before The People were due to return and, no longer able to deny her curiosity, Jane went in to see what they had been doing.

The window of the sleep-in room was boarded up, and there wasn't a single piece of furniture left. Monet prints that Martin had brought in had been taken from the powder blue walls. The men had fitted a peephole to the door, and changed the handle so that it locked only from the outside. Jane went to where the window had been. The board fitted perfectly and was nailed firmly, so that no natural light would ever enter that room again.

'Excellent,' said Della, filling the doorway and plunging the room into almost complete darkness. ' You see, this room is wasted during the day. The new fold-up bed will be stored in the utility room and only brought in here at night for the sleep-in. During the day this will make a perfect time-out room.'

-Chapter 48-

2nd October 1987
10.45 p.m.

Mickey's eyes were half shut as he held out an arm for Jamie to help him into his pyjama jacket.

'Sea air, Mick. Have you ever been to the seaside?'

'bubububub' said Mickey, in a tone of sleepy contentment.'

'Mind you, from what I remember from your file, you've travelled a bit haven't you?'

Jamie recalled with sadness what he had read in Mickey's file when he first met him, how Mickey had been born in Hong Kong to wealthy parents, how they had taken him all round the world to find a 'cure' and how, when their money, their health and their patience had begun to run low, they had left him at the hospital. In some research that Jamie had been undertaking about British mental handicap hospitals he found that Mickey was just one of eleven hundred children between the ages of five and ten who were admitted to institutions in nineteen sixty-six. Each of the eleven hundred children and families would have their own story of heartbreak. In Jamie's mind the advent of places like the Bungalow represented hope and a new start. But something was going wrong at the Bungalow, and if it was not righted soon it would end up providing the people with a life style as institutional and devaluing as anything the hospital had delivered.

'Bububububub,' said Mickey, bringing Jamie back from his train of thought.

'Sorry mate...where was I? Oh yes: travel. That's what I'm going to be doing next- travelling, seeing the world. With a bit of luck, Julie will come with me.'

Jamie swung Mickey's legs up into the bed and pulled the duvet over him.

' This time next year I should be in India. You've got to grab these things while you're young, Mick- you never know what's round the corner. But first I've got to make sure that you lot are O.K. When everything's settled I'll be off, and not before.'

As Mickey slipped into a peaceful sleep, Jamie reached a can of Red Stripe from his rucksack, and a book about travelling in Asia. He cracked open the can, and sat on his bed, thumbing through the book.

But that won't be before she's gone.

*

'Fa' off' screamed Rita, announcing her arrival. Jamie jumped from his semi-slumber as he heard a bedroom door bang shut, followed by the unmistakable sound of Rita hurling herself onto her bed, then bursting into tears. As Jamie leapt to his feet he heard Ruth trying to comfort her. Something was wrong. This was not a tantrum, but heartfelt sobbing.

'It's all right Rita,' said Ruth, as Jamie approached the bedroom, 'everything will be all right.'

'Fa' off, Ru.' Something thudded against the door. Jamie opened it to see a mangled Gideon Bible and Ruth, her eyes brimming with tears.

'What's wrong?'

'I'll see you later, Rita' said Ruth, closing the door behind her. 'Jamie, I need to talk to you.'

'So what happened?' asked Jamie, as they sat down on the settee. Ruth dabbed her eyes with a tissue.

' After you left, there was an accident.'

'Accident?'

'Eddie fell off a sea wall. Fortunately, he fell this way, onto the path. It's just the thought of what would have happened if he'd fallen the other way.'

'So where is he now?'

'He's gone to his room. Martin wanted to check him for bruises.'

Ruth began to sob and Jamie put his arm around her. 'So what's up with Rita?' he asked.

'Oh, she wanted to go and find that git she was with last night. When we told her it was too late she went apeshit and knocked Martin's glasses off.'

'So a good night was had by all.'

Ruth looked up. Her face, streaked with tears, was now smiling as Jamie hugged her.

Unseen by either of them, the door to Martin and Eddie's room was quietly closed.

*

Shit.

I hadn't had a good day. Ruth had ignored me for most of it, then I'd had to face the possibility of Eddie taking a dive over the sea-wall. I can't get the pictures out of my mind: Eddie, either with his head smashed against a rock, or drowned in an ice-cold sea, all because we weren't paying enough attention.

Then Rita, raging to see the loser I'd flattened the night before, swipes my specs off my face, cracking a lens. Now, to top the lot, I'm creeping from the bedroom so as not to wake Eddie, only to see Ruth and Jamie sitting on a chintzy settee in an amorous clinch.

Great. Fucking Great. I would have left London a long time ago, if it hadn't been for her. But she wasn't free was she? I get to come away with her for two nights, and each one is spent with a different bloke. Fucking Marvellous. Well, I'd better go in. And this time I'll let them know I'm coming.

'Goodnight Eddie, sleep well.' I call, closing the door.

'Sounds like you've had a sod of a night Martin,' says Jamie, 'perhaps you want to offload?'

'Either there's something wrong with the drains,' I say, sniffing the air, 'or the man from the bullshit farm's just delivered.'

'Point taken,' says Jamie, passing me a can, 'not that I should be encouraging you to drink on duty, but you look like you need it. So is Eddie O.K. now?'

'Not a bruise. It's shaken him though, but he's just dropped off.'
'So I'd heard,'
'Ha bloody Ha.'

'Sorry.'

' He seems O.K. now, but he's been doing the 'they killed him at Christmas' thing again.'

Ruth sits forward as if something I've just said has jolted her.

'What's up Ruth?' Asks Jamie, who also seems to have noticed her reaction.

'Nothing really, it's just that... you mean you've heard it before?'

'Well yes, but I didn't think anyone else had.'

Ruth takes a drink from her can and offers round a bag of doughnuts she'd bought from a stall by a pier. We wait for Jamie to comment, but he's unusually quiet, so   we just sit listening to the wind and, somewhere in the distance, the crashing of waves.

' He sometimes mentions it in his Mr. Hill chant,' says Ruth 'I thought it might have had something to do with Billy, because he says something like 'tied the socks, killed the man,' but I don't know what the socks have got to do with it...Jamie, are you O.K.?'

'What...oh yes, fine...it's just that I've got onto a train of thought and I don't like where it's taking me.'

There was more shouting from the bedroom:

'They killed him... they killed him at Christmas.'

We sit for a while in total silence, listening to the whistling sound from the old gas fire and the rattling of the window frames. Saying 'goodnight,' Jamie reminds me of a sleepwalker as he gets up to go to bed. Ruth and I share a look of concern, but I suddenly feel my face getting hot, and know that I'm blushing. For the first time since we'd met, I really don't want to be alone with her. I fiddle with my glasses, checking that the cracked lens isn't going to fall out.

'God, Martin,' says Ruth, 'I've never noticed what nice eyes you've got.'

'All the better to...I, er, don't want to be too late myself tonight' I say, starting to get up. 'Long journey tomorrow.'

'Hang on, Martin, when we were walking, before Eddie climbed onto the wall, you said you had something to tell me.'

I stop, look around, and say, 'it's not important now.'

*

At some point during the night I have a really vivid dream about the day I got Eddie to drive the car.

Simeon:	What's going on?
Eddie:	I'm going to set my dog on you.
Della:	Get him off me. Get him off.
Me:	NO. He's joking with you, you stupid...

In a brief gap of consciousness, like sunlight momentarily breaking through clouds, I'm aware that I'm awake, and that the voices are in the room.

Simeon:	Come on Eddie.
Me:	Where are you taking him?
Della:	In the absence of a time-out room it will have to be his bedroom- he needs a little time out to calm down.
Me:	Him calm down? It's not him that needs....

Amazed at the accuracy of Eddie's impressions, I try to listen to the rest, but all of the walking and sea air have tired me out. As I drift in and out of sleep, incidents from my time at the Bungalow play and re-play in my mind, Eddie's references to death and murder going round in a loop of constant background noise. At one point I see Colin, and he tells me he thinks that Eddie and Della have met before; next I'm with the fortune-teller, who is holding a badge and saying that its original owner witnessed a murder. As I finally fall into a restless sleep, I hear old Arthur's voice:

She's followed you boy, she's followed you here... and now she's found you she'll probably kill you... Eddie thought he was escaping. But he's been followed here. Now no one is safe.'

*

Jamie tossed and turned as Mickey snored softly in the bed next to him. Patterns were beginning to emerge in his mind which he was finding difficult to ignore. He had been a student at the hospital up to and after the Christmas of 1976. He remembered returning after the break to hear that a patient had died on Christmas Day. The patient was a man who wore socks as gloves.

It had become clear to him tonight that each member of staff had their own independent accounts of Eddie's references to a murder. He had heard things himself but, like everyone else, had dismissed them as the fantasies of a man with an imaginary dog.

Until tonight.

The night when it had become clear to him to whom the statements were related.

The night when Jamie finally remembered where he had first seen Della.

-Chapter 49-

3rd October 1987
6.15 a.m.

Madame Delores had woken from a troubled sleep. Her dreams had been filled with apocalyptic images, culminating in the world swirling in a vortex and disappearing down a giant plughole. Feeling that this was a weather dream, she pulled in a clump of seaweed and a large pinecone from her window ledge. The weed was limp and wet, the pinecone tightly closed. After consulting the star charts and the tarot, followed by a forty minute session focussing on her crystal ball, she felt that the warning was loud and clear: there was going to be a storm. A great storm.

4.15 p.m.

'You are turning it into the fucking hospital!'

'I would thank you for not swearing at me Jamie.' says Della, in her false calm manner. The argument is coming from the closed door to Della's office. There are no hushed voices and no attempt to stop the fight from spilling out. Jamie's professionalism can no longer stand up to such an onslaught on the things that mean so much to him and it's as if we've all sensed that when this happens it signals the beginning of the end.

'It's a time out room. People live here, it's their home and you have created a time out room.'

Jane, Ruth, Simeon and me sit around the kitchen table. Seeing Jamie's face when he spotted the spy-hole in the door, Howard,

295

who had been sent that day from the agency, had taken Rita for a walk. Oscar is out, and the rest of The People are either in their rooms or watching the T.V. Around the table all heads are down, nobody taking any pleasure in what they're hearing- it's as if a crack that we had always known was there has suddenly opened under too great a pressure, and a deluge is about to break through the growing gash.

'It is perfectly acceptable practice if used properly.'

'And when is it ever used properly?'

Jane sits next to me, holding her head in her hands. She looks like she's had enough.

'Has it been that bad?'

A tear wells in her eye.

'Well...yes....' She looks like she's got a lot to tell me, but Simeon's earwigging our conversation as well as the argument in the office. '...There was one highlight: we had a friend of yours here doing agency work,'

'A friend of mine?'

'Yes, your flatmate, Kevin.'

'Oh, right. Kevin.'

'Martin.'

'Yes?'

'Why does he...'

'We don't ask... so what's happened?'

She explains how Andrew had had a series of seizures and nearly been hospitalised again. He was still in bed, and Jane had got hold of one of those baby monitors, so that staff could hear if there were any more fits during the night. Rose was also having a day off from the centre. Last night she'd had a fall and yanked her stiff arm. Zuska had been over this morning and massaged it with a pungent oil. She'd said that although falling and hurting herself was not recommended procedure, Rose's flexibility would probably be improved in the long term.

'It's all going wrong, isn't it?' says Jane.

She has a tragic look, as if the Bungalow, or what it stands for, has been pronounced terminally ill. 'Just look at what it's done to Oscar,' she says, almost sobbing. 'He was so drunk when he came in last night he couldn't find his room. He's putting loads of weight on and I think he's getting depressed.'

'But,' I say, knowing I'm saying the wrong thing as it leaves my lips, 'Oscar is making his own choices...'

'Yes Martin, but how informed are those choices? People are unhappy and we have done it to them. Is this what it means to be part of the community- everybody has the right to drink themselves to death, so why not them?'

I take her hand, and say 'don't let it get to you. This isn't like you. Surely this is better than the hospital.'

'Is it?'

I look around at the drab decor, the dull corridors off the dining room, and the row of three doors- one the door to the dangerous and unaccepting outside world, the others the door to the time out room and Della's office: a punishment room and a nurse's station by any other name.

'Is it really?'

I notice for the first time that the carpet is a patchwork of stains and the ghosts of stains that the most thorough cleanings have failed to remove. Although they'd been able to splash out on the original building of the Bungalow, subsequent funding cuts had meant that repairs and maintenance were almost non-existent, and even Della's obsession with order and cleanliness has failed to impose itself, apart from the ever-present smell of bleach which is like a constant reminder of the hospital.

'But it doesn't work like that,' says Jamie. I've seen it. People are put in there for a few minutes, another incident happens and they are forgotten.'

'So it is up to us to make sure that staff do it properly.'

Della's voice has that fake tone of serenity, which I always find irritating. Each sentence is deeper and slower than the last, and I can tell that she's smiling.

'Sounds like bloody Margaret Thatcher' I blurt out.

'I think that's a bit unfair, Martin,' says Simeon. 'Jamie shouldn't really be talking to his manager like that'

O.K., so maybe I wouldn't have said what I did if I hadn't been so tired after the holiday, but I pause, take a deep breath, and decide to say it anyway:

'Well, Sim, if he spoke to her like you do she might have trouble understanding what he's saying.'

'What do you mean?'

'I mean,' and by now I'm shouting, 'that his voice would be muffled if he stuck his head so far up her arse.'

'Martin...' Jane has put her hand on my arm and is stroking it. 'It's not worth it.'

'That is not what we are here for.' shouts Jamie.

'Well well,' says Della, 'so if we are not here to train them to fit into the real world, what are we here for?'

There's a pause in which the whole of the Bungalow seems to be draining into that office, as if some black hole is threatening to drag it in, sucking it clear of colour, of light, and of sound. Then Jamie's voice, much quieter now:

'Perhaps we could... give them a home... give them dignity... even love them.'

'Oh no no no no no.' says Della, with a derisive laugh in her voice, 'that is certainly not within our remit.'

No more is said, then the door opens, and Jamie comes out, looking paler than ever, and slams it.

'I'm going home now,' he says to Ruth and me, 'and I suggest that you two do the same. I didn't sleep well last night. Perhaps things will look better in the morning.'

As Jamie gathers his things together, Jane tells him about the parcel that arrived while we were away, and hands him his copy of Colin's novel. An envelope addressed to him is sellotaped inside the front cover, and as he reads the letter I see his eyes widen with a look somewhere between disbelief and horror.

I'm distracted from Jamie by the front door, which flies open as Rita stomps in, with Howard close behind, a red slap-mark on his face. She storms into her bedroom, the slamming door shaking the whole Bungalow. As Simeon comforts Howard, Jamie leans over and whispers:

'Come to my place at about nine o'clock. Bring Ruth and Jane.'

'What's wrong?'

'I'm not sure,' he says, waving Colin's letter, 'but things suddenly seem to be slotting into place. There's someone else I need to check things out with first, but I can't talk about it here. Promise you'll come.'

'Yes of course, but...'

Sitting on the floor at the end of the corridor, Mickey starts to bawl, as Eddie appears at the entrance of the lounge, beads of sweat

298

running down his forehead. He stares into space, muttering feverishly, the only discernible words being 'Mr. Hill.' For most of the weekend he had been the fun loving Eddie we had first met at the hospital. The moment we stepped into the Bungalow he'd immediately taken on a pale and haunted look. I walk slowly towards him, but he looks past me, a wild glint of fear in his eyes.

'It's the Devil,' he says, signalling for Pansy to come to his side, 'it's the Devil...he's here.'

***

3rd October 1987
9.15 p.m.

Where I come from squatters are an underclass, they are people who take advantage of the hard work of others and sneak into your house and crap it up. Down here it's different. Jamie lives in a squat, and he's not the only care worker who lives there. He's even given me a squatters' handbook, which tells you how to do it without falling foul of the law, in an effort to help me out with my accommodation search. It's just that the pathetic outer London allowance comes nowhere near to making up the difference in the cost of living between North and South. Most of the guys at the factory were now buying their own council houses, just like Maggie (God bless her) intended, but if you're living down south and you're in some lowly trade like ours you have to settle for rented accommodation or squats, leaving the million pound broom cupboards to the yuppies.

Jamie's room is quite sparse. His bed is a mattress on the floor, and the only items of furniture are a wardrobe and a well-stocked bookshelf. Next to his mattress is a ghetto blaster and a cardboard box half filled with cassette tapes. He'd been selling off his cassettes and books to help fund a trip he's planning to India. The player would be the last thing to go. He believes in travelling light, and when he returns he will start again, acquiring only what he needs for the next phase of his life.

'I'll get straight to the point,' says Jamie, once he's handed us all a can of 'Red Stripe.'

299

TASTING THE WIND

'I think I know what this is about ' I say, interrupting him.

'I don't think you do,' says Jamie, a weak smile breaking his grave expression, 'but go on...'

And I can tell that I'm right by Jamie's open-mouthed expression when I say 'you've brought us here to tell us that you think that Eddie was witness to a murder.'

-Chapter 50-

Both Ruth and Jane sit in a stunned silence, looking from me to Jamie.

'You're right,' says Jamie, but there's more to it isn't there?'

'I think so,' I say, feeling uneasy now, 'but I was hoping you might have something resembling evidence for the next bit...'

'O.K. boys,' says Jane, 'do you think you could stop talking in riddles and fill us in?'

Taking a long swig from his can, Jamie begins:

'It's just that ever since Della came to the Bungalow I've had this feeling that I'd seen her somewhere before. It should have been obvious where that was, her being an ex-nurse and all, but recently it's come back to me: she worked at the hospital when I was a student there. In those days her name was Della Cahill. I only saw her at a distance- and although she was big then she's put on a hell of a lot of weight since.'

'So she already knew some of The People,' I say, 'yet she has never mentioned it.... Hang on a minute, if her name was Cahill then some poor sod must have married her.'

'Divorced.'

'That figures' says Ruth. 'So is that your great revelation- that Della got a shag once?'

'No,' says Jamie, 'it was that I remembered hearing about how she left. I phoned Julie today- she started at the hospital at about that time- and she confirmed what I vaguely remembered: Della left under a cloud. Someone had died on the ward and there was something not quite right about it. There was an enquiry, and she got off, but it was one of those things where a lot of people that knew her would have sworn that she was responsible.'

'That explains something,' says Ruth, 'the fact that in all the time she's managed the Bungalow she's never been to the hospital. Too many bad memories... or was she afraid of being recognised?'

'But if there was an enquiry,' says Jane,' and she got off, how can you be so sure now?'

'I can't' says Jamie, drawing his knees up under his chin,' it's just that the man who died was called Frankie. He used to wear socks as gloves like Billy did. Julie reckons that the case fell down through lack of witnesses. Recently I've started to think that there was at least one.'

'Who's in the cupboard?' chants Ruth, 'rang the bell, made the noise...tied the socks...killed the man.'

'I've heard Eddie mention a Frankie before,' I say.

'So have I,' says Jane, 'but I always thought he was referring to Billy, because the staff all called him 'Frankie.' But even if Eddie knew the original Frankie, it's a bit of a long jump to what you're suggesting. I once thought that Eddie was trying to tell me something, and believe me I would love to pin something like this on Della, but I think you're jumping the gun. What proof have we got?'

'We know that Della was at the hospital, and that she was the subject of an enquiry' says Jamie. 'After talking to Julie today, I now know that Eddie and Andrew were on that ward at the same time. We should find that their files bear this out.'

'And,' says Ruth ' there is something between Della and Eddie. Rita exhibits far more in the way of 'challenging behaviour' but Della's in no rush to send her back to the hospital.'

'It was Colin who first suspected that Della knew Eddie,' I say. 'And he was convinced she had the potential to be an abuser.'

'Yes, says Jane,' but a murderer?

'That's the other thing,' says Jamie, passing Colin's letter around. Its tone is disturbing, frightening even, particularly as it was written by the normally laid-back Colin. It mentions his suspicions about Della- the ones he had shared with me- but goes on to say that on the day he left he felt that Della came close to revealing something far more serious.

'But murder?' says Jane. 'Besides, how can you kill somebody with a pair of socks?'

'You could strangle them.' suggests Ruth.

'No,' says Jamie. 'That would have left marks. Anyway, Julie told me that another reason Della got off was because it was proven that Frankie choked on his own vomit. Now it's not impossible, but he had an advanced scoliosis- a curved spine- which meant that he had to lie on his side. You're more likely to aspirate if you're lying on your back, and Frankie couldn't do that...'

'Unless...' I say, 'unless we start taking Eddie at his word. He always says 'tied the socks'.'

'Just listen to yourselves,' says Jane, 'you're sitting here talking like the cast of 'Scooby-Doo.' How will it all end, with Della saying 'I would have got away with it if it wasn't for you pesky kids.'?'

'The intellectual I can take,' says Jamie, 'the satirist is a bit harder to cope with. You've spent too long with Martin.'

I don't know what it is about what Jamie said but I've never seen Jane blush before, or be so effectively silenced.

'So, says Jamie, 'she used the socks to tie Frankie to his bed. They would have been secured to his wrists with sellotape like Billy's were, to stop him from taking them off. If he'd started to vomit he would have choked. I suppose that technically it's not murder, but Della would have known there was a chance that her actions could lead to his death. That virus was rife that year. I picked it up. Frankie would have been violently sick, but unable to turn onto his side because he was tied, cruciform to the...'

'Oh my God.'

'What is it, Jane?'

'Cruciform?'

'Yes, like on a cross...'

'I know what it means...it's just that...' we watch as Jane struggles with some realisation which is starting to persuade her, reluctantly, that what we are saying need not be pure speculation.

'It's just that the time I mentioned earlier, when I dismissed what Eddie said as meaningless rambling- he said 'they stretched his arms out.' I thought he was talking about Jesus, but then he said 'they killed him at Christmas.' When did Frankie die?'

'1976,' says Jamie, 'Christmas Eve, 1976.'

'So,' I say to Jane, 'do you see what we're saying?'

'Yes, O.K., but how do we prove it?'

Ruth's beer can shakes in her hand. 'The bitch. The murdering bitch. She can't be allowed to get away with it. Should we ask Eddie?'

' I don't think he would be considered a reliable witness,' says Jamie. 'He sees the world in a different way to us. He sees dogs that aren't there, calls things by different names. We've got to find another way.'

We sit in absolute silence. I don't know what the others are thinking, but in my mind I see a sky full of straws. And they are all flying in the direction of Della Belk.

'So you're agreeing with us? asks Jamie.

'I suppose I am, yes,' says Jane, 'at least it's a sound hypothesis. But at the risk of repeating myself: how do we prove it?'

'There is only one way to prove it' says Jamie.

'And what's that?' we say, almost in unison.

'It's easy. All we need to do... is to get Della to confess.'

-Chapter 51-

6th October 1987

For the plan to work, Jamie explained, it had to be carried out on a shift where he, Della, and at least two others were present. It was preferable that The People were not at home, but even more essential that Simeon was not around. This, Martin pointed out, was not going to be easy, because Della had planned the work rota so that most of Simeon's shifts coincided with hers.

The day, when it came, was a Tuesday, on which Martin and Jane were working, Simeon was on sick leave, and Jamie had asked Della for a private meeting, which she had granted. The meeting was to take place at two o'clock. At a quarter to two, Della was sitting at her desk, updating her strategic plan and recording 'to-do' notes on her Dictaphone. Ribbons of mist drifted from a china cup containing 'Kopi Luak' coffee. She savoured the aroma, distinctive among coffees, as the beans had firstly passed through the digestive systems of civets. Suddenly a high-pitched scream came from somewhere in the direction of the bathroom. Della took a sip of her coffee. She couldn't make out who it was, but she knew that there were sufficient staff around to deal with it without disturbing her. Another scream, this time longer and louder, then another, until Della, feeling a growing annoyance that her tranquil break was being interrupted, sprang to her feet and headed for the bathroom.

TASTING THE WIND

Through a crack in the lounge door, Martin saw the great black mass disappear down the corridor, and once he was certain that he would not be seen he went quickly but quietly into the office. In his hand he held the plug-in microphone apparatus of the baby monitor.

'There is only one free socket in the office,' Jamie had said. The ones near to the desk are all taken up with the computer.'

Passing by the desk he noted the truth of Jamie's observation.

' It's also important that it's plugged in well out of sight. Della is a classic Obsessive Compulsive. Everything in that office has a place, and if anything was different she would notice it immediately.'

Martin had seen the inside of Della's office on rare occasions, and each time the files and books on the shelves had been arranged in size or alphabetical order, the equipment on her desk in a perfectly straight line.

Next to a Dictaphone was a half finished coffee in a china cup.

Smells like shit, thought Martin, resisting a strong urge to spit in it.

In the bathroom, Della was glaring at Jane who stood, fully dressed, in the bath, the showerhead in her hand.

'For God's sake what's wrong with you?'

Jane said nothing, but pointed the showerhead in the direction of the laundry basket.

'What?' said Della, advancing towards her, 'pull yourself together and tell me.'

'At the back of the room,' Jamie had said, talking as if he were mounting a guerrilla attack, 'in the corner next to the window you'll see last year's card-mounted year planner leaning against the wall. Behind it is a socket. Use that one.'

'Come on,' said Della impatiently, I haven't got all day.'

'It moved' whispered Ruth, putting on the performance of her life.

Martin knelt down and looked into the gap between the planner and the wall. There was a single plug socket but there was something already plugged into it: the coffee percolator, which Della had only that morning located in the window.

Shit.

'I think there's a frog in there,' said Jane

'A frog? How ridiculous. I'm far too busy for all of this. I suggest you calm down and get back to what you're being paid for, now...'

As Della made for the door, Jane let out another ear-piercing scream.

'Look...it moved.'

Still thrown by the presence of the plug, Martin heard the scream and recognised it as a signal that Della was about to return. *At least,* he thought, *if I unplug this it won't be seen.*

Obsessive Compulsive.

He knew what Jamie meant. But would she notice if the angle of the board had altered? On the off chance that she would, Martin decided not to move it, and instead lay on the floor and stretched his hand towards the plug. Removing it, he slowly let it drop to the floor, as small beads of sweat formed on his forehead. There was still noise coming from the bathroom, but he knew that in a split second Della could emerge and see him leaving her office.

Jamie had positioned himself in the corridor as the second line of distraction. He had originally assigned the job of placing the 'bug' to himself, arguing that if Della found him in the office he could say that he had turned up for the meeting and found the door open, but Martin suggested that if Della left the bathroom too soon, Jamie would have more of a chance of stopping her in her tracks than he would. Martin was starting to regret volunteering for this. 'Why can't you just take a Dictaphone in?' he'd asked. Jamie explained that he was aiming to make it a long meeting if he could, because it would take time to put

Della at her ease. Dictaphone tapes were not long enough, and the last thing he wanted was a telling 'click' at a crucial point.

The monitoring device was bulkier than Martin had thought, and was proving difficult to manoeuvre into the socket without knocking the board over. The socket was stiff and resistant as he slowly inserted the device and pushed it home.

'For God's sake get out of that bath,' bellowed Della.'

'You don't understand,' sobbed Jane, 'I'm not just a bit scared, it's a real phobia with me...'

Della grabbed the basket, turned it upside down and emptied its contents all over the tiled floor.

'Look, no frog,'

Martin was aware of a tremor in his breath as he looked around the room to see that everything was as he'd found it- nothing askew or out of place, and no marks on the pristine carpet. Certain that he had left no tracks he slipped out of the office and back into the lounge, just as the door to the bathroom slammed.

'Oh, Jamie' said Della, almost walking into him. 'I can see you now. And remind me to ask for mental health certificates the next time we recruit.'

As the office door closed, Jane joined Martin in the lounge where he sat next to the baby monitor, a cassette recorder on his lap and a finger to his lips.

'So Jamie,' said Della, her tone abrupt and formal, 'what do you wish to see me about?'

'It's about the other day, when I came back from Blackpool,' said Jamie with a feigned contrition, 'I would like to apologise unreservedly about how I behaved.'

Nice one! whispered Martin, *she'll love that.*

Della looked pleased, but bemused. This was the last thing she had expected.

'The thing is,' Jamie continued, 'and I know it's no excuse, but I'd had very little sleep, sharing a room with Mickey and all, so I was on a short fuse...'

'You're right. There is no excuse. A senior member of staff should set an example.'

'Yes, and I always try to. It was just that it had been a bit of a strain being responsible for everything when all you've got to work with are the likes of Martin and Ruth.'

Cheeky git!

'I can well understand that,' said Della, 'I live constantly with that strain, I just hadn't realised that you felt that way. Thank you for being so open with me. I accept your apology. Would you like a coffee?'

'Er, no thanks...'

Jamie made a mental note that if the meeting showed signs of faltering he would ask for a cup of the strange-smelling brew. Otherwise he would prefer to leave it alone.

'So, your views on time-out...do they still differ from mine?'

'Er, no,' said Jamie, straining for an answer, ' I've been giving the subject a lot of thought recently, and I've realised that it's not time out I disagree with per se. I think it's a tried and tested way of managing behaviour... when done properly. My only doubt is that when we're not around, the morons we have to work with will not do it by the book.'

Della smiled and took another sip of coffee. 'Quite right. That is exactly my fear, but I'm sure that with the right kind of training even a chimp could get it right. If they don't then they'll be down the road. You know, Jamie, I'd got you all wrong. I used to think you were quite pally with our little band of failed shelf-stackers.'

'No no no. They think that, but I just try to keep things professional.'

You know, said Martin, *he sounds like he means it, the bastard.*

309

'Professionalism,' said Della, 'there is a distinct lack of that around here, and it's not for lack of trying on my part... or yours. I think the problem comes with moving away from the medical model. If we just employed nurses, like ourselves, there would be a much greater degree of discipline.'

'Yes, I remember you saying that you'd had nursing experience,' said Jamie, 'and to be honest it does show in your practice...'

Go for it Jamie...

'...did you ever work at Oulston...'

Now reel her in.

'If you don't mind.' said Della, straightening in her chair, ' Like I said before, I spent most of my early career working in the North of England. Besides, I prefer not to discuss previous employment. It's all in the past as far as I'm concerned. I believe in concentrating on the here and now. Are you sure you don't want a coffee?'

Jamie looked towards the percolator, and for the first time noticed where its lead disappeared behind the year planner.

'What's wrong?'

'Oh nothing, I just need to take my inhaler. It must be the change in the weather.'

What's happening? whispered Jane.

Jamie was aware that his eyes had lingered for too long on the coffee percolator, and forced himself to meet Della's stare. Something had changed there; where there had been a momentary warmth, the hardness had returned. He wondered if she was beginning to suspect, or if Martin had decided not to go ahead when he saw that the socket was in use. In either case, the plan would fail. Unless he took a different approach. If Martin had not plugged in the device, what were the chances that he was, even now, outside the office door with the cassette recorder? If that were the case, then Della's volume would have to be turned up.

The plan had been to convince her that he saw things her way, make her believe that he was an ally, then gently draw out what he

310

wanted to know. But all of his instincts now told him that this was not the way.

'So while you're here,' said Della, her smile returning, 'is there anything else?'

'Yes,' said Jamie, putting his inhaler back into his pocket, 'yes there is. Ever since I met you I've been struggling to remember where I'd seen you. Are you sure our paths haven't crossed before?'

'What's he doing?' blurted Martin.

'Shhh,' whispered Jane, pointing to the cassette recorder.

'This isn't what he said he'd do. What's happened?'

'Absolutely,' said Della, ' like I said before, I think you must be mistaking me. Now if there is nothing else...'

'Maybe you don't remember me. I was a nursing student at the hospital. A friend of mine remembers you, too.'

'Look,' said Della, banging her fist on the desk and causing a drop of cold coffee to jump from its cup, ' even if that were so I fail to see its relevance to our work here...'

'It was Nurse Cahill, wasn't it?'

Silence.

'I know what he's doing' whispered Martin. *'If he gets her angry it might come out.'*

'Do you remember,' said Jamie, his voice now firm and controlled, 'a patient called Frankie?'

'No.' said Della, a tidal wave of red sweeping from her neck to cover her face.

'That's strange,' said Jamie. Because Eddie does. Have you not heard it?

'Who's in the cupboard

Rang the bell...'

'This is preposterous. I should have you sectioned together with that mental bitch Jane.'

'...Made the noise...'

'Get out. Get out...'

'Tied the socks

Killed the man...'

'Oh shit. This is it.'

In the lounge the monitor crackled with a threatening and ominous silence, which seemed to drag on for minutes. Apart from the beads of sweat that now ran down her face, Della sat across from Jamie in perfect stillness, like a predator who was about to pounce and completely devour her prey.

He knew.

Somehow, from things that he had remembered and things that Eddie had said, he knew. She pondered what her next move was to be, but as she did so a calm voice, one which had replaced the legion which for years had filled her head, said: *It doesn't matter.* And it didn't. Her name had been cleared, and since then she had received a sign from God that it was in fact her sacred mission to remove people like Frankie, people like Eddie, from their meaningless lives. And she would tell Jamie that. Here and now. And it would make no difference because it would be her word against his, the word of God's representative against that of the servant of the father of lies.

'Excuse me,' she said, her sweat-soaked blouse peeling from the back of her leather swivel chair, 'it is rather hot in here, and I think that if we are to continue our discussion without expiring I need to open a window.

'She's going to tell him,' said Martin, struggling to keep his voice down.

Della reached for the window latch, then froze. Something was wrong. Different. Her mind went back to just before the meeting, to Jane's bizarre display of fear. She had left the office. It had only been

312

for a short time, but in that time something had changed in the room. She looked down at the coffee percolator. It had been on when she left, and there had been a small red light to indicate this. Now there was no light. Someone had been in and unplugged it.

In the lounge the monitor clicked, and fell silent, devoid even of background hiss.

'What's happened?'

'I don't know,' said Martin, unable to keep the blind panic out of his voice. Probably a power cut, or maybe...'

'Oh my God...she's seen it, hasn't she?'

Della flung the year planner to one side, unplugged the device and thrust it into Jamie's hand. He felt the sudden shift in his heartbeat as adrenalin pumped around his body, but was unnerved when, instead of the anticipated rage, Della spluttered into a fit of giggles, like a schoolgirl who had just won a treasure hunt.

'Take your toy with you. I could dismiss you for this. All of you. But that would be too easy.'

And, she thought, *it would be a departure from my plan.*

Slamming the door behind Jamie, Della plugged the coffee percolator back in then sat at her desk and booted up her computer. So people were speculating about her past. A lesser person would see this as a setback, but not Della. This development made what she was about to do that little bit more exciting, and was obviously to be interpreted as the catalyst of the next stage.

Della had been disappointed at the outcome of omitting Eddie's medication. Soon she would be forced to empty the drawer, but in all that time he had not had the complete mental implosion she had expected. Perhaps, she was loath to admit, Eddie had been on much of the medication unnecessarily, and once the symptoms of withdrawal had completely passed he would be a healthier, more lucid person. She shuddered at the implications of what this could lead to, but re-introducing the drugs was now no longer an option. Now she knew that she had to move onto the next stage. Her hour had come.

TASTING THE WIND

What was it that the old priest at the hospital used to call the nurses? Instruments of God. If only he knew.

Calling up her shift rota she selected a date when she felt that the correct configuration of staff were present: the fifteenth of October. Martin and Ruth would be on a sleep-in. That night she would start it, and Jamie and his cronies would suspect what was happening but be totally unable to prove anything or to stop it.

That night she would begin the cleansing.

-Chapter 52-

15th October 1987

Again Madame Delores inspected the clump of seaweed that she kept on her window ledge. Although there had been no recent rain the weed was limp and wet, and had begun to rot. The pinecone was tightly closed, and Delores felt it was a powerful omen that a fly had somehow been trapped in it. From a black velvet bag she took a handful of twigs and cast them onto the floor. They formed a strangely uniform spiral shape.

'Of course...'

It was unheard of for so many of her predicting tools to agree, but on this occasion they could mean only one thing.

From beneath a dusty skull, Delores took a telephone directory and picked up her phone.

'Hello,' she said, talking as if the extra volume was needed to push her voice through the wires to the other side of the city, 'I would like to speak to Mr. Fish...Well I'm sure he's not too busy to hear what I have to say...oh, all right then... but please make sure that he gets this message... do you promise? Yes? Then tell Mr. Fish that the signs are unanimous and incontrovertible: London is going to be hit by a massive hurricane. Tonight.

*

TASTING THE WIND

'Martin, what on earth's the matter,' says Jane, hugging me as I enter the Bungalow, my face streaked with tears.

'It's O.K., I'm not having a breakdown- contact lenses.' I feel my way to a kitchen chair and, sitting down, pop out the lenses, and put them into a fluid filled container I carry in my pocket. My eyes feel like they've been through a sandstorm. The optician had said that they would feel better worn in fresh air, so I'd come the long way round instead of taking the short cut through the park. All through town, concerned mothers had pulled their children from the path of the dangerous red-eyed lunatic, and I now know how the traffic-dodging frog must feel in the video game they've got at the Lobster.

'Thought they'd be useful,' I lie, putting my glasses back on, 'number of times my specs get knocked off.'

And Ruth thinks I've got nice eyes.

There's an atmosphere in the Bungalow now, ever since our botched attempt to catch Della out. It was bad before, but now the unhealthy cocktail of anger, and oppression has had shaken into it a large shot of fear. Everything just seems to be going on as normal. But it's not normal. Della has never referred to what happened. In fact she's been almost friendly. And that is scary. I've even wondered if her failure to react means that she didn't know what we were trying to do, and is an indication that we got it wrong. But Jane sees it differently. She reckons that there's nowhere for us or Della to go. In any normal work place we'd be done for trying to bug our boss's office, but she's worried that if she takes action it will come out why we did it. But if we take the initiative and go to her boss, Des Machin, what proof have we got? So it's stalemate.

'What's this?'

There's a crumpled white envelope propped up against a milk bottle. It's addressed to me, care of the Bungalow, and although the writing looks familiar I can't quite place it.

'I found it in Rita's room,' says Jane, 'when I was helping her to tidy up. It was postmarked about three weeks ago.'

As I open the letter, I notice that it has a Stoke-on-Trent postmark, and it starts to dawn on me who it's from.

Dear Martin,

316

Sorry I've not written before. Dave gave me your work address ages ago, but things have been a bit mad. He said he was sure he'd remembered it correctly because he thought it was funny that it had the word 'moon' in it, and you work with 'loonies.' (The PC revolution has totally escaped him hasn't it?)

Anyway, I'm hoping you are reading this. If not, I hope you're a hunky millionaire, because I am a young, free and single blond, who would love to meet you.

So have you changed the world yet? I bet you're really good at it. I've now got a job as a 'personal banker,' so things are looking up, after one or two setbacks recently.

What I'm writing for, is to say that a lot of water has gone under the bridge since I saw you last, and I wondered if we could meet. I would come down there, but things are a bit busy at the moment. I thought we could talk over old times, and perhaps create some new ones.

Please give me a ring some time,

Yours, Jo.

There's an address and telephone number at the top of the page. *Jo.*

The very reason why I had come down to London in the first place.

Single. And blond.

'Who's it from?' asks Jane.

' Oh, an old friend... a friend in need... Jane?'

'Yes?'

' Do you mind if I pop out to make a phone call?'

'No. No problem. Is everything all right?'

'Yes, I think so...it's just somebody I used to know, and I'm off tomorrow and Saturday, so I'm going home... I mean, to Stoke.'

I return about ten minutes later, none the wiser, having left a message on Jo's answer machine. It was good to hear her voice again, even if it was only her telephone voice, and it's given me time to think:

1. Jo has dumped/ been dumped by Ken.

2. She wants me back.

3. Ruth is not with Rick the Prick any more, but

317

4. She would be more likely to have a relationship with Quasimodo- or even Simeon- than with me.

5. Della wants to get rid of me, and probably everybody else who was involved in the baby monitor stunt.

But do I still feel anything for Jo? The answer surprises me. It's funny, but I think we have some sort of defence mechanism about pain that stops us from formulating accurate memories of it. I had acute appendicitis when I was about fourteen. I know I was in a lot of pain, but unlike remembering a taste, or a smell, I can't bring to mind exactly how it felt. I know we had rough times, but when I try to think about them they don't seem that significant, and are overwhelmed by the good ones. So why should I stay here? Why not just turn my back on it, treat it like a game of computer chess and resign from a game with an inevitable outcome?

Somewhere in my newfound sense of belonging I realise that there is a widening gap. I could get on that train tomorrow and never come back.

'Oh,' says Jane, as she's about to leave, ' I nearly forgot- I've got to show you this.'

It's a memo from Della:

I am writing to instruct all staff and residents not to leave the Bungalow tonight, as there have been rumours of dangerous weather conditions. There is also a need to make some savings, as far too much is being spent at the local hostelry.

'Bloody cheek,' I say, 'there's bugger all else for anybody to do of an evening. And how do we stop Oscar from going out if he wants to?'

I hadn't realised, but tonight I'm on a sleep-in with Ruth. It strikes me that I always used to know when these were well in advance, but now something's changed. Since Blackpool there's been an awkwardness between us. Our conversation is polite and matter-of-fact, and it's as if each of us is trying to avoid double meanings, not knowing if things will be misinterpreted.

'Er, according to the handover sheet,' I say, 'Mickey needs a walk up and down the corridor, and Rose could do with an arm massage, to stop it from stiffening up again.'

'Right. I'll do Rose, shall I?'

'O.K. Andrew has had two grand mals today, but recovered well each time.'

'Right.'

I can see tears forming in her eyes.

' And Ruth looks like she could do with a hug.'

The tears come as she lets me take her into my arms. At last I can feel her soft hair against my face, smell her perfume, but all the time I can't help comparing this to the hug I'd got from Jane when I arrived. Her body had moulded itself to me, giving its softness and warmth, whereas Ruth, though needing the hug, seems sort of stiff, receiving but not giving. This is the exact point in time where I know once and for all that there could never be anything between us.

'What's wrong?' I ask.

'What's wrong? Did I imagine it, or did we just fail to prove that the person we're working under is a psychopath?'

'Apart from that?'

'It's Richard,' she sobs, 'I thought he was going to come back, but he hasn't, and I've found out why: he's seeing someone else.' She breaks away and dabs her reddening eyes. 'God, I bet I look like the very devil.'

'What?'

'The very devil. It's a quote from one of my favourite musicals-My Fair Lady. You know, when Eliza's all upset and you think he should be comforting her, it's what he calls her.'

'Oh,' I say 'I thought you looked more like a pound of tripe.'

She allows herself a small, spluttering laugh. I look at her pale, tear streaked face, and want to kiss the tears off, but know that she is longing for someone else to do that. It occurs to me that this is probably the only place we can really meet, us human beings, not at an intellectual level, but through the emotions. There are as many levels of intelligence as there are people, but when we hurt, we hurt the same. I remember Vicki at the 'Breakaways' club, crying over Neville. It was no different to what Ruth's feeling now. To what I'm feeling now. Only I don't cry. Haven't since I was a kid. And next week I could be back there, away from this nightmare, carrying on like the last year had never happened.

TASTING THE WIND

There's a knock on the door and when Ruth opens it a blast of wind blows leaves into the kitchen and with them, half stepping , half- blown, is a man who introduces himself as 'Edward's uncle.'

'It's such a shame that Jane has just missed you,' says Ruth, as we sit with cups of tea. 'She's really into the diaries, in fact she's taken one to read at home.'
'I would love the opportunity to tell you more about Edward,' says Uncle Ray, 'is he home?'
'Yes,' I say, 'he's watching the telly, I'll fetch him.'
In the lounge Eddie is rocking and mumbling to himself. I can pick out the word 'spinning game.' It had been months since Della had taken it from him, and weeks since he'd mentioned it.
'Eddie, you've got a visitor. Your Uncle Ray has come to see you.'
'Uncle Ray.'
As we leave the lounge, Michael Fish is reading the weather report. He's laughing at the fact that some woman had been phoning to say that there was going to be a hurricane. This, he assures the viewers, is definitely not the case.

*

In her bedsit, Jane was sitting on a beanbag, drinking Chablis and nibbling dark chocolate. She had lit candles around the room, and they flickered as the growing wind outside felt its way through the badly fitting windows. This was it:' 1971' the last of the ten, the one which mysteriously ended somewhere in August. Eddie's 'milestones' of walking and talking had still not been reached.
So what happened?
She read on, but as she flicked over the page her eye was drawn to a capitalised sentence half way down the next one:
AND THEN I WAS CERTAIN: HE HAD THE GIFT.
What was that about?
As she read the preceding paragraphs her eyes began to widen. Feeling her heart starting to race she gulped the remaining half glass of wine. The passage told of how 'Edward' was ill, of how his mother had taken him outside to massage his limbs in the fresh air, of how she

lifted him to the ground and how, lying in the grass, he had stuck out his tongue to taste the wind.

The wind was azure blue and tasted of caramel, as it patted the heads of the poppies which bobbed up and down like a hundred red balloons in the fields which surround Poppyfield farm.

...So this must mean that....

*

'What?' asked Ruth, who had just picked up the phone to find an unusually excitable Jane on the other end.

'The diaries,' said Jane, from her bedsit, 'we thought they were about Eddie, but they can't be. They're about Andrew...'

Before Jane could say any more her voice was replaced by an abrupt silence as the line went down, a casualty of the building storm. Already confused by what she had heard, Ruth turned round just in time to hear the visitor say:

'I'm sorry, but this isn't Edward.'

'Isn't Eddie? said Martin.

'Isn't Eddie' said Eddie.

In Eddie's mind it was 25th August 1971. He watched as a younger version of the man in front of him left the ward with his wife, leaving behind him the twisted little boy. The boy was part of the institution now. Safe from everything outside, he would be fitted into the routines of care, kept warm, dry, and fed, for the rest of his predictably short life.

In the office, Nurse Clare sat down with the boy's admission documents, and neurologist's report. She knew from the manner of the couple who had brought him in that she wouldn't be seeing them again, despite their declarations of intent. They were just glad that he was off their hands.

'They must think I'm stupid.'

'Bugger off.' said a voice from behind her.'

'Edward Sparrow' she said, trying to mask her surprise, 'we'll have less of that language in here. Where do you pick it up from? '

'I've got a dog at home.'

TASTING THE WIND

The nurse flicked back to the front sheet of the admissions form.

'Not another one.'

'What's that boy called?' asked Eddie.

'That's the problem. His name's Eddie, but there are already too many of you for my liking.'

There was already enough confusion having an Edward Sparrow, Edward Parsons, and Edward Barton on the same ward. Mistakes had already happened- no serious drug accidents yet, but Edward Parsons had within the last month, with a great deal of resistance, been given an enema meant for Edward Barton. So now there was an Edward Andrew Wellman. But not for long. The nurse took her pen, and crossed out the first name until it could no longer be discerned.

'From now on,' she declared, ' he will be known as Andrew Wellman.'

'Eddie.' Said Eddie.'

'No, Andrew. It will save a lot of confusion, and he won't know any difference anyway.'

'So...' said Martin, bringing Eddie back to the present, 'if this isn't Eddie...who is?'

-Chapter 53-

Uncle Ray stands at the side of Andrew's bed, watching his wheezing chest rise and fall.

'We use this' I whisper, pointing to the baby monitor, 'in case he has a fit.'

Ray strokes Andrew's thick, wavy hair.

'I'm sorry I've not seen you for so long. It's been difficult.'

'When did you last see him?'

'Oh it was years ago. Too long. I'd promised my sister, Miriam, that I'd look after him. I thought we had. Barb- that's my wife, couldn't cope, so we agreed we'd find somewhere to take him in. The hospital was all that was available   then.   The last time I saw him was a Christmas Day. I went to visit him so I could take him something to remind him of his mum and of home. Where they lived there were fields and fields full of poppies, and she used to take him out and lie him down amongst them in the grass, singing to him and massaging him...'

'It was you. You took him poppies in the hospital.'

'Yes, but how...'

'It's a hospital legend: Christmas Day and a bunch of poppies mysteriously appear on a patient's pillow.'

Ray laughs, and Andrew looks straight at him, still smiling. ' It wasn't exactly like that. I stood for ages ringing the bell to the ward, until eventually the door was opened by the boy I've just seen- Eddie. There were no staff around, so I put the poppies on Andrew's bed. And no, they weren't flowering poppies; it was a bag full of seed-heads. I had thought that they could scatter some in the hospital grounds so that Edward...Andrew, could have a poppy field to remind him of home.'

We stand in silence, and even the restless wind outside appears to still, as what Ray had just said sinks in. Then he stands up, kisses Andrew, and says that he has to go.

'I'll be back soon; I've left it far too long. It's Barb, her nerves. I was at Papaver the day you came- that was how I found where you were: we had the day centre's address on the booking form. I'm sorry about what happened, it's just that...' Ray looks at Andrew and, ruffling his hair, says 'I'll carry on outside if I may.'

Outside the bedroom door, Ray continues in hushed tones as the sound of Rita laughing at something she's watching on the telly echoes down the corridor. ' It's just that Barb blames Edward for his parents' deaths.'

'But how...'

There was a fire at the farm. When the fire engine arrived Miriam and James were dead. On the grass outside they found Edward wrapped in a blanket. Next to him were the diaries. They had sacrificed their own lives to save him. Their bodies were found just inside the window, which they had broken and thrown him through. Barb could never understand how they could have put the life of someone like Edward above their own. I could understand that. He was their son, after all. The one thing I can't grasp is why they threw out the diaries? I've tried to read them so many times, but given up. Miriam's style could be a bit inaccessible. I brought them here because I thought they belonged with Edward, and it might give you some idea about where he came from. Does he still do that thing with his tongue?'

'Yes,' I say, surprised that of all things he should mention that, 'does it mean something?'

'Miriam thought he had the family 'gift.' I haven't got it, but Miriam had an overlap of her senses- synaesthesia- she could smell colours, feel sounds, see flavour. She thought Edward had it. I think she may have been right. He used to, what she called, 'taste the wind.''

' He still does,' says Ruth, '

Ray smiles as if he's looking through a back catalogue of bitter-sweet memories.

'Just before she died she phoned me to ask me over. I hadn't seen her for months, as she and Barb just didn't get on. She said she didn't want to tell me over the phone, but that Edward had 'taken it further' and she wanted me to see for myself. I never did get to see what she meant. In fact, that was the last time we spoke.'

*

As Ray stepped out of the front door, another scattering of leaves blew in, covering the doormat. 'Looks like we're in for a rough night,' he said, then folding his collar up he leant into the wind and crunched along the gravel drive.

Uncle Ray had left his car on the Cat and Lobster car park. *Maybe just one for the road,* he thought, as he reached the front door.

As he sat at the bar drinking his half pint of bitter he noticed the return of a tremor in his left hand, which appeared whenever he had to make impossible choices, to face conflict, or tell untruths. He knew that he had been weak. It was true that his wife had had difficulties accepting Andrew, and that in a state of grieving for his sister he had backed down from wanting to take Andrew in. But if it had been up to him he would have visited him more often. He resolved that from that moment he would stand up to her and put things right, keeping the promise he had made to Miriam. He knocked back the drink, and got up to leave, pulling his raincoat tightly round himself; he would go back to Papaver and tell his wife that he was going to be Edward's uncle in the true sense. If she was in the right mood.

As he left he noticed an obese woman wearing a long black overcoat, staring through the pub window in the direction of the Bungalow. Reflected in the window, he could see piercing, dark eyes, and she was so still that for a moment he doubted if she were real. On the table in front her was a novel: 'Integrating Arthur' by Colin Macallan.

Ray glanced over her shoulder. The book was opened at the final section, which was entitled 'The Prince of the Power of the Air.'

Quite apt for tonight, he thought, as the wind howled like an incubus past the window, *quite apt.*

*

Della watched the starved-looking man leave. She had seen him come from the Bungalow, but despite her curiosity did not introduce herself, in case details of her whereabouts on this night of all nights got back to the wrong people. She was certain that no one from the Bungalow would enter the pub. The wind was beginning to rage and she had, after all, left a written order to that effect. Should Martin Peach ignore her instruction it would be a disciplinary issue; but she did not want that to happen tonight. No, for her plan to work in its fullness, he had to be in the building.

Della would watch the Bungalow until all of the lights had gone off or until the Lobster closed. Then, if she had to, she would wait in the hire car that she had parked a little way down the road, until she felt that the time was right. Entering quietly by the front door, she had the excuse ready if anyone was still awake that she could not sleep and had called in for some unfinished paperwork, and the Dictaphone, which she had deliberately left on her desk. But she did not intend to be disturbed. Her intention was to enter the building quietly. With a gloved hand she would close the door, which she herself had oiled that morning, then glide noiselessly down the corridor in the pale glow of the emergency lights. Only when she was in the bedroom of Eddie and Andrew would she don the mask.

Della felt the soft rubber in the large pocket of her overcoat. It was the face of a horned red devil.

Ironic, isn't it, she thought, *particularly in light of my calling, that when Eddie says the devil is after him I'm sure that it is his attempt to pronounce my name.*

Wearing the mask, she would find a hard object- maybe a wheelchair footplate or a lamp- and with that object would bring to an end another totally worthless subhuman life.

She had, only within the last twenty-four hours, been forced to radically revise her plan, but she was happy with the revision, as she felt that it was prompted by the spirit of God. It had been her intention to relieve Eddie of his life, but in light of what Jamie knew about her it was clear that she would be the prime suspect. It would be far more fruitful if, on a night when Martin Peach was in the Bungalow, she could make it look as if Eddie had killed Andrew Wellman.

There were risks, but she felt that God would protect his own. There was the risk that the method would be noisy, and alert the staff. Then there was the risk that Eddie might be awake, and would attack her as he had done all those years ago. But no, she had to put such thoughts out of her mind. If all went to plan, Eddie would awake in time to see just enough to be able to tell anyone who asked him that it was not him, but the devil who had done it.

Della closed her eyes and, concerned that the longer she waited the weaker would be her resolve, prayed for guidance. Where a babble had once tormented her she now heard one strong, domineering voice. She could not be entirely certain if its tones were angelic or satanic, but its meaning could not have been clearer:

Don't wait...do it ...do it now.

-Chapter 54-

Jane continued to read the final diary. 'How could I have missed the fact that they were about Andrew and not Eddie?' she said to herself. 'I've got degrees based on my ability to interpret two-thousand year old texts, yet I can't even get an angle on something written while I was alive.'

She had noted a sudden change in style in the entries she was now reading.   There was no use of ancient languages, and the synaesthetic descriptions were minimal. Instead the language was simpler, as if there was an urgency about its meaning being understood.

I was with Edward one day in the poppy field. A gentle breeze was heading towards us, the bowing poppy heads tracing its progress. When it arrived Edward, as I knew he would, held out his tongue. I did the same, and the breeze tasted like a scale of bright notes on a harp of cool spring water.

Then it came to me: Edward's use of his tongue was not a reflex or involuntary action: it was deliberate and intentional. Everything about Edward's movement, with the exception of his manner of eating- is involuntary. The lolling of his head, the spasms in his arms, the arching of his body.

But when he tastes the wind... it is because he chooses to do so.

Jane flicked through the following pages, observing how the diary format was now ignored in favour of a sustained explanation, written in a scribbled, urgent style, not over several days, but at one sitting.

Therefore, the diary concluded, *if Edward could control when he stuck out his tongue to taste the wind, he could learn to use his only controllable movement to communicate his thoughts.*

Jane read with fascination how Miriam Wellman had taught Andrew to use his tongue: one lick for 'yes' and two for 'no.' Her fascination turned to euphoria, as she read how Miriam learned that Andrew was not only capable of making basic choices, but had the capacity for subtle abstract expressions.

Jane's thoughts were taken to Eamon, whom she had met on only two occasions at the day centre. The second time his mother had been there and she had approached Jane and said: 'you must be the theologian. Jane, is it?'

'Er... yes. Who told you that?'

'Eamon. He doesn't miss a trick.'

She went on to explain how Eamon, immobile and silent as he was, could tell her anything through smiles and subtle facial gestures that only she could read.

You're smiling broadly Eamon. Something new happened at the centre today. Was it a party?... no... a new person? Yes...female?... yes...did her name begin with 'a?'...no...' d?' no... 'j?'...yes...'June?' No.. .'Jane?'...yes.'

Jane's euphoria slowly turned to horror as she thought about Andrew, whose mother had realised his capability but had never managed to pass it on. Andrew had an active, intelligent mind trapped in a body which would not respond. Apart from his tongue. And no one else knew.

At least, Jane thought, *we can change things for Andrew now. For the first time we will hear his voice. For the first time he will be able to express what it was like to live in the hospital and...*

Oh my God.

Jamie was certain that Andrew was on the ward the night that Frankie Adams died. Could Andrew be the witness they needed? Feeling a need to share this revelation, and an urgency to begin the process that would liberate Andrew from his silent prison, Jane picked up her phone.

No tone. She had forgotten: the line was dead.

Alone in her flat she felt an enforced empathy with the thin man at the other side of the city: a mind overflowing with ideas and revelations, unable to express itself as the storm of the century breaks around it. And she would have walked the length of that wind-ravaged city, had she received some premoniton that by the end of the night that mind, with all of its unspoken secrets, would probably be extinguished.

-Chapter 55-

'It's probably that the wind's brought down the lines near to Jane's place,' says Ruth, putting down the phone. 'I've tried her again and it's stone dead. Local lines seem all right though- I phoned my mum and there was no problem.'

We sit with Rita, Rose and Mickey, watching whatever comes onto the telly but not really taking it in, and the picture keeps flickering as if the aerial is taking a battering. There's something in the air tonight, a spooky sort of siege feeling a bit like the last bit of Alfred Hitchcock's 'The Birds.' The People are quiet, apart from Eddie, who is chanting rhythmically but unintelligibly in the kitchen. The monitor for Andrew's room is silent.

'Ruth?'

'Yes?'

'Why didn't we know that Andrew was called Edward?'

'Omigog,' blurts Rita, 'Aroo is Eggie?'

'Oh I think I've worked that one out,' says Ruth, 'remember the admittance form from the hospital?'

'Yes?'

'There was something obliterated from in front of Andrew's name. We thought they'd got his name wrong, but how about this: Aunt and Uncle bring Andrew in and give his details to a nurse. We know that Eddie was in that ward at the time. Nurse decides that another Eddie will be too confusing, so gets rid of the name. From then on he is Andrew.'

I think that's much too far-fetched, but say nothing. We sit again in silence, taking no notice of the droning telly. Outside there's a gate banging somewhere.

'Ruth?'

'Yes?'

'Have I got this right: Papaver Riding Stables used to be Poppyfield Farm, yes?'

'Yes.'

'When Andrew's mum and dad died it went to her brother, yes?'

'Yes.'

'Well shouldn't it have gone to Andrew?'

For no apparent reason, Mickey starts to bawl and Rita, in a way that seems quite out of character, holds him until he calms down and begins to doze.

'Martin?'

'Yes?'

'What do you think is going on?'

'How do you mean?'

'Well,' says Ruth, who for some reason is talking in a whisper, 'shouldn't it change how we view Andrew?'

'Why?'

'Think about it,' she says, stroking a lock of blond hair from her eyes, which she always does when she's getting intense, 'you've never thought that much was happening in Andrew's head.'

'No, I...'

'O.K., maybe not now, but at first you thought he was a totally blank page. As we've got to know him we've suspected there is more to him. Now, there's a possibility that he not only doesn't have sensory deficits, but that he may sense the world in a more complete way than we do....'

There's a loud banging as if a large fist is hammering on a door.

'Shit,' I shout, a bead of sweat suddenly running down my forehead, ' somebody's trying to break in.'

Ruth has collapsed in a fit of giggles. I know now that if hero status in her eyes was unreachable before, it has now been booted into outer space.

'Aren't you going to check it out?' she asks. The noise continues, and seems to actually be coming from the kitchen. Rita looks scared and cuddles closer to Mickey who is now asleep. The heavy metal callipers he now uses for walking are on the floor at his feet. I pick one of them up, and head out of the lounge, brandishing it like a club.

Eddie is standing with his back to Della's office door, shoving his backside into it like a battering ram, mumbling the words *spinning game* over and over again. Part of me wants to cheer him on, but thinking of the repercussions when Della next comes in, I decide to stop him. A loud crack and the splintering of wood tells me I'm too late, and by the time I get to Eddie he is in the office, rummaging through the things on Della's desk.

'Hang on Eddie,' I say, switching on the light, 'it's up there.' I reach the game down from the top of a cupboard and give it to him.

' I'll play good in the bedroom with Pansy.'

'O.K., but be quiet about it. Andrew needs his sleep.'

As Eddie retreats with his treasured possession, Ruth passes him in the doorway. The doorframe is beyond repair.

'Boy are we in for a bollocking,' she says,' How will we explain this?'

'I don't know. And Della will probably use it to get Eddie out. She said 'one more thing' didn't she?'

We look around the office. It could have belonged to the leader of any number of methodical and emotionally cold races, such as Vulcans or Daleks. The books on her shelves are all in alphabetical order, and the piles of paper in her in and out trays are squared up. The only area of disorganisation is the desk- there's a desk tidy, an electric pencil sharpener, a Walkman, and a pocket chess computer- all of which are usually in line, but Eddie has spread them round in his search for the spinning game. There are also two racks full of floppy discs.

'We might as well make the most of this,' I say, looking through the discs. Ruth, following my meaning, boots up the computer and I see a disc that looks like it has files on my disciplinary. I'm really disappointed when I find that it's password protected.

'What's this one?' asks Ruth.

The disc is labelled 'articles.' There are several long accounts of happenings in the Bungalow over the last year: *a community experiment with six ex-patients from a long-stay hospital... a successful sleep-pattern programme for a man of Oriental origin with a severe mental handicap... a successful walking programme ... a new look at the 'time out' method.* As we scan through the documents a clear pattern is emerging of how Della has set up a highly successful home, taught Mickey how to walk and sleep in a bed, as well as

333

modifying Eddie's and Rita's behaviour to enable them to live normal lives in the community.

'But wasn't it you who was there when Mickey first walked?'

'I thought so, but reading this I'm beginning to doubt it. Who are these for?'

Ruth nods to a shelf-full of books and magazines about mental handicap. 'Looks like she's planning to make her name out of our hard work.'

The temptation is too great. I change the occasional 'time out room' to 'punishment room,' staff 'meetings' to 'beatings,' and the potential for the phrase 'walking programmes' is much too good to miss.

Our sabotage is interrupted by the phone ringing in the kitchen. I answer it, hoping that the line to Jane's place has been restored, but I soon realise that it's a local call. Very local.

'Hello, is that the home?' says Mrs. Busby.

'No,' I say, 'this is the Bungalow. Can I help you?'

'No, but I am phoning to tell you something young man: One of your children has got out, and it's a frightful night. I am telling you so that you can see to his safety, but rest assured I shall be contacting the newspapers tomorrow.'

I can feel my face heating up, and see my knuckles turn white as I clutch the receiver.

'And let me tell you, Mrs. Busybody, that the man's name is Oscar, that he hasn't 'got out,' because he is a free agent, and you are either blind or stupid if you haven't noticed that he is not a child.'

I think I manage to put the phone down before she does. There would doubtless be another complaint.

I wander back into the lounge, where Ruth is trying to rouse Mickey, and relate to her what Mrs. Busby had said.

'Shows how observant I am,' says Ruth, 'I didn't see Oscar go out tonight.'

'Neither did I, but he's never around at this time so...'

Then it happens.

There's a dull thud on the baby monitor from Eddie and Andrew's room, followed by the loud crash of furniture being overturned and of breaking pottery. It all seems to happen in slow motion, like one of those dreams where you're running but getting nowhere, and as I pass through the kitchen on the way to Andrew and

334

Eddie's bedroom, Oscar appears, complaining that the noise has interrupted his snooze.

*

'Oh my God,' says Ruth, 'where are they?'

Andrew's bed is empty, and Eddie is nowhere to be seen. The room is freezing cold because the window's wide open, and a duvet has been placed over the ledge to prevent it from banging in the fierce wind. Andrew's bedside cabinet has been knocked over, and a red ceramic vase that had stood on it is in pieces on the floor. The squealing wind has blown a selection of leaves and paper bags into the room, and for a moment everything seems to be in motion around us.

Then Ruth notices the rhythmic fluttering of Andrew's duvet, which lies rolled up on the floor between his bed and the overturned cabinet. The top of the duvet cover is stained dark red. A sudden break in the wind leaves the room in silence, as we realise that amongst the wreckage, litter and scattered leaves, lies the shrouded body of Edward Andrew Wellman.

-Chapter 56-

As Ruth pulls back the duvet we see Andrew, his whole body shaking violently, his hair stained and matted with blood.

'Oh my God, Andrew, what's happened?'

She turns him onto his side and grabs a wad of tissues from a box on the floor.

'Martin, keep him in that position and hold these firm over the wound. I'm going to phone for an ambulance.'

For a moment Andrew's convulsions subside, and he appears to be fully conscious. As the wind begins another wave of attack upon London, Andrew sticks out his tongue to taste it. This time there is no look of satisfaction. Instead his face is contorted with fear as if his senses have confirmed that this is no ordinary wind.

'They're on their way.' says Ruth as she returns, but they've warned me they might be delayed, because branches are starting to come down.

'Ruth, I'm going to have to go out and find Eddie. Will you be O.K.?

'Yes, I'll stay here with Andrew. Ask Oscar to let the ambulance men in.'

Zipping up my leather jacket, I take a torch that's kept in the kitchen drawer and search the garden, before setting off along Moonfield Road. The wind howls around me, creating a blizzard of leaves and chip papers, and I have to stop in the doorway of the pub because it feels like the breath is being sucked from my lungs. For all I know, Eddie might have gone in the opposite direction. I'm about to turn that way when I see a flash of white carrier bag, and can just make out the shape of Eddie, bent double against the tempest, entering the park. The large torch has a powerful beam, and as I shine it down the path it picks out Eddie's bag, which billows behind him like a drogue chute, the wind carrying his voice as he shouts, *I can fly, I can fly.* Then the direction of the gale changes, and I find myself pitched forward onto my hands and knees.

Regaining my senses I find that I'm still clutching the torch, but I can no longer pick Eddie out with it. Damaged in the fall, its light flickers intermittently. Either side of the path trees creak and groan as I point the beam into the chaos of moving trunks and falling branches. Something else, something white, is moving. As it comes into focus, I see that it is an owl, limping helplessly, one wing trailing like a ragged white flag.

By the time I get to the other side of the park I'm half stooping, half crawling, all of my senses engaged in a battle with the elements. Passing through the gate I look up and see the tin tabernacle. And there's a light on. The garden that Eric tends so lovingly has been totally ravaged, bushes lying where they have been cast aside, plants flattened and pots overturned. It isn't until I reach the gate that I see Eddie, standing on the steps of the chapel, pinned to a wall by the wind.

'Eddie!'

And as I shout his name, it's like the wind creates an illusion, an echo, which screams 'Eddie' with the voice of a banshee, as a large urn hurtles through the air. Later, when I recount this to Ruth, it will be about how I made a heroic dive and brought Eddie down, saving his life. In reality it's more of an untidy, stumbling thing, twisting my ankle in an awkward fall to the ground and knocking Eddie aside. But whichever way it's told, I know as the urn shatters against the wall where Eddie had stood, that I have saved his life. But we're still exposed. Our only hope now is that for some reason there is somebody inside, and that the light has not been left on by mistake. I bang with both fists on the door, vainly trying to shout above the wind, in the hope that we will obtain sanctuary.

Eddie laughs manically, chanting:

'Mr. Hill smashed the plant pot.'

Then the world seems to cave in. Somebody had opened the door and, as we sprawl on the floor, strong hands help Eddie and me to our feet, then force the door shut.

'What on earth are you doing out on a night like this?'

'What the fuck are you doing here?'

337

'May I remind you,' says Eric, 'that this is a house of the Lord?'

'Sorry, I've had a bad day. But what *are* you doing here?'

Before Eric can answer, there's a deafening screech and groan of metal, as part of the corrugated roof begins to lift off like a can lid. White ceiling tiles whirl around us, then are sucked out into the blackness as if there's been a hull breach on a starship.

'Fuck me...' shouts Eric, then 'Sorry Lord.'

The lights flicker out, but in the beam of the torch a torrent of dust swirls like a desert Djinn.

'Give me the torch and follow me.'

Eric leads us to the front of the meeting room then, stooping down, he lifts up a metal ring from the floor, and with a heave pulls up a trapdoor.

'Quick, we can shelter in there.'

The flickering torchlight shows wooden steps descending into a large underground tank with white- tiled walls and floor.

'It's the tomb of our Lord,' says Eddie, excitedly.

I look down into the dark cell and up at the sky, which is now visible through part of the disappearing roof as another sheet of metal flaps around like paper in the wind.

'You two go first,' says Eric, 'and hurry.'

I'm weighing up what will happen if I refuse to enter the black hole when Eddie takes my hand and leads me down the steps. Eric follows with the board above his head, which he lowers until it clunks into place like a coffin lid, sealing us in.

It is, Eric reminds me, a baptistery, but at the moment it's being used to store bundles of newspaper that are being collected to raise funds for Ethiopia. Eric drags some of the bundles off the pile, and arranges them on the cold tile floor. The three of us lie back on our newspaper loungers, disturbed only by the occasional crash and muted sounds of the hurricane above. I close my eyes, knowing that I am shaking with fear, my hair, and every item of clothing drenched, not with rain, but with sweat.

'You all right?' asks Eric.

'Yes...fine...just don't like enclosed spaces... just glad you were here... why are you here?'

'I'd seen the weather forecast,' he says,' and some woman had been pestering Michael Fish all day about there being a hurricane. He said there wasn't, but there's no smoke without fire, so I kept an eye on things, and the wind was getting up, so I came to check that things were all right here, to batten down the hatches, so to speak. I'd have had better luck tying a Zeppelin down with a shoelace. So what are you doing here?'

I explain what's gone on at the Bungalow, and Eric wants to pray for Andrew. It's not something I'd ever do, but I suppose when you're stuck underground, sheltering from a hurricane, it certainly can't make things any worse. I close my eyes as Eric begins his prayer, and I see Jo's face. I had a normal life once- a girlfriend, a flat and a boring job. Look at me now, sheltering in an underground tank, and working for a boss that I suspect is a killer.

But tomorrow I will be saying goodbye to all of this forever.

'So tell me again,' I say when Eric's finished praying, 'what is this?'

'A baptistery,' says Eric, 'for full-immersion adult baptism. The Plymouth Brethren built this place and put a baptistery in it. When their numbers declined they merged with a Gospel Hall in another borough and sold it to the Salvationists. The Sally Army don't have baptism, so they use the baptistery for storage.'

'So this thing fills with water?'

'Yes.'

'Then we could drown in here?'

I can hear my own voice as if it belongs to somebody else, somebody tired and pathetic.

'No, not unless you trail a hosepipe from the kitchen taps.'

I close my eyes and take deep breaths of musty old newspaper. I can hear a dripping sound, and in my mind the water levels rise, the torch goes out, and I can't find the trapdoor as my lungs strain and my heartbeat thuds in my ears.

'I need to get out.'

'You what?'

'I need to get out.'

I try to stand up, desperate to get away from this entombment, but find it impossible, as Eric is holding me.

'No, Martin, it's not safe out there.'

But I'm still trying to pull away, preferring to face my chances with the hurricane, to rush out and face the devil I don't know instead of staying with the one I know only too well.

'Oh Lord,' prays Eric, 'defend your servants against the perils and dangers of this night, cover the people of this city with your protecting hand, and deliver Martin from his spirit of fear, I beseech you,'

I've stopped struggling. I'm looking at Eric's big eyed imploring face in the glow of the torch light, and something about the situation makes me burst into hysterical laughter.

'Praise the Lord for the spirit of laughter,' says Eric, who joins in, followed by Eddie. We laugh until our sides ache, and we're left lying exhausted on the bundles of newspaper.

For I while we sit with our own thoughts, as the wind whistles above us. When I was a kid my dad used to say that thunder was the sound of God moving his furniture around. Now it must be real furniture moving around and falling which sounds like thunder through the floorboards.

'Toilet,' says Eddie, 'where's the toilet?'

'Sorry, Eddie,' says Eric, 'they didn't install a toilet in the baptistery. Didn't think there'd be a call for it.'

'Where's the toilet?'

'Eddie, we'll have to clear a corner of newspapers. Is that O.K., Eric?'

'I'm sure the Lord would rather have Eddie wee in his baptistery than spend the night in discomfort. It'll be better if we clear that corner- it slopes that way towards the drain.'

Pulling out some bundles of paper we create a passageway to the corner. Despite initial protests- *I am not going there, I need a toilet bowl, I am not going on the floor*- the physical demand eventually succeeds in persuading Eddie to do what my arguments couldn't.

*

'It reminds me,' I think out loud, 'of camping out with my mates on a piece of waste-ground we called 'The Jungle.' But we always had food and drinks... and sweets.'

'Food and drinks... and sweets,' says Eddie.

'Sorry Eddie,' replies Eric 'that's something we can't make out of paper.'

There's a rustling sound. Eddie, reaching into his carrier bag, brings out a humbug, the one he had bought in Blackpool, and hands it to Eric, who smashes it against the tiles. Soon we're all sucking a sticky black and white chunk of the stuff.

'So what else have you got in there Eddie?'

Eddie looks at the bag, then at me and back to Eric. I'm trying to signal to Eric not to pursue this, as the last thing we want is Eddie kicking off in here, when Eddie says:

'Souvenirs.'

'Oh. Can I see them?'

Eddie looks into the bag, shaking his head, then at Eric. 'All right then.'

I've no idea why after all this time Eddie has agreed to this, but as I try to get a glimpse of the bag's contents in the flickering light it's like opening Tutankamun's tomb. Eddie reaches in and pulls out a book. It's an old children's hardback, 'The Jumblies' by Edward Lear. It contains the single poem, each scene heavily illustrated with bizarre and sometimes frightening characters with green faces and blue hands.

'Where's this from, Eddie?'

'Mummy.'

He then reaches in and takes out a figure of Peter Pan, which I recognise as the one from the model at the hospital.

'Hospital,' says Eddie, before anybody can ask.

'So wherever you've been,' I say, 'you always like to get a souvenir before you leave?'

'Yes.' He is digging deeply for the next one, and I can see that his 'spinning game' is also in there.

'Bungalow,' he says, as he hands the 'souvenir' to me. It's Della's Dictaphone.

*

I'm lying back on my newspaper bed, listening to Eric humming a hymn as I rub my sore left ankle with the heel of my right foot.

'I know that one. I know it from school.'

'You're not a believer are you, Martin?'

'No.'

The wind still whistles above us, and is joined by Eddie's gentle snoring.

'Can I ask why?'

'You can ask, but don't try to convert me.'

'I can't convert you- it's the Lord who converts. But what do you believe?'

I turn over on the crumpling paper stack. I don't remember being asked that before. What do I believe?

'It's not that I don't believe anything,' I say. 'I would like to believe. I really would. I would like to believe in a loving God, but I know that innocent people suffer in a way that anybody who loved them wouldn't allow. I would like to believe that I have an eternal soul, but I know that what I call 'me' can be altered by chemicals in my brain. I'd like to believe in an afterlife, but I know what strange things grief can make the mind do. But what do I actually believe? I believe that sometimes things happen too closely to be co-incidence, because everything is linked. They call it synchronicity.'

As my tired ramblings come to a halt, I hear Eric's snores join those of Eddie. I wish that I could talk to Jane now, because I realise that what I have just said has mainly come from her, but has somehow become part of me. Things happen. I know we sometimes see them where they don't exist, like the poppies, but I've heard enough people talk about these things 'that are too much of a coincidence' to be able to just dismiss it. Jane once said to me that there was a difference between what was happening and what was going on. What was happening was that we were trying to help a bunch of handicapped people live in the community. But there's something else going on at the Bungalow, and it's to do with Della and Eddie, with Andrew and the diaries and, somehow, with me. And right now it is all rushing to its conclusion, but it's as if I can only glimpse it out of the corner of my eye.

And to be honest it scares me so much that tomorrow I know I will just walk away from it all and never look back. I will resign, just like I do from computer chess, and all the pieces will be lined up like they were before. It will be that easy.

*

I'm about to turn over to try to get some sleep when I realise that I still have Della's Dictaphone. Holding it close to my ear I listen to the manly tones of her 'notes to self' until I start to drift off. I'd sort of hoped to find something incriminating, or evidence that she'd hidden it somewhere to record other people's conversations, but most of them are the boring everyday things that she had to do around the running of the Bungalow, or ideas for her articles. The click of the Dictaphone switching off brings me back with a jump to full consciousness. I turn the tape over and press the start button. Silence. Jo used to use one of these, but this looks like a far more expensive model. Della would miss it. On the side I recognise a sound activated setting.

'Mr. Hill' mumbles Eddie, and it occurs to me that my parting gift to the doubters could be conclusive proof that he does have an uncanny power of mimicry. I set the device, and place it at Eddie's side, before falling into a restless sleep.

-Chapter 57-

16th October 1987
7.45 a.m.

Rose had had a turbulent night. Although she had no words for them, she had been dreaming that wailing demons were banging on her window. She woke with a dry mouth and it felt like her heart had dislocated itself and was now beating loudly in her ears. She was wet, and the half lit room came in and out of focus. Her arm had a dull ache, more like a nagging toothache than the needle-sharp stabbing she had felt when she'd   first had the fall.

Rita mumbled to herself in the next bed. She was dreaming about the hospital. Don Maguire took her out into the fields, and undid his zip. She giggled at what she saw so he slapped her, pushed her down then, tearing at her tights and knickers he stuck it in her, stopping her screams with his mouth. She tried to tell a nurse.

What are you saying dear? Say that again sweetheart? No, I don't know what you're saying.

A roaring wind encircled them, and she could hardly hear her own words. The nurse turned her back, so Rita touched her to get her attention, then prodded her, then pushed her until she fell, and Rita awoke, her eyes stinging with tears as she repeatedly pounded her mattress.

*

When Ruth got back to her flat there were half a dozen empty lager cans on the floor, and two foil take-away cartons. Richard was back. She slowly opened the bedroom door. He lay there half covered by the duvet. His wavy black hair was tousled, and his chin was dark with stubble. This was the Richard she had fallen in love with- the potential rock-god, a faded 'Motorhead' tattoo wrinkled over muscle that hadn't yet lost all of its firmness. She carefully pulled back the duvet, and snuggled in beside him. Maybe they should give it one more try.

*

Mickey had spent his first night in several months under his bed. He didn't feel safe with all of the noises outside. Taking stock of his surroundings, he emerged slowly, and giggled as he pulled himself up into standing using his wheelchair. He pictured himself reaching the things in the high kitchen cupboards, the things in the fridge on top of the freezer, things that tasted better and were easier to eat than frozen burgers. He laughed again: he was on the up and up.

Oscar had woken early. Today was going to be a big day for him. He filled his sink and had a complete wash down, brushed his teeth, shaved, then splashed himself liberally with 'Brut.' Earlier he had heard voices from the kitchen. Ruth and Jamie, then Jane, Simeon and Della. Now he could only hear Jane and Jamie, and Jane was crying. This was out of the ordinary, but it had not been an ordinary night. At one point he had had to let in the ambulance men to take Andrew to hospital, then his radio had said something about a hurricane. Fortunately he had managed to sleep through it- he had a busy day ahead.

Oscar dressed in his best blue shirt and pullover, matching trousers, clean white socks, slip-on shoes, and the green jacket that had once been Don Maguire's.

I will go to places and see things that the Don can only dream of.

He lay on the floor and pulled his suitcase from under his bed. From an inside pocket he took a sock, and from the sock he took a bundle of notes and a handful of coins. Soon there would be silence, as the staff went to help the ones who needed it to get up. Then he would slip out. He would go to the supermarket, not to work, but to say goodbye.

*

345

'The water soon came in, it did,
The water soon came in:
So to keep them dry, they wrapped their feet
In a pinky paper all folded neat,
And they fastened it down with a pin.
And they passed the night in a crockery jar,
And each of them said 'how wise we are!'
Though the sky be dark and the voyage be long
Yet we never can think we were rash or wrong,
While round in our sieve we spin!'
Far and few, far and few,
Are the lands where the Jumblies live;
Their heads are green and their hands are blue
And they went to sea in a sieve.'

I wake up hearing a woman reciting nonsense verse, having had this really improbable dream where I'd spent a night with Eddie and Eric, sheltering in a baptistery from a hurricane. It isn't until I open my eyes that I realise it's true. The torch has dimmed, but there are hints of daylight around the edges of the trapdoor. The only sound is that of water dripping onto the tiles and piles of newspaper, and there's a strong smell of urine, as both Eric and me had had to follow Eddie's example during the night.

Eric and Eddie are still sleeping. I pick up the Dictaphone, hoping that it's caught Eddie's recital, but the tape had already reached the end of the second side and switched off. Winding it back, I press 'play,' but after ten minutes of recorded snoring I switch it off and put it in my pocket.

'You awake, Martin?'

Eric. He's sat up, putting his glasses on. I realise that I'd slept wearing mine. The lenses, like everything else, are mottled. I'd been half aware at one point of something heavy falling and dust showering us from the old floorboards above.

'Yes. It's morning.'

Eric cocks his head to one side, and listens. 'I think it's stopped.'

'Morning,' yawns Eddie, taking in the scene. He does a double take, then says: 'We're in the paper.'

I try to stand up, but drop back down, covering my face with my hands.

'Eric, will you do me a favour? If I try to lift the trap door and there's something blocking it, I'll just freak out.'

Standing up, Eric pushes with both hands. The door won't move so he presses his shoulders against it and starts to straighten up. A one-inch crack of light appears, until the straining Eric drops the door with a bang.

'There's something on it, isn't there?'

'Yes' says Eric, 'something heavy, I... hang on.'

'What's that noise?'

There are footsteps and voices above. Leaping up, I bang my head on the trapdoor, then start hammering it with my fists and shouting. Then Eddie joins in, laughing, as if it's a game. It's like being on the inside of a double bass when the bow is drawn across its strings as something is slowly pulled off the trapdoor. It takes three attempts before the job's finished, then daylight floods in as the board is lifted.

'Eric?'

The Salvation Army Captain and about half a dozen Salvationists, some of them in uniform, are looking over the edge. Stiff, cold, and covered in a light dust, the three of us emerge to the sound of Eric singing 'Up From the Grave he Arose.' No wonder Eddie feels so at home here.

I feel like I've woken up some time during the blitz. The building is totally open to the sky, the pulpit overturned, and the organ, less than a year old, has been smashed irreparably. Everything is splattered with soggy notice sheets, pages from hymnbooks, and brown leaves, as if nature itself has desecrated the place.

'Oh sh... sugar, I'm meant to be catching a train from Euston.'

'Euston?' Asks the Captain. Her uniform isn't in its usual pristine condition. Her face is ashen, her eyes heavy, and wisps of her normally tightly scraped-back hair drift across her face. 'Where to?'

'Stoke.'

'That will be difficult. I've been at Euston for most of the night helping the homeless who were caught outside. Word is you'll be lucky if one train goes North all day.'

*

347

TASTING THE WIND

Eric has insisted on giving us a lift back to the Bungalow. Even though it's in what would normally be easy walking distance, It turns out that the park's no longer a short cut, as hardly a tree is left standing. The ones that had lined the road have disappeared; council workmen had already made a start on moving the trunks, and the branches had been partly cleared, leaving space for a single line of traffic. But at the moment we're the only thing on this road, and there's an eerie silence. Pick any one of umpteen films or T.V. series where the world's population has been decimated by plague, alien invasion or nuclear holocaust: War of the Worlds, Terminator, Survivors, the Dalek Invasion of Earth- get the picture?

As we turn into Moonfield Road I see that Mrs. Busybody's house has lost several slates. She'll probably be in the paper next week, pointing mournfully at the house, and blaming the labour council for not restricting hurricanes to poorer countries. Outside the Bungalow the urns have been righted, but their contents have gone, dispersed in the wind. A climbing rose has been yanked from the front wall, and small pieces of glass which had been milk bottles are mixed in with the gravel.

Jane and Jamie are sitting at the table, at first looking frozen, as if under some evil spell. Seeing us they leap to their feet, Jane grabbing me and bursting into tears.

'Where have you been? I thought you were dead.' She stops short, and looks away, blushing.

'We've been in the tomb,' beams Eddie, 'the tomb of our Lord.'

The broken door of Della's office swings open, it's bent hinges grating, and Della steps out, wearing a long black overcoat and carrying a briefcase.

'So, the wanderers return.'

Eddie stares wildly, rocking backwards and forwards where he stands, mumbling unintelligibly.

'I have an important meeting to go to now, but by Monday I would like a written report about the events of last night.'

She opens the door to go out, then turns, saying, 'It will have to explain why a person in your care was seriously injured, why a door was destroyed...'

'There was a hurricane, don't you know?'

'...Why a member of staff went out with a resident when the weather was so obviously dangerous, having been instructed not to do so by myself in writing, and how personal property was stolen from my office.'

With that she left, slamming the door, not noticing my hand sliding down to hide the rectangular bulge in my pocket.

'Martin' says Jane with a note of urgency ' before we talk about anything else, there's something you need to know- in the last of the diaries it says that Andrew's mum taught him to communicate using his tongue- once for yes, twice for no. And she says he thinks just like we do.'

'And nobody knew?'

'No- she only worked it out a few weeks before she died...'

'Of course. She wanted to show Andrew's uncle, but he never went. That was why it was so important to throw the diaries out- so that someone would read them and find out how to communicate with him. But they never did.'

'There's more to it than that,' says Jamie. 'Supposing Andrew did see what Della did on the ward all those years ago. We've been seeing Eddie as the key, when all the time it might be Andrew.'

I feel too physically and mentally exhausted to take in all of the implications of this. Jane hands me a cup of tea, which I have difficulty holding still, and we exchange more information about the night before- me about my heroic dive to save Eddie from a flying urn, and our night underground, Jane about Andrew, and what we now know are Miriam Wellman's diaries.

'How is Andrew?'

Jane swirls the remainder of her tea around in her mug.

'He's been taken into hospital,' says Jamie. 'He had lost quite a bit of blood, and was having successive seizures. He's in intensive care. Simeon's sitting with him. Ruth's gone home. She hasn't slept all night and she's in a bit of a state.'

'So Della doesn't know what happened?'

'No,' says Jamie. 'I sent Ruth home before Della arrived. I told Della that you and Eddie had gone missing, and Andrew had got hurt. But she's come to her own conclusions.'

'Which are?'

'Not good. She has two ideas: either that you were stupid and went for an evening out in a hurricane, or that Eddie attacked Andrew and ran away.'

'But that's ridiculous, Eddie would never hurt Andrew!'

'I know that,' says Jamie, 'but if he didn't we've got to explain how it happened. Then there's the door.'

'That was Eddie. He knew his game was in there. And he took Della's Dictaphone. He took it as a souvenir. He wasn't coming back.'

Jane gives Jamie a meaningful look, like they've been talking about me and have to break some bad news.

'Martin,' he says 'I know you've not done anything wrong, but you do realise you're in deep shit don't you?'

'You don't say. Is that it?'

'No. Please hear me out. When you first came here I didn't rate you. I didn't think you'd ever do the job. But you've proved me wrong. Something happened, clicked into place, and now I think you're what The People need. I don't want to lose you.'

'Thanks Jamie. I appreciate that.'

'I won't ask you what the hell you were doing seeing Della on your own for your verbal warning. I'm union rep here, so next time I'm coming in with you.'

'And what will you say?'

'Fuck knows, but I'll think of something. You do know, with everything she's got on you that she'll try to go straight for a dismissal, don't you?'

But it won't come to that. It won't come to that because this is the fork- the position I had been in so many times: the knight threatens king and queen at the same time, causing the king to move, thus sacrificing the queen. If I say that Eddie broke the door and stole the Dictaphone she will use that as evidence that he was worked up and hurt Andrew. Then Eddie will be back on a secure unit. If I claim it is my fault, then I'm gone. But it won't come to that. I know what to do, I'll do what I'd already decided, what I always have done in this position: I resign; I walk away from the game, and get that northbound train.

As I leave the Bungalow for the last time, Jane follows me to the door.

'Martin, I just want to say I'm...here for you. Whatever happens.'

'Thanks Jane, I've enjoyed working with you...I mean 'enjoy' if you know what I...'

Jane's eyes glisten and her chin quivers slightly.

'Martin, please don't go.'

I swallow and look around at the scene of devastation outside the Bungalow.

'I can't do this any more. I just can't...Della will get rid of me, so I want to jump before I'm pushed. Besides, I've got some unfinished business.'

'But you're good at this, you've really made a difference here.'

I pause and look at Jane, whose tears have begun to spill down her cheeks.

'Thanks Jane. but I think you're bullshitting me.'

'No, I wouldn't, honestly; who was it who was there when Mickey walked for the first time? Do you know what Jamie said about that? He said it was nothing to do with the programme, but with Mickey feeling comfortable with you, with the relationship you'd built up. Surely that means something? And it was you who first took Eddie to church. Look what a difference that's made to him.'

I step back, crunching a piece of milk-bottle glass with my heel.

' You've changed your tune. Yesterday it was how it was all failing. What about Oscar? What about Andrew? I brought him out of the hospital for a better life, and where is he now?'

Jane puts her hand on my arm. 'That wasn't your fault. Just don't do anything rash. I...there are still people here who need you.'

We hold each other in silence, until I kiss her on the cheek and say 'goodbye.'

-Chapter 58-

16th October1987

8.10. P.M.

The Bungalow had the unmistakable smell of vegetable curry, and it was clear that a new spirit had somehow entered, however fleetingly, as Mickey rolled on the floor in the grip of uncontrollable turmeric stained laughter. 'Omigog' cried Rita, stomping out of the kitchen into the lounge, but in self-parody, only to peep round the door, giggling. Even Eddie, who seemed to have taken the previous night in his stride, was in high spirits and making an addition to his song:

'Whose under the table...?'

Della stood in the midst of it all, hands on hips, addressing the table.

'When you have quite finished, there are dishes to be done.'

'Yeah, but I'm communing with Mickey, what's more important?'

'What do you mean, 'more important'? You have duties to do.'

'Duty doesn't exist, man. I'm talking relationship. Mickey pays my wage, and this is what he wants to do.'

Della had had misgivings from the moment the man from the agency turned up. She told him she did not think that it was appropriate for him to come to work with half a beard, but he'd said 'do you think it's appropriate to come to work in leather shoes?' which had momentarily thrown her. She was on the verge of telling him that she didn't need him, but having quickly run through the options she realised that she did: Colin still hadn't been replaced, Ruth had phoned in sick, probably unable to cope after what had happened to Andrew, and Simeon was at the hospital and couldn't be contacted. So, loath as she was to admit it, she needed the half-bearded wonder. And he was not only half-bearded, but dressed offensively.

The night that Simeon returned from his meal at Della's flat, it wasn't long before he had started to enthuse about Della's culinary skills. When he mentioned that he had eaten frogs' legs, the normally calm Kevin had hit the roof. The diatribe had lasted at least fifteen minutes until he accused Simeon of 'feasting on the flesh of mutilated frogs,' and Martin, who had enjoyed the scene to that point, turned a shade of green and left the room. Knowing that he was to spend a shift at the Bungalow with Della, Kevin found his protest T-shirt, which featured frogs in wheelchairs and on crutches.

Kevin's face emerged slowly from under the table, his cheeks puffed out, causing Mickey to go again into paroxysms of mirth.

'May I remind you,' said Della, 'that we are in the middle of a crisis- Andrew Wellman is in intensive care, and Oscar Doyle has gone missing.'

Kevin pulled himself from underneath the table and, with a completely serious expression, stood up and leaned in very closely to Della.

'Exactly,' he said, 'so don't you think The People need a break from all of the dark vibes in here? I'm just trying to meet Mickey where he's at. Would you rather I went?'

Della glared at him, turning red from the edge of one ear to the other, and visibly shaking like a boiler about to burst. She could not bear to see such an antithesis to her way of working doing as he pleased in her Bungalow- if he had been a regular member of staff she would be getting rid of him- like she was getting rid of Martin Peach- but she knew that if she sent him away now she would be on her own until the next shift arrived.

'I'm going out for a short time,' she announced, 'all I expect you to do is clean up, then sit people in front of the television. Do you understand?'

'O.K. But I'll leave you the drying up.'

'Well...well...' she stammered, 'I won't be asking for you again.'

'Chill out man.'

' Don't you tell me to chill out...' She turned to Rita, who stood giggling in the doorway, then furiously back to Kevin '...and don't call me man!'

As she pulled on her black overcoat she wondered briefly at the wisdom of leaving her Bungalow in Kevin's care.

What damage could he do in the space of an hour?

She contemplated staying, but no. As well as feeling a need to escape from the chaos of the Bungalow to preserve her state of mind, she did have two important jobs to do. The first was to offer moral support to Simeon.

The second was to determine the chances of Andrew Wellman's survival.

-Chapter 59-

I wondered where that had got to.

I'm packing my holdall when I find the pen that the kids from the club had given me as a leaving present. After emptying a drawer full of single socks into the bag it seems to be already full. Next I lay all of my shirts on the bed, trying to decide if there's any that aren't worth taking. My vision blurs as I yawn and rubbing my eyes they feel like they're full of dust. Sprawling across the bed I sift through a pile of change from trouser pockets, picking out any large denomination coins. I keep losing count, and eventually lose the battle to keep my eyes open.

*

As I prop my 'Chopper' bike up in the back yard, the one that my dad bought me with his compensation from the pit just before he died, I recognise this as my recurring dream. I've been getting it regularly since the day I got locked in the punishment room at the hospital, but it's also got tied up with the 'locked in' feeling I get around Andrew. It's an exact re-enactment of something that happened one summer's day when I was about ten, the same day that Dave decapitated the frog.

I'm aware of the smell of fried bacon and the sound of raised voices through the open kitchen window.

'He's going to have to face up to it, Jean.'

'But I've tried,' he just changes the subject or runs out.'

'Then let me try again.'

Entering the kitchen I see Ricky stepping away from my mum, who quickly stuffs a white handkerchief up her sleeve. Her face is pale, her eyes puffy. 'Uncle' Ricky had been brought in to help me when my dad was ill, and I'd started misbehaving at school. Somehow, in a way that I never quite understood, he had now moved in.

'What's up, Mum?'

'Nothing,' she says, looking to Ricky for some sort of cue, which comes with a nod. Ricky opens a bottle of dandelion and burdock, and fills two glasses.

'Your Uncle Ricky wants a word with you in the front room while I finish tea off,' says mum, 'it's bacon, cheese and oatcakes. Your favourite.'

'Come on, son,' says 'uncle' Ricky. 'Lets go through to the lounge and have a glass of pop together.'

The man gives me a glass and, putting a hand on my shoulder, steers me from the kitchen to the living room (I was never *ever* going to call it a 'lounge.')

'Let's sit on the floor.'

I'm feeling uneasy at this, and Ricky seems equally uncomfortable because as he puts his glass down in the hearth his hand is shaking. I ignore him and sit staring at the glass door of the recently installed solid fuel fire. Its presence depresses me somehow. The coals are a uniform shape, and are obscured by the sooty glass, so you can't sit and pick out pictures the way my dad and me used to with the old open fire. It speaks of change, of growing up, of the triumph of functionality over imagination.

'Your mother and I are a bit worried about you, Martin.'

I say nothing.

'Your mother tells me you had a rabbit when you were a little boy. Do you remember?'

'Yes...' I say, wondering where this is leading. Maybe he's going to buy me a rabbit to win me over. It won't work, but I'll have the rabbit anyway.

'She said that one day you went out to feed it and it was still. Do you remember what had happened?'

'Yeah,' I say, taking a gulp of my dandelion and burdock, and fiddling with my shoelaces. 'It died.'

'And did you cry?'

'No. Crying's for girls.'

As I stroke the new fitted carpet I remember the red tiles underneath. When the council had modernised the house and put in central heating we had lived for weeks with cold, bare floors. Then there had been a day when the house had been full of people speaking in hushed tones and the tiles were sprinkled with small wet spots.

'It's not easy losing things, Mart, but it's better if you talk about it, and cry about it too.'

Only my friends called me 'Mart.' He had no right to. 'I think tea's ready,' I say, and make to get up, but the man stops me with a heavy hand on my shoulder, as with the other he reaches into his pocket and pulls out a red balloon. He inflates it, ties a knot in the end, and holds it towards me.

'This balloon is like a person isn't it?'

I shrug.

'I mean, it needs air to be a balloon, like we need air to live. It grows until it's as big as it can be, just like a baby grows into a little boy, then to a man. And it can make us happy.'

He knocks the balloon towards me. It bounces off my head and onto the carpet.

'But like us,' continues Ricky, retrieving the balloon, 'it is delicate and fragile. Like the balloon, we won't last forever. Sometimes we lose things we love. Sometimes we lose people we love...'

He holds the balloon to the fire, then presses it against its blackened glass. There is a loud bang, and all that's left of the balloon are remnants that hang from the door like a crematorium curtain.

'That's the nature of balloons, lad. They don't last forever.'

The sound ringing in my ears, I spring to my feet, glaring at the man as the flaccid rubber falls into the hearth. I turn to leave, but Ricky holds my wrist.

'He's dead, son.'

'I am not your fucking son,' I scream, kicking his shin and running into the hallway. Again the man grabs my wrist and bends down so that his mouth is almost touching my ear. The smell of beer reminds me of my dad coming back from the pub on Christmas Day and bending down to kiss my head.

'Your behaviour is making your mother unhappy,' whispers Ricky, 'and that makes me unhappy. Very unhappy'

'Let go of me you fucking bastard.'

'Martin,' shouts my mum from somewhere behind me, 'don't you dare talk to your Uncle Ricky like that, he's only trying to help you.'

At that I freeze. This is betrayal. She has sided against me. My reaction is barely conscious, as I launch myself at the man with my hands, my feet, my head, screaming in a frenzy until I am firmly seized by my hair.

'Ricky, don't hurt him.'

'I've no choice,' he snarls, as he drags me toward the stairs, ' just leave him to me.'

As the cupboard door slams and the key turns I step back and trip over something in the darkness, falling awkwardly into the unseen clutter of the cubbyhole. There's a searing pain in my right knee, and as I rub it, I find that it has already begun to swell. But I will not cry. I WILL NOT CRY. That's what Ricky wants.

And because of that l swear that I will never cry again.

*

I wake up shouting Andrew's name and I don't know if I'm on a sleep-in or still sheltering from the hurricane. Clicking on a lamp I realise that I'm on my own bed, surrounded by unpacked clothes. I remember getting back to the flat and phoning Euston Station. The Captain was right- there would be one train leaving at 6.30 tonight. I look at my watch. It's ten past eight. *Is that morning or night? It's dark. Must be night. I've lost a whole day. I wouldn't have caught it anyway.*

The white board at the home still reads:

Today is: 25th of June 1986.

The weather is warm

I wonder how this affects residents with senile dementia, as I'm having problems with place and time, and I'm just knackered from being out for one night in a hurricane.

I often think that I belong to another age, because I still have this sense of wonder that in a home for the elderly in London I can dial a number and make a bell ring two hundred miles away. A bell at Jo's

358

place. A bell that at this moment is probably disturbing her as she sits watching telly. *Shit, it's Friday night- she's probably out.* I count ten rings. Maybe the delay is that she's in the shower, so I wait a bit longer in the hope that she'll hear it and stand talking to me in a white towel.

After five minutes the phone is picked up.

'Hello,' snaps Jo.

'Oh, hello, sorry if I got you at the wrong moment.'

Silence.

'I'm sorry, I think you've got the wrong number.'

'Jo, it's me.'

Silence, then 'Martin?'

'I thought I'd better ring,' I say, 'just to let you know why I'm not there.'

'Here?'

'Yes, it's a long story, first there was the hurricane, but since then...'

'God yes, the hurricane, I saw it on the news. It never occurred to me, but you'd be caught up in that where you are, wouldn't you? Did you see it?'

'Well, yes and no, it's a long story, but I was just phoning to say...'

'God it looked awful. I've been watching it on the telly, but I only got back this morning, and I'm a bit jet-lagged.'

I'm starting to remember how she used to interrupt me, and her habit of not name-dropping, because she didn't know any names to drop, but of dropping in phrases like 'jet-lagged' and waiting for a response. I'm not going to bite.

'It's just that I'd got your letter, and I was meant to be coming up today, but I wanted to explain...'

'Letter? Today? Where are you now?'

'Still in London, I...'

'Thank God, I mean, thank God because I wasn't expecting you, and the place is a tip.'

'Didn't you get my message?

'Message? God no. I've been in the Caribbean for the last fortnight. I still haven't got round to checking them.'

'Right. It's just that I've realised that you've split with Ken, and...'

359

'Ken? Oh, Ken, he was months ago. I'd split with Mike.'

'You'd split with Mike?'

'Yes. We had a big bust up and he stormed out. I was feeling a bit sorry for myself, got drunk, and wrote to you...God, what did it say?'

'Oh not a lot, it's just that I was coming back, but I now realise...'

' Yes, Mike came back the next day clutching two tickets... Oh God, he's back. We'd realised that the Moet we'd got in wasn't chilled, so he'd just popped out to the late shop. Nice hearing from you Martin...'

But I'm still talking, because it has to be said, even if it's only to a humming phone. '...I now realise that even If things were different it would have been such a big mistake to come running back. I've found something here that disintegrated around me when I was ten: a sense of family. And I already know that it won't last, but I also know that this is not the time to turn my back on it. Sometimes you feel deep down that there's a place where you're meant to be. And this is it. And do you know what else has happened? I've finally realised that this story isn't about me. And it isn't about you, because there's somebody else I care for, somebody else I love, somebody who needs me...'

And I need to hear what he has to say...

-Chapter **60**-

There are chairs outside the intensive care ward where people can sit when they have had enough of watching a loved one gradually slipping out of reach, for when the emotional muscles have stretched just that bit too far in trying to hang onto them. As Jane took a break from the vigil at Andrew's bedside, the events of the last few days repeated again and again in her mind, and she wondered how she had let Martin go without telling him how she felt. The loop of thought was interrupted by a stab of guilt, chastising her for sitting in such a place and being so consumed with her own, comparatively miniscule sense of bereavement.

There is something about this room.

It was as if the place was haunted by the ghosts of too many goodbyes, immersed in so much sorrow that if years later it should be used for a different purpose, upon entering you would be overwhelmed with despair. Martin had once told her that he had been to Auschwitz, and that to this day there is an oppressive atmosphere. He had also heard of a place where there had been a wartime massacre, which was now a hotel where, on their first night, every newcomer dreams about the war. Martin's illogical willingness to accept old-wive's tales, his suggestibility and uncritical views made him her total opposite, but somehow endeared him to her, somehow contributed to whatever it was that had made her fall in love with him.

And despite her efforts to make him see things differently, with all of the events around Andrew and the diaries she knew that it was herself that had changed, and was now a little less logical. Perhaps it was a better way to be- despite her reputation for making acute observations wasn't it Martin who had recognised the patterns around Eddie, clues which had stared her in the face for months but which she had rejected?

Jane had been shocked at the stab of jealousy she had felt when she waved Martin and Ruth off as they left for Blackpool. Then they had returned and everything seemed to happen so quickly: things had definitely cooled down between them, but before she could do anything about it, Martin was leaving because, she guessed, he had been summoned back up North by some old flame. She wanted to hate him for it, but knew that she never could.

When she had first come out of the ward, leaving Simeon at Andrew's side, there had been an old lady in a crumpled heap, doubled up with grief and shaking uncontrollably. Jane had put her arm around her. The only words she could make out were 'Joe...losing,' and 'nearly sixty years.'

Lost for words, she remembered that the title of one of her first year college assignments had been: ' the God of a suffering world cannot be both all-powerful and all-loving. Discuss.' She realised painfully that her A- plus answer had not prepared her for this. The woman's shaking seemed to transmit itself to her, causing her own silent tears to start flowing down her cheeks, tickling where they collected under her chin, and dripping into the woman's cotton wool hair.

The woman had been gone for ten minutes when Jane, trying to decide whether or not to go back into the ward, heard the first faint sound, something like the rhythmic pounding of a hammer, in the distance. Then she realised that the sound was not hammering at all, but footsteps slowly descending the stairs at the end of the narrow corridor. They paused before their owner came into view, and in a sudden irrational rush of apprehension, Jane felt goose bumps rise on her arms and a growing sickness in the pit of her stomach.

Jane didn't know why, but every time she tried to find an explanation for what had happened in the Bungalow on the night of the hurricane her mind kept returning to the feeling that Della was somehow involved. She wanted to get rid of Eddie. What if she had set him up as a suspect for attacking Andrew, when it was actually her handiwork? Della had killed before- despite their inability to come up with cast-iron proof Jane was now convinced of it- so what was to stop her from doing it again? And what would Della do if she found out that Andrew could communicate?

What if this is her now, coming to finish the job?

Della had been a nurse. All she would have to do was to add something to Andrew's drip, and any information he held would die with him. Looking at the shadow in the doorway, Jane felt a surge of primal fear, which took her back to her Sunday School days when an over-zealous preacher had talked of how the devil stalked believers like a lion, waiting to devour those that wavered. She knew that she was the only thing standing between Della and Andrew. But she knew, and with the utmost certainty, that If she had to, even taking into account the physical differences between them, she would fight like a she-wolf protecting her cubs to prevent Andrew from coming to further harm.

The figure stepped out of the shadows and walked towards her. He had red hair and wore a leather jacket.

'Martin?'

'I had to come back. I needed to see Andrew. See how he was.'

'I thought you'd gone... I thought I wouldn't see you again.'

'Oh you're not getting rid of me that quickly. So, how is he?'

'Not good. Not good at all,' said Jane, rubbing her cheek, which was sticky with drying tears. 'Sim's in there with him.'

'Sim?'

'Yes, Della seems to be letting him have whatever shifts he wants to sit at Andrew's side. I don't know who it's for though; I think he's getting some sort of perverse Mother Theresa kick from it all. Now you're here I'll get off. I've not been home yet and I'm on the early shift tomorrow. It's just so awful there at the moment. And Oscar's gone missing.

'Jane,' said Martin, her last statement hardly registering with him, ' is he really that bad? I mean, people come here to be nursed, and they get better don't they?'

'Yes, yes, but he looks so... go and see him. And Martin, there's something I have to tell you...' She looked up and kissed him on the cheek, 'I... I think Andrew will be pleased that you came back.'

Picking up her coat, Jane headed for the exit, but as she reached the first step she happened to turn around to see Martin, looking as pale as a sheet, his head down and his hand visibly shaking as he clutched the handle of the door. For a moment she wondered if she should pretend that she hadn't witnessed this, knowing that Martin would be painfully embarrassed that his cool, macho front had dropped, but seeing him there, looking so vulnerable, she couldn't resist the urge to run back and hug him.

'Martin, are you all right?'

'No,' he mumbled, 'no... I can't do this.'

-Chapter 61-

I stand at the door of the intensive care unit, overwhelmed by images and emotions that I'd not encountered since the last time I was in such a place. I can see my Dad, but he looks more like a copy, something made by an alien race. Edging closer to the bed my Mum urges me talk to him. I say 'hello,' but he continues to lie motionless, a white sheet pulled up to his chest, the blue coal scars on his arms more prominent than they had ever been against his pale skin.

'Martin,' says Jane, bringing me back to the present, 'you don't have to do this you know.'

'But I do,' I say, my voice faltering, ' it's why I came back.'

Jane takes my hand from the handle and squeezes it, then opens the door, which a moment ago had seemed as fixed as a tombstone.

'In that case,' she says, 'I'm coming with you.'

Light green curtains, some of them blown gently by fans, separate the beds, in one of which lies an emaciated, toothless old man, grey skin stretched over his skeleton. We walk carefully, as if entering a shrine, where the boundary between life and death is as perfectly defined as the difference between a wave and a straight line on a monitor. Through a half-opened curtain a figure draped in a stiff white sheet is propped up on a pile of pillows. Its face is a shapeless blur of reds, purples and blues, like a distant, ravaged planet, covered in a white mist of lubricant. The only indication of where a mouth once had been is where a tube enters. There's nothing left to indicate gender or identity.

At the bottom of the ward, Simeon sits at the side of a bed. It has a single white sheet, tucked in tightly and turned over under

365

Andrew's bent arms, which rises and falls with each breath, like a balloon repeatedly failing to fully inflate. It's as if the breath of life itself is clinging desperately to his frame. He lies almost flat, flatter than I'd ever seen him, enabled by the arrangement of white pillows. Tubes extend from his nose and mouth; his eyes are slits, the gash above the left one stitched.

As Simeon seems to be praying, we sit quietly on the plastic chairs on the other side of the bed. Andrew, who had spent so many years of his life in hospital, is now back in hospital. From living in a world where he was seen as characterised by his needs and stood out because of his deformities, he now lies, one among many, an equal. It's funny how for so long I'd viewed him as inert, a blank page, as having no interface with the outside world, and only now, seeing him truly detached and lifeless, do I realise how energetic, active and alert he had always been.

'Excuse me.'

A male nurse in a white tunic is standing at the head of Andrew's bed.

'Oh, sorry' says Simeon, moving his chair. 'Martin, I didn't realise you were here. Isn't this your day off?"

The nurse puts a tray down on Andrew's table, removes the tubes from his mouth and carefully brushes his teeth, before moving on to the next patient.

'Yes. But I don't think the rules apply any more, do they?'

' No, no, it's just that I'm supposed to be off today, you see. Della asked me to come in to support Andrew. I'm getting paid.'

'Yes. Kevin once said that we were a very strange breed of prostitute. I disagreed- the pay isn't this shite for getting rogered up the arse by some sweaty businessman.'

'I'm glad you're here,' says Sim, rising, 'I need to nip out for some fresh air.'

Jane gives me a disapproving look as Simeon leaves, and I find myself trying to fight back a huge pang of guilt that I've offended him, and that I've done it here.

And there he lies, Edward Andrew Wellman. I stroke his arm and feel his cold, papery skin and bone. Out loud I say 'Hi Andrew... What are you up to, giving us a scare? I want to see you up and about and riding that horse again... you won't be ready for the Grand National at this rate.' But in his ear I whisper 'I love you, mate.'

They say that the last thing to go is your hearing. I don't know how they know that, but assuming it to be true I talk to Andrew about everything that's happened: about the hurricane, about how Eddie jumped out of the window, of how I saved him from a flying urn, and how we spent the night underground in a giant bath. And about his mum's diaries.

Then Andrew's eyes flicker. They flicker.

'Jane, did you see that?'

'Yes, but I think it was just a tremor caused by...'

But slowly and surely his eyes begin to open. And he's looking straight at me.

'*Andrew, can you hear me?*'

He sticks out the tip of his tongue, then pulls it back into his mouth.

'Andrew, I know this may be difficult, but there's something we have to know: did Della...'

'Martin, what the hell do you think you're doing?' says Jane, pulling me away from the bed.

'I have to find out if it's true...'

'*You* have to find out? Since when did this become about you? Don't you think he's been through enough?'

I look back at Andrew who is staring intently at us, fixing us in a way I had never thought him capable of.

'Look at him, Jane,' I whisper, 'he's conscious now, but can we guarantee he'll pull through this? If he did see what we think he saw, that will have been burning inside him all of those years. If he can communicate to us like his mum said, then he needs to let it out. We owe it to him.'

Jane looks at Andrew, then back to me, and even though I know she's doubting my motives, she says:

'Yes. O.K. But don't just go blundering in there with the question. You need to ask a few things to ascertain if this yes-no response is definite.'

I approach the bed and pull my chair up.

'Andrew. Can you hear me?'

The tip of his tongue begins to emerge, protrudes beyond his lips, then is abruptly withdrawn.

'Is my name Simeon?'

TASTING THE WIND

The tongue comes out twice, and there is a sigh as if he is getting bored with what I'm doing.

'Is this lady called Jane?'

One lick.

'Andrew... did your mum call you 'Andrew'?'

This time he sticks his tongue out twice.

'O.K. then... Edward...'

If such a thing exists, there is a silent gasp, and you can see his head trembling with strain as he forces it to face me.

'Edward...' I look to Jane, a question in my eyes, and she nods, 'Edward...did you see Della kill Frankie?'

Andrew's eyes widen as a large tear rolls down his cheek. Then his face, which had been deathly white, begins to redden as if he is attempting to do something that requires monumental effort. Then it happens: his tongue is forced out, slowly and emphatically, and as he pulls it back he almost succeeds in closing his lips, something he has never done, but is trying now as if to make his answer unmistakable:

YES.

'We're going to get her, Andrew. We're going to make her pay for what she did. Once you're better you can tell us how...'

'What do you think you're doing?'

Della.

I don't know how long she had stood behind the curtain through which she now emerges, but from the look of panic on her face I can only guess that she has heard enough. I try desperately to think of something to say, as Della stands, glaring at us, but the standoff is cut short as Andrew's eyes turn up into his head and his normally stiff arms extend. Then his whole body arches, and jerks violently as if some unseen demon has closed its jaws and is savaging him. I've seen his fits so many times before, but this is different, and as we exit the ward, leaving the nurses to do their stuff, I wonder if this is what is meant by 'death throes' and if this is the last time we will see Andrew alive.

And I can tell by the way that the look of panic on Della's face has been replaced by a satisfied smile, that she thinks the same.

-Chapter 62-

18th October 1987

Synaesthesia.

Today I think that for the first time I can almost grasp what it means, how it feels for your senses to overlap, as the cold rain runs down my neck, making me shiver, a shivering which seems to go to my core, to my bones, to my soul, and I can hardly tell where the dullness of the day ends and my internal bleakness begins. I'm trying out my contact lenses again, but although my view of the park is bleary, I can see that it is a scene of desolation, with hardly a tree left standing. Somebody has cleared away the uprooted trunks and fallen branches, making a barricade along almost the entire length of the path. Each breath makes me feel like there are splinters of glass in my lungs. I've either got a cold or I'm suffering from getting a gob full of dust during my night under the floorboards. *Don't go down the pit,* my dad had said. *If you do you'll be coughing up dust til you die.* So I go into the caring profession, which may lead to baptistery related pneumoconiosis. And that's nothing to what I expect is ahead of me over the next few weeks. But I have to go to the Bungalow today, no matter what. I have to know how the story- Andrew's, Eddie's... mine... ends.

A distant patch of red in the grey wash landscape catches my eye. Because I'm still not used to my contact lenses it is blurred, indistinct. I carry on walking, but seem to get no closer. My trainers have let water in and each step feels heavy and uncomfortable. Looking up, I see the bobbing red shape again, and realise that somebody is holding it. Distracted by a patch of white in the dam of smashed trees, I stop, and have to bend down to be close enough to focus. Set in mud, and made mosaic by the crisscrossed branches, is the body of the owl. When I look up, both the man and the bobbing red blob have gone.

The bottom of my jacket is now underlined in dark blue, where water has collected on my jeans. I'm feeling that itchy wetness you get when it has finally soaked through to your underpants, and it reminds me of when I got covered in coffee at the hospital. That all seems so long ago.

I get to where the man had stood. For a moment I think I see a poppy out of the corner of my eye, bobbing up and down in the wind. I turn to see a red balloon, floating on the other side of the barricade of branches, a piece of white string trailing from it to the ground. I remember the balloon that Eddie brought with him from the hospital. Was that Eddie I saw just now? Surely it couldn't be the same balloon? No, that one had good luck messages written on it, and it was months ago. I wonder if there has been a children's party, or fete somewhere over the weekend.

The balloon is partly deflated, and struggling to fly away. At first I thought it was tangled in the branches, but now I see that the string is trailing through the wet grass, and it seems as if it is only the weight of the string that is anchoring it. For a moment it shakes, then changes direction, strangely out of time with the wind- it wants to fly.

Not yet Andrew... please... not yet. And why not? Do I want him to live for himself, or for the information he's holding in his head?

I get an irrational urge to clamber over to it, to untie the cord, and let it go. Then it comes back to me that I am just a soaking wet bloke, in a muddy park, watching a balloon.

*

When I get to the Bungalow, Ruth and Jamie are there. As I'd guessed, there's a letter waiting for me, summoning me to a disciplinary hearing. Della and Des Machin, the area manager, will attend it, and I have the right to take my union rep, Jamie, along to support me.

'He just didn't come back from work,' says Jamie, as he tells me how Oscar went missing. ' Della phoned the supermarket manager, he said that Oscar had turned up that morning and announced that he didn't need to work any more because he had done what he needed to achieve his IPP.'

'You don't think,' I ask, 'that he'd somehow got it into his head that he only had to stay here until he'd done everything in his first IPP do you?'

'I don't know,' says Ruth, 'but I'm worried to death about him. He could get into trouble out there.'

'What has Della done about it?' I ask.

'She called the police,' says Jamie. 'They said there was nothing they could do at the moment. There is some good news, though. I've been making some visits today. I went to see Andrew, and he's starting to come to.'

I feel my heart start to race. I thought I'd seen Andrew for the last time, but it seems like his life force has clung on by its fingernails, and has survived. Jane had told Ruth and Jamie about what we had seen Andrew do at the hospital, but our elation at the possibilities that this points to is overshadowed by a feeling which I am the first to voice:

'I'm pretty sure that Della heard everything, and knows what we were trying to do. If that's the case, and Andrew does recover, I don't think that this is a safe place for him to come back to.'

'You're right,' says Jamie. 'What I intend to do is contact Des Machin and tell him everything.'

'What do you think Des will do?' asks Ruth.

'I've met Des a few times. He's got a real intuition when it comes to recognising the truth. He will probably suspend Della, and involve the police. If Andrew's communication is as clear as you say they will probably do a few tests to establish that he is a reliable witness, then take it from there. I'm confident we'll get a result this time.'

'You said 'visits",' says Ruth.

'Oh yes. I realised that if we had mixed up Andrew's parents with Eddie's, it was Eddie that we knew nothing about, not Andrew. So I went back to the flat that Sim had been to where he got no reply, and there was someone in- Mrs. Sparrow. I spoke to her for a long time through the safety chain. When she eventually let me in it was an education. Mrs. Sparrow had struggled to bring Eddie up there on her own. The place was tidy, but it was like a museum- all of the furniture you see in plays about the fifties and sixties, and the wallpaper. She told me that she hardly left the flat, because she was agoraphobic. She'd had to let Eddie go when he was a child. She reckoned that they were distantly related to Edward Lear, and that Eddie was named after him. She used to read him 'The Jumblies' every night before he went to bed.'

I'm still trying to take this in when I hear somebody putting a key in the door. I feel my muscles tensing, thinking that it must be Della. The door opens, and a beaming Oscar breezes in.

'Oscar,' says Jamie, obviously trying not to over-react. 'We were worried. Where you been mate?'

Oscar heads straight for Jamie and hugs him.

'Jamie, I'm glad you're here. Remember my IPP.'

'Yes?'

'Well, I want you to know I've completed it.'

'Completed it? Which bit?'

'Which bit? The important bit. I had to work in that shop, but I've scrimped and saved and cadged beer, and finally I'd got enough. The money's run out, so I had to come back. But I've done it.'

'Done what?' asks Jane.

'Last night I, Oscar Doyle, went out... and shagged a tart. And it was great. When do I get another IPP?'

It's the first time I've seen Jamie smile since Blackpool. And no wonder: Oscar is safe, we know more about Eddie, and Andrew is on the road to recovery.

Which means that Della is on the way to justice.

-Chapter 63-

18th October 1987
10.45pm

As I load the chess program on my Sinclair 48K I take a swig of 'Special Brew,' and catch a glimpse of myself in the wardrobe mirror, illuminated in the ghoulish green light of the TV screen. God, that burglar must have shit himself. The bedroom is infused with the pungent aroma of large doner kebab with chilli sauce and jalapenos. It lounges on my knee like a smelly pup on a blanket of greasy paper. This is a deliberate and concerted blitz on the senses. Somehow I have to get the Bungalow out of my mind, just for one night. Try as I might, I can't share Jamie's confidence that we will now get rid of Della so easily. And even if we do, these things always take time- time in which I could be out of a job and Eddie could be back in the hospital.

I have to concentrate, because the black bishop has already checked my king, causing it to move into the only available space. Another deep swig from the can to aid the thought processes, and it starts to wash over me, numbing my senses from the feet up. Another bite from the kebab, and a whole jalapeno bursts on my tongue, filling my mouth with its juice. I can do this. It is a battle of man v. machine, like 'Terminator,' and in the end man has to be superior.

The black king's left flank is badly defended, so I move my rook down the board to take a pawn, before taking another confident bite of the kebab and washing it down with a gulp of beer. The black knight makes its move.

Shit.

It's done it again. I have allowed it to do it again. The fork. I never learn. The knight checks the king at the same time as threatening the queen. All that's left to do *again* is for me to resign. Walk away. Press the 'New Game' button as I always do, and it'll be like it never happened.

But what happens if I don't? What if I carry on, and play to win? This time I'll go for it. I'll feel the force and face the dark side. I have to move the king out of check. If I move it to the queen I could take the black knight once it has taken. Whatever happens, to carry on requires a sacrifice, and it cannot be the king. If I say that Eddie broke the door down and ran away, Della will argue that he also attacked Andrew. Did Mr. Hill attack Andrew? If I say that I went out with Eddie that night, she will argue that I was irresponsible. But if Eddie didn't push Andrew out of bed, who did? This is something else which only Andrew has the answer to, and soon we will be able to ask him. I take another drink, and finish the last strip of cold doner meat, then move the king forward.

The king. Who is the king, the one to be protected?

I wait, but it doesn't, as usual, immediately take the queen. After a minute it moves a pawn for no apparent reason. Then I see it. I've got black under threat without realising it. The black queen is in front of its king, which is blocked in. I move the white rook across, threatening the black queen, which takes the attacking rook . The black queen is now diagonally in line with the white... I take it, and the black king is under attack, but hemmed in with no pieces to defend it. Check Mate.

As I start a new game and open another can, somebody knocks on the door, which leads to the Willows. Probably some old dear after the toilet. I move the queen's pawn two spaces. The banging gets louder.

At the door is Paul, one of the staff at the home.

'There's a phone call in the office for you- says it's urgent.'

It takes me a while to get down the corridor, having to wait for an old lady in a nightie to negotiate her way on a zimmer. When I get there, the phone waits on the desk.

'Hello?'

It's Jamie. He sounds subdued. Everything seems to slow down, as if I'm underwater, as I hear the words:

'Sit down, mate, I've got some bad news.'

I breathe in steadily, trying to clear my mind of the affects of the alcohol. I know that I'm squeezing the telephone, and I can hear my own heart beat echo in the earpiece.

'He's dead, isn't he?

'No, he's... he's dying.'

Jamie tells me how, earlier that evening, things had taken a turn for the worst, as Andrew's body was shaken by one seizure after another. The hospital had decided to call for his next of kin and Simeon, having recently become party to the information, told them that it was Ray and Barb at the Papaver riding stables.

'Why did he do that?' I hear myself blurt out, 'they don't care for Andrew.'

'Martin mate, I know what you think of Sim, but he had no choice. They had to ask the next of kin if they could turn the machines off.'

'So he is dead?

'It's... it's not like that. They turn things off bit by bit. Andrew won't know it's happening...'

'So how long...'

'They said he'd be dead by eleven.'

Ten minutes.

Ten minutes and a human life will be gone.

'Why have we only just been told?' shouts my voice, 'did Simeon want to keep this all to himself?' Somebody, I guess it must be Paul, closes the office door.

'No, Martin, he has been trying to phone. Mickey's got into this habit of playing with the phone lead and must have yanked it out of the socket. I'd only just seen it. Simeon really wanted you to be there.'

Ten minutes become nine...

Not enough time to get to the hospital.

'Martin, do you want to come back to the Bungalow, so you don't have to be on your own?'

'No, no thanks, I'll be O.K.' I hear sobbing in the background. 'Give Jane my love. Have you spoken to Ruth?'

'No. I phoned her and got that git of a boyfriend. He wasn't very helpful.'

On the office clock, nine minutes has become eight minutes. In eight minutes time Andrew's life would end.

375

'I have to go. I think they need the office.'

'O.K. I'll see you tomorrow. Take care Martin.'

Jamie puts down the receiver, leaving an empty tone where a voice had been and leaving me with a feeling of loneliness I had only ever felt in dreams, or when I was locked in a cupboard, refusing to cry because some bastard thought it was the 'appropriate' thing to do.

Eight minutes become seven...

There should be a way to stop time and go back. When Lois Lane died, Superman reversed the rotation of the earth and brought her back to life. Somewhere Andrew is seeping away. And what has his life been for? All of that suffering, the physical deformity, the loss of his parents and hospitalisation, the witnessing of a murder which can now never be proven, the brief time he had spent at the Bungalow, then this, all for no reason.

Seven minutes become six...

Ruth was staying with her old friend, Bridget. They had worked their way through a bottle of Frascati, when at a quarter to eleven she had felt a need to phone the Bungalow. The phone was engaged. As it got closer to eleven she phoned again and was told the news.

Andrew.

Six minutes become five...

In the early hours of Friday morning Ruth had made herself believe that she wanted Richard back. She had snuggled beside him as the wind howled outside her window, allowing herself to be encompassed by his aura of whisky and nicotine. She had drifted off, but as she slept she'd had a dream that Andrew was lying, dead, on a lawn. Then he moved. She shouted to Richard for help, but he just stood there with the look of disgust he had shown when he told her how Andrew had regurgitated his food the day he walked in to the Bungalow. When she woke up, she knew that the seed that had been planted then had now germinated, and would grow. Things would never be the same again.

As Bridget opened the second bottle, Ruth looked at her watch.

Five minutes become four...

At the same time as Colin Macallan was raising a glass of his namesake whisky to toast Andrew, or 'Arthur' as he tended to think of him, Uncle Ray was slipping his wedding ring from his finger and shoving it into his pocket.

Four minutes become three...

In the corridor outside the Intensive Care Unit a nurse passed by a young man who was mumbling prayers, and for a moment thought that she heard a string of swear words, but concluded it must have been Latin. As Simeon's world slipped into chaos, he tried to contain the rage he felt towards God. He had had cause to be frank in his prayers in the past, but this time it was different. This time it ended with 'if you exist.'

Three minutes become two...

Jamie held Jane tightly. He had seen this before, but somehow had never felt it so keenly.

'You just have to grab everything that life offers,' he said. One month from now, he vowed, he would be in India. 'You never know what's round the corner... that's why you've got to tell him how you feel.'

Two minutes become one...

*

Through the open window of the office, I hear a church clock beginning to chime eleven. I can't describe this. It feels like a large serpent has been coiled up inside me, squeezing my stomach. As it uncoils I feel nauseous. As it reaches my chest I gasp for breath. I feel my throat tighten, and my face seems hot as pressure builds up behind my eyes. Then the reservoir of tears bursts, and flows thickly down my cheeks onto the desk.

'Goodbye, Andrew...'

*

Della returned home to find a recorded message from Jamie to ring the Bungalow. She would erase it and pretend that it had not recorded. She guessed what it was about. It was another piece of ammunition that she could use to get rid of either Martin or Eddie.

The past few days had brought to Della a realisation: that her new, god-given role had brought with it unexpected powers. On the night of the hurricane she had planned to enter the Bungalow unobserved, and to euthanase Andrew in a way which would make Eddie the prime suspect. But all had gone wrong, or so she thought, because of the hurricane. The voice which had nagged her not to wait she had decided was that of the devil, but because conditions were becoming dangerous, and because the lights in the Bungalow remained on, she had reluctantly postponed her plan until a more convenient time.

But that was no ordinary hurricane, was it? It was God almighty himself passing by and blessing my endeavours.

Arriving the next day to find that the outcome she was planning had occurred without her having to lift a finger, she could only conclude that she now had the power to achieve her ends through thought alone. Without her intervention one of the two witnesses to Frankie Adams' death had been removed. Now nothing could stop her from creating her perfectly functioning unit, whatever it took.

Tomorrow she would have to check her list of patients, erase Andrew from it, and contact the hospital to arrange Eddie's return.

-Chapter 64-

26th October 1987

Everyone was in the lounge, apart from Jamie, who was at the kitchen table making a few additions to the accounts book. There was a loud knock at the door, and when Jamie opened it he saw Ben, who supplied and maintained wheelchairs from the central store. He also took them away when they were no longer needed.

'Wellman,' he said, with his usual broad smile, 'I'm taking a wheelchair away for Wellman. Jamie said nothing, but in that instant, Ben saw the black tie, and the wreath on the table.

'Oh no, I am so sorry. They never tell me. I got to a place once and there was a hearse outside, so I had to wait round the corner...'

'It's O.K.,' said Jamie, 'you weren't to know.'

The wheelchair stood at the side of Andrew's bed. It would go now and have new fittings for its next user. Jamie would make sure that Della didn't immediately remove every reminder of Andrew, as he'd seen done in the hospital. He had to be remembered. It was the last thing they could do for him. As he wheeled the chair out, Jamie prayed that no one would see it leave.

The funeral took place at the local crematorium, and was presided over by the Salvation Army Captain, who had sought the opinions of everyone who knew Andrew, so that the words she said would be apt. Andrew's Uncle Ray sat at the back of the church. Simeon was in the opposite pew. When Jamie sat next to him he started to mumble.

'It's all right Sim,' whispered Jamie, 'you did more than any of us. He wasn't alone. You stuck by him to the end.'

TASTING THE WIND

'I wasn't with him at the end,' said Simeon, looking straight ahead. 'They made me leave. Said it had to be next of kin. I went to see his body at the Chapel of Rest. I wanted to see him with no pain at last. But his mouth was open. They don't have to display them like that, do they? I've heard they break their jaws if they need to. And the other thing: Andrew's arms were straight. He must have died having a seizure. His arms only straightened in a seizure.'

They sat in silence, then Jamie said: 'it's times like these, Sim, when you have an advantage. Because you have a faith you believe that Andrew's body isn't really Andrew. You believe that Andrew is somewhere else where he's happy.'

Simeon looked down. 'Do I?'

During the funeral arrangements Jamie had talked of ways in which people who are non-verbal can be included in a service that to them might be just a stream of meaningless sounds. It was decided that they could place objects that reminded them of Andrew on the coffin, so they lined up in the aisle, slowly and silently placing their objects of reminiscence. Rita placed a cake. She had once helped to feed him sponge and custard. Oscar placed some coins, saying that he wished he could buy him a drink. Eddie had been very definite. It had to be a red balloon, with messages written on it. Everyone had contributed to that, and Jamie helped him to place it, with the cake and coins holding down the string. Jane placed one of the diaries. Martin helped Mickey to take up some photos of Andrew on a horse at Papaver, and Uncle Ray placed some poppy heads.

*

And that was that. Afterwards I'm sitting on the steps of the church, unable to join in with the pleasantries, as Della poses in an ugly black hat that makes her look like a fat toadstool. I'm looking at the sky, when somebody sits beside me and puts an arm round my shoulder.

'Fuck me, what's Godzdella wearing?'

'Kev.'

'You just look like you need a hug man. How goes it?'

I scratch at a piece of red confetti which is stuck on the step.

'You know, it just doesn't seem fair, the sort of life somebody like Andrew gets. And all for what? You know, I'm not in any way religious, but I was just sitting here thinking that if everything was like in the books then he'd send us some sort of sign, something to tell us he's all right, that he didn't live and die for no reason.'

Kevin shook his head. 'First law of synchronicity.'

'What's that?'

'They never happen when you're looking for them.'

-Chapter 65-

2nd November 1987

Della made a big deal about postponing my disciplinary hearing until a week after the funeral. ' Out of respect for the deceased,' she had said, and ' I have to take account of your feelings.' *Bollocks.* It was more likely that she wanted to prolong the agony, make me sweat. Jamie reckons it was probably done at the suggestion of the area manager.

Des Machin is a lean, silver haired man in a dark grey suit and precisely knotted tie, one of those people who has 'ex-forces' written all over him.

'So what exactly are the allegations,' asks Des, as he peers over his half-moon glasses at a letter with Della's signature at the bottom. The meeting is taking place around the kitchen table at the Bungalow. Everybody is at the day centre, apart from Oscar who has been bribed with money to see a matinee at the local pictures (or, more likely, wander the streets and put the money towards something more enjoyable.) Della has had professional cleaners in, giving the place a sanitised, hospital smell.

'It is difficult to highlight one single offence,' says Della, her expression steely, ' as there have been so many in such a short space of time, and other things from the past have now come to my attention. In view of the fact that he has already had a verbal warning...'

'Can I just say on Martin's behalf,' says Jamie, 'that it is unfair and in contravention of policy if he does not know the precise details of what he is supposed to have done.'

'Della?'

Della thumbs through a wad of papers, a brief smile rippling across her face.

'Firstly,' she says, taking a deep breath, 'there is another complaint from a member of the public, a Mrs. Busby.'

'How do you spell that?' asks Des's secretary.

'As in the headgear of the Coldstream Guards,' says Della.

'Or Sir Matt, or the bird on the telephone advert,' I add.

'Mrs. Busby says that on the night of the hurricane she phoned here to say that one of our residents was out in the storm, and that the man she spoke to, a man with a Northern accent, called her a stupid busy body. That night the staff on duty were Mr. Peach and Ms. Cassel.'

'Is this true?' asks Des, turning to me.

'It wasn't exactly like that, no. Yes, I probably sounded rude, but she'd said something like 'one of the children has escaped.' I said something like it was stupid to mistake one of The People for a child. I just found it offensive, and sometimes it's difficult to bite your tongue.'

'And would you be willing to apologise to Mrs. Busby?' asks Des, 'and perhaps explain your position more civilly, if you had the chance?'

I look at Des, then at Della, 'I don't think...'

'Yes,' says Jamie, ' I'm sure he would, wouldn't you, Martin. I'd be happy to accompany him.'

'I don't believe this,' hisses Della.

'I would suggest,' says Des, 'that owing to the pressure you work under here, such an indiscretion should be allowed some form of absolution, don't you think?'

I'm not quite sure what he means, but I nod anyway, because that's what Jamie's doing. I hadn't expected the thing with Mrs. Busby to come up, in fact I'd forgotten all about it with everything else that had gone on. But this was just Della bringing out her pawns to see what damage and minor irritation she can cause before mounting the real attack.

'On the subject of there being a resident out in the storm,' says Della, 'there may be reason to question Martin Peach's competence.

The problem is, his colleague who was on the shift with him that night seems to be reluctant to say what the circumstances were whereby Edward Sparrow came to be outside of the Bungalow. I was hoping that we might clarify this today.'

'Mr Peach,' says Des, 'would you like to give me an ordered account of everything that happened on the night of the hurricane, just so that I can establish the course of events.'

All I can do is fiddle with my watch, and it feels like a hand is pushing my head down, making it physically impossible to look any of them in the eye.

'Des,' says Della, 'on a related matter, can I just ask at what stage my office door was broken down, personal property stolen from it, and by whom?'

I take a deep breath, but the combination of my lingering cold/ baptistery dust disease, and the strong smell of disinfectant, catches in my throat.

'I...I...'I splutter, and each time I try to catch my breath I go into a coughing fit. As Jamie jumps up to get me a glass of water, I see a look of satisfaction on Della's face.

'Just tell the truth,' says Jamie, handing me the glass, 'I promise you you'll be OK.'

I know that he has no reason at all to believe this, but I get what he's saying. Jamie knows that we've lost but somehow the truth has to be said, doesn't it? Otherwise, how can you live with yourself? I remember seeing once a cartoon, I think it was in 'Private Eye.' It was of Gladiators saluting Caesar, and saying:

We who are about to die salute you... you fat slob.

So in the same spirit, I look Della in the eye, and start at the very beginning:

'Eddie broke your door down. Do you want to know why? If you're talking about stealing property: you stole his spinning game and he had to break your door down to get it back.'

'No no no... you see Eddie consented to give up the game. We have a policy about age- appropriateness, it didn't do him any good to have a childish game.'

'He needed that game. He was agitated, and wanted something familiar, but you had taken it and locked it away.'

The secretary is feverishly taking everything down in shorthand. Della turns to Des.

'Can I just ask whose hearing this is? I resent this questioning of my managerial decisions.'

Des leans forward, looking over his glasses.

'Yes, may I remind you that if you have any issues with Mrs. Belk, there is a grievance procedure. Please keep to explaining your own behaviour... so Edward was agitated that night?'

'Yes. How do I say he was agitated without saying that Della's treatment was the cause of it?'

'You were working that night,' says Della, 'not me. He was agitated when you were working with him. He broke my door down, went to the bedroom and attacked Andrew Wellman when you were working with him.'

'No.'

'So what happened?'

'Eddie went back to his bedroom with the game. After that the phone rang.'

'This was before you heard the crash from the room?' asks Des.

'Yes.'

Des scratches his head and turns to Della.

'Forgive me if I'm being simplistic, but I would have thought that it was obvious that Eddie didn't attack Andrew.'

'What?' Then how else could it have happened?'

'That is not for me to say, but can I just ask, where was Eddie when Mrs....' he looks down at his notes, 'Mrs Busby phoned.'

'He must have been passing her house,' I say, ' because he went through the park.'

'And how did you know that Andrew had fallen?'

'It was the baby monitor. We heard a crash.'

'After the call?'

'Yes.'

'So how did Eddie, who by that time was passing Mrs. Busby's house, push Andrew out of bed?'

Della is shaking her head. 'Des, I really don't think we can rely on this information. Andrew Wellman could not move. If Eddie did not push him out of bed, then someone else did.'

'There is another solution,' I say, my voice like that of a sleepwalker. 'Zuska had been working with Andrew to get him to turn himself, and she said she'd seen him do it.'

'And did you?' asks Des.

'No.'

'I'm surprised that you didn't' snorts Della, ' you seem to inhabit the same uncritical world as Zuska. There is absolutely no reason to believe that Andrew flung himself out of bed. Why would he do such a thing?'

I look down the corridor to Eddie and Andrew's room, then through the open door to the lounge at the baby monitor in the socket.

'He did it to tell us that Eddie was in danger...'

'Oh come on,' blurts Della, 'this is pure fantasy. Des, let me put this into perspective, Andrew Wellman was a profoundly handicapped man who had little movement and very low cognitive ability...'

'How do you know that?' Now I am standing up and shouting, 'How the hell can you know that?'

'And how can you prove that he was anything else?'

'Because Andrew could tell us things, and you know that, but we found out too late...'

'Will you please both sit down,' says Des, ' we all need to remain calm. We must not digress from the real business of today, which is to discuss the accusation that Martin Peach has committed professional misconduct. Can we please concentrate on this issue?'

At this, Della closes her eyes, then puts the piece of paper she's been referring to aside. Underneath it I recognise my job application and a handwritten letter, which I guess is my forged reference. There are circles around the loops of g's and y's, and notes in the margins with arrows pointing to underlined words and spaces, crossings and dots. She moves it to one side, revealing another letter. It has the factory logo, and is written with a fountain pen. Two of Foster's many (and I'm using a Jane word here) idiosyncrasies, were an obsession with the poor quality of the handwriting of modern youth, and his use of a fountain pen, which he carried constantly in his breast pocket. Somehow Della had got through to him.

'I don't feel well,'

'What?' grunts Della.

'I don't feel well,' I repeat, ' all this, and Andrew, it's been stressing me out.'

Della tuts and shakes her head.

I imagine my face, my ten-year-old face, reflected in orange canal water.

'I have to object, Des, this is just a ploy for sympathy. I have evidence here that will demonstrate what Martin Peach is really like.'

Through the shiny surface of the water, the soft yellow underbelly begins to emerge, then the whole body is visible, life juices seeping through the hole where the head should be.

'And I have to object,' said Jamie, 'This is showing us what Della Belk is really like.'

Della scoops the frog from the water. As she removes the legs with kitchen scissors its innards splash down her apron. Still twitching, the legs are dropped onto a plate of tomato sauce.

The vomit lands accurately upon the paper, thin blue veins of ink immediately running into it, the rest splashing up onto Della, who runs down the corridor to the bathroom, holding a hand over her mouth.

'Perhaps,' says Des, 'we could take a short break.'

***

'I'm fucked,' I say, pacing up and down outside the Bungalow, ' I'm totally fucked, and you're not helping by insisting that I keep to the truth. You do realise, don't you, that she's managed to get through to my ex- boss?'

'Yes,' says Jamie, 'but I don't think his letter will be fit to use now, do you? Are you feeling all right?'

'Yes, I'm fine. It was almost worth it to see her face. But I am fucked aren't I?'

'Martin, just relax, and trust me. Des is no fool, and whatever happens, I don't think Della's going to come out of this smelling of roses.'

I can't stop the laughter bursting from my lips when I imagine what Della must be smelling of right now, and Jamie dodges, thinking I'm going to puke again.

'Sorry Jamie, but have you seen 'Return of the Jedi?' There's a bit where the goodies are about to be plunged into the gut of a monster, which will digest them over hundreds of years. Luke Skywalker is walking the plank. He looks at Jabba the Hutt and says something like 'this is your last chance, let us go or you die.' Jabba laughs his head off. Then the tables are turned and Jabba dies. But that's because Luke has Jedi powers and a lightsabre. What have we got?'

When I was at school and at the factory I had this knack for getting justice through playing humiliating pranks: like clingfilming toilets, or the swapped calendar that got Foster a black eye. But for the first time I'm at a loss, because there's something about Della that's different, something that scares me. Playing a prank on Della would be the equivalent of placing a whoopee cushion on the Fuhrer's chair at the Nuremberg rally.

I can't work out what Jamie is staring at. It might be the Cat and Lobster, because of an unconscious desire to get pissed. He may be looking beyond it to the park, which, until the storm, was totally hidden with shrubs and trees. You can even see the still roofless building on the other side, where I'd spent the night underground with Eddie and Eric.

'We have to blame it on Della,' he says.

'What?'

'Just tell the truth. Des has already worked out that Eddie couldn't have pushed Andrew, so Andrew must have turned himself over. We've got the minutes from Andrew's IPP, saying that Della refused professional advice to get cotsides for his bed, which means that she has to take some responsibility. So what were you saying about Jabba the Hutt?'

'But Eddie still trashed her door. Won't that be enough evidence that he's out of control? Oh, and there's this,' I say, taking Della's Dictaphone from my pocket.

'What the hell are you doing still carrying that around?'

'Bad habit of mine,' I say. 'Every time I put on a new pair of trousers I just dump the contents of the old ones into the pockets. I'd meant to stuff it down the side of a settee or something, make it look like Della had lost it.'

By the look on Jamie's face I can see that an idea is brewing.

'What's on that? Have you listened to it?'

'I know exactly what you're thinking,' I say, 'and no, she hasn't used it to record our private conversations. It was just a load of boring stuff. It's even more boring now. On the night of the hurricane I set it to record Eddie as he slept, hoping it might prove that he does the voices. All I got was a load of snoring.'

Laughing, Jamie takes the Dictaphone and switches it on.

'How did you sleep through that? The hurricane was quieter.'

The snoring starts to fade, and is replaced by low moaning, then by the sound of a woman's voice:

'Far and few, far and few, are the lands where the Jumblies live...'

Now silence.

'I obviously didn't listen long enough.'

'When I met Eddie's mum,' says Jamie, ' that was exactly how she talked.'

'Well, if there's only one good thing to come out of this,' I say, ' it's that it'll wipe the smirk off Della's face. I've got proof now.'

'If you'd been a bit more patient you'd have heard it before. And if you'd been a bit cleverer, you'd have done this...'

Pressing the fast forward button, Jamie listens to a few seconds of silence, until he reaches a section of speeded up chatter and presses 'play.' I am totally unprepared for what comes next, and as we hear the rest of what was said that night as I sheltered with Eddie from the hurricane above, I know exactly what must be done.

The final straw has come to rest.

-Chapter 66-

When we go back in, Des and Della seem to have had a disagreement: they aren't talking, and Della is turned away from him, clutching what's left of her wad of papers.

'I hope you are feeling better now Martin.'

'Yes thanks, Mr. Machin,' I say, 'much better.'

'Right,' says Della, 'let's get on with it. Although the letter from Mr. Foster has been totally destroyed by your...accident, I have here a copy of your original app...'

'Just a moment,' interrupts Jamie, ' can I just say that before we go on, something's come to my attention which may speed things up a little.'

Della puts her papers down. Des peers over his glasses, and the secretary stops writing. All eyes are on Jamie.

'It's about the theft of Della's Dictaphone.'

'Yes, says Della, I would like an explanation of that.'

Jamie takes the Dictaphone from his pocket. 'Martin has just given this to me.'

'I thought so,' says Della. 'And what is your explanation?'

'Just tell her how you came by it,' says Jamie, 'and keep to the facts.'

I clear my throat. ' Eddie took it. The night he broke your door down to get his game back he saw it on the desk, and put it into his bag.'

'What on earth could Eddie want with it?'

'He wanted it as a souvenir. He was leaving. Every time he leaves anywhere he takes a souvenir. He was leaving here because of you, because you have shown your dislike of him since he came, and he knows you're trying to get rid of him.'

'Des!' whines Della, 'I am not the one being judged here.'

'No,' says Des. 'Can I ask, Jamie, what the relevance of this is?'

'It is evidence of the pressure that staff have been working under,' says Jamie, ' it is evidence of Della's management style. Some of the staff have wondered if it has been used to record their private conversations. They may be wrong, but this is just symptomatic of how Della is viewed. I think that if Martin is found guilty of any misconduct, the way that he has been treated and the atmosphere we all have to work in- and that the residents are forced to live in- should be taken into account.'

Della is laughing. 'You are so wrong, and you will take that back.'

'What do you use the Dictaphone for?' asks Des.

'All I use it for is reminders- about jobs that need doing, and ideas for some research I am undertaking.'

'So you wouldn't mind if we played it? You are under no obligation.'

'I don't think you have any right to...'

'No...' I interrupt, there's no need to play it.'

The corner of Della's mouth twitches, like somebody's just tugged on a fishhook. 'So what exactly have you been doing with it?'

'Nothing, I just don't think...'

'Then yes,' she says triumphantly, 'yes, we will listen to it.'

Des motions to Jamie, who presses a button on the Dictaphone. *'What's going on?'* asks Sim.

Jamie pauses the tape. 'Do you recognise that voice?'

'Yes, of course I do,' says Della. 'Its Simeon. But how has his voice gotten on to there?'

'And what about this one?'

'I'm going to set my dog on you.'

'That is Eddie of course. But how...'

'Jamie,' I plead,' this is going against me, whose side are you on?'

'Just play it,' shouts Della, her fist crashing down on the table.

'What about this voice? Asks Jamie.'

'*... Get him off me. Get him off.'*

'That's me of course.'

'And do you recognise the incident?'

'Yes, of course I do, it was when Peach did that ludicrous stunt with the car. The only thing I don't understand is how it got onto the tape.'

'*I'm going to set my dog on you.'*

'Do we have to listen to this?'

' Yes Martin, we do,' says Della, sitting back with hands behind her head, 'you'll probably hear him swearing at me next.'

'*Martin, get him away from me.'*

'*NO. He's joking with you, you stupid...'*

'I think we've heard enough now,' I say, Turn it off Jamie, it's not doing my case any...'

'No!' shouts the real Della, 'leave it on. Let's see what he doesn't want us to hear...'

'*Come on Eddie,' says 'Simeon'*

'*Where are you taking him?'*

' *In the absence of a time-out room it will have to be his bedroom- he needs a little time out to calm down,'*

'*Him calm down? It's not him that needs....'*

'You see,' says Della, an ugly grin spreading across her face, 'this is proof of what I'm saying. Thank you Jamie, I...'

She is interrupted by her own voice.

'*Simeon, go and tell Martin to take Mickey for a walk.'*

Her eyes widening, Della leans forward and grips the edge of the table. 'Where was the Dictaphone? I thought...'

'*You've had it now you fucking little freak- get in there. You had better learn how to behave...'*

'Switch it off, switch it off now,' screams the real Della, but Des gestures for it to continue.'

'*...Or you'll die like Frankie did.'*

Click.

In the silence, everybody seems to freeze. I don't know what this feeling is, but it has been churning inside me since hearing the tape outside: one minute it's disbelief, the next shock, and then something like relief. As one, we look at Della, who has turned white, a vein on her neck standing out, and her left eye twitching.

'Could I just ask,' says Des, 'Who was Frankie?'

The Bungalow is silent, and for a moment I feel like I did when I stood by Andrew's coffin. But this time it's like I'm paying my respects to someone I never knew, someone who died many years ago.

'I knew him,' says Jamie. 'When I was a student nurse at the hospital. He died. He died when Della was doing a night shift.'

And Andrew knew him. He knew him, and carried the secret of his death for all that time. But now it seems to me that he played his part in ensuring that justice can at last be done: if he hadn't brought us rushing to the bedroom that night I would never have found Eddie, never have come by the Dictaphone, never have recorded the damning evidence. Eddie's power of perfect mimicry, Andrew's ability to turn himself over: Della denied them both, but they have now come together on her like sharp, effective scissor blades.

'Mrs. Belk,' says Des,' this is most irregular, but I think that in the light of what has happened I must close this meeting.'

Della stands and reaches out, thrusting her huge hand towards Jamie:

'Give that to me.'

But it is Des who takes the Dictaphone.

'I must insist on taking this as evidence. I have to inform you that you are accused of gross professional misconduct, and are from this moment suspended from duty. I would like you to collect your belongings, and then I will escort you from the building. After that, I will be putting matters into the hands of the police.'

Della is struggling to speak. As she gets up and shuffles towards her office door I can't believe that she could look so small. It's as if gravity itself is seizing on her vast bulk and pulling her down; and for all I care it could pull her down to the darkest pit of Hell. Turning slowly to face us, she speaks, but with a frail, pleading voice, which is that of someone who years of guilt have entombed like a collapsed building. And the only word she can say is: 'how?'

Looking at her I cannot believe that it's over, that we have won, if 'winning' is the right word. And I cannot believe, as the door to the outside opens, that she is about to be delivered the means to execute a tragic and devastating endgame.

-Chapter 67-

As Della was about to enter her office the front door of the Bungalow opened and Eddie breezed through it, closely followed by Zuska.

'Sorry to interrupt...' said Zuska, who immediately picked up from the faces around the table that she was not interrupting a social gathering, '...but I was just about to take Eddie swimming when we realised he hadn't got his...'

As Eddie walked between Della and the office door the same thought passed, like a hideous premonition, through the minds of both Martin and Jamie, but from where they sat behind the table there was no time to react.

In that single moment a cold light came back into Della's eyes and she seemed to grow from the shuffling, defeated thing she had become, to her previous stature. In one move she barged Eddie into the office, slammed the door shut and locked it.

'I'll set my dog on you.' shouted Eddie.'

'Shut up...shut up...I'm no longer afraid of you,' rasped Della in a voice that was hardly recognisable as her own, 'God has taken away my fear.'

Martin jumped over the table and hurled himself at the door, but it seemed to be made of stronger stuff than the one that Eddie had destroyed. Preparing to make a further assault, he was stopped in his tracks by the words:

'I have a knife.'

Des put his hand on Martin's shoulder. 'I think we need to back off. It's important that she calms down. I'll call the police.'

'But we can't wait that long,' yelled Martin, 'you don't know what she's capable of.'

'Exactly,' said Des, 'we can't afford to panic her.'

Des picked up the handset, put it to his ear, then rattled the receiver.

'It's dead.'

'Oh that'll be Mickey again,' said Jamie, 'he's been playing with the cables and... oh shit... looks like he got a bit carried away this time.' Above the skirting board, where there had once been a socket, there were now bare wires.

'Is there another phone in here?' asked Des.

'Only the one in the office,' said Jamie.'

'Then, Miss Frobisher,' said Des to his secretary, 'would you go to the phone box at the end of the road please and call the police.'

'So what do we do now?' asked Martin as he paced up and down in the kitchen, 'do we just leave her to kill him?'

'Martin, she says she has a knife, and her mind is in a very fragile state. We have no choice but to...'

'It's all right for you,' said Martin, choking back the tears of anger and frustration, 'you don't know Eddie, what he's been through. It's like he's spent his whole life behind a door, with people just inches away, but unable to help him. Andrew gave his life to save Eddie. If we don't save him now, that will all have been in vain.'

'I know, Martin, I know, but there's nothing we can...'

'It can't end like this!'

Through the office door came the sound of Della's laughter. 'You see- the house of Satan is a house divided.'

'Des is right,' said Jamie, putting an arm around Martin. 'I'll go round the front and see if I can get a view of them through the office window, get a better idea of what we're up against.'

'I'll try to talk to her,' whispered Zuska, 'it might keep her attention away from the window.'

As Jamie quietly left by the front door, Zuska closed her eyes as if in prayer and, pressing her ear against the office door, said:

'Della, it's me, Zuska...why are you doing this?'

'I am doing the will of God. You would not understand.'

'But how can it be the will of God. God would not want to hurt Eddie would he?'

TASTING THE WIND

There was a brief pause, then in a voice filled with raw and uncontrolled anger, Della shouted:

'What would you know about the will of God? You are a practitioner of witchcraft. Now leave my presence before I call down his wrath upon you.'

As Zuska backed away from the door Jamie entered and beckoned to her, Des and Martin.

'The blinds were down,' he whispered, but I managed to see them through a gap. I could just see their heads above the desk. Della is sitting on the floor with her back to the door, so we're not going to get in that way. Eddie is sitting between her legs and she is holding something to his throat. It looks like a scalpel. A drawer has been pulled out of her desk- she probably keeps it in there, but God knows why. When she wasn't talking to you she seemed to be praying, and there's this crazy smile on her face.'

'How's Eddie looking?' asked Martin,' and as he spoke Eddie's voice came through the door:

'Who's in the cupboard?'

'Shut up...shut up with your imbecilic songs. They mean nothing, nothing, nothing.'

'Eddie's looking quite calm, considering,' said Jamie. 'I think he's switched off. We just have to hope he stays that way or...'

From the office came a voice that Jamie and Martin had heard before. It was the voice of an Irish woman, and it said:

'Their heads were green,
Their hands were blue.'

'Is there someone else in there?' asked Des.

'No,' said Martin, 'that's Eddie. It's something he does...'

But Martin's explanation was interrupted by something that no one there had heard before or would ever wish to hear again. It began as a low whining sound, almost like an angry wasp, trapped in a jar, then rose to a loud, bestial roar of anguish, followed by low, breathless chanting.

'What is she saying?' asked Des.

'I don't know,' said Zuska, pressing her ear to the door again, 'it sounds like...'nemesis."

'We've got to get in there,' said Martin.

'No,' said Des, 'we must wait for the police.'

'But where the hell are they?'

*

Miss Frobisher had been only too glad to get out of the Bungalow. She was a competent secretary who had only just returned to work after a period of sickness with her 'nervous complaint' to find herself in someone else's nightmare.

Even before she had entered the red phone box she suspected that there would be a problem. The box was plastered with graffiti and its windows were smashed. When she opened the door she saw that the phone had been ripped out, leaving a hanging wire. Walking as quickly as she could she came back to the Cat and Lobster pub. It was closed, and according to a sign on the door would be so until six o'clock.

The next idea was to knock on a door, any door and explain that this was an emergency. She felt her heart begin to race at this prospect, but found her way to a large detached house and pounded heavily with the ornate knocker.

Mrs. Busby opened the door to see the frail, bespectacled secretary standing breathlessly on her doorstep.

'I'm sorry to disturb you,' said Miss Frobisher who, whatever the situation, always felt it important to remain polite, 'but I'm from the Bungalow at the end of the road and...'

Miss Frobisher could not have been expected to understand the woman's response, knowing none of the history behind it, but the string of abuse about the Bungalow staff, and the slammed door, made her decide against seeking help from any more of the inhabitants of Moonfield Road.

She knew that if she were to enter the park it would take her at least fifteen minutes to reach the telephone at the tube station on the other side. Surely that would not make much difference. Surely, what was happening at the Bungalow would not have escalated in that time.

But she was not to know that by the time she had made it half way across the park, she would already be too late.

*

397

'I don't like this,' said Martin, 'It's too quiet.'

'How long,' said Des, ' have you known...suspected things weren't quite right with Mrs. Belk?'

'Only a couple of weeks really,' said Jamie, but there was nothing we could call proof, nothing we could bring to you or to the police.'

'And what about the tape? How did that come about?'

'It's a long story. Once this is all over I'll get Martin to...'

'Their heads are green
Their hands are blue...'

'You do know,' said Des, 'that it probably wouldn't be accepted as evidence?'

'Yes,' said Jamie, 'but I don't suppose we need it now, do we?'

Martin crept up to the door of the office, and pressed his ear against it. At first he heard nothing, but then there was something that sounded to him like heavy, laboured breathing.

Jamie approached him. 'What can you hear?'

'I'm not sure, it sounds like...'

'Martin...'

'What?'

'What's that?'

Following the line of Jamie's eyes, Martin looked at the floor. The carpet was green, but from underneath the door came a semi-circle of black, upon which he was standing. And it was spreading. Without a word passing between them, the two men raced out of the door and round to the front of the building. Jamie picked up an urn, which had lain empty since the night of the storm, and used it to smash the window. Reaching round the jagged remnants of the glass, he opened the window, and tore down the blind, causing Della's coffee percolator to crash to the floor. Followed by Martin, he climbed in, neither of them knowing what they would find, or whose blood had been shed. Somewhere beyond the desk and filing cabinets which obscured them were Eddie and Della. Slowly, they moved forward, but stopped when they heard:

' Who's in the cupboard,
Tied the socks
Killed the man...'

'Eddie?'

Eddie sat, cross-legged in a corner of the room. His T-shirt was smeared with blood.

'Who's in the cupboard,' he began again,

'Made the noise
Ate the sweets
Stabbed the knife...'

Della was slumped against the door, her blood, the blood that stained Eddie's shirt, draining from her and staining the carpet black. A scalpel lay at her side, her thighs and wrists slashed to gory ribbons. In front of her was the desk drawer, which contained a mixture of loose pills, all of them instantly recognisable as the cocktail prescribed to Eddie. As Martin cradled Eddie in his arms, Jamie checked Della's vital signs, noticing that from her mouth there was a stream of multi-coloured saliva.

'Looks like she meant to complete the job.'

As police cars pulled into the forecourt, Eddie chanted about Mr. Hill, only at times it came out in a different form, and sounded more like 'Nurse Cahill.' It told of how she had once killed a man, and had now killed herself. It was interspersed with his mother's voice, reciting the words:

'Their heads were green
Their hands were blue.'

No one knew the significance of the voice to what had happened in the room, apart from Della, who would never speak to, or harm, or kill anyone ever again. That voice was the last thing she had heard, her nemesis, and no matter how or where she cut herself it would not go away.

Looking at the scene that was materialising around him, Eddie sensed that the story he had been telling for the last decade was now, on the blood-stained floor of Della's office, somehow complete. He would recite his chant   again and again for the rest of the day, for everyone to hear. Then he would stop, and 'Mr. Hill' would be gone forever.

-Epilogue-

August 24th 2007

And in twenty years they all came back,
In twenty years or more,
And everyone said, 'How tall they've grown!
For they've been to the lakes and the Terrible Zone,
And the hills of Chankly Bore.'
And they drank their health, and gave them a feast
Of dumplings made of beautiful yeast;
And everyone said, 'if only we live,
We too will go to sea in a sieve,
To the hills of Chankly Bore!'
Far and few, far and few,
Are the lands where the Jumblies live;
Their heads are green, and their hands are blue
And they went to sea in a sieve.

'Turn right at the T- junction.'
'Thank you dear.'
My wife had said that she would file for divorce if I continued my blatant flirtation with the satellite navigation system, but I am so grateful for her/its assistance today that I could shag the little darling.

It's getting on for twenty years since I left London. During that time I think you develop false memories of distances, and the relationships between things. And even happenings. You forget that things change, that trees grow, buildings go up, are altered, are knocked down.

'You have now reached your destination.'

'I don't know what I'd do without you, duck. I'll make it up to you later. Wear something comfortable.'

I couldn't have found my way to it, but there it is, the Day Centre. It's still recognisable, although it must have had a paint job shortly after I'd left, so is now back to looking a bit tired again. There's no longer the big 'Day Centre' sign at the gate. Instead, on the wall next to an 'Investors in People' plaque, is a smaller one, which says: '21st Century Options.'

'Can I help you?' says a small, bright eyed, curly-haired woman in jeans and a white t-shirt as she meets me at the door.

'Er, yes, my name is Martin Peach, I'd arranged to visit today.'

'Oh hello,' she says, 'I'm Anne, I'm assistant manager here. The manager is expecting you.'

Inside the foyer there's a reception desk, a green fitted carpet and rubber plant- a little more business-like and less schooly than I remember it.

'Has my wife arrived yet?'

'No,' says Anne, 'How's she getting here?'

'Tube. She was at a conference yesterday, so we thought we'd combine the two.'

'I'll keep an eye out for her. The manager's office is through there.'

The door to the office is open. Behind the desk is a 2007 year planner, and a poster of the Floyd's 'Dark Side of the Moon' cover, the one where a prism is splitting white light into its component colours.

'Hello?'

'Hello, please come in,' says a voice to my left. A man in a blue suit stands with his back to me, closing a filing cabinet. I think I recognise something about his voice, but as he turns round I'm not sure whether or not I know the balding, clean-shaven man.

'Please sit down Mr...'

'Please call me Martin.'

'Martin?'

'Yes.'

'Martin. It's me, Kev.'

I'm not aware that I've changed so much, but Kevin certainly has.

'So where's the...the...' I stroke my chin.

'Oh that went years ago. I was trying to make a point, but for some reason nobody ever asked me about it.'

I wait, but the answer is not forthcoming. 'So,' I say, ' what was your point?'

'Well it seems a bit silly now, but I was young and idealistic. If anyone said 'why have you only got half a beard?' I would say 'it's to show that it doesn't matter how you look, because what's on the inside is more important.'

'Oh.'

'See, not very impressive in the light of day. I was stoned when I had the idea.'

'We all have our foibles,' I say. I remember how I used to think I would do something really world changing.'

We sit, and Kevin gets two white coffees from the machine outside his door.

'You've changed,' is all that I can think to say.

'You mean sold out?'

'No no no. People do change, and if you taught me anything it was what you said just now, that how you are is nobody else's business. I just imagined that you would still be the same. Daft idea really. Looks like you've been successful.'

'In one sense. Better pay, more kudos. But sometimes I feel like I'm a one-ulcer man in a two-ulcer job. At least I'm still in touch with the service users. That makes it worthwhile.' Kevin takes a sip from his plastic cup. There's a sadness about him compared to how he used to be. Not depressive sadness, but that of one who had been carefree, but who experience had dragged to the extreme before he could find the mid point we all straddle for most of the time.

'We're planning to close it down you know.'

'I did wonder. That's partly why I'm here; I'm doing some research for my organisation about new initiatives to improve people's lifestyles.'

Kevin sighs. 'Sounds familiar doesn't it? Like we were doing when The People came from the hospital, only we've somehow managed to slip over to the other side of the line in some sort of dialectic. It's us and our ways of doing things that are old hat now.'

I take a drink. The coffee tastes as plastic as the cup, and I realise for the first time that Kev now takes milk.

'So,' I say, trying to casually introduce the question I'm really dying to ask, 'are you still in touch with The People from the Bungalow?'

'You do know that there is no Bungalow now?'

'Yes. Or at least it's changed its function.'

I'd realised this when I'd phoned and found that it was now a respite care facility.

'All The People are living in ordinary houses, some of them have jobs.'

'Oscar?'

'Yes, but he tends to go from one to another, jacking it in when he gets bored or has built up a big enough stash, whichever comes first. And would you believe he's not many years off retirement?'

'Do you remember Andrew?'

'Of course I do. I didn't know him as well as you, but his death had a profound effect on me. I'm not sure if it was for the good, but it was then that I decided that I wanted to have influence, not to leave it to the Dellas of this world. To be honest, I'd seen such deaths before, but it was his that gnawed away at me and made me realise that things...don't always work out for the good.'

I wonder how long Kevin has waited to pour this out. I'd remained at the Bungalow for less than a year, when the possibility of advancement, and the realisation that 'up North' held a better standard of living for the low waged, led me back there. I had gathered that the staff group had slowly disintegrated, and that agency workers like Kevin were heavily relied on.

'The 'stable home environment' didn't last long, did it?'

'That was the problem with Rita,' says Kevin 'I tried to tell the new manager that. It was after you left when they got one. He was nothing like Della, but coming in new he couldn't see beyond Rita's challenging behaviour and realise that her new family, the one that had promised her a brave new world, had so quickly disintegrated.'

'So where is she now?'

'Don't know. She went from the Bungalow to a Behavioural Unit. And the only suitable one when she went was out of borough. I knew that if I'd been manager I wouldn't have allowed it to happen. She nearly got sent back to the hospital.'

'Did it close?'

'Yes. And you won't believe what I got from a website recently.'

Kevin reaches a piece of paper from a desk drawer and hands it to me. It's from an estate agent's website, and describes a luxury block of flats in the middle of the countryside, boasting a unique feature in its original Victorian hospital frontage.

I feel a shudder at the thought of what that fine piece of architecture represented to the thousands of earlier residents, and hope for their sakes and for the new residents that their ghosts have now been laid to rest.

Unlike mine...

'And Eddie?'

' Oh, Eddie helps out with gardens. It all started when he went to the old Sally Army chapel- the one that got knocked down by the hurricane- did you know about that? Since then he's been supported in gardening all over the place.' Kevin draws the blind to his office window, ' you can see some of his handiwork out there.'

The garden is well kept, and amongst the shrubs and bedding plants are hundreds and hundreds of poppies of different varieties.

Poppies...

That year at Moonfield Road is never far from my thoughts. It amazes me that between us there were so many interpretations about what actually happened there. Simeon had gone for an Andrew who was as I'd first seen him: profoundly disabled, unable to move, understanding nothing of what went on around him. The rest of us could accept, after what his mum wrote, that he shared her unique sensory perspective, although we had to admit that we wanted to believe that he had something to raise him out of his situation.

There was one thing that only Jane and I knew for certain, because we saw it: Andrew could communicate what was in his mind through pointing his tongue. And that was how we knew the truth about what happened to Frankie Adams.

And when Andrew sensed something wrong on the night of the hurricane, he risked himself to alert us to Eddie's danger. I still believe that, although it will always be impossible to prove. Jane said it was the best example of unconditional love she had ever witnessed: 'greater love hath no man than he lay down his life for a friend.' She reckoned that anything else we do always has a payback, either in praise or returned love. But if you risk your life, you're accepting the possibility that you might lose everything, and not even see the results of what you've done.

When I worked with Andrew, I naively thought that I was showing him unconditional love. It was probably the other way round. And I did feel it, I can swear that I did, on a day when I massaged Andew's feet, and had a vision of redness, like a poppy field on a summer's day.

There's a knock at the door, and Anne, the deputy manager opens it.

'Your wife's here,' she announces.

'Oh, right. Kevin, you do remember my wife, don't you?'

Jane enters, looking the least changed of us all.

'Of course I do,' says Kevin, standing up to kiss her cheek. 'We could have a class of '87 reunion. Talking of which, I think the bus has just arrived.'

We hear him first, that familiar deep throated giggle. Then come the footsteps, and a small oriental face appears around the door. When he sees us, Mickey squeals with delight and runs to us. His gait is still wide and awkward, but he runs, his legs no longer in callipers.

'I haven't a clue,' the driver is saying to Anne. He didn't get on with it, and it wasn't there before- I only gave the bus a good clear out this morning. But there has to be some explanation for it.'

Behind Mickey, trailing from a string that he holds in his hand is a red balloon. And it doesn't matter to me or Jane or Kev that nobody else understands its significance. What matters is that the balloon is colourful and causes smiles and laughter wherever it goes.

Giggling, Mickey walks to the door at the back of the centre, the balloon bobbing behind him. Glancing back at us he opens the door. The strong sun silhouettes him in the doorframe, and with the light and the birdsong that enter the building from Eddie's garden comes the smell of lavender. As I look on I remember Mickey at the hospital- bum-shuffling with shreds of denim trailing behind him, the bruises on his face, his life governed by the rigid, soulless routines of the institution. And I remember what Eric said about poppies, how they can lie dormant in the darkness for years but as soon as the ground is disturbed, as soon as light sheds on them, they grow tall and burst into beautiful colour.

TASTING THE WIND

ALLAN MAYER

Printed in the United Kingdom by
Lightning Source UK Ltd., Milton Keynes
137230UK00002B/49-51/P